Back to the Island

Copyright © 2015 by Timothy P. Munkeby

Two Harbors Press
322 First Avenue N, 5th floor
Minneapolis, MN 55401
612.455.2293
www.TwoHarborsPress.com

All rights reserved. No part of this publication may be reproduced, stored in a retrieval system, or transmitted, in any form or by any means, electronic, mechanical, photocopying, recording, or otherwise, without the prior written permission of the author.

ISBN-13: 978-1-63413-290-9
LCCN: 2014922902

Distributed by Itasca Books

Cover Design by B. Cook
Typeset by James Arneson

Printed in the United States of America

Back to the Island

a novel

Timothy P. Munkeby

TWO HARBORS PRESS
MINNEAPOLIS, MN

"I hope you understand, I just had to go back to the island"
—from *Back to the Island* by Leon Russell

Acknowledgments

Front Cover Photo (of an actual Elbow Cay beach) by Mary Munkeby

Back Cover Photo (Lake Vermilion in distance) by Lisa Munkeby

Sketches by Heidi Spurlin; poems based on poems by Heidi Spurlin (except those of the 'Rashi' character in the novel)

Special thanks to Lisa Munkeby, my remarkable daughter-in-law, for all her help. And to Susan Krasaway, my typist … and for her "Novel Notes"

We all have our island -- some person, place, or comfort we need...must return to.

PART I

It's Not Gonna Happen . . . Maybe

CHAPTER 1

BEING DECEMBER, the breeze off the sea had a little nip. M, comfortable in flannels and a sweatshirt, took a sip of his coffee and looked over at Sara's profile, noticing her nose took a little downturn … just like Kate's. He set his cup down and decided to end what was not, actually, an uncomfortable silence: "All right, today's simply going to play itself out. It should be exciting as hell. Really, I don't see any reason to stress over it, you know? Whatever is going to happen is going to happen. And, somehow I don't feel a need to worry about Peewee." He kept trying to convince himself of this. "Sara, just think how exciting today … imagine: Spense *and* Lottie, again! And Nassau, the British government, Interpol—who knows what kind of adventure that'll involve."

"Not sure I share your enthusiastic optimism, but, yes excitement awaits. Speaking of 'adventure,' what you going to do about Lottie?" Sara asked, looking out at the lighthouse and then chuckling to herself a tad derisively.

He noticed her apparent amusement, followed her eyes, and wondered what that was about. Then, back to her: "Do? Whaddya mean?"

"Any feelings still there? The way I understand it, you two didn't actually have closure."

He looked over at her, wondering what she was up to. "Play it by ear, I suppose. Lottie's totally cool, a great person."

CHAPTER 1

"Not too bad looking, either," Sara slipped in, a little caustically for her he thought.

"I'd like to be friends, really," M went on obliviously. "But, obviously, that'll be up to her. She's pretty pissed. I suppose she should be. I wouldn't have slept with her if I'd thought it'd hurt her. Really, she was pretty much the aggressor. But," he smiled crookedly, "she *is* the second most alluring woman I know."

Sara frowned, ignoring who might be the first, but she moved on to the second: "You think you'd sleep with Lottie again?"

"God no! Apparently I never shoulda in the first place, I guess."

"Oh, I don't know ... *if* she's the aggressive one? She can be pretty *alluring*, to use your word. What about when you see her again? Can you contain yourself?" Was this a taunt, he wondered? If so, what was she doing?

"You know, Lottie's with Spense now, sailing with him. I wouldn't even consider interfering with that, not that she'd even be interested now anyway. If anything, I hope at least it could be friends with us. But, like I said, believe me—she's plenty pissed, so probably no banana."

"No banana? What the devil does that reference mean, eh? Oh. Never mind. I'm beginning to understand Kate's 'off the wall' references about you. Anyway, those two would be unlikely bedmates. Do they have something going on?" Sara asked, eyebrows raised, looking over at M for the first time. "Can Spense still get it up? He's getting up there."

She was still surprising him ... not unpleasantly. "I've wondered that myself. I certainly hope so. But he had said his and Lottie's relationship was platonic."

"Betcha I know what he means by 'platonic'," Sara said, a wry smile curling her lips, a smile he thought he'd never seen before ... a somewhat acerbic side he hadn't seen before, either.

M looked at her with one eye closed, curious about what she was going to say. "OK?"

"Older guys, after a certain age, can still, you know, you'd probably say 'get off,' even if they can't get it as hard as they need for coitus. And I've noticed his remarkable fingers manipulating buttons and toggles on that keyboard ... he's definitely got the touch. I doubt that's not all he knows how to manipulate, if ya get my drift? I'm guessing he'd have no trouble handling a couple 'toggles' and 'buttons' simultaneously. I don't how old Plato was before he died, but I betcha that's how he woulda done it if he had to."

M almost fell out of his chair. Was she talking about what he thought she was talking about? Definitely a new slant on 'platonic.' This wasn't at all the Sara he thought she was. And how the hell did she even know about what old guys could or couldn't do? "O—o—k. Now what do we talk about?"

"What! *You* embarrassed?" she retorted, looking over at him, grinning.

She was actually reminding him of Kate. "OK, listen," he said, changing the subject and attempting to get serious. "Even though we got a whole lot to talk about, and I *have* to say it one more time: I can't thank you enough for gettin' me down here and coming along. I really didn't expect that. But I love that you're doing it. But, OK, let's put all that aside for now, and how 'bout I start a different conversation we absolutely need to have? First of all, though, just to set the record straight, I'm doing my darnedest to think of you as my sister, even half-sister. I'm trying, in spite of blood and

CHAPTER 1

genes—well lack of, naturally— um, will you always see me as a brother ... your half-brother?"

"All right, speaking of that, while alleging you were our brother, Kate had nicknamed you Mick. Now that we are *all* aware that that is not the case, what do I call you? 'M' or 'MP'?"

"I told you once, you can call me whatever you like. 'Darlin' would do."

Sara smiled and looked out over the flowers, the bushes, the low-slung roofs of the cottages below barely visible through the coconut palms, out into the Abaco Sea. "Gosh, it's beautiful here," she said, but thinking: Oh, God, I should be Kate. Kate should be here.

"Exactly, word for word what Barney said sitting in that very chair. He even said 'gosh.'"

"Really? I didn't think he noticed much of the world outside his intimate, little cubicle in the library."

M peered intently at Sara, who was camped next to him, adorned in the splendor of her fuchsia terry cloth warm-up suit. He used to dislike terry cloth, thinking it totally out of fashion, passé, especially in running suits, more especially in fuchsia. But, he couldn't help but register how the soft, delicate fabric flowed subtly around her not-so-subtle curves. "You sure do have nice tits, sis."

Sara shook her head, not taking her eyes off the horizon and the now half-sunlit lighthouse across the harbor as the sun rose behind them. "Great line. That one work for ya all the time, buddy? There you go again: absolutely no filter. I know you know where the line is because you frequently, indelicately, and intentionally take several giant steps over it. But ... thank you, I guess. I'm glad that you like my breasts."

"I didn't say I 'liked' them." M and Sara were side-by-side on the front porch seated in Adirondack chairs. The biting breeze off the sea slacking as the sun climbed, creeping down the lighthouse. The palm leaves, which had been entertaining them with a scratchy, mesmerizing symphony, quietly were settling in for what looked like a promising day.

Sara pulled her feet up under her, pointing her terry-clothed knees at him. "Umm ... if you think they're nice, wouldn't that imply you liked them? My God! I can't believe I'm sitting here debating my breasts with you."

"Barney liked them. He likes big boobs. I just think they're nice. If I try to think of you as my sister," which he figured he might as well give up on, "I can hardly 'like' them, for cripes sake," he lied. "They just ... look nice on you."

"But, as you now know, I'm not your sister."

He was going to have to learn not to get into these little insinuation games with her. She was good. She was always going to turn the tables he knew. Make him look like the dumbshit he was. "No, really, ah, they just look great on you," he fumbled out, wondering how to escape gracefully.

Sara looked over at M. She was trying not to laugh. "Like I just happen to be wearing these breasts well today?"

"Yes, as a matter of fact," he answered, attempting to remain straight-faced. "Of course not just today. No, I'd say generally ..."

"Generally!?"

"Yeah, well, no, I mean," he stumbled, "yeah, all the time, probably."

"Probably!? But not just some of the time?"

She seemed to be enjoying this turning of the tables ... torturing him, again, like Kate would. "You know," he said,

CHAPTER 1

steering the conversation back to Kate. He was becoming aware he was over-matched with this new version of the previously sweet Sara. "I felt guilty the entire time with your sister. I feared I might like Kate's little twin dollops. But I thought I couldn't, right? I mean if I thought she's my sister, right? Well, *now* I suppose I wouldn't have to feel guilty, right? I could now, you know, actually allow myself to, well you know, because, although, obviously she's your sister, now I know she's not mine. So … "

"Dollops!?" Sara interjected, trying to save him before he fell flat on his face. "My God, she'd kill you if she heard you say that. Dollops! My Lord. Where'd you come up with that one? You might be able to say that about a real little sister, maybe, but no, now she would kill you. She did what she did to keep you interested in her, you know? That's what she thought she was doing. She does not think of you as a brother—never did. You don't think of her as a sister anymore, do you?"

"You know, I keep trying to convince myself of that … that she's not my sister … but not having very much luck, I'm afraid." M was looking out into the Sea of Abaco as well, watching a distant sailboat now glowing in the morning sun. It looked like it was floating above the turquoise sea, like his mind seemed to be doing.

Sara turned and gazed off to the left, again toward the candy-cane-striped lighthouse.

M again followed her eyes. "Just so you know, it was the lighthouse Barney was impressed with."

Sara laughed. "Well, not very subtle, I guess. A big red and white phallic symbol's bound to catch a guy's attention, even Barney's."

"You'll have to work on his atrophied sense of aesthetics. Get him out of that cubicle once in a while."

"No. Please drop it. Not me. I think he'd need something more—more of an attraction than me to drag him out of that library."

"No way. If you can't do it, nobody can. You are aware of how alluring *you* are?" He looked over at Sara and noticed she was suppressing a smile, which gave him confidence that he was still on the safe side of the line. "And, as I told you, *he* likes big boobs," … as well as terry cloth, ponytails, and old-fashioned ideologies, he thought, realizing he was suddenly growing somewhat fond of terry cloth himself. He had always thought ponytails were cute, and definitely so on Sara, but … hmm … big boobs?

"You know when you said you were starting the conversation we needed to have, I assumed, erroneously it appears, that it was Kate's, not my bosoms that we needed to talk about?" She reached up behind her head and undid a matching fuchsia ribbon and shook her head, splaying her hair loose. Then, reaching back and up, she re-pulled her hair into a ponytail, re-secured it, turned, and smiled over at him innocuously.

M couldn't look away, even though he thought he should, considering what he'd been unabashedly looking at … not her pony tail. Should he feel guilty? What if she knew what she was doing to him? "OK then, now that we have yours out of the way, let's focus on Kate's," which wasn't going to be easy having just surveyed Sara's. "Of course, hers aren't here."

"You realize," she said, poking him in the arm, "I don't have these kinds of conversations with men … heck, with anybody."

"Never had a brother before, real or otherwise."

CHAPTER 1

"True. True. Still don't, right? And, OK, I'm not actually complaining. My conversations with you are, I have to admit, much more ... umm ... interesting let's say, more fun than most of my conversations. Like with Barney."

"Really? You two were going nose to nose when he was down here."

"Yes, yes, he's a great guy, don't get me wrong, but frustrating. Like my sister, once they get something in their minds there's no changing it."

"I once heard a line from a movie: 'Only the narrow-minded are certain.'" Proud of his little quote, M tried sitting like Sara, she looked so comfortable with her legs tucked under her; but not being limber enough, he grimaced and crossed his legs instead.

"Nice try there," Sara said, smiling, nodding at his crossed legs. "That is a great line, though. I believe that. Barney *is* a pretty 'certain' guy."

"Yeah, but you seemed to hold your own with him."

"Sure. But I always seemed to be playing the devil's advocate. He's rather oxymoron-ish. He's really quite compassionate, a great listener, but he'd say something like it was a law of the universe. Even if I sort of agreed, I had this craving to point out an opposite point of view. Rather like you just said about certainty. It bothered me. Barney was a little too 'certain.'"

M studied her for a while. In his fascination with Kate's overwhelming randomness, had he, because of Sara's previous unobtrusiveness, her apparent pleasant and appealing sweetness, overlooked or misread Sara's brass, her chutzpah? "You said that my conversations were more fun than 'most.' I want to be number one. Ours have to be the *most* fun of not most but *any* of your conversations," he announced, resolutely.

Sara laughed. "Oh, I can see why it always looked like there could be fireworks whenever you and Kate bumped up against each other, philosophically or physically—you and my pugnacious sister."

"Better fireworks than no spark at all?" M queried, standing and walking to the porch railing, leaning forward, looking up and down the sandy, narrow lane each way.

Sara smiled, noticing how, like an exuberant child, he leaned way out, stretching his neck. "I don't know, really, if I felt a spark with Barney or not," she mumbled, almost to herself.

M turned, leaning his butt against the railing. "What you talkin'? You two almost went up in flames that night, the way I picture it."

"There you go again." Sara untucked her legs and leaned forward in her chair, pointing a finger at him. "The line! There'll be no 'picturing' anything of the sort. Out of your mind, OK? But I do admit I respect the man. Going to bed drunk with a man, and then to get naked! My Lord. That is not me."

"It was."

"Sure, under the influence."

"Of what?"

"Goombay squash, or whatever that concoction was, Kate ... *you*!"

"Me? What? Barney gets off scot-free? I'm sure it was him—it wasn't Kate or I—that slipped that conservative little nighty off?" Like a little slap, it hit him: best friend or not, he really didn't want to picture Barney and Sara naked together.

Sara was giving up on trying not to laugh. "The man *was* righteous, I've got to say! Screwing, excuse my language ..."

CHAPTER 1

"You're excusing the word 'screwing?' My God, you are the *good* sister."

"*Proper*!" She shifted closer to the end of the chair. "The proper sister. As I was saying: screwing was not the proper … no, *right* thing to be doing that night, that soon, but I might have. Kate and you have this no-holds-barred, let-it-all-hang-out aura that rubs off. Tempts me to do things I shouldn't."

M turned and looked again, both ways up and down the lane. "My mother had this saying: 'The only thing I can't resist is temptation,' but, you're right, my friend is righteous. I'd like to think I am, but especially under the influence I'da screwed ya, I'm afeared. You're just too fecking adorable."

"What happened to 'will you always be my sister?'" Her smile still a little suppressed.

"I believe that was: 'Will you always think of me as your brother?'" he replied, again turning his back to her. "But, good point. Those are rather interesting considerations there … yours and mine."

"Who or what are you looking for?" she asked, shifting closer to the edge of her chair. "Are we expecting company?"

"When I used to look that way, to the north, I couldn't wait to catch sight of Heidi, meandering out of the morning light toward the cottage, folder in hand; or she'd already be sitting on the steps; or on cool mornings, wrapped in her poncho-like thing, cuddled up on the settee. Or I might see a giant of a man come strolling down the lane smiling like a huge fool … a huge man, a huge fool of a man, damn it!"

"We'll get Peewee back," Sara entreated. "I'm sure he's OK. You know him. Everything'll be OK, M. I really believe that. Don't you?"

"Or this way, toward town," he said, ignoring and not wanting to consider her question, "it might be Spense's colossal cart, bouncing down the lane. Lottie—stunning as always—alongside him, both laughing, yelling some fool stuff. Oh man, I miss that. Then throw Barney ... and you ... into the mix. It was so much frickin' fun."

"And Kate? Where was she in this picture?" Sara stood and sidled over to M at the railing, brushing her shoulder lightly against his. They matched up, height-wise, perfectly.

M instinctively dropped his arm around her as they stood side-by-side. "Oh, you know: sitting here on the porch, probably braless, of course, under her T-shirt, whining: 'Oh my shoulders. They are so tight! Give me a little rub, would ya?' And then whipping her T-shirt off. And if I'd catch a glimpse of those little titties, I'd feel like a pervert. You know, when I think of her now, think of those times, the thought of her moves through my blood like cold oil."

Sara frowned, wondering what he meant. M's throat tightened, his eyes inadvertently watering.

She looked over at him, noticing, and turned and hugged him. "If you say I have nice tits now, I'll slap you. Just want to warn you."

M leaned back, rubbed noses, and kissed her on the forehead. "So, what are we going to do, sis?"

"Kate would like to be here, you know," Sara said without a lot of conviction and laid her head against his shoulder, surprising him.

"Oh? Lottie's not around now. That was her excuse before."

She gave him a little push away, crossed her arms, and leaned out against the railing herself, gazing both ways up and down the lane as M had done. "You two should be able to

CHAPTER 1

work this out. I mean, running into each other like you did. It's amazing. It's certainly like fate brought you two together for a reason."

"Brought all three of us together," M pointed out, leaning his butt against the railing again, his shoulder still brushing Sara's.

"I don't know. Won't it seem tragic if you two can't give it a shot?"

"Star-crossed lovers?" he asked, looking sideways at her. "Where's that flaw, do you suppose?"

"Flaw?" she asked, looking at him, squinting.

"Like you said, if things don't work out for two people, like with my—well, our—dad, and my mom. Isn't there always a tragic flaw behind it? They obviously had something flawed going on between 'em. Don't we all have our tragic flaw?"

Sara turned and faced him, hands on hips. "Yes, of course, but what? Pride you mean? Is it that you two are too proud to allow yourselves to admit you love each other?"

M turned, placed his hands on the small of her back, gently pulled her back to him, and squeezed a little. Sara leaned into the hug and gently squeezed back. It was remarkable how eminently squeezable she was. Holding her seemed to soothe him. He wondered if this was what having a sister would have been like, although at the moment he wasn't feeling exactly 'brotherly.' "I don't know," M sighed in her ear. "What if I just don't love her that way? Anyway, it's more complicated than that. Being proud should be good. We should be happy with who we are, proud to be who we are."

"Excessive pride?" Sara countered, leaning her head back but causing a more interesting part to nudge forward, alarming M. "Blindly egotistical? Narcissistic even?"

They looked into each other. Sara didn't pull away. "I don't know," M almost whispered. "But is there a more tragic flaw than one that keeps two people who might love each other from spending their lives together?"

Sara didn't say anything.

"So, you won't be moving to Minnesota to settle with Barney?"

"Not gonna happen," she whispered back, slowly shaking her head.

"So, no Minnesota in Kate's or your future?"

She hesitated and, not uncomfortably connected to him at the pelvis, searched his eyes, wondering what was in them. "Maybe," she finally said.

"It's not gonna happen … maybe?" he repeated, and it almost seemed to echo.

PART II

Serious at Sears

CHAPTER 2

MP HAD felt lost, aimless, and angry. On a recommendation and a whim he had decided to move to Elbow Cay, one of the outer Abacos islands in the Bahamas, settle, and buy a place. He had found a colorful hillside cottage: two bedrooms, one and a half baths, and a covered wraparound porch to, hopefully, defend his freckles against peeling off in the tropical sun. It was a little more than he wanted to spend, but since there was no real estate tax in the Bahamas, the more expensive the property, the better the deal, he figured. There was a property tax, but minimal in his price range.

He considered just trying to live off the income from the proceeds of the fairly substantial life insurance policy and from the sale of his house in the States, but why not work a little if he could get a work permit? He was only fifty-two. His assets would continue to grow if left alone, and the big Wall Street banks hadn't entirely destroyed the economy. There was no income tax, either, if you lived and worked in the Bahamas. The islands gathered the necessary revenues from consumer taxes, making the resorting a bit expensive for tourists and part timers. Cool, he thought: exploit the exploiters and nurture the natives ... much like the Indians with the casinos. A woman friend of his had married a full-blooded member of the tribe that ran a very successful casino outside Minneapolis. He had told MP something he had

CHAPTER 2

loved: "The white man stole our land; now we are buying it back with their money."

M could live with the high consumer taxes: he consumed little himself, rarely ate out … ate little anyways. So, let the visitors consume and foot the bill. Not a bad plan, he figured, possible only in a small island nation like the Bahamas. A place where he felt he could hide out comfortably.

He wanted to add a covered gazebo on the very top of the cottage so, while he scribbled away, he would have both a view of the harbor and turquoise sea to the west and, over the dune behind, the mottled blue ocean to the east. He had figured he'd want to spend much of his time writing. Although he had taught creative writing and had found students who he had thought had the artist's touch, he wasn't sure he could find an artist in himself.

After Martha and their baby had died, the second baby to do so, he felt he wanted to escape it all and that he needed more than a little catharsis. Everything seemed to upset him. He wasn't much in favor of the direction the current system was taking the US, much less the world. Excess, debt, greed, entitlement—all that shit upset him. Of course the Great Recession caused by all that shit, with a little fraud by Wall Street thrown in, had upset a lot of people a lot more than it had him: jobs, houses, futures, dreams—lost. Too many poor sods had expected a gold mine but got the shaft. MP figured he could be fine in these, so far it seemed, pristine isles. Exploit the system a bit, why not? The system deserved it—but nurture the island.

Development, and the excesses that accompany, seemed to be everywhere. It was already too late for the neighbor to the east: Florida. Even here on too many of the islands, especially down in Nassau, too much of the natural shoreline, coral reefs, and wildlife habitat had already been despoiled and destroyed—and the word was, more was on the way. All in search of the big bang—the almighty buck. But, at what cost, of course? So, before it was too late on this tucked-away little isle, why keep his mouth shut his and pencil idle?

For work, he had initially considered the most available part-time job: waiter or bartender at any of the numerous eating or drinking holes scattered around the islands. But this worried him. He had never been very comfortable around a bar crowd ... unless he was drinking. Actually, he rarely got into the flirty contusion of bar discourse unless he was drunk. And, when he hit the fifties, he lost his appetite for hangovers; up was not worth the price of down. Nor was he ready for a relationship, at least not yet, and probably not the kind of relationship spawned in gin. He had considered a non-drinking establishment, but there weren't many and, of course, drunks tipped better. At this time in his life, he felt it best to avoid the temptation of spirits, and when you lose your family, that temptation could be consuming. He discovered, anyway, when he contacted some of the interesting restaurants and watering holes, that if a Bahamian citizen wanted the job, he or she would be considered first. This was cool and why, he had noticed, that the bartenders and wait staff were mostly Bahamian—white, black, or in between—and all citizens of the Bahamas. So this was fine, he figured, as his Irish blood summoned decadence when alcohol was streaming through his veins.

One day while in Marsh Harbour, a bigger town a short ferry ride from his cottage in Hope Town, searching for tools to construct his bird's-eye perch, he had discovered that the

CHAPTER 2

best selection was at Sears, of all places. His father had always used Craftsman tools from Sears, so he liked the symmetry. He was surprised, actually, to discover Sears still thriving in the islands, as well as in Newfoundland, oddly enough. One of the TV stations on the islands was Newfoundland-based, and they advertised Sears all the time. He was also surprised to discover that *land* was the stressed syllable in Newfoundland, not *Newf*—sorta like most people don't stress the *Or* in Oregon, saying instead Ore*gone*. With a name like Mulcahy, his adoptive name, with the *Mul* stressed, which nobody did, he was, his wife had accused, unwholesomely sensitive to stress—stressed and unstressed syllables only, he had argued.

If the confusion with the surname wasn't bad enough, his mother, the renegade she apparently had been, named him Mikael: not pronounced Michael, of course, but *Me*-cale. And, just to muck things up even more, rather than Patrick for his middle name, she engendered him with simply Pat. An uncle, who was more reprobate than renegade but had been military police in the marines, decided to dub him MP, or 'Empy' as his first-grade teacher had started to spell it in school, or "Empy-headed" as his classmates initially liked to taunt him with. This wasn't as bad as 'Sue,' as in Johnny Cash's 'A Boy Named Sue,' but it had had the same effect. MP had to frequently defend himself ... and his name.

Being a little on the short side, MP had quickly learned a caveat: when insulted, especially by a larger defamer, assault immediately and brutally—at least as brutal as a first-grader can. Flail away assertively, especially if a flail can catch a nose, which usually causes blood to flow—an effective way to end a potentially ugly encounter immediately. These conquests had put an end to the name abuse—until fourth grade when a kid who had flunked two grades and was twice as big as MP decided, at recess, to taunt him with the old moniker. MP never hesitated and ferociously attacked. The oversized mogul, Todd by name, easily mollified MP and neutralized the attack by placing his right hand on MP's empty head, smiling down at him almost kindly. Meanwhile MP flailed away at what could have been gnats, possibly bloodying one or two, but not the giant, and had only the effect of humiliating himself. Everyone laughed and immediately started to chant, "Empy-headed, Empy-headed." Except for the ostensibly now-gentle giant, who, while holding the still-flailing, still-short MP at arm's length, told them all to "shut up or I'll mash you all into little flesh balls."

This gruesome image quickly evoked total silence, and for a moment all you could hear was the swishing of short arms and tiny fists, which gradually slowed and then stopped altogether. The giant continued to hold MP at bay, not trusting the hot-headed midget to have cooled down sufficiently to *not* be empty-headed and come to the realization it was probably a good idea to succumb if he wanted to subsist.

This became what MP thought was the first 'defining moment' in his life. It was true, his history of having to defend the moniker had created a strong sense of confidence: the realization that he didn't have to take shit from anybody, that he could and would stand up for himself, but also: 1) That an untamed temper could lead to humiliation as well as potential holocaust. 2) It was best to be friends with people that could not only harm you but assist you in life, as oddly he and Todd—the gentle giant, who had started to refer to him simply as 'M'—had become great friends after. The only person after who was ever allowed to taunt him with 'Empy-headed'

CHAPTER 2

was indeed Todd, usually when he was giving M some shit he deserved. 3) It was a weakness to be defensive. Since he wasn't dumb, he needn't get all worked up over a taunt with no truth to it. It was like calling a big guy 'little,' like Little John in Robin Hood or calling Todd 'Peewee,' as MP took to doing after they became friends and Peewee his protector. Peewee always seemed to be around when MP's temper got him into a confrontation in which he was overmatched.

For example, one day at a city beach, a bigger, older bully had tried to confiscate the little rubber football MP and his friends were playing catch with in the water. MP had foolishly attempted to tackle the showboating interloper and had managed to grab the ball back, but found himself lifted by the back of the neck with feet dangling just above the water, ball tucked firmly against his chest by both hands. As he dangled there, at a loss as to how he was going to get out of this one, he heard a crunch, a deep-throated yell, and he was suddenly freed, dropped into the water. When he surfaced, there was Peewee asking: "You OK, little guy?"

And 4) last and most important: he learned that because you didn't do well in school, didn't mean you were dumb. Even though Peewee had flunked two grades, he was the smartest guy MP knew. Peewee had trouble with trivial shit like deportment or a report card, but he seemed to be able to see the bigger picture. Peewee had told MP to go ahead and get good grades himself, as he was going to have to start using his head to remain alive and well when Peewee wasn't around to protect him. But, to succeed in life, MP had realized, an A on your report card didn't mean crap in the real world. To MP, Peewee seemed to have an understanding of life you didn't acquire in school. MP didn't get it or know why it was this way, but it gave him a wary apprehension about the system at his early age. That apprehension never went away, and possibly, as far as he could tell now, was why he was living on a remote island and standing in Sears, as it happened, in front of the women's shoe department, thinking: commissions?

When walking through the store, he had seen and heard several sales clerks whose appearance, speech, and accents had not seemed Bahamian. Maybe the rules with an international company were different. So he had sought out the administrative offices. There he found an island eighth-generation Bahamian loyalist: white, named Ajax, who owned the franchise. Ajax dismissed MP immediately without even really looking at him, saying they weren't hiring. MP then asked if he could fill out an application anyway and have an interview, hoping it could lead to something. Ajax finally cast a look at him, smiling, more like sneering—a large eye tooth escaping from under a curled lip—and snarled, "I believe I said we aren't hiring."

"Well, you know, if something opens up, somebody gets sick or something ..." MP tried.

"Apparently ..."

"I wouldn't even cost the store anything," MP inserted, cutting him off. "I'd work entirely on commissions."

" ... you didn't hear me," Ajax finished.

"Like the women's shoe department ... ," MP started.

"Hey!" Ajax yelled sharply. "I ..."

Suddenly a face stuck itself around the corner of Ajax's office. "Ajax," the face implored with tentative urgency.

"What!" he snapped, not sounding too happy with MP, the face, himself, or all three.

"We've got a problem," the face said.

CHAPTER 2

"Well, take care of it," Ajax growled.

The face hesitated. "It's Marilyn. She's pissed."

"Oooh. Marilyn. OK, I'll be right there." Obviously, Ajax didn't relish the idea of facing this Marilyn either. He turned back to MP and hissed, "It's been sweet," and followed the face around the corner. He was hitching up his pants by the waist, looking more like he was hitching up his courage as he strutted out of the office.

Ajax was probably one of the many loyalists (loyal to the king or queen, of course) who had scuffled off to the Bahamas after the mostly successful American Revolution. MP wondered if he seemed too much like a Yankee, a Yankee tourist at that. Anyway, it looked like Sears was not in MP's future. On his way out of the store, MP decided to wander through the women's department and stopped several women who looked like they had some bucks, or at least 'bucks' with money. They told him that the selection of shoes was great, that they liked to buy shoes from this Marilyn. But she had been promoted to manager of the entire Women's Department and a not-so-popular 'Arthur' had just become the new shoe dog. The service had gone to the dogs, even though the selection was still remarkable, as, apparently, Marilyn did the buying.

When he had asked them why they thought Sears didn't get rid of Arthur, they glanced at each other, and one responded, "Well, Arthur is Ajax's brother and, although Arthur is an absolute ass, rude and condescending, Ajax certainly wouldn't fire him."

So MP had wandered back to the women's shoe department to get a little better look at this Arthur. He couldn't remember seeing a man when he had walked by the department before, just several women wandering around, fondling the merchandise.

This time the department was empty. Some ladies were scurrying away with shoes scattered on the floor and awry on the displays. From the back room he could hear two whiny male voices overriding each other, rising in pitch, punctuated with a soft but firm woman's voice saying, "No." The "nos" stayed calm and firm, even as the pitch and timbre of the simpering crescendoed.

Finally, there was a thud, like something hard had struck something soft, and a male voice screamed, "Shit! Goddammit, Ajax, you gonna let her do that to me?"

No answer. Silence abruptly settled in.

"Well?" came another shrill cry.

No answer.

MP was dying of curiosity, especially about the firm "no" lady. He could give a shit about the whiners. He hated whiners. Who didn't? There was a lot of whining going on these days in the States, what with political correctness running rampant. Totally irritating. He was, though, very curious about what these little whiney whimperers would look like, but most curious about the female. How had she managed to stay so calm with those sniveling dickheads? Who had done what to whom? What was the thud?

Then, calm as could be, she appeared from the back. At first glimpse MP thought she looked stunning, beautiful ... but then, not. She had short, dark hair. It looked ... he couldn't tell what ... but not quite right. She was fairly short, and he thought, stocky. But as she strode confidently toward him, he saw her long, conservative skirt had an incongruous slit up the side almost all the way to her hip, and the leg, of which quite a bit was exposed, was surprisingly pleasant and firm, like her voice. Was this the Marilyn?

CHAPTER 2

Behind her the weasely, high-pitched voices started up again. As she approached MP, she greeted him with, as they say in Ireland, a 'lovely' smile. It seemed sweet, natural, yet with maybe a tinge of lampoon sprinkled somewhere in the sweetness. That interested him. "Can I help you?" Yup, the same calm, steady source of the "nos" from the backroom.

"Are you Marilyn?" MP asked, returning the smile.

"Why, yes," she said looking quizzical, but not losing the shine.

"We—e—ll," he said, not sure he should be bucking what he had assumed was the store manager, namely Ajax, "I'd like to be your shoe salesman, or one of them."

"Men's or women's?"

Now you don't have to be a shoe 'salesman' generally with a man. Usually he'll just come in, pick up a shoe, say: "Size nine?" You either got it or you don't. "Want to try it on?" "It's a size nine?" "Yup." "Just box 'em up." No fun in that. Now women … women you need to tempt and tease; you gotta sell. And not just one thing. And not something they don't want—why 'sales' got a bad rep. That's what MP had found was fun about sales: finding out what someone, especially women, wanted and helping them get it. There were always new outfits, new colors, new occasions, new relationships, new husbands … so always a need for something new, especially shoes it seemed. MP had learned this working at an upscale shoe store while in college. "Women's," he responded, without hesitation.

"When can you start?" she said, still shining an interesting, engaging little smile.

"Now," MP said, shrugging. "But what about the work permit rule, though?"

| 25

"Now?" she exclaimed, laughing. "Tomorrow would be fine. I'll take care of the work permit. What hours would you prefer to work?"

"Would, like, four to close be OK?" MP asked, grimacing.

"Hmm," she said now, the shine ebbing to smirk, "only the busiest hours, eh?"

He registered the "eh." Where in the hell was she from, Canada? "Well, I need to spend time, uh, well, I'm writing a book. By four I'm burnt out anyway, and … well, I think I'll surprise you at how good a shoe-dog I am."

"I've already got one hound working here. Did you hear him howling in the back?"

"Well, let me rephrase that: I am the consummate pedestrian pedagogue, a professional podiatribe of the highest pedigree."

The smirk sank to the depth of grimace. "A lot of p's in there, even for a writer. Let me guess, your name starts with a 'p'?"

"Nope. Ends with one though."

"What … Skip?"

"Please!"

"Nip?"

"Nope."

"Kip?"

"Never?"

"Rip?"

"Like your skirt?" He had noticed several times that the slit up the side was no slit, but a frazzled tear. The skirt was long, and it looked like, at one time, had been tightly tailored.

"Oh, God. I forgot." And she ineffectively tried to hold the seams together while standing her ground on two feet. Finally, the only way it would work was if she crossed her feet, thus holding her legs tightly together and pinching the frayed edges with one hand. Of course then she started to lean, sway, to tip—apparently she didn't have the best balance. So MP found himself sticking out an arm and tipping her back into balance.

She acted as if this was quite natural and thanked him the first time, nodding her approval each time after.

"Tip?"

"Like Tip over?"

"Exactly," she said, now stifling a smile, a pretty darn cute one.

"Nope."

"Flip?"

"Like Wilson?" Another gentle tap to straighten the little lady.

"Sure," she said.

"Nope."

"Well, then ... hmmm, not Pip?" she said expectantly, like she had it, adding, "Like in *Great Expectations*?"

"Speaking of expectations, you expect me to keep righting you here?"

"Yes. Of course. If you don't mind. So I give up. Can't think of another man's name that ends in 'p'," she said, swaying.

"You did pretty good, actually. I'm not sure I could have come up with that many."

"Yeah? Then you must not be much of a writer. So what comes before your 'p'?" she inquired, her tiny burst of sarcasm almost toppling her.

"Pressure. Initially a slight discomfort." MP grinned, crossing his feet and swaying with her, after another righting tap.

"OK, wise guy—thank you—you know what I mean. Don't get cute. We hardly know each other. It *must* be 'Tip'?" she asked, again continuing to succeed at being cute, herself.

"Nope, yet here we are getting tipsy together," as she nonchalantly tapped him back into balance. Realizing, as we all eventually do, that he had carried the cuteness far enough, he told her: "MP."

"MP!? What the hell kind of name? How do you even spell 'MP'?"

Suddenly the two whiney wimps wound their way around the corner and out of the back room, the second one still whining. The first, to MP's dismay, was Ajax himself. Ajax was trotting determinedly away from the man MP assumed must be Arthur, both of them ignoring both Marilyn and MP.

"Ajax!" Marilyn called firmly, stabilizing herself and once again exposing almost an entire limb. "Shut up for a second, Arthur, for crying out loud." MP was pleasantly startled by the quasi-controlled temper in Marilyn's command.

Ajax stopped without looking back. Arthur quieted immediately, turned his head, obviously with apprehension toward Marilyn and, while also appearing to be wondering who the stranger was, ran smack dab into Ajax. "For Christ's sake, Arthur!" Ajax carped. "What, Marilyn?" he shot back, taking a deep breath and letting go a huge sigh, now noticing MP.

Realizing her leg was again exposed, she returned to the more modest but unstable pose. Marilyn cleared her throat and nicely and calmly stated: "Meet Mr.... P. He'll be starting in women's shoes tomorrow."

As MP, still swaying a bit himself, gave Marilyn another gentle righting nudge, she returned the favor. Ajax yelled in exasperation, "Whatever!"

Another shrill "What?" escaped from Arthur. "No way, and you gonna let her talk to me like that?" The whimpering

CHAPTER 2

continued as Ajax and Arthur continued to wind their way, now around displays of women's bras and ladies' undergarments, until they were out of sight.

MP uncrossed his arms and ankles, reached out, and put a hand on each of Marilyn's swaying shoulders. He smiled and said, "Thank you, I think. You're going to have to stabilize yourself now."

Marilyn nodded and returned the smile. "See you tomorrow then."

"Uh, I feel I must tell you … Ajax told me Sears wasn't hiring."

"If you're as good as you say you are, you won't cost the store a dime. There's minimum wage paid against commissions, not on top of commissions. So, you sell enough, you'll always make more than the wage."

"Uh, right," MP said. "Actually, I already tried that tact."

"Don't worry," she said. "You can let go of me now." She turned toward a young lady who had wandered into the department. "Hello, I'll be right with you," she chirped with an almost cynical cheerfulness. Looking back at MP: "Tomorrow, then. Bring an ID. We'll have to fill out the official paperwork. Bye, Mr. P."

MP turned and walked away but looked back as he was leaving. Marilyn had once again uncrossed her ankles. He gave her the thumbs-up at the, again, manifested member.

She looked toward him, faked indignation, and pulled her slit together as well as she could, nodded, mouthed "Bye," and turned to help the browser.

MP left, unable to suppress a wide grin. He hadn't felt this much gleeful anticipation since … his honeymoon, he supposed.

DATE: Wednesday, Jan.18, 2012, 6:33 p.m.

M: Hey, Barn. Looks like yur online or whatever. Sorry it's taken me awhile to get to you. I'm getting settled in, and until a few days ago, I didn't have Internet access. So, how's things? You there in your library cubicle on your computer? Got time for a chat?

Barn: Yeah, yeah, I'm here, of course. Shit, man there is such a thing as a telephone. You OK?

M: Yeah, I'm good. Can't make overseas calls on my cell yet, tho. Too expensive. I've bought a little place, got a job selling women's shoes again, no less.

Barn: You frickin bought a place? Where? On Crooked Key or wherever you said you were headed?

M: It's Elbow Cay, dumbshit, and, as you can see it's Cay but pronounced key.

Barn: So, shit man. Does that mean you actually plan on staying there for a while?

M: Yup. It looks like it. It's a great place: far from the maddening crowds. C'mon down.

Barn: Don't get going on our destructive human race but, yah. Good. I will, definitely.

M: When?

Barn: Well, it'll probably have to be summer break.

M: What about that stall in the library where you pretty much live, writing your exciting lectures on, what was that fascinating topic? Oh yeah—taxes! You gonna sublet it out in the summer?

Barn: Ha, ha! Very funny. No, seriously, can I come? You got room?

M: Yeah. But we'll have to sleep together, Big Boy. That bother you?

Barn: Well, we've done it before on trips, but you were married and so, not horny. What about now? Think you could stay away from me?

M: What! Does suddenly being single make me gay? You ought to know you latent homophobic pedagogue.

Barn: Hey! Just because I never married doesn't mean I'm a homo—whatever, either.

M: What does marriage have to do with sexual preference these days, huh, you nonliterate tax professor? Anyway, just kidding, about sleeping together that is. I have two bedrooms, so you can stop getting excited. But I have discovered a very interesting lady down here who I am excited about.

Barn: You ready for a relationship already? Kind of quick, isn't it?

M: I don't know. Maybe.

Barn: So, you sleeping with her yet?

M: Thanks for the positive thought. No, not even close. I'm not even sure if she's interested in me. I'll keep you posted. Gotta go, big boy. Bye. Let me know if you can get down here sooner.

CHAPTER 3

MP HAD many reasons behind wanting to write: to be a writer, or really 'an author.' Writers write; authors are published. For one, he liked the idea: "What do you do?" "I'm an author." People have no idea what to think of an author or anyone who makes a living as an artist, probably. Anyone can write or paint or sculpt, but can you make a living at it? The premise, he supposed, was that if you can make a living at it, somebody must appreciate it, and if someone buys it, it must be good. Of course, that's not necessarily true. Well, not entirely, he thought. It's a lot about marketing, right? If nobody sees it or hears about it, how can they buy it?

First things first: what should he write about? He had heard a writer should write about what he or she knows. Kind of a 'duh!' He did have some devils to exorcize: like about being a little short. Who has written about the prejudices against and tribulations of short people? Like being embarrassed when you discretely *hide*, out of *your* and obviously your wife's sight you dumbly assume, a bottle of personal warming lubricant on top of your refrigerator where *you* can't see it. Of course it's in plain sight of any normal-sized person, and then they ask, eyebrows raised, why you have it in the kitchen to begin with. Or the curiously emasculating look you get when a taller female clerk, who reminds you of nuns that used to twist your ear in grade school, asks if you'd like her to grab you a package of Preparation H you've unfortunately been unable to reach on a high shelf—as if short people don't have hemorrhoids! Or the humiliation and unfairness of being told senior year of high school that you can't be the quarterback anymore, the position you've played quite successfully all your life to date, not because you're not good enough, but because *you're too fucking short*!

Or, maybe write about a little more imposing demon: illuminating how screwed the young generation is. The happy-go-borrowing baby boomers, first bequeathing their sense of entitlement to their offspring, who are unfortunately following right in their fickle footprints, and then, even if inadvertently, exploiting their own grandbabies, for crying out loud, who will be inheriting the burden of their debt and of caring, financially, for the generations ahead of them who have spent all their money.

Whether MP was any good at writing or not he didn't really know, but he figured he'd try to write something interesting, even fun, so that it would get read, and might make a difference. It appeared the system in the islands would allow him to nurture, not exploit. There was yet, it also appeared, no concept here of planned obsolescence, thus planned waste. On Elbow Cay there wasn't even a need for a car. You could get anywhere you wanted with a bike or electric golf cart. His only boat for now, a kayak. With a good garden of veggies and fruit, he could almost, with no taxation, be self-sufficient. Seemed like a plan. For two years since Martha and his baby's death he'd done little but drift, grumbling and muttering through his days.

He figured he had something to say, so this is what he thought he wanted to do with the rest of his life: write about shit that bugged him. He enjoyed most of the ironies: how the people composing the system in the States had, ironically, exploited *themselves*. They worked to earn money, and even if they made a lot of it, they were poor because they paid everyone but themselves. The irony of affluence: abundance is dependent on resources, and the sources are being exhausted. Dumb shits. Parasites. The system, created by us short-sighted humans, was simply exploitative; and even if it was likely too late to quell the inevitable apocalyptic tsunami caused by the eruption of these consummate consumers, he felt he had to say something about it. Try, maybe in vain, to temper the system by appealing to the sensibilities of young people. Made him think of Todd 'Peewee,' the smartest guy he'd ever known, yet who failed out of high school at eighteen when he was only a sophomore. The system simply sucked.

Marilyn did not, however. Yet something nagged at him: behind the attraction, the seemingly rosy glow and lovely smile, he sensed a simmering of ... something: an edge, an edge that if you went over you might find darkness, something seething below. He didn't know why he felt this way, but it fascinated him. Enticed him. She had seemed entirely wholesome, honest, straightforward, and completely in charge of her life and the women's department at Sears. This included women's shoes, fortunately, since Ajax and Arthur were double-A adversaries. He had been immediately drawn to her, but there was something awry he couldn't put his finger on.

In the interview the next day, basically filling out the official application, Marilyn had gotten MP's vitals: he was fifty-two years old; had been an economics teacher but also had taught elective creative writing classes, indeed an odd combo she had pointed out; had gotten a securities license to help fellow teachers

CHAPTER 3

with their financial planning; had been married for thirty years. He didn't know why—he had surprised himself—but he had even shared with her, off the record, his family history. He had never known his biological father, a Mac McGennity; his mother had not lived with this Mac but had married and divorced him the same day. As MP's wife used to say, "In a vain attempt to prevent MP from being a bastard." She instead married Robert Mulcahy, apparently her real boyfriend, before MP was even born, and had adopted him.

Right after MP and his wife, Martha, were married, Martha had almost died giving birth to their first baby, who had only lived a few hours. After that they had kept on trying and, finally, "a little too late in life" they were told, had gotten pregnant again. But both mother and baby had died this time, almost two years ago. There had been a variety of health and insurance problems all along with a multitude of medications and procedures that had left not only a sour taste in MP's mouth but distaste, again, for the entire system, including the health insurance and medical professions. He wasn't sure why this had all spilled out of him to pretty much a perfect, well a seemingly perfect, stranger except, maybe it was because he was alone and a stranger far from his estranged home?

So Marilyn, who told him her last name was Chambers, had gotten even more than the vital statistics on MP, now in the Sears culture known as Mr. P. By the time MP was done, Marilyn had turned stone silent and had an almost dazed look. Finally she had said, distractedly, that MP was the most pathetic excuse for a name she had ever heard. So, for now, until something better came up, it was Mr. P. As he left, he looked back to find her sitting there, staring off at nothing in particular.

CHAPTER 4

DATE: Thursday, Jan. 19, 2012, 7:15 p.m.

Kate: Hey, Sis. How's things in Spokane? You there at your pretty purple laptop? Got time for a chat? Wow, you're not going to believe what I just found out! You're not going to believe it.

Sara: Yeah! Hi, Katie. I'm here. Good, good. How are you doing? I'm just finishing up some business emails. What am I not going to believe? But, first, have you heard from them? Or *HIM*?

Kate: I haven't, thank God. You?

Sara: Well—yes.

Kate: And?

Sara: Richard says he'll never give up looking for you. He gives me the creeps.

Kate: No shit, Sadie. Your email is safe, isn't it?

Sara: I don't know how he could get my password. Except it sounds like he's getting desperate, so with the tech resources at his company, who knows what he can do?

Kate: Well, he hasn't found me yet. I don't know how he could find me down here.

Sara: Marilyn? I've been thinking—why'd you pick that one? LOL. I just can't picture you as a Marilyn.

CHAPTER 4

Kate: And I've picked Chambers as my surname.

Sara: No! You're terrible!

Kate: Nobody's picked up on it yet. Otherwise, yeah, well, I'm laying low. No confidences with anyone. Nobody knows anything about me. I dress like a Marilyn, bad hair and all. You know: "Marilyn, Marilyn, Madam Librarian from *Music Man*. So I try to look and act like one.

Sara: I know it's from *Music Man* but it's Marion, fool. Sounds kind of lonely, babe. Well, what's this great news?

Kate: Well, that's the real reason I e'd. You remember Dad talking about being married to this crazy lady before Mom? Didn't live with her but had a kid? Well, this guy comes into Sears just when I'm having it out with Arthur & Ajax and so, out of spite, I tell him I'd hire him to sell women's shoes. I had no idea why I was doing it. It was like the devil made me do it, and, well, now I guess maybe I know why he did. Does the name Mikael Pat Mulcahy ring a bell?

Sara: Kind of.

Kate: Who would have been born Mikael Pat McGennity?

Sara: What!? No freaking way. Really? No crap. Is it really him? After all these years of wondering about him? It's right, isn't it? When Dad told us about him, he was adopted Mulcahy. Mulcahy's right, right?

Kate: Yeah, it's got to be him, our long lost sorta-half-brother. He was born in Duluth, where Dad said he married the mystery woman. This guy, MP he calls himself, says he never met his birth father, that he heard he was a brawling, drunken Irishman, and his mother remarried

37

right away, a Robert Mulcahy, and he doesn't remember, well, Dad, at all.

Sara: LOL. A brawling, drunken Irishman, eh? I've heard some stories, even considering the way he died, so it doesn't really surprise me. So, what's he like?

Kate: Well, that's just it—it's weird. I felt a connection right away, before I knew. He's cute, funny, and engaging, I guess I'd say. I just sort of felt like I was comfortable and could trust him right away.

Sara: You haven't told him anything, have you?

Kate: No, but it's like I want to. When he was talking about not knowing his father, I almost told him I understood because we never knew our real father either, and since Dad left him behind, I wanted him to know that he didn't abandon *us*, that he married Mom, adopted us, and was a good father.

Sara: Well, you better not. The more people that know anything about you, the more likely you'll be discovered. But, God, I can't believe it. I've got to get down there and at least see him. Holy crap! I can't believe it. No way. And hey, Sis, it's been long enough. I miss you. When should I come? God, I want to come right now.

Kate: Well, put it on hold for a little while. I miss you, too. Gotta go. I'll keep you informed. Mum's the word for now. Bye, hon.

Back at Sears, Mr. P., on the other hand, had been unable to discover anything about Marilyn. Wait, had she said her last name was Chambers? Marilyn Chambers! No feckin' way! The porn queen? Who'd name their daughter Marilyn Chambers?

CHAPTER 4

He didn't know anything about her: how old she was, if she was single, married, divorced, widowed, straight, or gay. He couldn't consider asking Ajax or Arthur, as neither was on speaking terms with him.

Marilyn had gotten Sears to pay for the work permit, which would be for one year. MP, Mr. P., had been forced to agree to a succession of weekly assessments. Ajax insisted that Mr. P. was on 'probation' for that first year. It would need to be assumed by the government that he was training another employee, a Haitian named Vernal—although a citizen of the Bahamas—to supposedly be taking over his job for him. This ruse seemed a bit subversive to MP, but apparently the AA brothers had money and, thus, pull. This was one of the ways Sears got around having to hire Bahamians, but MP was surprised that Ajax had let *his* hiring happen. He guessed a fear of Marilyn's ire was behind it, as he knew Ajax wasn't happy about it at all.

The only concession by the 'system' at Sears was that Marilyn was to do the assessments. Apparently, Ajax didn't have the time. So MP was delighted. He figured with Marilyn's domination over the less-than-august Ajax, his job was safe, in spite of Arthur's sputtering. Also, since he didn't see Marilyn as much as he would have liked since she was either diligent in her management responsibilities or sequestered searching out new and exciting merchandise to buy, the assessments would give him the opportunities to assess her as well. Knowing absolutely nothing of her personal life, he was exasperatingly intrigued, almost haunted. Marilyn Chambers … yeah, right! Something definitely smelled fishy.

For the first weekly appraisal, they were to meet at a local eatery by the ferry dock at the water's edge called, appropriately, Water's Edge.

He had gotten there twenty minutes late. "Sorry. Sorry. I got wrapped up in something I was writing, missed the ferry," he apologized as he sat, breathing hard to demonstrate his sincerity.

She had only a hint of her usual convivial smile. "Not a good idea to show up late when I'm supposed to fire you." She went on to tell him she had bought him another week, due to that in the first week sales had quadrupled, of course quadrupling Arthur's irritation. "You're going to have to make some concessions to Arthur," she told him. "He's especially unnerved by the prospect that by you training Vernal to sell on the floor that he'd actually have to treat him as an equal. Up until now Vernal has always been in the back running shoes, so he's been able to treat him as a subordinate, you know, his slave."

"You're aware Vernal has no ambitions to *sell* shoes, only to *stock* them?" MP said.

"Sure. Of course I know that. It's just how to beat the system. Vernal's got a different agenda anyway. You are aware, officially, we have to place three ads to see if a Bahamian could fill the position?"

"Yeah. I know. Why wouldn't that happen?"

"There's no way Ajax would allow a Haitian or native Bahamian to be selling on the floor. They all have to be out of sight doing menial jobs like Vernal's. The only way I got away with hiring you is under the premise that you're training Vernal for your position."

"Yeah, I know. A little underhanded, isn't it? I almost wish I *was* training him to take over for me."

Marilyn smiled, almost with a hint of … could it be affection? Or maybe it was affection he was feeling. Was there such a thing as 'affection at first sight?' "Sure," she answered, "but

CHAPTER 4

that's the reality of the system at Sears." Another system he was sure he wouldn't want to be part of—if it weren't for Marilyn.

"So, what are these concessions I have to make to Arthur?" MP asked, knowing this was going to piss him off.

"Anything. Just to ward off his incessant complaints to Ajax."

"Again, like what?"

"Don't get defensive," she said. "Maybe just help Vernal stock some shoes when you come in.

"I do."

Vernal is not a native islander but a Haitian initially hired to run the shoes for Arthur." He wasn't the speediest worker, even by Sears' standards, but MP was starting to realize Vernal did have bigger things on his mind than running shoes. MP had been paying more attention to him. He had discovered that Vernal acted coy intentionally, almost like a disguise.

"Arthur probably has only five or six customers all day before you come in and the rush starts. You seem to get more sales in your first hour than poor Arthur has customers all day. Did you say you already help Vernal stock shoes?" she asked, seeming surprised.

"Yeah. Why?"

She hesitated. "Well, Arthur told me you don't."

"Don't what?"

"Stock shoes," she finished, holding her breath.

"Why, that …"

"Watch it!" she said, though smiling. "I have delicate ears."

" … that pimply-assed-lying-lizard son-of-a-dick-fart!"

"There's an original one," she said, laughing. "You really have been stocking shoes?"

"Yes!" he said, now pissed and defensive.

| 41

"You know, hiring you hasn't made me real popular. I stepped over the line quite a ways that day. I'm actually on probation myself. I'm pretty sure Ajax would love to get rid of me as well. I don't believe he enjoys women he can't control."

"No way. The women's department is by far the best, most profitable in the entire store. If Sears had any brains, they'd fire Ajax and Arthur and make you the store manager."

Marilyn said nothing right away, just gazed at Mr. P. "Actually, Ajax and Arthur own the stupid franchise," she finally said. "They belong to a well-heeled family ... lotsa money. Like I said, I stepped over the line. Ajax went to the regional guy in Miami. He knows the store's numbers, but he is a good ole boy from way back ... and so did give me a reprimand. I'm sure Ajax and the family control him, anyway."

"A reprimand? What the hell for?" MP asked. "Exactly what line did you step over?"

"The day I hired you, I got sick of those two, especially Arthur. He had just offended a friend of mine. He's apparently got this trick: he pulls his stool up close when slipping on a shoe, causing the woman to have to lift her knee up too high and, if she happens to be wearing a dress, Arthur gets what he hopes is a 'beaver shot.' Well, my friend does not shop without undergarments, but she did have on a short summer dress and became fully aware of what that sneaky little prick was doing. So she took off the shoe, threw it at him, and found me. I was giving Arthur hell in the back when he went and got Ajax to come to his defense and lied about what he had done. Finally I got so frustrated I ... I just hauled off and put my foot halfway up that asshole's asshole."

"Ajax's or Arthur's?"

"Arthur's, although I would have liked to have booted both."

CHAPTER 4

MP couldn't keep a shit-eating grin off his face. "And so the thud I heard, and the sexy slit?"

She looked back at MP again, a little grin on her face. "Right. The sexy slit ... ," and she started to lean, tipping over in the booth.

MP laughed harder than he had in a long time, reached out, and tapped her back to upright. Then, surprising himself, he did something he didn't think he had ever done to anyone: lightly pinched her nose before withdrawing his hand. He still couldn't figure it out. She had these almost alarmingly beautiful bright yet biting eyes, but her hair framed her face awkwardly. It was not a fashionable cut, definitely not flattering. Her nose turned down a little; her cheekbones were a little too sharp; her face a little too gaunt; her mouth too large. He had originally thought she looked stocky, but it must have been due to the clothes she wore. They didn't flatter her in the least. He could tell she had an athletic build: slender but strong upper arms and definition to her calves. The leg he had seen quite a bit of that first day had been also slender, but not skinny. The clothes she wore simply did not complement her figure, accentuate her breasts, or display what he imagined was a cute little tush. None of the parts seemed to match, but she seemed comfortable in them. She did not carry herself in a masculine way, yet she offered no sensuality in demeanor or appearance. No come-on ... but no go-away either.

"Hey, no freebies," she said and knocked her nose with her finger. "And the slit showed more than you'll ever hope to see again."

"Ever? Hey, I can hope all I want. Or is there a rule against that in Ajax's system?"

She simply smiled back. "We'd better get back to the store. Finish your watered-down tea."

"Wait. I know absolutely nothing about you. Not fair. You got my history."

"OK, one question."

"One question?" he protested. "At one question every week, you'll die of old age before I know much of anything. We'll just have to have dinner."

"No fraternizing with the hired help. Rules of the store."

"Uh-uh. Doesn't work. You're hired help too."

"I'm your manager."

"So?"

"That's the system," she said, squinting at him.

"I don't think much of any system," he said. "I doubt you do either."

"Hmmm ... ," was all she said, smiling.

"So, dinner?"

"We'll see." She seemed to be holding something back, he could tell.

"Well, until 'we see,' then two questions; two per week."

She stared at him for a while. "OK. Shoot," she finally said.

"All right. Let's see: how old?" It hit him he had no idea. She could have been maybe late twenties, maybe late-thirties.

"None of your business."

"Again, not fair. You know how old I am."

She paused, again smiling, but seeming distracted. "OK, forty-five."

"Really!" he said, honestly surprised.

"Watch it," she warned, still smiling.

"No. Sorry. No offense. You just don't look forty-anything."

"Watch it!"

"It's a compliment!" he expounded. "Are you married?"

CHAPTER 4

"No," she said without hesitating and started to slide out of the booth.

"Ever been married?" he asked immediately.

"Uh-uh. Only two questions."

"What? No fair. That's part of the same question."

"Let's go," she said, definitively putting an end to the quiz, and started to walk out. The last thing she said to him as they entered Sears was not to get into it with Arthur about the lie about stocking shoes. She would deal with it.

THE WEEK went fine: MP got more comfortable with the stock and making friends with an extremely private Vernal, discovering he had a couple children—a boy and a girl—and that he and his wife had been involved in protests against a crooked and ineffectual Haitian government and had been forced to flee to the Abacos for safety. MP was also enjoying the interaction with the variety of lady shoppers, and avoided any interaction and altercations with Arthur, who was around less, thankfully. Unfortunately, so was Marilyn. He had begun to wonder if she was avoiding him. For the second weekly appraisal, MP came in early again because he had to meet with Marilyn in the women's shoe department this time, as Arthur was in some kind of meeting with Ajax. MP had stopped and picked up a couple of lattes.

Being an island and beach environ, MP wasn't sure how casually he could dress: he avoided shorts and flip-flops and generally wore a buttoned short-sleeve shirt and light, quick-dry nylon pants, sometimes with leather sandals or Crocs. He really took his lead from Marilyn, who always dressed conservatively, almost matronly, like the full-length skirt of the revealing rip, and nothing low-cut or tight. So MP went

[45

with inoffensive and conservative. No reason to give Ajax any ammunition anyway.

Today, though, was a little different. Marilyn was arranging shoes on the racks when he entered the department. He stopped and scrutinized the scene unfolding in front of him. Her blouse today was a draping, clinging fabric and her skirt more brightly colored and rather short. For the first time he could tell she had breasts … and two knees. He wondered if she had dressed a little more breezy for the meeting with him? Hopeful thinking, but … maybe.

"Well, do I still have a job?" he said as he approached her.

She turned, smiled, and started tapping the shoe she was holding in the palm of her other hand. "I thought I felt someone standing there. What were you doing? How long have you been there?"

"What makes you think I've been standing here for a while?"

"You have that guileless look like you just performed some indiscretion."

MP laughed. "My, my, how perceptive. I was simply admiring how you look today. Is that OK?"

"No," she said, stifling her grin. "Let's sit and do our assessment before a customer comes in." She reached out and snatched her latte.

"I got an idea," MP said. "You pretend you're my customer and I'll demonstrate just how profound my shoe-dog skills are by bringing out four shoes, which I'll bet three of which are your favorites, and all will fit you to a T."

Marilyn laughed and said, "You're on. What's the bet?"

"Well, let's say I win—you pay for dinner; you win—I pay."

"Nice try, Romeo. How about you win, I pay for lunch at our next assessment? Vice versa, hot dog."

CHAPTER 4

"Not much of a bet! But settle in this here chair and let me see that foot."

She settled and crossed her legs, holding her right foot out to him. As he sat on his stool and slipped her Capezio flat off with his right hand, holding her Achilles gently with his left, he was struck with an odd, erogenous sensation. He had taken hundreds of shoes off in this exact manner and had never really thought much of it, except a little anticipation regarding what the paw would look like. In his experience, he had found feet to be the universal equalizer. Many a beautiful woman had the ugliest feet: veiny, second toe curled and longer than the biggie, knobby, bunions; while many not-so-attractive prospects had smooth, well-shaped, beautiful feet. So there always was some fun in the unveiling, but this time the exposure knocked him for a loop. He had never thought of an Achilles as sensual, or the sliding off of a slipper as compelling.

"You having a little problem there?" Marilyn inquired, a hint of mockery in her tone.

"Ah, no. No. Just have to estimate the right size: length and width, you know? Looks like we have a narrow one."

"You always cradle and caress your customers' Achilles to size their feet?" she asked, eyebrows and sarcasm raised.

He hadn't planned to, but after taking her shoe off, he had reestablished his hold on her foot, albeit gingerly, in his right hand, the left hand still cupping the Achilles.

MP laughed a little nervously and set the foot on his stool's slope between his legs where he'd had, again, hundreds of feet—sweet feet, grotesque feet—but had never, never realized that they were naked and that close to … 'home.' "OK," he caught himself, "you look like a 7, A or AA depending on the shoe."

"Very good. I'm impressed. Of course, after groping it for a while ..."

MP stood, a bit disconcerted. He couldn't believe it. What was wrong with him? A foot had never done this to him before, naked or not. Get a grip, he told himself. "Be right back. Be ready to continue to be impressed." Lame, he thought, but he trotted off to the backroom. *What the hell was that all about? It was just a fecking foot*, he thought as he disappeared into the shoe archives.

He wandered around, trying to focus. Four shoes: one, maybe a dress heel; then a more daring new look—an oversized platform maybe; then a comfort casual; and, finally, a walking shoe?

He came back out, satisfied with his choices, and sat on his stool, setting four boxes on the floor to his right. "OK. We'll start with the most difficult to fit first: an evening dress sandal."

"Oh my. I'm dying to see your choice. A shoe someone might wear out to dinner I assume?"

"Exactly," he said, grinning, holding but not opening the box. "This choice assumes you have at least a somewhat glamorous side yet to be revealed?"

She smiled, sarcastically of course. "Excuse me if I don't dress glamorously at Sears. I mean, ya think I got the hots for Arthur?"

"Where is the SOB, anyway?"

"He and Ajax have been in a lot of meetings lately ... with guys in expensive suits. I'm not sure what that's all about."

"Ajax seems to be gone a lot lately, not that I mind," MP said, knitting his brow.

CHAPTER 4

Marilyn returned the knit. "Yeah, right. He's been leaving the store a lot during the day, usually dressed to the nines, especially lately. I don't know what they're up to, but I don't trust either of those …"

"A-holes?" MP interjected.

Marilyn laughed. "That is good: 'A-holes.' Yes, I just know they're up to no good. You know? And the pricks have money, too, you remember? Family money."

"What the hell are they doing working at Sears?"

"They're not just working here, fool; they, or the family, own the franchise. They still own stores all over."

"Where?"

"I don't know. Ajax is always bragging about the family corporation and acting like they're royalty … developing this, buying that. You know how he acts: like you're shit under his shoe."

"What could they be up to around here?"

"I don't know, but they have a big cruiser in the harbor. Vernal says they go out in it a lot, usually with those guys in expensive suits. They also keep a plane at the airport."

"Vernal?" MP said. "How does he know?"

"Vernal plays dumb; he's not, you know?"

"I'm just starting to figure that out. Why, do you suppose?"

Marilyn leaned toward him conspiratorially, and said quietly, "Vernal is well-connected. There are Haitians all throughout the islands. They keep in contact with each other, almost like a brotherhood. And I've heard Vernal is one of the chief guys. All I know, even though he doesn't talk much, as you know, is that he and the other Haitians hate both Ajax and Arthur. You probably don't know, but besides running shoes, he cleans the offices. I get the feeling he spies on especially

| 49

Ajax, which he can easily do, as they pretend he isn't even there, like he doesn't exist."

"Well, let's talk to him."

"He keeps everything pretty close to the cuff. I'm management so he may not believe he can trust me. But he likes you. You treat him well. Maybe he'll talk to you."

MP was clutching the shoe box to his chest like he was protecting a rubber football.

"OK, Mr. Shoe Dog of the highest pedigree. Let's see what you've got there."

MP smiled slyly, hid the box behind him as he took the shoe out, and looked at her over the top of his tortoise shell glasses. "Ready?"

"Oh, I can hardly wait," she said with her hand over her heart.

He whipped the shoe around and she broke out in laughter. "Well, good choice, I guess, since I already own these. Only," she said, "my heel slips out of the back strap."

"Well, try these on. I'm willing to bet yours are an A width?"

"Uh, yeah, I think they are." She could tell by the way he was trying not to grin and looking at her over his glasses that he was up to something.

"Let's slip on these AAs and see what happens," he said, covertly cagy, and pulled his stool closer. Still looking up at her over the top of his glasses, obviously smothering a grin, he lifted her foot, and thus the knee, to slip the shoe on, and suddenly Marilyn realized it was Arthur's trick and that if he were looking other than at her face, he would know whether she was wearing undies—or not. She grinned back at him, swiftly lowering and extending her foot, stopping perilously close to his boys' 'home' and her heel frighteningly near the

CHAPTER 4

front door. "Watchit, hot dog, if ya wanna walk out of here," she warned.

Just then a couple resorters came strolling into the department. Smothering a laugh, Marilyn said, "You better go and check on those two, wise guy."

He hadn't flinched and she hadn't removed her foot. He looked down at her, yes, still naked foot and laid his hand on the instep: "Fortunately, but just barely, I am able to." He looked up and their eyes caught, and for a moment neither faltered, grins fading. He put a little downward pressure on the instep, her big toe close to ringing the doorbell.

"Go, fool," she said, slapping his hand away and leaning forward, sliding the shoe on and adjusting the straps.

He sat for a second, watching her hands delicately diddle with the strap inches from …"Go," she said again, hushed.

After greeting the pair and deciphering they were shoppers, not buyers, he started back to Marilyn, but heard another couple entering and stopped.

Marilyn now was standing once again, hands on hips in pseudo indignation. "Our meeting is over, buddy. And, yes, the AA doesn't slip and I have two of the other three already. If I wore a walking shoe, I'd probably get this one. So, even though I should fire you for indecent foot-fondling and other sneaky, underhanded offenses, you pass the second assessment. You are, indeed, a consummate podiatribe of the highest pedigree."

"Well, thank you." And they both turned away smiling, thinking, for the time being, similar thoughts.

MP ALMOST made it through the week upholding Marilyn's request to avoid confrontation with Arthur, and so helped Vernal stock shoes in the back. He used the opportunity to get to know Vernal even better. Vernal definitely had another agenda other than running shoes, but he wasn't ready to share it with MP yet. But it was obvious he had no love for Ajax and Arthur.

Then one day after running shoes in the back, MP came out and found Arthur sitting in one of the chairs, his feet up and crossed on a stool, his eyes closed, and several women just leaving the shoe department. It pissed MP off so much he walked over and kicked the stool out from under Arthur's feet.

This, of course, startled Arthur awake. "Huh? What the hell! Whaddya think you're doing?"

Arthur just pissed him off. He couldn't help himself. In spite of what Marilyn had requested, he spit, "Why'd you tell Marilyn I don't stock shoes, asshole?"

"What? Huh?"

"You heard me, shithead. Why'd you lie to Marilyn?"

"I ... I didn't," he stammered.

"Bullshit. You're telling me Marilyn lied to me?"

Arthur jerked to a stand and huffed, "I don't have to answer to you," and stomped off toward the backroom.

Just then a young island girl strolled into the store. MP yelled to Arthur that he was "up." Arthur took a look and said, "You can have her" loud enough for her to hear. On her heels a wealthy older woman walked in and took a seat as the young island girl sulked away. As MP passed Arthur in the back on his way to get shoes to show the wealthy woman, Arthur hissed, "It was my ups!"

MP was proud of himself: although he wanted very badly to smack him for his behavior toward the island girl, he didn't. "Sorry, old boy, I'd say you gave up your 'ups.' Besides, this

CHAPTER 4

one, apparently a better prospect in your sniveling little mind, requested me."

"What do you mean 'requested you'?"

"She said a friend of hers told her to come in and ask for me."

Arthur started to sputter something.

"Hey, watch the saliva spatter, you dumb mutt," MP said, now trying to piss him off.

"You can't do that!" he spat out.

"Do what? Whoa! You ever hear of breath fresheners?"

"Tell people to ask for you," Arthur cried petulantly.

"Well, in this case I didn't tell her friend to have her ask for me, but why the hell not?"

"Then I miss my 'ups!'"

MP had no sympathy for this little mongrel. "You wishy-washy wimp ... you entitled little moron prick. You sit on your ass and because you and your worthless brother own the store you think you get 'ups' you don't deserve ... or even need. Just piss off, asshole. With that he left Arthur standing there whimpering, hoping he hadn't gone too far.

HE HAD. The 'entitled' apparently can be decent schemers. They have to do something to validate themselves. When MP next came in to work, he was met at the door by Ajax.

"You're fired," he announced proudly.

MP didn't bother to argue or protest. "Where's Marilyn?" he demanded.

Ajax sneered gleefully. "This is way over Marilyn's head. It'll teach you to call me a 'worthless prick!'"

"I ... ," he started to argue, to say that it was Arthur he called a worthless prick ... or did he say something like that about Ajax as well? Probably. It was true. "Where's Marilyn?" he repeated.

Still the gleeful sneer: "She's not here."

"Where is she then?"

"She's gone."

"Gone?" MP asked suspiciously, with one eye closed.

"Yes. Your savior left you crucified."

MP was surprised at the play on words. Must be an accident, he figured. "Gone where?"

"Wouldn't you like to know? With the wind," Ajax said, enjoying his cruel attempt at humor.

"C'mon, you ... Ajax." MP figured calling him an asshole at this juncture would get him nowhere. "When will she be back?"

"Not sure she's coming back."

"What! What do you mean?"

"Sorry. It's been nice knowing ya! Now get the hell out of here."

MP thought of wringing it out of him. What did he mean by "not sure she's coming back?" Instead he summoned up one last acerbic, almost pitiful smile, shook his head, and walked away. He had just started a writing project that got him excited ... so, fine. He'd just go home and dive right back into the writing. But ... what the hell was up with Marilyn? And how was he going to find out? He had no way to contact her.

DATE: Monday, Feb. 20, 2012, 8:20 p.m.

Kate: Sara, hon, did I catch you at your computer? Time for a chat?

Sara: Yeah, I'm still doing some work. Seems like I'm stuck on this darn computer a lot lately. What's up?

Kate: I'm taking some time off work and I'm staying over at a friend's on Treasure Cay. Sara, I saw him today in Marsh Harbour!

Sara: What? He knows you're down there? How? What are you going to do? That means ... How the hell did he find out where you are?

Kate: I don't know, Sara. He didn't come to my apartment and I didn't see him at Sears. So he probably doesn't know where I live yet, or hopefully where I work. But he must know I'm here or why would he be?

Sara: Well, what happened? He didn't see you?

Kate: No, he must not have.

Sara: What are you going to do about work? What if that's how he found out where you are?

Kate: Could be, I suppose. I told Ajax, the store manager, that if someone looking like him—I showed him a photo—came into the store asking if someone like me worked here, to tell him no! But Ajax's a total ass, except he's not dumb. I could just see the greasy wheels turning in his head and he got all suspicious and started asking questions. I think he felt he had something on me. He was almost gloating because he could tell I was worried and uncomfortable. I don't know why I even considered talking to him. It hit me that if Richard came in asking about me, Ajax would be more than happy to accommodate if he felt he was getting me into some sort of trouble.

Sara: Jeez, Katie. What'd you do to get on his bad side?

Kate: Never mind, it's a long story and has something to do with our newly discovered "brother." Ajax hates him more than he hates me. He fired him. Hey, hmmm. You know, I think I just got an idea. Family helps each other out, right?

Sara: Yeah, of course. I'll do anything you want.

Kate: No, how about our new family?

Sara: New? Oh. What you thinking, Sis?

Kate: Well, I can't stay at my friend's in Treasure Cay for too long, and I'm scared to keep coming into work in case he knows. I'm taking a few days off and putting everything from my apartment in a storage locker, not that I've got that much. I've avoided MP (God, what a stupid name!) not wanting to involve him. I don't want him in any danger. But Ajax says he's going to fire me as well if I take too much time off. Hmmm.

Sara: So you haven't seen MP?

Kate: Not for a while, since Ajax fired him. I don't know what he's thinking. He hasn't contacted me. Of course, I don't know how he could. But if he comes in the store—I suppose I have to go back in—and I'm there? I don't know.

Sara: Shoot, I've gotta go, Katie. What if it is our emails that gave it away? What do we need to do? Do we change our passwords? We'd better, you suppose? Keep me informed. Tell me what I can do. God, I can't just leave you hanging.

Kate: What you think you can do up there with me down here? No. Really. I think I have an idea. But, Sara, I am concerned about us emailing. What if that is how he knows I am here? I'll think about it. See what you can find out as well. I've got to go, too, hon. I'll keep you informed somehow. Later.

CHAPTER 5

SEVERAL DAYS ambled by. MP tried to immerse himself in his writing, but he couldn't get Marilyn off his mind. He had assumed she would contact him, but she hadn't. He had given his cell number and email for his file, so she should be able to reach him. Where was she? What was going on? He didn't really know her all that well, but still he really felt they had connected and this didn't seem right. Why would she just disappear? Was she embarrassed she let him get fired? Was she pissed he had gone and yelled at Arthur when she had asked him not to? But Ajax had said she might not be back! She couldn't have just walked out of his life, could she? He had really liked her and, at the least, wanted to be friends. He had his good friends back in the States, but she was the first person he had met down here that he thought he wanted to be close to.

He figured he'd have to go back to Sears and see if she was there or, at least, find where she had gone. But what if she was there? Why wouldn't she have contacted him? Maybe she didn't share his feelings. But, being a cocky Irishman, he couldn't help but presume he was simply irresistible. He assumed if she was gone or something was wrong, he'd never get anything out of the asshole brothers. Would some of the other employees know anything? Could he find the regional guy in Miami? He would know. But would he be willing to provide that kind of information? What the hell was going on? Was she OK?

MP had set aside his rough draft of his novel, *A Little Short*, and had started a nonfiction piece he thought he'd call *If I Had a Million Dollars*. Because of his economics background and financial planning experience, he had perspective on what had caused the most dramatic recession since the Great Depression. What he also knew, having taught that generation, is not only how oblivious the children and young adults were to what they were inheriting, but how ill-prepared and uninformed they were to deal with the challenges facing them. They were the generation, more than any other, that would have to take care of themselves financially ... yet ironically and dangerously, they were the generation that had been the most taken care of. Coddled in their parents' misguided economic optimism and search for abundance, they had definitely caught a disease—affluenza—and so were obsequious and susceptible to failing.

So, MP thought, why not write to them in their language, a readable, understandable, and hopefully motivational little book to enlighten them. He also knew enough about financial planning to give them the fundamentals. Everyone in the States was clamoring for financial literacy, fearing that each successive financial crisis would get cumulatively worse if those habits that had gotten them into this mess weren't corrected.

He wanted to encourage young adults to do things like informational interviews. In one of MP's own informational interviews when he was pursuing the idea of becoming an ad exec, the CEO of an ad agency had just returned tanned and excited from Hope Town on Elbow Cay in the Abacos. He didn't have a job to offer, but he sure had been excited about

CHAPTER 5

Hope Town. It seemed like a good name and spot for someone losing faith in his destiny.

Now, here he was on a cloudy, windy day, bundled up on his perch, looking out at the not-so-topaz Abaco Sea with the bleak, relentless Atlantic waves pounding a message behind him, contemplating just how happy and contented he was with where his search had led him. So why not write what he had learned about career literacy as well? It might help some new graduates, maybe.

But scribble as he might, gaze as longingly as he did, feel as self-righteous as he tried, he couldn't completely lose himself. He always found himself wondering: what the hell was going on with Marilyn?

He started having trouble getting to sleep. The thought of Marilyn buried like a burr in the back of his mind—scratchy, snagged on some distant amnesic nerve. He found having a martini helped, two did the trick. He thought of another saying his mother always delivered with a crinkle in the corners of her eyes: "Martinis are like women's breasts—one's not enough and three's too many." Two would do for now.

He tried masturbating to how he imagined he would make love to Marilyn, but he couldn't sustain an erection. He felt like he was trespassing, an interloper in an inviolable place. He could get hard but he couldn't sustain an erotic image. The memory of his peek at her exposed leg would get him excited, but he couldn't get himself to exploit her erotically. The thought that she must have nipples would arouse him, but he didn't ... couldn't ... touch them in his imagination. The anticipation of his tongue mingling with her tongue would excite him, but the speculation of a clitoris would render him soft.

Oddly, the same thing happened with the memory of his wife. He had loved to make love to her, but now that she was dead he felt it was almost sacrilegious to think of her carnally. Was this normal? He so wanted to rekindle the sensation of her touch, the sensuousness of her body against his. But, since this didn't seem right, why couldn't he replace Martha with Marilyn? What was wrong with that? He felt Marilyn had been attracted to him. Yet, no matter how graceful or tender his fantasy would be, it was like he was trying to just have sex, when what he missed was making love. Where the hell was Marilyn? He wondered if she had any notions of possibly making love to him. He felt something was there. He believed all would be well 'in the flesh'—if they could ever get there.

He had no trouble fantasizing about Lottie, though. Lottie was the bartender at Cap'n Jack's, a watering hole on a pier overlooking the harbor. Lottie was gorgeous, freckled, and fun—a red-headed anomaly with generous breasts but narrow waist, compact tush, and slender legs. One cool night, the wind whipping the palm trees against the roof of Cap'n Jack's, MP started on his third breast, talking and toying with Lottie. This was about the third time he had outlasted all the other guys to closing and finally got the nerve to ask her if she wanted a peek at his little perch. Of course, to last 'til closing, he had had to break his mother's rule, and so he was surprised when she accepted, fully aware that in his condition, if it got down and dirty, he might be seeing three breasts.

When they got to his place, she hadn't encouraged him, and so, although inebriated, he did his best to be the consummate gentleman. Although she spent the night, cuddled warmly in his bed, he ended up swathed in blankets in the hammock on his chilly perch, thinking not of Lottie, but of Marilyn.

CHAPTER 5

MP woke in the morning to Lottie gently swinging him in the hammock. She was wrapped in one of his sweaters, an old rolled-neck cardigan, smoking a joint. His back was killing him from sleeping all night in the hammock, but when he realized she was naked behind his cardigan, the pain dissipated magically. One shoulder was exposed, tanned and freckled, as was plenty of cleavage, tanned and freckled. A lot of thigh, more tenderly tanned and, naturally, less freckled, was showing below the sweater. He feckin' loved freckles.

"Morning, buckaroo," she rasped while holding in a lungful. "Care for a hit?"

"The way you look this morning, I'd like to hit on you." MP and Martha used to smoke pot before making love, but he hadn't had an opportunity for stoned sex since ... well, since awhile before she ... he tried to push the memory of Martha from his mind.

"That'd be just dandy," she said and sat down in his writing chair, lifting her leg, putting her foot up against him, and swinging the hammock with it.

Well, she definitely didn't have underpants on under the sweater. MP's first reaction, after getting one of Arthur's beaver shots, a rare red beaver at that, was to quickly avert his eyes.

"What's the matter? Don't like what you see?" she said, obviously toying with him and taking another puff. "Here," she said and leaned forward, handing him the joint, the sweater falling forward, exposing not three, but two perfect martinis.

This time he didn't avert anything, and she had to lead his hand to the joint. He took it, looked to see what was in her eyes, and sucked too hard on the joint, thinking it was going out. He started hacking, uncooly, and tipped the hammock, also uncooly. He managed to land on his feet but tripped up in the blankets. She stood and caught him with her arms out and the unbuttoned cardigan wide open. They were about the same height, and they stood there nose to nose, breasts to breast.

"Why didn't we do this last night?" MP asked, freeing an arm to take another drag on the joint but finding it out.

"Here," she said, removing one of her arms from around him, pulling out a lighter from the cardigan pocket, and lighting the joint while he inhaled.

He almost coughed again but managed to hold it in, eyes watering.

"You're OK," Lottie said, laughing. "You'd had too many last night. If you'd come on to me, I would have left. If a female bartender learns anything, it's that late-night drunk lovemaking is seldom rewarding."

MP laughed. "You're OK, too."

With that, she leaned in and gave him a slow, soft kiss with lips slightly parted. Why was he thinking about Martha and Marilyn right now? No Martha, no Marilyn; no Martha, no Marilyn.

"But a slow, stoned lovemaking in the morning, fully delightful for both … now that's another story," she said and leaned into him again. This time she found his tongue and, although he felt his heart speed "up," he wondered why nothing else was.

CHAPTER 6

ALL RIGHT! After trying unsuccessfully to write all day, MP decided that he had waited long enough for Marilyn to contact him. He was going to go back into Sears and get serious with Ajax and Arthur. If Marilyn was there, he didn't know what he'd do. If she wasn't, he didn't know what he'd do. But he decided he wouldn't leave until he found out what was going on, if not from the A-hole brothers, then from some other employee. But first he had to go see Lottie, and ... what? Apologize?

When he walked into Cap'n's it was Saturday night, happy hour, and the place was crowded with only Lottie on, tending bar. She paid no attention to him. She was busy keeping everyone at the bar up-to-date on their poison. Finally she glanced at him, but no smile, and turned to satisfy another thirsty patron. The gulls seemed a little more aggressive tonight as several were landing near some of the tables out near the edge of the pier. He went and shooed them away and then came back and stepped behind the bar, helping himself to a glass of Hendrick's and some rocks, looking to her for approval.

"Want a job?" Lottie asked as she whisked by to grab a few limes from under the bar.

"What?" MP asked and followed her with his eyes as she floated to the other end, grabbing two Coronas on the way.

"Jerry quit this morning," she yelled to him. "I can't handle this all by myself. Jack told me to find a replacement. Interested?"

A guy named Jack was actually the owner, although not the original Cap'n Jack. "Free punch part of the bargain?"

She came and stood by him, washing out some glasses. "Gin, you mean?" She was all business, sarcasm aside. He couldn't get a read on her reaction to seeing him any more than he could figure out what he should do or how to act. For one of the first times in his life, he felt meek, humbled. Not his usual cocky self.

"You serious?" he asked just as she left with a clean glass and started the blender. "What about a permit?"

She said something, but he couldn't hear her over the noise of the blender.

When it stopped, he yelled a little too loudly, "What?"

She sidled over to him and intently asked, "Have you tended before?"

"Yeah, a little."

"Can you handle a crowd?"

What did she mean by that? Just because he was inadequate this morning didn't mean he was an impotent bartender.

"Well?"

"What do you mean?"

"What the hell do you think I mean? I'm getting killed here," she said as two guys started pounding their empty Red Stripes on the bar. "Can you? Do you want a job? Don't worry about the work permit. Just a sec, gentlemen!" she yelled over her shoulder.

"Sure. Yeah, I guess so."

"Then grab a Cap'n Jack's T-shirt under there and get your ass in gear."

CHAPTER 6

He had an ominous feeling as he took off his 'The Beatings Will Continue Until Morale Improves' T-shirt and put on the Cap'n's. He felt like he was abandoning Marilyn. He had assumed he would eventually get his shoe day job back. Now? And how was the captain going to handle the work permit? He wasn't sure he felt OK with this underhanded bullshit.

The bar was jammed all night, this being a Saturday, and he had no time to consider his situation with the permit, Lottie, or Marilyn. The only times they talked before closing was when he had trouble with the cash register or he needed some instructions on mixing some more ultra-exotic, umbrella'd, blended drinks the resorters seem to love. He decided multi-tasking with decisive drunkards might be a hell of a lot easier than indecisive sober shoppers. And, he wouldn't have to deal with the A-hole brothers.

As the last of the stragglers was almost forcibly escorted to the door, MP wasn't sure how he was going to face reality himself. He poured himself a glass of Hendrick's as Lottie wiped the last of the glasses. "This OK?" he asked, holding up the glass.

"I won't tell if you don't," she said dismissively, MP felt.

"Well, tonight went a lot better than this morning," he ventured, unsure of what to say, how to act, so he swigged the gin.

She didn't smile. "Don't worry about it. It's happened before."

"Not to me," MP lied.

"Well, you passed the test tonight, so it looks like we'll be working together. Not a good idea to be messing around with someone you work with anyway. Jack will start paying you under the table. If no one complains to immigration, you'll be fine for now. See ya tomorrow."

"What! No second chance? I'm sober as a judge tonight."

"Like I said, judge, keep the shirt and grab a couple more. I'll let Jack know tomorrow. Come on in a little early to fill out the forms and shit. Take it easy. See you around four o'clock." And with that he was dismissed.

He poured another shot of Hendrick's and threw it down, hoping it would help him get to sleep. When he got home after a somewhat wobbly golf-cart ride, he lay on his bed and considered trying again with Lottie in his dreams, but he couldn't shake the feeling that he would be cheating on Marilyn … or was it Martha? Why the hell did he feel like this? Martha had been gone long enough. No one, including Martha, would hold it against him if he started dating. It had been long enough. So why did he feel dirty masturbating? And Lottie? My God, she was every capable male's wet dream. And there she had been in all her carnal splendor. What the hell was wrong with him? *Thank God for gin* was the last thought he had as he dropped off.

HE AND LOTTIE had made it through a Saturday at Cap'n's—not an easy chore. Sundays the entire cay mostly shut down—little was open but the churches, so the local folks as well as the tourists made the most of Saturday nights. Lottie was great to work with as well as be served by: easy on the eyes, efficient, always cheerful and accommodating … as long as there was no sexual tension. MP figured that was probably A-OK since this was, actually, a work relationship now. But today was Sunday. The ferries still ran to Marsh Harbour, and Sears was as serious on Sunday as every other day. He was

CHAPTER 6

going to get to the bottom of the Marilyn mystery or else. Or else what, he didn't know.

It was about a three-block walk from the ferry pier at Marsh Harbour to Sears. The sun had come out and it was a hot Sunday sidewalk stroll. It felt good to get into the air-conditioned store, until he saw Marilyn repositioning a mannequin that was attired in only a bra and panties, in the, obviously, women's department. He moseyed up behind her and waited, wondering what he was going to say. Was he pissed? He was conflicted: was he happy she was here or angry?

She stood back, almost into him, pondering the positioning of the barely clad prototype. She … it … had nipples that showed through the almost-bare brassiere.

"Don't you think that's a little bizarre?" he asked quietly, almost in her ear.

She jumped as if he had yelled it. "Shit! You scared the hell out of me! There you go sneaking up on me again? At least you finally showed up."

"What do you mean: '*I* finally showed up?' Where have *you* been?" he said, a trifle petulantly.

"We need to talk," she said. "Let's go get a coffee."

"A coffee?" he said, making no attempt to conceal his Irish ire. "How about a line of boilermakers?"

She looked shaken. He had never seen her lose her composure before. "C'mon. Follow me," she whispered and grabbed his arm.

"Really?" he responded, not budging. "Follow you? Where?"

"MP, I'll explain. C'mon. Let's go somewhere we can talk."

"Somewhere? Like where?"

"Umm, how about your place?" she popped on him, like she thought there was nothing unusual about the suggestion.

He did, though. "My place? You don't even know where my place is. It's not in Marsh Harbour."

"Well, of course, I know you don't live in Marsh Harbour. I know you're on Elbow Cay."

He took a couple of deep breaths. "OK, of course, the application. We've just really never talked about where I live."

"There's a lot we haven't talked about, but I know a lot more about you than you realize."

"What the hell does that mean?" he howled.

"C'mon. Let's get out of here," she said, hooking her arm through his and dragging him toward the door. She stopped and grabbed her bag from behind a counter on the way. This was starting to appear to him like something she had planned beforehand.

He let her lead him out of the women's department, out of the store, and to her car, an old VW Vanagon Westphalia, packed to the brim. They climbed in without a word of protest from MP, and she drove to the ferry. He had no idea what was happening or why it was happening, but what the hell he figured? Go with the flow.

"What are we doing?" he finally had to ask as she parked the VW at the far end of the parking lot for the ferry.

"We're going to your place, remember?"

"My place! We're going to my place?" This was about as muddled, and … enticed he supposed … as he'd been in quite some while, maybe ever so, again, what the hell?

"Yeah, so shut up and let's get on the ferry before it leaves without us."

The ferry ride from Marsh Harbour, a town big enough to have an airport to Hope Town on Elbow Cay, a settlement just big enough to have a ferry dock, took about twenty minutes.

CHAPTER 6

They barely spoke, Marilyn seeming nervous. MP just shut up like she had told him. He figured this was way beyond him. Her purse, perched on her lap, was more of a duffel, a woven island bag, and she was hugging it. It was full, of what MP couldn't even guess. It looked heavy.

When they pulled into the harbor, the tide was out, so they had to climb up several rungs of the ladder to get onto the dock. Kate went first, MP grabbing her bag and stifling the urge for a furtive upward ogle. On the dock Marilyn cracked the silence with, "Cart or walk?"

"No. I've got a cart. It's not a real long walk, but the road is sand to the north end and is a dusty walk … a dusty cart ride too, I'm afraid."

"Good. I wasn't expecting a walk today, so I don't have those good walking shoes on," she said, always with that tinge of sarcasm.

Being the old shoe dog, he had noticed her sandals: multi-colored straps forming a creative island flip-flop. "Cool sandals," MP said. "New from the Sears women's shoe department?"

She didn't answer, just looked at him with a slightly twisted smile as they climbed into his cart.

"How are sales?" he asked, just to make conversation as he pulled the cart onto the cobbled path that ran through the settlement of the mostly small, brightly painted island cottages, past the harbor entrance, to the dusty, rutted road leading to the north end of the island.

"Down, of course," she answered.

"Arthur any better?"

"No."

"Well then, why the hell did you leave me fired, stranded, 'crucified by my own savior' is the pithy phrase Ajax used?"

"That's what we're going to talk about," she said, looking away to the right up at the sand hills that overlooked the ocean. "Today was my first day back to the store. I didn't have your cell number written on my hand … or anywhere else. I couldn't call you, but I was going to, today."

MP looked to his left at the sparkling water of the Abaco Sea peeking through the lawns of the cottages as they zipped by. He figured he'd just wait for the explanation from this beguiling woman he was trying to be annoyed at. But he just couldn't muster up any of the displeasure he wanted to feel. There was something deeper, he felt, with her. It just felt good to be with her, but with the unexplained hiatus he was still pissed off … a rather curiously not-unpleasant cacophony of emotions.

PART III

Women

CHAPTER 7

MP PULLED the cart through the open gate into his small but colorful backyard and parked in his usual spot next to a large hibiscus bush. "Well, here we are," he said, the first words aired in a while. He dared look at her, also for the first time in a while.

She just sat there, looking down, pensive, not at him, the yard, or cottage.

"So what do you think?" he asked as he climbed out of the cart.

"Huh? Oh, um ... yeah, cool. It's really private back here. So many bushes," she said, distracted, still not looking at him, even when she spoke. She was wearing the colorful sleeveless sundress over a scrunchy tank top, worked both at Sears and here on the island. He noticed she was more tan than usual and her exposed upper arms weren't thin but firm, almost muscular, like he recalled that leg. Actually he didn't really have to recall it; it frequently popped into his mind uninvited.

"Well," he asked, "you want to come in or sit on the porch around front facing the Abaco? I can make us a drink or whatever."

She looked at him, finally, lifted her eyebrows, and said, "Let's take a look at the interior of your humble abode."

"OK, follow me." He led her up onto the back of the wraparound porch and in the back door through a little room

CHAPTER 7

full of beach shit and right into the living room. It had had bare pine walls when he bought it, but he had stained them golden oak to look like the knotty pine interiors of the old cabins he had spent summers in on northern Minnesota lakes. There was a lounge and other chairs set haphazardly amid driftwood tables, with books scattered everywhere on the floor. The one especially comfortable-looking lounging chair sat facing a TV with an old pole lamp from the sixties next to it. One piece of driftwood that resembled a dog sat obediently on the other side of the lounge.

"Very interesting décor, my dear," she said, frisking the room with her eyes.

"My dear?" MP parroted, closing one eye, lifting the other. "Well, my dear, I might have straightened a bit if I had known I was having company."

She laughed and said, "I'm especially interested in the kitchen."

"Huh? Why the kitchen?"

"You'll see." And she walked down the step from the living room toward the front of the cottage. The kitchen was on the left. Not large, but a counter separated it from the eating area, which was over on the right, providing ample counter space. The dining table was piled full of books, shells, sand dollars, 'found' glass, pieces of 'found' wood. "Use the table a lot, do you?"

"Ahh, not for eating, no," he said. "I usually eat out on the veranda." He opened the French doors and led her out onto a huge covered porch with a hammock back left and to the side, a ceiling fan hanging over several deck chairs up front by the porch railing, and another fan over a fairly large rectangular glass-topped table on the right, with only a closed computer

73

and empty glass on it. A settee sat in the middle back. The sun was blinding, just starting to drop beneath the protection of the porch roof.

"So, facing the sunset, eh?" she said, squinting and looking out at the harbor and the lighthouse in the distance to the left with the glimmering Abaco Sea straight ahead beyond the beach cottages down the hill.

"Eh? They have verandas in Canada, do they, eh?" MP mocked as he lowered the sun shades at the front of the porch. "That where you're from?"

"This is where you do your writing?" Marilyn asked, ignoring his question, and sat at the table. "I didn't think you typed."

"I don't."

"Then what's the computer for?"

"Mostly to peck out emails. And when I write, it's pencil to paper. Then I have it typed and emailed to me. Then edit and rewrite from there on the computer. But this isn't where I do most of my writing."

"Oh, let's see where you do. And I imagine you have at least one bedroom somewhere, and I could use a bathroom. Got one of those?"

"Two, as a matter of fact; well, one full, up, and another half, down. But two bedrooms."

"Good," she said. "Perfect. Now where's the closest bathroom?"

"Good? Perfect? What's that supposed to mean?" MP sputtered, continuing to wonder what the hell was going on but not really caring or worrying.

"Ah … you'll see. Now, that bathroom?"

He stood for a moment, brow furrowed, considering … what? He had no idea.

CHAPTER 7

"It's getting a little urgent," she said, crossing her legs.

"Don't start that again," he said, smiling. "Off the living room, around behind the stairs. I'll run upstairs and pick up a bit. Come up when you're done."

"Gotta hide those girlie magazines you got scattered around your bedroom, I suppose?" she said as she headed toward the bathroom.

"Yeah, right," he answered, then realizing she was right, and she knew he knew. He scurried up the stairs into his room, stacked the *Playboys* and *Esquires* on his nightstand with a *TIME* placed strategically on top, and halfheartedly threw the covers up over the pillows. He made a quick trip into the upstairs bath to see how disgusting it was and realized he had to pee too.

Just as he got the stream going, he heard her coming up the stairs. The flow was showing no signs of abating and he had left the door open. He gritted his teeth, shut the flow off midstream, and scurried quickly to close the door just as she arrived. He froze, penis in hand.

He turned and tried to stuff it back in through his fly, but it wasn't ready to be stuffed anywhere and, engorged with urgent urine, started squirting. So he scuttled back to the toilet, dick in hand, and let go a wild spurt that only partially got the toilet bowl.

He sighed with relief, and as he started to shake it free of dribbles, realized she was still standing there and, also, that more than dribbles covered the front of his jeans.

"You're going to have to be a better shot than that," she said as he unhunched, tucked it back in, peacefully this time, and looked over his shoulder to see her casually leaning against the door frame.

This was not normal behavior for the Marilyn he used to know. And he was not terribly proud to show off the wet stains all down the front of his pants. "Do you mind?" MP said over his shoulder, trying to muster the indignation he assumed he should feel.

"Why aren't you turning around? You dribble?"

"Not funny!" he retorted. "Why are you just standing there watching me?"

"Well, if we're going to be living together, we'd better get used to each other's foibles. Where's that second bedroom?"

"It's around ... what? Living together? What the ..."

She walked up behind him, put her hand on his shoulder, pulled the hair dryer off a hook, and handed it to him. "Here. This is what I'd do if I dribbled." She peeked over his shoulder and said, "But you may need a clothes dryer for that one, baby."

He covered his fly, although now zipped, with both hands and sputtered, "What! Wait! What do you mean? You're ... what?"

"Dry yourself and I'll explain in the bedroom. My bedroom, by the way, not yours. If we're living together, there'll be no explaining anything in your bedroom."

He heard her walk across the hall to where his bedroom was. "Oops!" he heard her say. "By the way, nice try putting the *TIME* on top of your *Playboys*. My room must be the other one. And what is this ladder going up to?" He stood there several seconds, paralyzed with confusion, looking at himself in the medicine cabinet mirror to ensure it was him this was happening to. Finally he switched on the blow dryer and realized this was something he'd never done before—drying pee off his crotch—and had an odd dawning that his life was going to change and he'd be doing a lot of things he'd never done before.

CHAPTER 7

He found her up on the perch sitting in *his* chair at *his* table perusing *his* view. "Cool. Really cool," she said, swiveling in his chair in all directions.

"It took me and a carpenter on the island several days —and Craftsman tools from your Sears—to get it done. That's why I was there, by the way, the day of the kickin' slit."

"Very clever! This is the sense of humor I have to learn to live with?" Just about everything she said had a little sarcastic sting. "But, great job. This is really cool. You're obviously handier than you let on. You can see out past the masts and lighthouse almost all the way to Marsh Harbour. And, over here, the sinister Atlantic."

"What's sinister is you; that's what's sinister," MP retorted.

"What, bro?" she cooed. This was definitely not the Marilyn he used to know at Sears. Who the hell was this?

"Just what's going on in that ... what do you mean, 'bro'? You're definitely acting different, but you're still Caucasian."

"Why can't I call my brother 'bro'?" She was trying to act casual, wry, comedic, but he could tell she was nervous.

"Yeah, if I had an Afro ... I mean, what do you mean, *brother*?"

She looked at him, calmly, an uneasy smile stuck on her face. "Here, pull over your chair and have a seat."

"*My* chair is the one you're sitting on. I can pull over a chair for you ... wait, wait a minute! What the hell is going on?"

"C'mon. You're going to have to relearn to share," she said. "You want to sit here and I'll pull over a chair?"

He slid over the only other chair, a rickety bamboo he had salvaged from Cap'n Jack's, next to his. "Here. You sit in this one. I'll sit in mine." He had no idea why he felt suddenly protective of his chair, but he was starting to get an inkling he should be protective of more than just his chair.

"My, my. You're going to have to get over that territorial attitude if we're to coexist comfortably," she said as she swiveled in his chair. "You can close your mouth. You look like a Venus flytrap."

He tried to say something, but only a little gurgle came out. She got up, relinquishing his chair to him, sat in the wobbly wicker, and put her feet on the edge of his chair. "So, sit," she said, "and I'll explain."

"Your feet are on my chair."

"There's still plenty of room for that skinny little ass of yours."

Who was this person? he thought. Did Marilyn have an evil twin? But he sat down on his chair, wanting to say: "My chair! My chair!" Which he was aware would've sounded really stupid, but IT WAS HIS CHAIR!

She kicked off her sandals, leaned dangerously back, the wicker creaking, and put her bare feet in his lap when he tentatively sat. Her naked, slender, sandy feet now not only close to home but more than just her toe knocking on the door. He looked at them, looked at her, and back at the feet, skinny and a little dusty, and then back at her. What the hell kind of reversal had happened? It was like the *Twilight Zone*. He had always been the one to play with her, make suggestive cute little comments. Now her feet were in his lap, which yesterday he would have welcomed—welcomed any physical contact for that matter—and now he sat rigid, tense, almost afraid to look at her feet, much less touch them. Then suddenly he felt a charley horse starting to seize his calf.

"What's wrong? You look constipated," she said.

Suddenly the calf convulsed in an intense spasm. He leapt out of the chair, sending her feet flying, and first pounded on his calf with both fists and then stomped around, screaming silently.

CHAPTER 7

By now she was bent over laughing, a little too hysterically he felt. It wasn't *that* funny. As a matter of fact, it wasn't funny at all. "Oh my, oh my," she said through tears. "Here, sit down and put your leg in my lap. I assume ... oh my ... I assume you have a cramp. I'll rub it out."

"No way! No way!" he yelled, but he couldn't believe himself. Hadn't he fantasized a number of means to acceptable physical contact with her? Now she was offering a massage, be it just his calf, and he was terrified. He slowed his stomping, finally, as the cramp abated.

Still laughing little hiccups, she asked, "You all right now? Can we talk?"

"Go ahead, talk," he said as he kept pacing around the perch. "I'm dying to hear whatever you have to say."

"You looked like it," she said and started laughing again. "Dying, yes, oh my, my ..." she trailed off. "OK, can you sit down again? I think it'd be best if you were sitting when I tell you this."

"Tell me what?" MP said warily, still pacing, still feeling the pull of the cramp.

"You're sure you don't want to sit down? I promise not to hurt you this time."

"You didn't. OK, OK, just kidding, right?" as he sat cautiously down.

"Yup. But now sit tight. I'm getting serious. Hold on to that chair. You remember that day we met?" she started.

"Of course, whaddya talkin' about?"

"Well, I have to admit I thought you were kinda cute. You know, felt a connection; you know what I mean?"

"Uh, yeah!" Boy, did he ever know what she meant. But from what she was implying so far, he wondered at what kind

| 79

of connection she was now referring to.

"It was more how you acted that I thought was cute ... not that you're a mutt or anything."

"Gee, thanks. A dog, but a purebred, huh?"

She didn't smile or laugh. "Just shut up and listen, OK? This isn't easy. I liked you right away, OK? Didn't know why. But I wasn't going to get interested, even if you were Sean Connery ... well, maybe more like Johnny Depp. I was escaping a bad deal and the last thing I wanted was a relationship. And that, as it turns out, is a good thing."

"A good th—?"

"You gonna shut up or do I have to hurt you again?"

MP closed his mouth, figured "what the hell," kicked off his Crocs, lounged back in *his* chair, feigned nonchalance, and crossed his feet in *her* lap. Let her deal with that! "All right, go ahead. Not another word."

To his surprise, she grasped his feet gently, pulled them down deep into her lap, shifted to get comfortable, and continued: "Well, anyway, let's say your wanting to work at Sears seemed to be ... fortuitous."

He opened his mouth to say something, but she squeezed his feet and glared.

"Then," she continued, "you filled out the paperwork."

Then, he thought, things changed. He had felt the first day she had returned his flirts. But after that it was all business ... well, mostly business. He had thought that since he was now officially an employee, she was trying to act professional. He raised his eyebrows, waiting for her to continue.

"'Mikael Pat Mulcahy' it said," Marilyn not only pronouncing it correctly but getting the inflections right. "When I asked you about your father, you said you had never met him. Your mother had divorced him, a Mac McGennity, before you were

CHAPTER 7

even born, then married your stepfather, who adopted you."

It was like a lightning strike screamed through his veins. He tried to sit up, but she held his feet firm.

"What do you know about him?" she asked. "Mac McGennity, your biological father?"

He was sitting, uncomfortably now, up straight, his feet secured firmly in her hands, and, rare in his life, speechless.

"OK, you can talk. What do you know about him?"

"Well, my uncle, who I guess knew him pretty good, said if he had one night to live, he'd go out on the town with him."

"That's ... nice," she said.

"But a good friend of my mother's, as I believe I already told you, told me he was a brawling, drunken Irishman."

She smiled a little sadly. "They're both right, I suppose."

"I also believe I have two half-sisters?" he said slowly.

She looked at him expectantly. "Yes, you do. One is now holding your feet, and she's in a bit o' trouble."

He looked at her, into her really, not knowing who he was seeing: a lovely woman that he thought he had desired or a frightening woman he suddenly had to believe was his sister? She squeezed his feet tightly and looked down. He felt warm drops on his toes.

CHAPTER 8

DATE: Sunday, Feb. 26, 2002, 10:30 a.m.

M: Barn, you there? I desperately need a chat. You're not going to believe this. You know that woman I was talking about down here? You know: she hired me and I kinda liked her? Well, she's my sister, well half-sister, I guess. Can you fuckin' believe that? Really!

Barn: Yeah, yeah, I'm here. I'm always here. Wait, wait. This woman, I thought you were sleeping with her?

M: No, no, dumbshit. I said I was interested in her. Really, she was sorta oddly good-lookin', and we, like, flirted, but something didn't seem right about… I don't know… although attracted to her, I hadn't come to really seeing myself being with her, you know—in the biblical sense. I just couldn't think lewdly, you know—that way—about her. And, shit, it's a good thing!

Barn: OK, wait just a minute. I guess I remember you telling me that a guy called Mac-something was your genetic father, but I don't remember anything about sisters. That's just too weird. How do you know this? Where'd you meet her?

M: Remember, I told you I was selling women's shoes again at Sears? Well, she hired me, remember? And, of course, I had to fill out an application and shit. So, when

CHAPTER 8

I told her my history—more than she needed ... I don't know why, I just went runnin' off at the mouth—she figured it out.

Barn: Wait just a minute. Why didn't you recognize her name? Why didn't you know? This is just too bizarre. Why does this kind of shit always happen to you? Where's the other sister?

M: I know, I'm totally freaked out. She doesn't go by McGennity, which should be her name—unless she's married, or was. She said she wasn't, but I suppose she might have been. I really don't know anything about her ... YET. And, when I think about it, she doesn't look like a Marilyn. Well, there is Marilyn Monroe. I just bet her name is not even Marilyn. Now don't fall out of your cubicle, but something weird, and I mean *weird!* is going on with her. I just found this out today, and now *my sister* is taking a bath! In my tub!

Barn: I thought you weren't ... what is she doing taking a ... what the hell's going on?

M: Exactly. I don't fricking know. But she says she's moving in with me. Something's wrong, I guess. All she'd say is that she's hiding from someone.

Barn: What? Why? From who? What's wrong?

M: Again, I don't know! She has only told me that she saw this person in Marsh Harbour and that's why she's here with me. I hear her coming down the stairs; I'd better go. When I find out what the hell's going on, I'll let you know. Bye.

Barn: Wait. M? Shit. You can't leave me hanging like this.

M: Later. Bye.

Barn: M?

Barn: Shit.

MP HAD had to leave for work. Jack's wasn't open for business, it being a Sunday, but he had said he'd come in in the afternoon and help Ma give the kitchen a good cleaning. When he got home it was a little late and he had come up the stairs quietly so not to wake her. But, as he slipped into bed, he thought he could hear her crying in her room. So what was he supposed to do? If he even resembled a gentleman, he had to offer, at the least ... consolation? But what if she was in bed, even worse in her pajamas? He couldn't go hugging her or whatever in her pajamas, could he? He had let himself be attracted to her. She's feckin' *attractive* so something would be wrong with him if he wasn't ... but, Jesus, she was his half-sister! Could he be attracted to just the 'good' half? Oh hell, he decided: she sure sounded like she needed a hug or something. So he slipped back into his clothes and ventured across the hall.

He put his ear to the door and could hear quiet sobbing. He opened the door slowly, knocking as he did so, and peeked in at her. Sure as shit! Not even jammies: T-shirt and panties! Now what? Shit! She was sitting up, against the back of the bed in the standard crying pose with her knees up and head buried between them. She didn't look up even after he knocked again, lightly.

He walked over to the bed ... hesitantly. She had stopped sobbing but still had her head between her knees. He kneeled on the bed, crawled over to her, and tried to figure ... how the hell was he going to hug her? She didn't really look like she

CHAPTER 8

was inviting a hug. He knelt there for a second, figuring. She didn't move or acknowledge his presence. Finally he reached one arm across her knees to her far shoulder, a light hand on the nearer one, and placed the side of his face against the back of her neck. He felt lame; it was an awkward as hell hug, but he didn't know what else to do.

Finally, she lifted her head, tear lines running down her cheeks, dripping onto her Victoria Secrets, and asked him what he thought he was doing.

"Uh ... I guess ... umm ... I guess I'm trying to hug ya. Sorry."

"You call that a hug? Come here, you moron. Can't you see I need a real damn hug?" With that she grabbed him, pretty much threw him back down on the bed, slid up next to him, buried her head in his neck, wrapped her arms around him, and squeezed pretty darn hard.

Which was exactly what he was afraid of getting. He cautiously hugged back, not wanting to acknowledge to himself that there was no bra strap. She wouldn't be? Nahh. He waited, vigilant, but fortunately no message was sent from his brain to his balls ... or maybe it was the other way around? Anyway, good.

She started quivering and his neck got wet. Uh-oh. Tears again. She was sobbing softly. He squeezed harder; she squeezed harder. He was afraid he felt breasts. He closed his eyes, started counting the coconuts he could see dangling in the palm out the window, which of course reminded him of what he was trying to ignore.

The next thing he knew, she was leaning over him, wild bed hair and bags under red-rimmed eyes, shaking him with both her hands against his shoulders, yelling, "What are you doing on my bed? I'm in my underwear for crying out loud! I'm your sister, you pervert. Get out of here."

Not being much of a morning person, MP muttered, moped, mumbled, and kind of stumbled off her bed and to the door. When he hit the doorway, he came around to the thought that this hadn't been *his* idea. When he turned to say something, he saw her smiling at him.

"Thanks for last night. I needed that. See you in a minute. Breakfast?"

As he did every morning, he stepped out, still shaking his head about what was going on, onto the front porch to take his usual six breaths: three good airs in; three bad airs out. He decided to double it this morning. It was a bright, cool morning, as most were this time of year, and the rising sun, although still behind his dune, was lighting up the red and white striped lighthouse across the harbor. The rigging on the masts of the rocking sailboats clanked in the post dawn still as various morning dories passed carrying claustrophobic boaters ashore. With the quaintness of the town, the famous lighthouse, and well-protected harbor, plenty of boats were always moored. Many were quite large, as they had to maneuver the Atlantic before entering the quieter Abaco Sea and safety of the harbor. One huge modern white monstrosity stuck out among the others.

Marilyn walked down into the kitchen as he was staring blankly into the refrigerator. He didn't know what to think about this morning, but it certainly wasn't about breakfast, or this morning, but a little further into a suddenly fuzzy future.

"I don't smell any coffee. Aren't you a coffee drinker?" she asked.

"Uh, yeah, actually I am. I'm having a little trouble concentrating this morning. You might understand why?"

CHAPTER 8

"Well, let's get some coffee brewing and see if that helps," she said as she walked out onto the porch. "Oooh, is that pretty! The masts are glistening and the lighthouse glowing … gorgeous. And the sea right out there. Nice spot, bro!"

"Will you quit calling me 'bro'!" He turned and aimed for the coffeemaker.

She came back in, leaned on the kitchen counter, and he realized she was wearing Lottie's cardigan. Well, his sweater, but the one Lottie had worn quite glamorously that unglamorous morning. Fortunately, as it fell forward this time, he could see she was wearing one of his T-shirts under and, fortunately, a pair of his sweatpants. He wanted to see no skin, anywhere. "Well, we have to figure something out, because I'm not calling you MP."

"I would suggest we have other things to figure out before we mess with my name." Why did women always look so alluring when wearing men's clothes, especially if they were yours?

"Right. Get out of the way and let me get this coffee going. You look like you're pretty helpless in the kitchen. Looks like you need a woman around the house."

"I've been doing just fine, thank you," he said, but regretted it immediately, as she didn't respond. "Sorry. You're actually right. Martha did all the cooking. She was a really good cook and I was fabulous at loading the dishwasher."

She still didn't respond, silently getting the pot going.

He was getting nervous. He had a million questions to ask but didn't know where to start, and the first thing he did say was something stupid, making her feel unwelcome. These recent turn of events were all no small surprise to him and rather threw a curve into what he thought would be his new routine. A routine had almost seemed a consolation after

87

the haphazard, willy-nilly, unmethodical, undesigned, almost reckless developments in his life since Martha had died. But, if he had a sister—half, quarter, whatever—and she needed help, he would help. And, of course, since he already liked her—of course, this also threw a curve into *how* he had thought he liked her—he was willing, more than willing to at least attempt to oblige.

She got the pot going and turned and looked at him. "Where do you keep the cups?"

He pointed to a cabinet across the room over by the table that was covered with beach debris.

"Men!" she said, pulling the cardigan tight and walking by him to the cabinet.

"Whaddya mean, 'men'?"

"Never mind."

"No, tell me," he said. "I think we need to communicate here."

She came back by him into the kitchen, smirking. "Mind if we keep at least a couple cups over here by the pot? Or is that how you get your morning exercise, traipsing back and forth?"

"Hey, you can arrange this kitchen any way you want. I mean, wait! We need to talk."

She poured two cups and said, "Why don't we sit out on the porch and I'll … I'll explain."

"OK. It sounds like you're here to stay, I assume, at least for a while. So one of the first things I'll tell you: I have no sense of humor in the morning. I am *not* a morning person. I don't even like to talk to myself before noon."

"So, how we going to talk now?"

"Well, number one: you're the one it would seem that will be doing the talking, and … and …"

CHAPTER 8

"So there is a number two?"

"I got an idea. I usually walk next door toward town a ways where there's a little bakery and get a muffin or something, take my coffee, and sit by one of the steps goin' down to the beach and watch the sun rise out of the morning fog over the Atlantic."

"Really! I'm impressed. I can't think of a better way to start the day. Except the sun's already up and I'll be skipping the muffin."

"Why?"

"You are clueless, aren't you? If I had a muffin every morning, you'd have to get me a bigger bed. If I ate a muffin every morning, I'd end up looking like a muffin: squeezable, like my sister."

"Hmm ... OK. Now I know you have a sister. A squeezable sister?"

"Don't get any ideas. I'm sure she'll be coming down. So watch yourself."

"That right? What would I have to watch—she's my sister then too, right?"

"Right, natch. I'll thermos up some coffee, you go get your muffin."

"Okee dokee. You can have a nibble of mine if you like."

"A nibble would be good. I'll be right back." He watched her walk up the stairs in his sweater, wondering why everything she said sounded like a tease.

THEY WRIGGLED their butts into the sand and leaned against the bottom of one of the steps that led down the dune to the beach. To get there they'd had to walk by several cottages—some small, some big with porches and balconies—all brightly colored and all with names: Bahamian Breezes, Beachcombers Bungalow, Crow's Nest. Mostly they just read all the names and laughed at how the smaller ones had the more pretentious names: like Mandalay Sunsets—a tiny one-bedroom shack facing the east.

Now they were quiet, looking out at the ocean. One lone woman was on the beach running at the edge of the waves, her dog splashing in and out. The waves came in and out. MP and Marilyn breathed in, but nothing coming out. Neither knew where to begin, and the momentousness of the situation was settling in. It would seem their lives were going to change. A brother and a sister that had never met … until now. The unlikeliness of this happening. He now assuming they were expected and bound to at least like each other, if not love each other, yet due to how they had met, was still attracted to her. Neither knew what to think, what to say, what to expect, what to intend … fate having brought them to be sitting together on this beach, incarcerated in what MP was assuming would have to become an undeniable affinity.

MP broke the silence. "First thing, I suppose, is what I call you. I'm assuming for some reason it ain't Marilyn?"

"Kate."

"Just Kate? Not Katherine or … ?"

"Simply Kate."

"Kate. Kate fits you."

"Well, I'm glad you think so."

"Marilyn? Why'd you pick Marilyn? You don't look like a Marilyn. What am I saying? Why'd you need an alias at all, for Christ's sake? And Marilyn *Chambers*! I knew something was fishy when that dawned on me."

"Well, *secondly*," she said, smiling at him. "What do I call you?"

CHAPTER 8

"Everyone's called me MP since ... well, I can't remember being anyone but MP."

"Hmmm. Well, let's see. How about M?"

"Nah. Barney calls me that sometimes, and an old friend from grade school did, but it sounds like a girls' name ... you know, short for Emily. I had a friend named Emily, so I called her Em."

"Hmmm. I suppose P doesn't work. I'd say "I gotta go, P." And you'd think you had to escort me to the ladies' room."

He started chuckling. "It'll have to be your decision. You can call me anything you want."

"You mean like dumbass?"

"If you like. I certainly feel like one. I have absolutely no idea what to think or feel about what's going on."

"Now? Or most of the time?"

"Most of the time, I suppose," he said, still chuckling.

"Hmmm. Well, dumbass might be kind of embarrassing, like in front of your parents."

"No parents," he said.

"No parents? Everybody's got parents."

"Yeah, well I did. Just like I had a wife."

"Oh crap. Sorry. You know that really bothered me. When I found out you were my brother ..."

"Half. Half-brother."

"OK, so sorry. Does that make a difference? Oh, never mind. I really felt like I lost a sister-in-law, even if I didn't know her. It made me sad."

"No, I'm thinking it doesn't make a difference," he said, answering her question and moving on. "My parents died young. My dad, Mulcahy dad, had a heart attack, and my mother died zip lining in Costa Rica."

This sent Kate into a choking-laughter fit. "Zip lining?

| 91

Sorry, but hell, what a way to go."

He was laughing now too. "That's my line. I use it all the time when telling people how she passed. She just kinda zipped through life, until the zipper failed."

"Well, it's true. My God. If I gotta go, why not flying through the air? That's great. Well, I mean, I'm sorry you lost your mom, but it sure beats the hell out of cancer. My dad, your dad, died pretty young too, and rather dramatically as well."

"I guess I should have been more proactive, looking into where these siblings were I was told I had. I thought about it. All my mother told me about your father—our father—was that he was out with another woman the day I was born. She made me promise for my adopted dad's sake not to seek him out. Apparently I resemble him? She didn't want him in our lives."

"Huh. Weird the way it works. Yes, it's a little creepy, but I'm afeared one of the reasons I was attracted to you was that you're a lot like him: looks ... and behavior, unfortunately. Dad was pretty angry with your mother, too. He told us she demanded the divorce and then didn't tell him about you. Someone else told him they had seen her pregnant."

"So, out with another woman on the day I was born," MP said. "Getting back at each other."

"Dad was a strong person. Very confident, cocky really. Sound familiar? Everybody liked him, though. He was a good father. Probably a better father than husband. Sounds like your mother was a strong woman, too."

"Yeah, she was. A good mother, for sure."

"Our mother died in an auto crash. How'd you know about us?"

CHAPTER 8

"Your father would call my mother every year around my birthday and check up on me and what I was up to. He must have told her about you because when I got married she told me the whole story, including that I had two sisters ... half-sisters. How'd he die?"

"This is going to kill you, no pun intended. He was skiing in the mountains, drunk as a skunk. He shot down his last run, at dusk, straight, as fast as he could. They say he was going like seventy, eighty miles an hour and he never stopped. Went right through the fence at the bottom, bounced off a car or two, and ended up in the chalet bar. Went right through one of the windows."

MP was stuffing a laugh. "The same bar he got wasted in? He must have really needed another drink."

They both burst out laughing, and although still sitting, suddenly, spontaneously threw their arms around each other. The unwieldy, awkward attempt at a hug caused them to lose their balance, Kate falling over on top of MP and both rolling down the sand bank, sand flying, arms cinched around each other. When they stopped rolling and spitting sand, they sat up, held hands, and contemplated each other, crying a little and laughing a lot. He was confused by what he saw in her eyes, and he guessed she might feel the same.

"Well, crap. I don't know about you, but if I'm going to be able to clue you in on why you've found me on your doorstep, I'm going to have to get all this sand out of my teeth, hair, ears, eyes ... you name it, it's full of sand."

"Well," MP said, "let's go back then and shower."

"Shower? There's a huge bathtub out there and nobody in sight now. I'm going in." And with that she was off running.

"But, I don't have my suit on!" Which was pretty obvious since he still had his clothes on from last night at Cap'n Jack's.

He stood up to see her run toward the water yelling: "Well, avert your eyes, bucko!" Wasn't that what Lottie had called him that morning? To his amazement, while running, first off came his sweater, which she was still wearing, and which she flung with abandon. Next, tossed off into the breeze, his Cap'n Jack's T-shirt. He noticed with horror—well, horror mixed with a little demented delight—that she was not wearing a bra, or he assumed since he was gawking at a bare back. She then turned and confirmed his horror and delight, waving to him to "Come on, chicken shit!" then turned, kicked off her sweats and her undies, revealing a completely tanned ass, ran into the water, and dove into a wave.

She swam a ways, past the breaking waves, then turned, bobbing up and down and yelled, "You gonna just stand there? Come on in!"

"You're the pervert," he shouted. "You're my sister, for crying out loud!"

"Only half," she yelled back.

"Well, I could see *all* of this sister," he hollered as he started to make his way cautiously toward the water.

"All you can see is my head, fool."

"That was a hell of a lot more than a head I saw a second ago."

"Big deal, whoopee! It's not like I'm coming on to you. Aren't you really going to come in?"

His brain was totally fucked. There was a beautiful, naked woman yelling at him to join her. And this woman had to be his sister. As he walked, sand fell out of his hair into his eyes. He stopped, bent over, and tried to blink the sand out.

"Whaddya doing? Praying for forgiveness?" she hooted.

He looked up, thought "what the hell," carefully took his clothes off and folded them neatly—why, he didn't know—on

CHAPTER 8

a washed-up log half buried in the sand, and scurried into the water. Trying to cover his privies in both hands, he got smacked full frontal by a wave and knocked backward, providing her with a full view, as the wave rolled by him up onto the beach, of what he had intended on keeping private.

"Dive into the wave, fool," she yelled, laughing at him.

"I know, I know," he hollered, trying to lie low in the water. "I just didn't enter with quite the same abandon as you did."

"I already have seen your little peni, you know," she said while still undulating up and down in the waves. "You embarrassed?"

"Well, I am certainly not used to being em-bare-assed with my sister," he said as he ducked into the next breaker. He had unfortunately inherited his mother's puerile sense of humor.

"Bare-balled you mean?" she laughed, drifting toward him as he rolled and dove through the next wave. "How do you know what you're used to? You never had a sister before."

"Well, if I had, I wouldn't have been swimming with her naked."

"Oh, boo hoo. Why not?" She had bobbed over to him and their two heads swayed up and down just beyond the breakers. The water was crystal clear and he had a very difficult time not perusing through crystal clear water, a body he had previously been dreaming about. Of course that body at that time hadn't belonged to his sister.

"I suppose you and your brother saw each other naked all the time?"

"No brother," she said. "At least not until now. But my sister and I skinny dip, and, well, we have no problem being 'nekked' around each other."

"Yeah, but you're two women. There's no sexual ... tension."

"So? That we're brother and sister should mean there's no sexual tension I hope, anyway. Or are you the pervert?"

He knew she was teasing. And maybe she was right! There should be no sexual tension. Yet her undulating next to him there, naked as could be, brushing against him as the waves rolled by, was causing his brain to short-circuit about halfway on the way to his toes. Maybe he *was* a pervert.

MP rolled in with the waves, laid flat, face down in the water, letting the waves wash him up onto shore, then he scurried over to his clothes, screening from her his ebbing erection. God, he would have been embarrassed if Mar— Kate had noticed. It embarrassed himself. What was wrong with him? He tried quickly pulling his undies on, clumsily, and tripping a couple of times, then hopping as his wet skin caught in his pants leg, and finally tumbling face first into the sand, pretty much negating why he had taken the stressful dip to begin with. He scrambled back to his feet, keeping his back to the water ... and Kate. He more carefully slid each pants leg on, feeling like he was dressing in sandpaper, his skin immediately starting to itch. He heard her behind him, hoping like hell she was having more success reapplying his clothes to her previously naked body.

"Shall we head back?" he yelled, not looking back at her, not wanting any more shocks from his obvious *mix*-conception of 'Marilyn.' This 'Kate' was certainly something else. He didn't know if he should be enticed by her apparent lack of propriety or dismayed. What he was was perplexed. He had always thought of himself as a free spirit, sexually sovereign without a lot of hang-ups ... as he believed he had always had good intentions. He had freely flirted with Martha's friends,

CHAPTER 8

girlfriends that is, and the wives of his good friends, even Barney's series of dates, because he had benign intentions, and he assumed they, everyone, including Martha, knew that. He felt he was letting them know that even if no one else found them desirable, he did. And all freely flirted back, making him feel desirable and bone fide. All safe and sound because all intentions were honorable.

But what about now? This predicament? Just what were his intentions? It *was* all about intentions, right? His intentions with Marilyn may not have been entirely honorable. C'mon, she was a babe—funny, nice, and, as he'd already felt: although he didn't sense a come-on, he hadn't felt a go-away either. But this was not Marilyn. This was Kate, and her toned little body might be totally exposed, she buck-naked, right behind him, and he couldn't look … because she was *his sister*! He decided he needed to get a grip: all intentions toward Kate would be noble. NOBLE! This was apparently going to be made difficult by her apparent bohemian-ness. So, if she was going to be this free spirit, he would have to regress and find asylum in restraint … because Mar— … no, Kate … *was his sister*!

"I'm dressed. You can turn around now so I can hear you," she yelled out over the slap of the waves on the sand.

He turned to speak to her, but of course she was carrying his sweater and his sweats. She now looked like she was entering a wet T-shirt contest with nipples aplomb. He whipped back around and waited for her to catch up to him.

"OK, OK. I'll wear your sweater until my, your T-shirt, dries. Sorry. Please realize I'm not coming on to you, will ya? I mean," she said as she pulled up next to him and took his arm, "if I can't be open and free with you, with whom could I be?"

"Your sister, maybe!" he said, emphasizing "sister."

"Why just my sister? Why not my brother? Our relationship should be open, natural, unconditional … no?"

"No," he answered immediately.

"Why not? It's not like I'm turning you on, right?" she said, tugging him toward the wooden beach steps.

"Right!" he responded, way too quickly.

"I mean, it's not like you got all excited just because you saw your sister naked?"

"No. Of course not," he lied.

"Well then, let's just be who we are. I am very free and open with my sister, maybe more so than she is with me. She's more conservative … she has the looks, the body—nymphish to say the least, not skinny and flat like me. So why not be free and open with our brother? You don't seem like the overly modest, prudish type. Right?"

He tried to squelch the thought that there was another sister, especially the one she just described. But why should he be trying to repress it? He thought, really, isn't that silly? "Uh, right. Great. Another sister. Tell me about her."

They had reached the steps but stopped. She let go of his arm and they faced each other. "We're twins. Can't remember if I told you that?"

"You haven't told me anything … yet."

"Well, let's head back. I'll get dressed more respectfully, and I'll tell you my tale of woe."

With that she headed up the wooden steps, taking each step gracefully and athletically. "We really don't look much alike," she said over her shoulder. "She's more … full-bodied than I am."

"What's that mean?" he asked, following behind her up the steps, bending to snatch the bag of uneaten muffin and undrunk coffee.

CHAPTER 8

"Big tits, fool. Whaddya think? She got the brains and the boobs; I got the athletic bod and sports stuff. She's always been considered the hot twin. I've been meaning to tell you about her because she wants to come visit. Think it's OK if she stays with us for a few days?"

He pushed that thought right out of his mind. A more attractive twin, especially if anywhere near as free-spirited, might push him right over the edge. "Uh, what sports did you play?" he asked as a diversion.

"You name it," she replied, "I played it. But being a little short, I eventually concentrated on soccer and softball."

"You look like you'd be fast?"

"Why d'ya say that?" she said as they reached the top of the steps.

"Strong legs, strong body," he replied. He couldn't help but notice that her butt, quite apparent since her undies were a bikini variety, not much different than a bikini suit bottom he kept trying to tell himself, was pretty much muscle, "I coached women's soccer. I recognize an athlete when I see one."

"Telling me I have soccer thighs?"

"Looks like you maybe used to," he said, starting to get a little uncomfortable talking about thighs.

"What's that supposed to mean?" she challenged, yet smiling.

"No, you look like you're still in good shape, but no bulging muscles ... anywhere."

"Well, thanks, I guess. See, you can talk about my body in a respectable context, right?"

"Right," he lied.

"What you've seen is a body you can admire for its physical prowess. Right, MP?"

"Uh, right," he lied again.

| 99

"Well," she said, grabbing his free hand. "Let's head back. You can eat your muffin; we'll reheat the coffee, sit on your lanai, and I'll do the talking. Whatcha say?"

"Fine, if ya put those sweats back on." They headed off, backtracking by the cottages, MP feeling mentally a little unzipped, but oddly contented and happy.

When they got back, they both headed to their rooms and Kate found an email from Sara:

Date: Feb. 28, 2012

To: Kate

From: Sara

Subject: Small world

Hey Katie, you there? No? Well I changed my password. Is there some other way we should be communicating? I mean, I'm amazed someone, he, anyone, can interlope into someone else's personal stuff. It blows my mind. I guess everything is encrypted at work, I'm told, so harder to hack in. Anyway, hope this is safe now. Even if it isn't safe, if we don't say where you are, it doesn't matter, does it? I mean, he can't tell where you are when you email, can he? I'm so stupid about this stuff. I should—no I will—talk to one of the tech guys, see what they say.

Anyway, I just have to tell you this; you'll love it:

I was telling this cool person at our office in NY—actually she edits and publishes all our journals—about you finding a long-lost brother, and when I told her his name, she says: "No shit! Mr. Mulcahy? Mr. Meecal Mulcahy? He was the least favorite teacher I ever had and I hated

CHAPTER 8

him. He was my writing teacher in high school. But I don't want to tell you about it; it'll be a pretty long tale. So, I'll write it like a story. To demonstrate that I can, indeed, write."

I'm going to myself : she's a well-known publicist. Why wouldn't I think she can write? Well, the next day she sent me this (see the attachment):

I wasn't popular in high school, sort of what they called a 'dirtball.' I hated school and I especially hated English. I hated writing, double especially. Grammar, specifically. It always made me feel dumb. I just couldn't grasp nouns, subjects, verbs, objects, adjectives, adverbs, prepositional phrases. They were Greek to me. Then my teacher, who pissed me off royally because he was always on my ass: 'You can do this. You can do that.' Well, I couldn't, at first. Then one day he tells us he's not going to waste a lot of class time on grammar because it was boring and everyone could get it quick and easy if they applied themselves. Yeah, well, not me. I said to myself I'd like to apply tar and feathers, quick and easy, to my English teacher. Pretty much everyone liked him. He was young and nice to everyone but me, I had felt. I have to admit he was pretty funny-- if I had had a sense of humor about English class, which I didn't.

Then he tells us that we don't get a passing grade in English this quarter unless we pass the mastery test in grammar! He said he was supposed to teach us how to write decently, which he said would be necessary if we wanted to go to college or get any kind of decent job, but we'd have to understand how to structure a sentence. Well, I thought: 'He could be the master of himself, not me.' Basically, I didn't believe him. He wouldn't give me an F for the entire quarter just because I couldn't understand grammar. I mean, I turned in all my homework, for crying out loud. He had made a deal with our class, which was a 'skills' English class: if we all handed in our homework on time, he wouldn't assign work on weekends or holidays. So, basically, if I didn't want the entire class angry with me, I had to do his stupid, difficult homework. The other classes he taught were the creative writing classes with all the top students, so I thought he already expected too much of us anyway.

He had already blackmailed us by MAKING us read what I initially thought would be these stupid novels, at home, on our own time, again if we wanted to pass! He said it was also homework and we were supposed to read out of a book of our choice every night before falling to sleep rather than watching the boob tube. Any book I had tried to read before in other classes, like Romeo and Juliet, put me immediately to sleep no matter where I was, which made it difficult to actually finish a book. I mean, my boyfriend at the time felt a drug by any name smelled as sweet, so I hadn't figured roses were relevant. At first I tried to fake that I was reading at home; it was some stupid romance novel I had found lying around the house. It was a really stupid book, but I figured I'd just fake reading it anyway. But he'd have these reading days during class time and it wasn't too difficult for him to figure out I was full of shit. I had to admit he was no dummy, like most of my teachers. He didn't get pissed.

CHAPTER 8

Just said, "Nice try. Why don't we try a book you might like?" I told him I'd never seen a book I was the least interested in. So he went into his little closet and came back with "One Flew Over the Cuckoo's Nest." I looked at it and told him he was cuckoo if he thought I was going to like a book, any book. Then he made me promise I'd give it a try. PROMISE! Another blackmail! Of course I had to come to school dead tired the next day because I couldn't put the blasted book down until I had finished it. The damn thing had kept me up all night. I yelled at him the next day and he handed me "To Kill a Mockingbird." I asked him if he thought I was a bird lover or something. He smiled and said not to stay up all night with this one: apparently I had bags under my eyes or something. He said I should spend some time preparing for the grammar test. Of course I flunked the test. Total humiliation. I was the only one. It was his fault anyway, I figured, for giving me those damn books. To kill the damn mockingbird was as good or better than the cuckoo book.

So, I asked him: "You know, I understand the mechanics of a car engine. You're not really going to flunk me this quarter just because I can't understand the mechanics of a sentence ... because grammar is beyond me?"

He answered: "Understanding the mechanics of a sentence is simple next to understanding the mechanics of an engine."

"Well, not to me," I said. "You're really not going to flunk me just because I can't pass a stupid grammar test?"

He goes: "Well, yeah. What do you think? Isn't that what I said?"

I go: "Well, yeah, but it has to be a bluff."

He goes: "We aren't playing poker."

I mean, I did respect the son-of-a-bitch. So I was almost ready to cry, not something in character with my rep, and he says to come in after school for like half an hour.

I go: "I'm a high school senior. I never got grammar yet; I never will."

He says: "See ya after school tonight."

So I show up a little late, hoping maybe he wouldn't wait for me. I thought I'd rather flunk than be humiliated. I really didn't want to sit there like a total dumb shit in front of this sorta cool adult male. I knew I could never understand GRAMMAR!

He sits me in a desk chair; he sits next to me on the desk. Way too close for comfort. He writes on my paper:

"The girl," and says, "This 'girl' is a noun, right? Person, place, or thing? And she's going to do something. That'll be the verb. Somebody's got to do something. In this case, the 'girl' is going to 'hate' the man."

So I'm going, OK, he's got my attention. This sounds a little weird.

Then he says, "So the girl does something to the man. The 'subject' does something to the 'object.' Make sense?"

"Sure," I say. "Why can't the 'object' do something to the 'subject'?"

"It sure can. Only then the object—the 'man'—would become the subject, so the 'man' would 'hate' the 'girl.' Only he doesn't. 'She' hates 'him.' See, we have the pronouns taking the place of the nouns."

CHAPTER 8

"Like 'you' and 'me'?" I say, probing a little for what I'm afraid he's getting at.

"Hey," he says, "way to go. See, you're smarter than you look."

Wait a minute, I thought. But that was one of the things I liked about him, even if I hated him. He wasn't usually serious. He joked around a lot. One of the reasons I thought he had been bluffing.

Then he says: "But this isn't just any girl. This is a 'pretty girl.' Could be an 'old' girl, a 'short' girl (I'm tall), a 'dumb' girl, but, no, this girl's not dumb, she's 'pretty.'"

What, now he's hitting on me? What would my mother think?

"So," he continues, "'pretty' describes the girl, so it's an ..." he waits for me to answer.

"Yes, yes, I know: an adjective. I've heard it a million times. This girl can remember, just not understand."

"Oh," he says. "So we have a different verb; rather than this pretty girl 'hating' the man, she 'doesn't understand' the man."

"So what's 'doesn't'?" I say.

"So you know 'understand' is a verb, right?"

"But 'understand' is not an action" I say.

"Oh, but isn't to 'understand' to 'do' something?"

"Yeah, sure," I say to shut him up, but I actually do follow.

"So 'doesn't' is a contraction ..."

"Yeah, yeah, I know what a contraction is."

"See, you are ..."

| 105

"Yeah, yeah, I know, I'm smarter ... just get on with it, will ya?" And I'm thinking: this is actually kinda fun.

"So 'doesn't' or 'does not' describes what?"

"Understand, of course," I say.

"And since 'understand' is a verb ... "

"Yeah, yeah, I know," I interrupt, getting cocky. "It's an 'adverb.'"

"Maybe you aren't smarter ... "

"Don't get smart with me," I say, all in good humor, which he 'does' understand. "So what is it then?"

"Think of it as just all part of the verb 'does understand,' 'can't understand,' or how about 'won't understand'?"

"OK, OK," I say. "Let's get back to 'doesn't understand.' So the 'pretty girl' doesn't understand the 'old man.'" I say this, of course, to let him know that he's a lot 'older' than me and not to get fresh.

"Hey. All right. Pretty quick. So 'old' describes?"

"You," I say. "I mean 'man'!" I couldn't believe I had said that.

"Hmm," he goes. "'You' would have been a ... "

"Yeah, yeah, I know ... a stupid pronoun. But I thought pronouns had to be subjects: you know, 'she' for the 'gorgeous girl'?"

"Well, let's not let this girl get conceited," he says. "The older man ... "

"I thought he was 'old'!" I interrupt.

"No, no, this man is just 'older' and 'does understand'

CHAPTER 8

the 'pretty girl.' So, either because they're nouns, could be 'subject' or 'object,' and the same with the pronouns. Depends on whether she did it to him or he did it to her."

Oh, so I think, is he really flirting with me or what? I'd never seen him act familiar with a student before. But, I had to admit, he had my attention.

"Then, of course," he says, "She could be a 'very pretty girl.'"

"Could be, maybe," I say.

"Oh, no, definitely," he says.

I actually blushed. I'd never had a teacher, an older man, make me blush before.

"'Very' describes what?" he asks me.

"Well, of course, 'very' describes the girl."

"There we go again," he says.

"What?" I say, defensive.

"It's a 'very girl'?" he asks, raising his stupid eyebrows.

"No! No, of course not," I say, because it hits me: 'very' describes 'pretty.' "It's an adverb because it describes an adjective."

"So, you have heard all this before?"

"Yeah, yeah." I didn't really want to let on I was understanding this.

"The very pretty 'young'?"

"Uh," I said, fast as I could, "describes girl ... a noun—so it's an adjective."

107

"The very pretty young girl never understands the wise older man."

"Oh, but she does." She did.

So he was my least favorite teacher and I hated him because he got me to understand something I knew I could never understand. Who'd he think he was? He got me to enjoy books and understand two things: one, how to structure a sentence. Yes, by the time he was done, I did get it. Still do, apparently. Second, I don't know how he did it, but 'the very pretty young girl' also understood that she was 'very pretty.' And not only to dirtballs and slackers, like I had been going with, but to, maybe: a doctor, a lawyer, an author, a teacher. It's weird, but it gave me confidence. I still wonder or maybe it's 'wish,' at the time, he was hitting on me. I realize he wasn't. He always gave me this smile, after, that almost made me blush all over again. I mean, it reminded me that I was pretty. I have always wondered how much those 30 minutes contributed to what I am today: an editor of a major publishing house and a very pretty older woman married to an author, of all things.

So, Katie, she sends me this, and, well, what do you think? He sounds like he was a pretty decent teacher ... and guy. And, although I'm not sure about his sense of boundaries—something you should be aware of—he's certainly not afraid to charm a lady. You two could be a volatile combination. Watch it, ya hear!

Kate read the email and emailed Sara right back.

CHAPTER 8

DATE: Tuesday, Feb. 28, 2012, 4:10 p.m.

Kate: You there? I'm here, I'm here.

Sara: Yup. I thought that'd be you. I'm really worried about you and MP. Something tells me it's not going to be easy for you to keep a sisterly distance.

Kate: Sis, I suppose this could be a problem. He did definitely flirt with me before he thought we were brother and sister. I really do like the dufus. It doesn't surprise me—this little story. I read it while you were finishing. I haven't told him that we really aren't sister-brother. I've alluded to our mother and that we call his birth father 'Dad' but didn't tell him Dad adopted us after he married Mom or, naturally, that our 'real' Dad took off before we were even one. Then here he tells me about not knowing *his* real dad, and we never knew ours. It's just too weird, too fateful.

Sara: I don't like the way you're sounding here, especially with you living with him! I think you'd better level with him.

Kate: No, don't you see. If he thinks I'm really his sister—if only half—it can be cool. We can live together because there is no sexual tension. I agree it's confusing to him. Hell, it's confusing to me. But until he eventually knows the truth, I think I want him to, I don't know, desire me, I guess. I definitely want to keep him interested. I don't want to risk losing him. And, even though I think I'm starting to, you know, maybe love him—really, I'd love to make love to him now—but that'd be way too awkward. When I have to leave, get back to NY, I'll tell

BACK TO THE ISLAND

him. If he knows now I'm not really a blood sister, I can tell—it wouldn't work.

Sara: BUT: YOU KNOW!

Kate: Yeah, yeah, I know, I know. I almost wish I didn't. I just don't know what else to do. It's actually kind of fun. I can be free and easy about it all without worrying about him wanting to jump my bones. He's a good guy and this will make it easy for him to keep it ... unmessy for now. We do have to make sure, though, I, we, aren't discovered here. I couldn't forgive myself if something happened to him.

Sara: So, you haven't told him why you're down there yet?

Kate: No. I don't know if I should. I can tell: he's going to want to protect his little sister. It may be better that he doesn't know.

Sara: Well, I disagree, Sis. The whole thing doesn't seem fair to him. You do have to make sure he isn't discovered too, I agree. What if Richard finds out you're staying with MP? (It's not really that stupid a name.) But you're there; I'm here. So I hope you know what you're doing. What if those jerks at Sears remember MP's address? It sounds like that Ajax wouldn't hesitate to expose you both if he had the chance.

Kate: Yup. As a matter of fact I think I'll go back into the store one more time. Maybe I can get my last paycheck. I'll drop that I'm staying somewhere—not here, of course—somewhere I'm not, anyway, to throw Ajax off in case he has a chance to give me away. I'll try to cop MP's file, somehow, just to be safe. Hopefully Ajax won't remember where he lives.

CHAPTER 8

Sara: What if Richard has already found out you are, were, working at Sears and sees you?

Kate: I'll take that chance. I've gotta go, Sara. The dufus can't even make toast. But then he's working, I'm not, so—I don't mind cooking. It's kinda fun cooking for two.

Sara: Oh, Sis. It just sounds like trouble. And I know you. Please be aware we're not all as uninhibited as you. I've always felt sorry for your men, especially now with poor MP. And, of course, Richard is totally screwed. I'm worried.

Kate: What's new? I wish I could say don't worry, but we all knew what I was getting into. I know you agree I need to do this. At least I'm feeling safe at the moment and having fun. I'll keep in touch. Let me know when you can get away. I've already asked if you could visit. You'll like MP—although I'll have a new name for him by the time you get here, regardless of what you think. Let's see what you can come up with. Bye, hon.

CHAPTER 9

MP HAD gone into work a little early, hoping to find Lottie there and talk to her. It felt like there was no longer any sexual tension between them, thankfully, since he had all he could handle at home, and the humiliation of the attempted hook-up, or lack of hook, had softened in their new working relationship. She was good to work with: usually upbeat, funny, and, seemingly very comfortable in her tanned, freckled skin. She appeared to MP as a natural beauty: she wore no makeup that was apparent to him, and her auburn hair, which MP now also knew was natural, was a potpourri of styles, somehow different every day. Although he had never been to her place, he knew it was toward the south end of the island in a more prestigious, newer subdivision. How she managed that on a waitress's salary was a wonder to MP. She was quite well-educated, he could tell. A native of Boston he had found out. He had also discovered that she understood technology much better than he did. What he needed today was some knowledgeable feedback to a sudden, urgent quandary.

When he walked into the Cap'n's, the place was empty except for Lottie and a gray-haired man sitting at a table at the edge of the dock looking out over the harbor. "Hiya, hon. You're in early," MP said as he approached, not interrupting them, as they weren't talking.

CHAPTER 9

Lottie, without turning, their voices now second nature to both of them after several nights of working together, in her typical satirical splendor responded, "I'm usually here early, but you'd hardly know that now, would ya, you laggard? Spense, meet the slacker scribe I've been telling you about. MP, this is Spense, who has once again sailed into our quaint little harbor."

Without rising, the gentleman turned and stuck out his hand. "Howd'ya do, mate? Pleased to make your acquaintance."

MP paused, startled. The hand was gnarled, as was the face garbled. He was an extremely incongruous hodgepodge of features: the hand with twisted fingers and polished nails; the face framed by long but groomed peppered-gray hair; the nose crooked; cheekbones high and pronounced; eyes sunken yet alert and piercing. The gray, almost silver mustache and goatee were trimmed expertly. Then quickly MP extended his own hand and, unfortunately, did not maneuver for a firm handshake due to apprehension at grasping the misshapen paw and found his limp hand crushed in an iron grip. "Nice to … ahh, yah … meet you," he said as he retracted his hand and tried not to grimace.

"Spense returns about this time every year from wintering in Santa Marta on the Guajira Peninsula in Colombia," Lottie explained, enjoying MP's surprise at Spense's appearance. "He's our intermittent entertainment entering our spring juncture before he heads off to cooler climes like—where'd you go last year, Spense, Prince Edward Island?"

"Aye, I did indeed, my astute little stunner. Thanks for remembering. If you recall, I did my best to recruit you as my companion."

Hmm, interesting! MP thought. "Uh, before anyone comes, can I ask you a question, Lottie?" MP considered

| 113

requesting privacy but couldn't figure out how without appearing rude.

"Sure, shoot."

"Well, you know how technologically illiterate I am, right?"

"Just technologically ..."

"Yeah, yeah ... but this is actually quite serious," he cut her off. "I mean, I'm talking maybe life or death."

"No shit?" Lottie said, turning to face MP and seriousing herself up. "Sit down and let's see what we can do."

"Would you like me to excuse myself?" the man with the fascinating face asked.

"No," said Lottie. "If it's a tech question, you'd be the one likely to provide the answer." Lottie looked at MP. "That fifty-foot futuristic yawl out there is Spense's. You have to be a techno-genius to sail that sucker by yourself. It would ordinarily take a crew of seven to ten to handle it on the open seas. Spense does it all by himself, via technology."

Apparently his was the extravagant-looking yacht MP had noticed moored at the harbor's entrance. He had wondered what species of mankind would own such a monstrosity, and here he was. "Well," MP started, "I've got a challenge for you two, then. Let's say someone has to stay clandestine, I mean almost like witness protection. How could another someone find this someone?"

"Does this 'someone' happen to be a mysterious woman I've heard has been around your place? Someone you have neglected to mention to me?" Lottie said, not masking the irritation in her voice.

"Well, yes, but later. I'll explain later. This woman, my sister by the way, just told me this. She has to stay ... well, undiscovered. Yet a person looking for her has been seen in

CHAPTER 9

Marsh Harbour where she had an apartment and worked—at Sears. How could this person have found out where she was?"

Spense uncrossed his legs, swiveled in his chair to face MP, and leaned intently toward him. "My, how cryptic. This is not hypothetical? This is veritably real? Sorry for the redundancy."

"Yes, unfortunately, very real," MP said.

"And this woman, your sister, is in danger?"

"I'm afraid she may be. Yes."

"Does this person know she's staying with you?" Lottie interrupted. "If she's in danger, doesn't this put you in danger as well?"

"That doesn't really matter. She *is* my sister. But, no. I don't believe this person knows she is with me … now. And we'd like to keep it that way. But we have to figure out how he discovered she was not only in the Bahamas, but in Marsh Harbour."

"You say she worked at Sears?" Spense asked. "Maybe he had access to Sears' human resources files?"

"I don't think so. She happened to see him, at least I'm guessing it's a him, but he hadn't come into the store nor had he, apparently, known where she lived. He hadn't been to her apartment, as far as she knew. And she's using a pseudonym."

"Why does this person want to find her or even to harm her?" Lottie asked.

"I'll explain that later," MP said. "First, I've got to make sure he doesn't trace her to here. So I've got to figure out how he did trace her to Marsh Harbour."

"It all depends what type of information he—if it is a he—had access to," mulled Spense, basically thinking out loud, the wheels turning. "If she used a credit card, which might leave a trail."

"No, that's not it. She changed her name, even her appearance a little. Her sister got her a new passport; basically, she created a new identity. But she did not even get a new card in her new name."

"Hmmm, how about phone calls?" Spense mused.

"No, she's avoided phone calls entirely. I don't even know if she has a

cell. I suppose she does. Besides, calling internationally on a cell is way too expensive, isn't it?"

"Has she tried to communicate with anyone? Certainly she didn't use email?" Spense asked expectantly.

"Well, yes. She and her twin sister, who lives in Spokane, Washington, but works in New York and Washington DC, too, have emailed each other but have been very careful not to mention anything about where she was."

Spense sat up, slapped his thighs, and said, "That wasn't very smart. That's most likely how he located her."

"They've changed their passwords. Do you think he actually figured out, like, her sister's password? And even if he did, if there was no reference to where she was, what good would that have done?"

"Has your sister used her computer to email since she has come to stay with you?" Spense asked, seeming suddenly alarmed.

"No. I don't think so. Well, maybe. She moved out of her apartment and has stored all her stuff. She had been staying at a friend's on Treasure Cay."

"How about your computer?" Lottie asked, sounding almost accusatory.

"No ... no, I don't think so, yet. But she might. Actually, I wouldn't be surprised if she's not emailing right now. She's

CHAPTER 9

gonna want to tell her sister what's going on. But, why? Her sister changed her password and he can't hack into her's or mine, can he?"

"I'd go home now and tell her not to use either laptop." Lottie stood up and put her hands on her hips.

"It's probably a good idea not to use email right now," Spense said. "This miscreant must have access to some decent technological resources. What probably happened, the way it sounds, is that he did somehow hack into the sister's email and, although they didn't indicate where your sister was exactly, he would have been able to trace the server to the Bahamas and probably even to Marsh Harbour. That would explain him being here but not knowing how to find her."

"She's going to need to communicate with her sister, I know that," MP said.

"He could have the sister's phone bugged, wherever—at her work, at home, her cell—if he had knowledge and access. But if the sister gets a prepaid cell phone, that can't be traced, I don't believe. She should probably even keep disposing of them and getting new ones. Might be a trite expensive, but maybe worth the expense. If she uses a public telephone, I believe it may be traceable."

"Go tell her right now," Lottie said, starting to pace. "It's not just her that'll be in danger, if this really is danger we're talking about. Go!"

"Wait, wait just a moment," Spense said. "This malefactor should only be able to trace either of yours to Marsh Harbour as well. Is there any other way this villain can discover where you live?"

"Well … yeah, I guess. If he finds out I worked at Sears. They have my records."

"Does the Sears human resources department know you and …"

"Marilyn … well, Kate, actually …"

Spense and Lottie looked at each other: "… Kate, then, are brother-sister?" Spense said, standing up and starting to pace, chin cupped in hand.

"No, but the human resources department in Sears, namely Ajax, it's hard to explain, but he knew that Marilyn, Marilyn Chambers—that's her name in the Sears world—and I were … friends."

"Ajax?" Spense and Lottie yelled at the same time. "Not Ajax and Arthur Mandelsung?" Spense finished.

"Umm, yeah. Why?" MP asked pensively. Obviously this wasn't good.

"The Mandelsungs are an old, wealthy family who owned a chain of haberdasheries way back in England, even before the revolution," Spense said. "I've had some serious run-ins with them, and thus the radically provincial government of Great Britain, myself. Now I hear they're conspiring with the Chinese, who are responsible for the casinos and the dire excesses in Nassau and Providence Island. These two are consummate buggers. Last season I came across their yacht grounded on the edge of the reef on the west side. I didn't know it was them or whose it was, but it's a seaman's duty to assist another mariner in distress. So I pulled them off the reef even though I didn't feel they should have been there. Some other boaters saw us and reported it to the authorities. Everyone is well aware of both our vessels. When the Bahamian Coast Guard questioned the Mandelsungs, they reversed the tale and told them I had been grounded on the reef and they had rescued me!" Spense was spitting ire by this time. "The lowly buggers!"

CHAPTER 9

"What happened?" MP asked.

"To make a long story short, the authorities surveyed both our vessels and found the damage on the Mandelsung's hull."

"Then what?"

"I think they may have gotten their hands slapped for damaging the coral, not much more."

"No shit! I guess money talks," MP said, standing. "The revolution, you said? What revolution?"

"The American Revolution, you fool!" Lottie almost shouted, all worked up. "The family were Tories and all escaped to the Bahamas. They live all over the islands and, along with the Chinese, are behind most of the construction and development destroying the islands."

"That's correct," Spense confirmed. "I have since come to realize why they were there on the west side. But somebody has been sabotaging their sites—even recently here on Elbow Cay I was told. By where they ran aground." He looked at Lottie, who nodded. "If this villain were to discover that you both worked at Sears, I'd assume these two miscreants would dispose of the information gleefully!"

"Totally. They hate Mar … Kate, and me even more. As a matter of fact, Kate asked them that if someone came looking for her, would they respect her privacy."

"And …" both Lottie and Spense queried.

"Let's just say either of those assholes would give her away, yes—gleefully—in a second," MP said as all three were now pacing in a circle, MP following Lottie, Lottie following Spense.

Spense stopped abruptly, causing a three stooges scene as Lottie bumped into Spense and MP into Lottie. Spense turned, a quick little kiss given to Lottie as he held her aside, grabbed MP by the shoulders, and said: "Did you say she's using Marilyn Chambers as her alias?"

| 119

"That's right," MP answered with a grin.

Spense laughed heartily. "Well, she must have a sense of humor. I'm very interested to meet your Kate. All right, my good fellow. Mañana we start to plan and we visit Sears. Lottie, you in on this?"

"They've been destroying the islands for years, and now they're after *my* island? Of course I'm in. Anything I can do to fuck up these fuckers."

"Ah, good. Another little redundancy, my dear, but tomorrow we will have a plan. Lottie will create a distraction. Can't think of anyone more qualified."

"I'll take that as a compliment," Lottie said, smirking.

"And we will furtively expunge those records from the annals of Sears. Let's convene tomorrow at nine thirty here, and we'll catch the ten o'clock ferry."

"What if Ajax remembers that I live on Elbow Cay?"

"He may, but with the calamity he's facing at all his construction sites, where you live will not be on his list of priorities. Anyway, he certainly will not remember your address. And hopefully your files are not on a computer, so if they go missing, it will possibly make finding you more difficult. If this villain happens to show up on Elbow Cay, we will dispatch with him somehow, anyway, gracefully and quietly. Now, several thirsty resorters have wandered into the Cap'n's and are searching desperately for someone to assist them in their quest to quench that endless thirst. Mr. MP, you run home and ensure your sister does not try to contact her sister via either email, just in case, and Miss Lottie and I will assist these patrons in their quest until you return."

"Uh, yeah, right," MP stammered, a million thoughts stampeding through his head, and started to head for the

CHAPTER 9

door. Then he stopped, turned, and stuck out his hand, and before the gnarled claw could grip, he cupped his palm firmly in the shake. "Thank you," he said, nodding solemnly. For some reason he felt he was in good hands, gnarled or not, with Spense, whom he remarkably already felt like he had known all his life or in a previous one.

MP then trotted out the door, climbed into his cart, and sped as fast as the electric whir could carry him toward the dusty, rutted road leading to the north end and his cottage.

THE MORNING was humid and windy, blowing hot out of the south. The moored boats were listing back and forth more than usual in the harbor, and waves were breaking strong out past the point. MP and Kate arrived at Cap'n Jack's a little early to find Lottie and Spense in intense conference at the door.

"Morning," MP greeted, climbing off the cart and walking up, Kate in tow right behind. "Kate, this is Spense and Lottie. This is my sister Kate."

Kate pulled up next to MP and gave him a furtive little pinch in the back of the arm, whispering aggressively in his ear: "I can see why you didn't mention anything about Lottie."

"Ow!" MP complained, holding his arm, then looked at Kate and frowned.

"Very nice to meet you both," Kate said, smiling innocently.

"My, my, what an enticing sister you have," Spense said. "My pleasure, I'm sure." Rather than offer her his gnarled claw, he gave her a gentle hug and kissed both her cheeks.

Lottie said, very businesslike: "Nice to meet you, Kate," and offered her hand. "MP has told me so much about you," she said, shooting a visual dart at MP.

"Oh, really?" Kate answered, looking at MP, who, as usual, was clueless as to the point of the dart, as well as the pinch, as well as to women in general.

"No, not really," Lottie said. "MP actually hasn't mentioned you. I had just heard there was a new woman around the house. Word travels fast in Hope Town on our little cay."

"Well, to be honest, he hadn't mentioned you, either." Lottie was dressed unusually spicy even for her: a remarkably diminutive summer shift revealing an abundance of thigh and cleavage. "And I can see why," Kate said, looking at MP.

"What?" was all the addled MP could come up with.

"I believe Lottie will take that as a compliment," the more urbane Spense chuckled. "Lottie is dressed a little more, suggestively shall we say, today ... even for her. She is to be our distraction at Sears, so we have ample access in which to pilfer Mr. MP's file from Sears' dockets. We were just discussing how to create this diversion."

"Well, I'll tell ya," Kate said, "with the way Lottie looks—and believe me, dear, you look hot—Arthur, the shoe dog, would be drooling if you were to enter the women's shoe department. Hey, I have a suggestion: you see, this Arthur has this nasty little trick ..."

"Great idea!" MP burst out with.

"... he will certainly try to utilize," Kate continued, "looking the way you do."

Lottie smiled. "Let's hear about this. Sounds fun."

"You ask to try on a couple pairs of shoes you pick out. When he goes to put them on your foot, he'll, um, may I ask if you're wearing undergarments, well, let me rephrase that: underpants?"

Lottie laughed. "Getting a little personal, aren't we?"

CHAPTER 9

"Well, the reason I'm asking, he—Arthur—is going to pull his stool up real close to your chair, and when you pull your foot up for him to slip on the merchandise, with a dress that short, he'll be able to peruse *your* merchandise. And *he'll* know whether you're wearing undies or not. He calls what he's hoping for a 'beaver shot.'"

"Ahhh!" Lottie shrieked. "You're shittin' me?"

"No, unfortunately, or maybe fortunately in this situation, I'm not."

"My Lord!" Spense roared. "What an uncouth, peripatetic arse."

"Yup, you said it, I think. Both Ajax and Arthur are the complete arsehole deal," MP added.

"So, what you do, Lottie," Kate continued, "is raise a big enough stink that every customer and salesperson within earshot hears. Someone will fetch Ajax, and he'll come running to Arthur's rescue, leaving the stage open for the heist."

"God, this sounds like fun. Can I draw blood?" Lottie asked, actually sounding serious. "Hey, why don't I write 'asshole' or 'fuck you' on the front of my thong? You know, a little foreshadowing."

Everyone, even Kate, was stricken speechless as this concept dangled in the morning air. Nobody, even the usually verbose and witty Spense, could muster a response.

"Maybe ask to try on some spike heels," Kate finally suggested, also sounding serious. "They could do some serious damage, drawing some blood if you like."

"Let's assuage the feline vengeance a tad," Spense suggested, laughing. "We don't want the authorities involved. Remember, our mission is not to reap retribution symbolically on this Arthur, who I agree sounds like he could represent all the male recreants worldwide, but to escape with Mr. MP's records—unscathed and undiscovered, might I add."

"Well, this prick Arthur will not escape unscathed, I promise. I'll leave him alive, but a sorry bastard."

"The way I met Mar … Kate—God, I've got to get used to that—is she had just planted her foot halfway up his skinny arse for doing the same thing to a friend of hers."

Lottie high-fived Kate. "This is going to be fun," she said, and MP was almost, but not quite, feeling sorry for Arthur. As laid back as Lottie might appear, MP was learning she had a high-spirited side, as she was demonstrating, and it appeared this scene was going to bring out the higher spirits.

"OK," Spense said, "we'd better get going or we'll miss the ferry. MP, you know where your files are?"

"Yup. They're right in the open, in a file cabinet next to Ajax's desk, easily accessed."

"No backup anywhere? Like computer files?"

MP looked at Kate. "Nah," she answered. "Not a lot of recordkeeping gets done. The file is labeled 'Mr. P.' After what I now know about Ajax and his real estate exploits, the lack of concern for filing and office protocal all makes sense. His role at Sears almost seemed secondary. He was gone all the time and often had suits in his office behind closed doors. It even makes sense why he's been so out-of-sorts lately with what MP told me about somebody sabotaging his development and construction sites. But, no, there's no backup. I can go right to the files and in a second have all MP's records."

"Well," Spense said, shrugging, "the reason I asked if MP knew where the files are is that I think it's safer for you, the way it sounds, to stay away from Marsh Harbour and, especially, Sears."

CHAPTER 9

"No way! I got a feeling Lottie's going to make these two A-holes pay, big time. I don't wanna miss it."

"A-holes?' Spence laughed. Very amusing. I certainly understand, dear, but I think it's best if you settle for a narrated version. Lottie's a great re-creator ... she's had a multitude of exploits and adventures that she's entertained us with in the past."

"Hey, watch it, buster!" Lottie warned, laughing.

"So, why don't you lay low; Lottie will provide the diversion. I will provide the lookout; and MP—yes, MP?—hmm, you will have to fill me in on the origin of that one—will do the actual heist. Agreed?"

"Ah, all right," Kate agreed and high-fived Lottie this time: "Get 'em good, girl!"

"Don't worry," Lottie said. "This is gonna be fun."

l 125

CHAPTER 10

KATE WAS sitting up on MP's perch staring out past the harbor in the direction of Spokane. She had stopped at the public phone by the ferry dock and had phoned Sally, one of her and Sara's best friends in Spokane, and left a message to tell Sara to get a prepaid cell phone and to call Kate at eleven, Kate's time, which would be seven Sara's, the next morning. She knew Sara would be going nuts by now. Suddenly the sound of a loud, gas-powered cart pulling up in front of the cottage broke her reverie. Peeking down, she saw MP, Lottie, and Spense climbing out of a huge, multi-seated golf cart, all laughing loudly and carrying drinks. A large jug of dangerous-looking elixir sat on the floor of the cart. Kate climbed down the ladder, ran down the stairs, and met them at the porch door.

With a drink raised in one hand and a folder in the other, MP yelled, "Mission accomplished, and I mean accomplished!"

Kate held her hand low for a low-five from Lottie who accommodated her enthusiastically. Spense stood back, holding two drinks, grinning and shaking his head. "Yes, it was quite a scene," he told Kate. "While MP was lifting his file, I had to go observe this most exciting, exceptional event."

Kate looked at MP. "Don't look at me," he said. "I was off appropriating my records. I missed the whole damn thing."

"Well, what happened? Tell me!" Kate shouted.

CHAPTER 10

Spense, excited, jumped in before Lottie had a chance: "When I arrived on the scene, after providing lookout to ensure Ajax was, indeed, dispatched from his office, I found what may have been the entire store, maybe people off the street, all surrounding the women's shoe department, all mouths and eyes wide open. Apparently our Lottie had stiff-legged Arthur in the middle of his deplorable little ploy involving a spike heel, meaning, I imagine, he got the spike. Ohhh, I can't even bear to think. His screams not only attracted a crowd but Ajax as well, who fared no better than Arthur upon arriving at the scene. When I arrived, both of those two, Ajax and Arthur, were rolling on the floor clutching—well, how shall I say—their delicacies, moaning rather magnificently. Lottie was standing over them vociferating phrases I've never had the horror of hearing in my life, words that would make a sailor blush. She was threatening to involve the CEO of Sears, the governor of the Bahamas, the Coast Guard, her old military police friends, à la reminiscent of our unfortunately absent friend, MP, all of whom would be involved in her retribution.

I had assumed, correctly, that their privates had been adequately violated, as the two miscreants continued to emit no other sounds but those beastly groans and grunts. They were still in the fetal position, rocking, knees uplifted, hands shielding groins, as if fearing another possible assault, when I decided it best we exit the scene before the authorities might arrive, having to convey our most passionate little Lottie away by hoisting her with my arm around her midsection. Her dangling feet were still addressing kicks in the direction of the two unfortunates on the floor as I imparted her toward the exit."

MP infringed on the tale by impulsively and exuberantly giving Lottie a huge hug, lifting her off the floor.

Kate slapped MP on the back of the head, said "my turn," and gave Lottie a big hug herself. Spense grinned crookedly, whispering to MP, "A little territorial for a sister?" Then to Lottie: "Sorry to steal your thunder, dear, but I could not restrain myself from imparting this most delicious adventure."

"Oh, Lottie, it sounds like I couldn't have done better myself," Kate whooped. "Thanks so much to all of you. All right, now, where's *my* drink?" Kate demanded, letting Lottie loose.

"Both of these aren't mine, my dear," Spense said. "Here you go. Hope you like Long Island iced teas or Elbow Cay iced teas, as they're known on our little isle."

"Oh, shit. I've had some misadventures with these," she said grabbing one from Spense.

"Who hasn't?" Lottie yelled. "Cheers!" And the foursome tapped their glasses together. MP led them out to the front porch, where, after consuming several more, they were randomly sprawled, out cold, before the sun dropped beneath the porch overhang.

Spense was the first to wake to the tapping on the veranda post. "Uggh ... uh, oh my, Jack. What time is it?"

Jack, not the original Cap'n Jack but the current, spoke quietly as if not wanting to wake the dead. "Well, well. My barmaid, bartender, and entertainer all cozy here together. How fortunate. Who, might I ask, is the spare chick propped up against your hammock?"

"What time is it?" Spense managed again, squinting into the fading light.

"Closing in on the aft of happy hour, my matey, although it would appear you've had one of your own right here."

CHAPTER 10

MP was the next to stir. He had passed out rear to rear with Lottie on the narrow settee. Spense was in the hammock and Kate on a cushion on the floor propped up precariously against the hammock. If Spense were to move, Kate would plop onto the deck. MP tried to move, but a screeching pain bounded around in his cranium. "Oh, man," he said. "Is that you, Jack?"

"Yes, it is. The Jack that writes out your paycheck. Lottie's got the night off, and it looks fortunate. You and Spense, on the other hand, are late for work."

"It would appear I'm held hostage here in the hammock," Spense ventured. "If I were to move, this lovely creature would tumble."

"What day is it?" MP moaned. "Isn't it Tuesday? Who goes out drinking on Tuesdays?"

"Apparently, you do," Jack responded, talking a little louder now. "And yes, it's a lighter crowd on Tuesday. I left Ma, Roland, and two rookies alone to handle the 'tweeners,' but you know what happens after the dinner hour. It's the happiest hours, even on Tuesdays. Tell you what, MP, come in for the rush and you can go home early and sleep it off. Ma and I'll clean up. Spense, you just stay there until … ?"

"Kate," MP answered. "My sister."

"Sister! Didn't know you had one," Jack said.

"Me either," MP replied as he rolled over and sat up. It felt like someone had poked needles into his voodoo replica. "Ah, shit, man. That hurts."

"What poison you guys been swallowing?" the understanding Jack asked knowingly. He'd been there … many times.

"Frickin' Elbow Cay long teas," Lottie grunted, sitting up. She looked at MP. "What you doin' in my bed?"

"Your bed? It's my bed."

"Then whaddya doin' in your bed with me?"

"I have no idea how I got here or you got here, but I don't remember having any fun."

"Well you wouldn't then, would you?" And with that Lottie stood up, groaning an "Oh my God."

MP cringed. The memory of that first Lottie morning was still very sensitive. Was that what she was referring to? Did it still bother her? Was he just being too sensitive? That much thinking hurt his head. He stood up too.

"Well, while you guys figure out your musical beds, as I was saying: Spense you can start tomorrow night. MP, c'mon in and help out for a while."

"Screw it," Lottie said. "You're being good about this, Jack. I'll come. MP, you stay here and nurse your sister."

"It's OK. It's your day off," MP protested, weakly.

"Ah, hell. I've got to get outta here anyways. It's cool," Lottie said.

"Well, whoever, come on, hop on the cart, and let's get going before Ma fires all of us." Jack's mom was a barmaid from way back and, although in her nineties, hung around helping out in the kitchen or bar when needed. She wasn't literally the boss anymore, but nobody argued with her.

Kate started to stir. "My God. What happened? Oh, shit, I think I'm stuck in this position."

"Well, if you're stuck, I'm stuck," laughed Spense.

"Oh, crap. Sorry, Spense." And with that she crawled over to the now-abandoned settee, climbed on, and fell facedown, groaning.

"Uh, Kate. Before you slip back into oo-oo land again, can I borrow some shorts?" Lottie asked. "I can't go in like this. Ma'd shoot me."

CHAPTER 10

"Grab anything you want," was the muffled reply,
"You want one of my T-shirts?" MP asked.

"I'll pick a fresh one up at the bar. Thanks."

MP led Lottie upstairs. She grabbed a pair of stretchy sweat-shorts, since she had a few more curves, hips in this case, than Kate, and headed back down.

"I'll be right behind," Spense said as Lottie climbed onto Jack's cart. "Now that I'm liberated, I'll head down to the boat. If I'm able, I'll grab my smaller keyboard and guitar and head back in. Maybe I can handle a short set."

"Well, don't worry," Jack yelled as he and Lottie left. "Anybody new die lately?" drifted away as they disappeared into the dusk.

"What do you suppose Jack meant by that?" MP queried, more to himself than Kate and Spense.

"Later," Spense said as he cautiously fumbled to his supercart and awakened the night, rumbling off down the road, leaving the dusk dustier.

"Can I help you to bed?" MP asked Kate. All he got was an indistinguishable, muffled reply, and almost immediately a dainty snore mixed with the sounds of night birds and the wind whispering through the palms and an insect-like humming in distant riggings.

MP stumbled back upstairs. His head hurt, but somehow it didn't matter; he felt good. He fell onto his bed, still in his clothes and, like Kate, was asleep in a second.

| 131

CHAPTER 11

MP AWOKE to the smell of fresh coffee wafting up the stairs and a pleasant breeze drifting in through the window. He wondered if he should shower and brush his teeth before breakfast now that he had a guest to be concerned with. But the odor of the coffee pulled him downstairs where he found Kate leaning on the counter, cup in hand.

"Morning," she greeted as he came around the corner. "You look like shit."

"Thanks. May I return the compliment?"

"Sure can. I certainly feel like shit … except this java is starting to help. And I'm tellin' ya, the next tea I have will have nothing but ice in it. My God!"

It looked like she hadn't made it up to brush and refresh herself, either. Even though her hair was disheveled, clothes rumpled, eyes red with sagging bags under, she managed to look considerably better than shit.

"Here. Pour yourself a cup and let's go out on the porch and do your little ritual breathing in the good and out the bad, which you ought to have plenty of this morning. It's actually a lovely day to take in."

After sitting down and settling in quietly for several minutes, Kate said, "OK, I've waited long enough. What am I going to call you?"

"My name."

CHAPTER 11

"You mean MP?"

"That's my name."

"Boy, you are a talkative one in the morning. Actually, that's not your name. I've been reviewing your files here, and you had indicated that your real name was M-i-k-a-e-l, pronounce MEE-cale. Correct?"

"You want to call me that?"

"Uh, no. I'd prefer MP, which, as you know, I don't like."

"Well, then?"

"Pat is the middle name, right?"

"Yup."

"That's easy. I like Pat," she said.

"Nope."

"No? Well, I suppose after probably being the only MP in the world, Pat is a little mundane."

"Yup, and Barney is Pat."

"Oh, OK. And 'M-u-l-c-a-h-y. MUL-cahy, right?"

"Yup."

"Well, let me *mull* that one over."

He looked at her over his coffee mug. Even his eyes weren't smiling. Too early in the morning, especially with a hangover, for dumb, dry humor.

"OK, I agree, that'd even be bad comin' out of your mouth," she said, but still mulling: "If you're gonna be my brother ..."

"Do I have a choice?"

"My, my. It's one thing to be laconic in the morning. It's another to be downright nasty."

"Sorry," he said, taking another sip. "I already told ya."

"Right," she interrupted. "So, my brother. It would have to be an endearing name. Something friendly, family-brother-like. Hey, I think I got it."

"Uh-oh."

"Well, it's nothing unusual, like MP."

"So, what is it?" he asked.

"Nah, wait. I'll try calling you this later and see how or if you respond."

"The tension and suspense will be riveting."

"Now don't get all sarcastic on me," she said. "It's especially too early for sarcasm."

"Agreed."

"OK, something else, Mick, I've got to contact Sara. She'll be going nuts wondering what's going on and if I'm OK." Oddly, the "Mick" slid right past MP.

"Can't you just call and tell someone …"

"I already did," she interrupted again. "I called a good friend of ours from the pay phone by the pier and left her a message to tell Sara to get a prepaid cell phone. I figured Sara could call me at the pay phone. Is that OK? Spense says that prepaid jobbie can't be traced, right? You know, I haven't made a lot out of this, but I am worried about putting you in danger as well, especially if now they know I'm here with you."

"I told you," Mick said, putting his coffee down, "you're my sister. If you didn't let me help, I'd be pissed. And how would they know you're here with me? Who's 'they?'"

"I think it's just that guy I showed you a picture of. I just want to be extra careful and not do anything that would lead him here."

"If he, whoever he is, finds us, we'll have to deal with it."

"Well, if he finds us, he's not going to just say 'howdy.'"

"Really? What do you think he wants to do if he finds you?"

"Oh … I don't know. I don't know if he plans on just wanting to talk to me, abduct me, or just get rid of me, reaping

CHAPTER 11

his revenge. Seriously, he probably just wants to try to talk me out of ..."

"Yeah? Out of what?"

Oh, never mind. I'll explain when Sara's here. Please don't ask more."

"Well, just in case sose ya know, until I finally get the whole story from you ... you've noticed those island kids, a lot of 'em with dreads, who walk by all the time either bouncing a basketball or kicking a soccer ball?" Mick asked.

"Yeah. So what?"

"Well, they came to talk to me and I've enlisted 'em to keep an eye out. One of them, at least for now, walks by on the hour, every hour, I guess even at night. I've shown them the picture you have of him."

"Really? How can we afford that?"

"Hey, they're island kids. Few have real jobs and no money. They don't care about money. They should be in high school, I think, but they have to go into Marsh Harbour for high school. I think they are attracted to the low-key world of Elbow Cay and just don't want to leave the island. To them this 'boyfriend' of yours is like the evil that lurks out there, that they don't want here. I can't believe you had a boyfriend you're afraid of."

"That's *ex*-boyfriend, by the way."

She had told him the guy had been a boyfriend. Why did it bug him that she had had a boyfriend? "So, anyway, they won't take any money. To them this is exciting. They take this guy and the evil outside influence he represents very seriously. They want to catch him."

"Well, we can't let them do that."

"No. You're probably right. Who knows what they'd do to him. But they say they know someone who is 'big, strong,

135

and smart.' I guess he's the one who sent them to talk to me and has them on this vigilance thing. So, I told the boys about the dude—what's his name?"

"Richard."

"Yeah, Richard. They listened and left but stopped back the next day. Apparently they had talked to this big, smart guy and he had them all organized on a schedule. I wonder who the heck he is. Anyway, they actually seemed excited about it."

"Well, can we count on them? What would they even do if Richard showed up?" Kate asked.

"Oh, I think we can count on them for sure. I can tell. I know nothing about the big, smart guy, of course. So for now they would just alert him, us and the islanders. By now, these guys will have let all the Bahamians on the island know about it, including the ferry guys and harbormaster. Your guy could not get on or off the island without them, and so us, knowing it."

"Off? After he shoots us, you mean?"

"Well, we'd know if he's on the island before he could even reach us, and he couldn't get off the island with you, for sure. And I suspect he doesn't want to get caught. I'm working on it. I don't know what else to do … for now. But, I wish there was some way to reciprocate, to pay them."

"You say they're school age, but not, like, going to, like, high school?" Kate asked.

"Right. It's kinda hard to tell their ages. I mean, you probably noticed: some are huge with great wide faces, some with dreads so long you can't really see their faces, and this one short little guy seems to be the spokesman. But I'm guessing they're like seventeen to twenty. Their ages almost don't matter. They could be twenty-five. It's that they haven't gone to school past eighth or maybe ninth grade. Why?"

CHAPTER 11

"Well, why don't I, like, teach them? I'm not doing anything right now anyway. It'd give me something to do."

"Whaddya mean?"

"Whaddya mean, whadd'I mean? Like home school or something. You know. Think they'd go for it?"

"You'd really do that?"

"Think they'd want to?"

"Uh, I don't know. But, why not? Really? What a cool idea, Kate. Where would you have these ... students?"

"Oh, shoot, Mick, speaking of students, I forgot to tell you. I don't know where my head is. When I got up this morning, there was a small, youngish girl sitting on the steps out front here. At first I thought she was only a child because she was so small. But as I was noticing her, she walked up and handed me this folder, and I could tell she was older ... like sixteen or even twenty. She spoke very good English with just a hint of island lilt. Her message was strange. She said she wanted to be a writer and that her dad told her that 'although you're a midget, you would be able to help her.' What's that all about?"

"I haven't a clue," Mick said. "Where's the folder?"

"On the counter in the kitchen."

Mick went in, picked up the folder, and came back out onto the porch. He opened the folder and found, first, a note: "I want to be a writer. My father says you could help. He also says you're a midget, like me. But I've seen you, and you're just a little short, like I am. If you could, please read my writing and tell me what you think and leave it in the folder on your porch by the steps. I'll pick it up sometime during the day and then come by tomorrow morning, and, if you agree, I'll leave you another. Thank you. H.S."

BACK TO THE ISLAND

For some reason, MP felt himself tremble as he read the poem:

> I looked at life to find
> That life was looking at me.
> And life looked at me exactly
> As I had looked at life.
> Life saw me filled
> With anger and pain.
> —H.S.

"Holy shit!" Mick expounded, startling Kate. "Listen to this!" and he read her the poem. "I can't tell if it's a mistake."

"Read it again," Kate said. So he did.

"What do you mean 'a mistake'?" Kate asked.

"Well, it's only six lines, but really, doesn't it say in so few words what sometimes it takes almost a novel to say? And it's perfectly, well, I don't know, symmetrical."

"It's remarkably sad," Kate said. "And the sketch. My God! Simple but really … sad, I guess."

"'Sad,' yes, I suppose, and the sketch is really as remarkable as the poem. But more …"

"More what?" Kate asked.

"I don't know. I wonder, one, if a young girl actually wrote this by herself and, two, if, maybe she's written a ton of stuff and her father or whoever told her that this one was good. It could be just an accident. I don't know. But if she did this, well, intentionally, it's kinda scary, I mean for a young girl, you know? It's simplistic but pretty darn good."

Kate laughed. "Once a teacher, always a teacher. What are you going to do about it, Mick?"

"I don't know. Whad'dyou call me?"

CHAPTER 11

"You mean 'Mick'?"

"Yeah."

"I've actually called you that before … and you didn't even notice."

"Well, I did, I think."

"Well, you sure took it in stride. You didn't even act surprised. You better get used to Mick, bro. I believe Mick it is."

Mick's attention drifted back to H.S. and the poem. He walked back inside without responding, went over to the bureau by the cluttered table, grabbed a notepad, came back outside, and wrote: "Is that all life sees?" He put it in the folder, keeping her poem and sketch.

"Whaddya write?" Kate asked.

"Do you mind if I keep it between her and me?"

"No, not at all. It's probably a good idea. Breakfast?"

THAT NIGHT when Mick sauntered into Cap'n's, he found Lottie already behind the bar, Jack, Roland, and Ma in the kitchen, and Spense setting up his keyboard with the name Dead Man on it. The keyboard looked extremely complicated with several levels of keys and a huge board of switches, toggles, and buttons.

"What's with 'Dead Man?' Seems a little ominous," Mick asked Lottie.

She laughed as she was washing out some glasses. It was early and, being a Wednesday, actually the slowest night, the place was almost empty. "I'm assuming you've already figured out Spense is a little ... eccentric, let's say?"

Mick laughed as well. "No, I haven't noticed. By the way, thanks for covering last night."

"Well," Lottie nodded and continued, smiling into the next clean glass, "he doesn't have that great a voice, but, like him, it's interesting and he is charismatic. He flirts with the ladies, cool—none of them get offended—and gives the guys shit. Everyone loves him."

"That's quite the keyboard."

"Oh, you have no idea. Sometimes it sounds like he has an entire orchestra behind him. Other times a rock band or sometimes just a Flamenco guitar. It's frickin' amazing, MP."

"Oh, by the way, you decide: Kate has decided to call me Mick. I'm not sure what I think about that. But when you get to know Kate, you'll see she tends to be a little strong-minded."

CHAPTER 11

"I've noticed," Lottie answered. "I like her, but I'm not sure how she feels about me."

"What? You two looked like you totally hit it off, especially yesterday. What ya talkin' about?"

Lottie didn't answer, just kept busying herself behind the bar. "Want a drink? Hair of the dog?" Lottie asked.

"God, no. You know what sounds good? A real iced tea."

"Well, get your ass in gear. Make yourself one. Mick, huh?"

Mick made himself his iced tea and started to arrange stuff behind the bar. "So, what kind of music does Spense play?"

"You name it. Well, actually, if you name it—make a request—it has to be a song either written or made famous by a person who has died."

"Huh?" Mick stopped, took an order from a guy at the bar, picked up a blender, and looked at Lottie.

"You heard me. He'll take requests and can play just about anything. He spends a lot of time alone at sea and that's what he does. He's apparently always practicing new songs, especially, you know, if someone good dies."

Mick finished mixing the resorter a blended drink, smiling the entire time. "Does he write any of his own stuff?" he asked when he was done.

"No. It's all covers, but he does some very interesting twists on popular songs."

"As long as the original singer is dead?" Mick asked, incredulous, still holding the blender and looking at Lottie. "Thus, I take it: Dead Man?"

"Yup, you got it," Lottie said, taking the blender and pouring the drink into a fancy glass, adding an umbrella, and taking it to the lonely looking patron. After getting him to laugh at something, she came back and leaned on the bar. "He says he feels guilty fuckin' around with a song while the singer's still alive; same with the songwriter."

"Interesting. Very interesting," Mick said, washing out the blender and putting it back in its place behind the bar.

"He's actually kind of famous. I know in Colombia and Prince Edward Island, they want him to cut a CD, but he won't."

"Why?"

"You'll have to ask him that. He's in demand here in the islands, but he won't do big venues like Nassau. Absolutely refuses. I don't know why. He does play on occasion at Kipper's, a popular drinking hole on Big Guana Cay, a ways out in the Abaco. They'll have like a big-deal pig roast once in a while and sometimes he'll play. I know in one of the islands on his way to or from Colombia—somewhere in the Virgin Islands, I think—they moor him outside a friend's high-end resort and he does a light show and blasts from aboard his boat or ship or whatever you call that intergalactic-looking vessel."

"Cool. Why not here?"

"We've tried to talk him into it, but he won't. In this little harbor, he says it would be intrusive to his neighbors."

Just then Spense walked up to the bar. "Hello, Mr. MP. Have you recovered sufficiently?"

"Took several cups of coffee and, well, I got a little head and shoulder rub from Kate—really helped I have to admit."

"A 'sisterly' rub?" Lottie asked, returning to her bar-ly labors.

"Oh, sounds wonderful," Spense mused. "I wish I had such an accommodating sister."

"Right!" Lottie shot back. "Give me a dinghy ride out to your ocean mansion after work tonight and I'll give you a good rubdown, including your dinghy if you so desire."

CHAPTER 11

"Whoa. Sounds a little titillating," Mick said, frowning, returning to his tasks as well.

Spense laughed. "You're on, honey. I'll gleefully surrender to your touch. MP, please understand, although sounding titillating as you say, Lottie and I go way back ... almost to Plato. Got it, my new friend? No 'tits' involved in the titillation, nor 'dinghies,' I doubt, albeit unfortunately."

Mick laughed. "Sorry. Got it. The same with Kate naturally." Although he had not been able to relax the entire shoulder rub—maybe a little with the head rub—it had felt marvelous. But he knew in his previous "rubs" and massages, especially with Martha, one of the enjoyments was the feminine touch. He had once had a massage by a guy and it wasn't the same and, as with Kate, he couldn't give in and just enjoy. Kate was, after all, his *sister*! He should have offered return compensation but just couldn't get himself to do it. He felt guilty. It wasn't fair; but this was *his sister*!

"Oh, by the way, Spense," Lottie kind of hissed, "Kate has dubbed MP 'Mick.' Whaddya think?"

"Well, won't this be fun. We can decide what moniker fits the occasion. That OK with you, Mr. MP?" Spense asked.

"Only if you drop the Mr.," Mick replied.

"Done. Guess I'll leave you two to your chores. I see some more patrons heading this way. I'll go get warmed up. Later, my friends."

The crowd ended up bigger than usual for a Wednesday. The word had gotten out that Spense would be on. Apparently there had been a few disappointed patrons the night before, as Spense never made it back once he had eyed his bed. But they, and more, were back tonight, and in good spirits. Lottie and Mick barely talked as they split time between the bar and serving food. Jack, Ma, and their cook, Roland, did a good job for a bar menu. When Spense ended the night with "Hit the Road, Jack," the crowd, to Mick's delight, dutifully filed out into the balmy night.

Mick got home a little earlier than usual and sat on the porch enjoying the night's salty breeze. It was the first time he had had time to think. He knew Kate had tried her and Sara's friend, Sally, again earlier, but again had to leave a message. Kate was only able to hope that she had given Sara the number of the public pay phone and the set time: eleven o'clock tomorrow morning, Eastern Standard Time. That would put Sara at seven o'clock, before her day would start and she got busy. Kate knew Sara would be biting her nails. Kate had gone to bed early. He hoped she was able to sleep.

Mick woke a little before his usual time to the clinking of coffee cups. He had been pleasantly surprised the night before as, apparently, Spense usually ended his routine right at closing time and always did his version of Ray Charles's "Hit the Road, Jack." He added "says" after "Jack," and instead of "don't ya come back no more, no more, no more, " he sang: "Ya better come back some more, some more, some more, some more." The song worked both because Ray was, indeed, dead and because all the patrons, juiced or not, respected that by the time Spense finished the song, they had to have "hit the road." If any hadn't, they were subjected to the biting wit of Spense, biting but all in good fun, yet with an obvious message, and the word had gotten out. Drunken newcomers were ushered out by their experienced compatriots, making the ordeal of closing up much more enjoyable.

Mick came downstairs feeling a tad more well-rested than usual and Kate, already up, handed him both a cup of java

CHAPTER 11

and the folder, which had seemed to just disappear off the porch yesterday. Mick immediately headed out to the porch, but Kate told him the little poet was gone. She had been there when Kate got up and had handed her the folder with a smile and the words: "For MP—My dad says to say thank you. He appreciates it and said he knew you would help. I thank you too."

"She's very unusual, Mick. I can't tell how old she is. She has this quiet, shy smile that emanates more from her eyes than her mouth. She speaks softly but is very articulate. She reminds me of a precious little bird."

"Well, let's take a look at what we got today." First there was a side note: "Does this answer your question?" Then no title, just:

> How silly and senseless life
> Can be ...
> Having something, but never
> Holding it close.
> Having a friend, but never
> Holding his hand.
> Having a leader, and not
> Being willing to follow.
> Having a father, but afraid
> To be his child.
>
> —H.S.

He handed it to Kate and explained, "I had asked her: 'Is that all life sees?' from her last poem."

"You sure you want me to read it?" Kate asked.

"I think I'd like you to see them all, and tell me what you think. What I write I may not show you, if that's OK?"

"Well, don't know why, but sure. Let's see it." Kate read it and looked up at Mick. "I think if she did write this, she's a lot older than her years. And, once again, did you look at the sketch? It's a poem in itself."

"Yes," Mick said, and scribbled the note: "Tell me about your father." Once again he kept the poem and put the folder out front. He was getting really curious about her. It wasn't like the poem was earth-shattering, but again, it said a lot in just a few simple words. And, of course, it was driving him nuts—referring to him as MP, and who the hell was her father? He'd have to catch her next time.

After breakfast, Mick went up to his perch to write. With everything going on the last few days, his routine was shot and discipline had slipped. He needed to catch up. Kate had found a Carl Hiaasen book, retired to the settee on the porch, and almost instantly had started to giggle. They both filled time pleasantly until Kate yelled up to Mick that it was ten thirty and that she wanted to get to the phone early to ensure it was not in use at eleven. Mick had had a little trouble getting back to the novel and had been mostly back-reading

CHAPTER 11

to catch the scent of where the story was headed, and so was a little irritated to be interrupted. But, what the hell, he figured. He better get used to it. Having Kate around was definitely going to disrupt any notion of a routine, and then Sara was coming to visit, he assumed, and Barney would be coming, so he'd better learn to live with disorder, at least for a while ... or maybe for a long time?

They sped down the lane, dust trailing them. Mick looked more at Kate than the road. He noticed that she still had bags under her eyes and wondered if she was having trouble sleeping. Kate, deep in thought, appeared to be searching the windshield for an answer to something. They arrived early. Nobody was looking to use the phone, fortunately, and so they stood securing it: Mick taking a good look at Spense's vessel out in the harbor, Kate staring at the phone, hopping back and forth from one foot to another.

When the phone rang, they both jumped. Kate snatched up the receiver immediately and dropped in several coins in response to the operator. "Hello? Hello, Sara? Oh hi, hon. How are you? I'm fine, fine. No, I haven't seen *him*. As you know I'm on a small cay, Elbow Cay, at ... er ... MP's—now known, to me at least—as Mick. Yes, yes, it is an improvement." Kate looked over at Mick and smiled guiltily. "He's ... we're ... just outside of a little settlement called Hope Town. No, no, not far from Marsh Harbour, just a twenty-minute ferry ride. Yes, yes, it's far enough from Marsh Harbour. There's no way Richard would connect Marsh Harbour to Elbow Cay. When are you coming down? Oh, that soon? No, no, that's OK. Are you sure you can get away? I don't know. Stay as long as you can get away for." Kate again looked at Mick, giving him a grimacing smile. "A week's good. Yes, that's fine." Mick

| 147

smiled and nodded his head. "OK, hon. Since you're coming so soon, call again tomorrow, same time to give me the details. Someone, probably Mick, will meet you at the airport. They aren't allowing me anywhere near Marsh Harbour. What? You want to talk to him? Well, sure, just a sec," and she handed the phone to Mick.

Mick looked at the phone, took it hesitantly, not knowing what to expect, and said, "Hello?"

"Hello, Mick?"

"I guess that's who I am now."

Sara laughed. A good, pleasing laugh, he thought. "You want me to call you MP?"

"You can call me anything you want."

"Well then, get ready honey, darling, any expletive I can think of."

"I thought expletives had to be cuss words … like son-of-a-bitch?"

Sara burst out laughing. "No, actually I believe an expletive can be any interjection, good or bad, and mine will all be good, you can count on it. I just want to thank you for taking care of my sister."

"Our sister, you mean?"

"Uh, right. You're right. Gotta get used to that one. But thank you so much. You are our savior."

"Uh, I wouldn't go that far." Mick had especially taken a disliking of that term since Ajax's use of it.

"Well, I think so. But I suppose we're going to need more coins here soon. I just want to say I'm dying to meet you. I'm nothing like Kate. I'm fat, boring—a number cruncher. Watch Kate. She doesn't always demonstrate … uh … the most rational approach to solving problems. You might say

CHAPTER 11

she's a bit impulsive and a spirit often too free for her own good. Please take care of her. I'll figure out what to call you when I see you. I can't wait. Bye, honey, darling, sweetie, son-of-a-bitch if you prefer. Oh, there's the operator. See you soon, bye."

Mick was more than favorably disposed toward Sara when they hung up. He felt almost like they had been on a blind date. "Cool. I like her already," he told Kate.

"Oh, you'll love her. She's very bright, as I think I already told you, and sweet, easy to live with—not like me."

"What's that supposed to mean?"

"Oh, I don't know. She just always seems to know the right thing to do. I have a habit of opening my big mouth before I consider, well, the effects of what I might do or say."

"She said she was boring. A 'number cruncher'?"

"She would say something like that. She's very unassuming. Again, not like me, I'm afraid."

Mick smiled at her. "Sounds like you're a little self-deprecating yourself."

"No, just honest."

"What does Sara do exactly?"

"Well, she has an arsenal of number crunchers that answer to her. She works with the SEC—Securities and Exchange Com—"

"I know what SEC means. If you recall, I taught economics and was a financial adviser," interrupted Mick.

"Right, of course. She's a bigwig. Makes tons of money. Hangs onto it, too. She's loaded. Takes huge chunks of time off, which is why she can just hop on down here for a week. Travels and takes vacations all by herself. Right now she's investigating insider trading and the use, or I should say abuse, of several products the big banks and wire houses were peddling, helping to cause the Great Recession."

"No shit? That's one of my pet peeves. Really? She's after the Wall Street cock-suckers? Sounds like my kind of gal. I don't think those suckers even understood those frickin' complex products," Mick spit out, "or I'd like to think they didn't. And they all made millions peddling them."

"Oh, no," Kate answered, a taste of bitterness in her voice. "The big guys understood perfectly what they were doing. Believe me, I know."

Mick raised his eyebrows. "Just how do you know? No one's been able to pin anything on those assholes. How you? You know you've ducked the question and put off answering me every time I have asked you what you did in the States or why, exactly, someone's chasing you. Fess up. Something tells me it's related to this?"

"Never mind," Kate said dismissively. "I can't tell you."

"Screw that!" he almost shouted. "If I'm going to protect my little sister, I think I should know why … and who from!"

Several resorters and island folk strolling by started to take notice of the ruckus. "Shh. Yes, I understand," Kate whispered. "Be patient. Let's wait until Sara is here and we'll explain completely."

"We? Is Sara involved in this too?"

Kate looked pleadingly at Mick. She looked almost ready to cry. "Indirectly …" she started to say, when they heard Spense's hulking cart grumble up to them. They hadn't noticed his dory had pulled up to the pier.

"Hello, my most esteemed set of siblings. I was just heading out to your quaint little abode. I believe I have good news."

CHAPTER 11

Mick and Kate were quiet for a moment. They just stood there staring at the ground.

"Oh, dear," Spense said. "I fear I have interloped on a private moment?"

Mick and Kate looked at Spense, back to each other, then back at Spense, and answered simultaneously, "No." Mick finished with, "It's OK. What's up?"

"I have an idea," Spense posed. "What if I dory you two out to my humble floating abode, give you a tour, provide a little lunch, and show you my good news."

"Humble?" they said again, concurrently.

"How quaint a set of siblings you are. Do you frequently respond simultaneously?"

"No," they both said at the same time, and all three burst out laughing.

"I was wondering when I was going to get a tour of your not-so-humble floating mansion," Kate said.

"Well, I'm in for some supplies. How about I do my shopping and swing by when I'm done and pick you two up?"

"Great!" they both said again at the same time. All laughed and the tension dissipated into the salty air.

SPENSE PULLED his teak dory parallel up to the aft of his yacht, pointed a remote at it, and suddenly from below invisible arms started to lift them. Both Mick and Kate grabbed at the benches they were seated on, unsettled by the sudden jolt. Spense chuckled. "Sorry, I should have warned you. We will be deposited momentarily on deck. There is a hydraulic cradle that will be very gentle. No need to worry."

The cradle settled the dory, gently as promised, next to a shining wooden platform. Spense grabbed a brass railing and stepped out easily onto a gleaming mahogany deck. When Mick and Kate followed and they headed into the interior, they were taken aback. The hull and fly, the only aspects visible from outside, were galactic looking: high-gloss white, molded in smooth, rounded shapes with a touch of navy and red trimmings, including, among a variety, a US flag flying high on the immense mast. But the interior was all highly polished beautiful woods accented with brass, stainless steel, and glass. Any material they could see on cushions and benches was a subtle khaki color, blending wonderfully with the hue of the woods. It was stunning. The incongruity of the ultramodern exterior and classic, tasteful interior was almost a shock.

Spense led them down a brass-railed, carpeted stairway to what appeared to be a den, or library. Books, DVDs, and CDs lined the walls, a desk in one corner with a green leather office chair, and a burgundy-colored leather love seat against one wall bracketed by matching leather lounge chairs. A shell-shaped glass end table accompanied each chair.

"Wow!" both Mick and Kate spurted.

"This totally blows me away!" Kate howled, mouth gaping.

"Shit, Spense," was all Mick could say.

"Please, be seated," and Spense pointed to the deep-red leather chairs. "I brought you down here to explain what I deem likely to be welcome news. We'll tour the entire vessel later. But, first ..." he walked over to a wall and slid open a panel, exposing a mini, high-tech-looking office. Computer screens, buttons, blinking lights, and toggles were everywhere. He turned, holding an ultramodern-looking little black box. "I've been tinkering. I'm hoping this little remote bridge here works. Rather than have you putt into Hope Town every time you need to communicate with family and friends, would it

CHAPTER 11

not be better to have use of email again?"

Kate and Mick looked at each other. "Well, yeah," Mick said, "but I thought this guy could trace it here?"

"Yes," Spense said, "if you use a server here in the Bahamas. I don't want to get too technical, but it has to do with your service provider having your IP address available. If he's really good, it's apparently possible for him to follow it here to Marsh Harbour—I'm not sure about Elbow Cay. *But*, if you use this here little gadget, a special modem, and plug it into your computer, you should be wirelessly connected to my server."

"But," Kate said, "you're here in Hope Town's harbor?"

"You've noticed the loft of my mast? It needs to be quite high due to the rather extensive LWL—that's an acronym for load waterline, or length. Another reason I have it so high is for reception. I have a need for a vast range of reception, especially BBC news—don't ask. It also functions as a transmitter for my computer and Internet. I have a gyroscope, GPS, and also a dish. I can face it in any direction to pick up another server ... like I do in Prince Edward Island. As a matter of fact, I have it aimed at a satellite in geosynchronous orbit currently with that portion of Canada right now, a direction I plan on heading when it heats up down here. Hopefully you will be served by Canada, as well. Your antagonist may be sent on a wild Canada goose chase if this works to connect you into my server. You'll be safe to email your sister to your heart's content. And vice-versa, of course. Her emails—you'd still be wise to ensure the mail's content doesn't give anything away—couldn't be traced to here, on Elbow. If this contraption I rigged up works, that is. And if it does, I may be able

| 153

to lead him to believe since the server was in Prince Edward Island, Canada, that you are, as well. *Or*, at another time even in Santa Marta, Colombia. Wouldn't that, how you two might say, 'fuck 'em up'?"

After a tasty little lunch in the galley and a tour that mostly involved Kate and Mick wandering through a maze of rooms on a multitude of levels, eyes wide and mouths hanging open, they all headed back to Mick's—and Kate's—cottage. There they plugged this new modem-like-bridge-thing into Mick's computer, and Spense deemed that it would work.

"This calls for a celebration," Mick applauded. "I've got a stash of 'goombay smash' saved for just such an occasion."

"Ah, yes. The favored poison in these fair outer isles of the Abacos," Spense said, clapping his twisted hands.

"You two settle on the front porch and I'll pour us all a glass of the fruity concoction," Mick directed.

"This reminds me of my friend, Mark, on Treasure Cay," Kate said. "He professes to make the best smash—has his own recipe. It's made with a special rum and he won't tell anybody what mixture of fresh fruits he uses. He has been taking tourists out for years on fishing and snorkeling excursions, and they generally come back at their limit: smashed. He's quite the character. The best beard I've ever seen. Cornrows reaching his waist."

"Is that who you stayed with?" Mick asked.

"Yup," Kate answered. "I need to get back there to get some of the stuff I left, mostly just clothes, and Mark has been caring for my Vanagon. Of course I have no use for it here, so for now I'll just let him use it. But I'd also like to get back to that storage unit in Marsh Harbour. I've got more clothes and other stuff there. Maybe there's something we could use

CHAPTER 11

around here? You are living a little Spartan, and I won't have to be wearing your clothes all the time."

"Yeah, but you look so cute in them," Mick said.

"You are so comme il faut, my man. Right on, as you boomers used to say. Nothing is sexier than a woman dressed in man's clothing," commented Spense, talking and raising his eyebrows up and down, Groucho style.

"Can I remind you that I am the *sister* here?"

"Well, I was just kidding," Mick lied once again.

"You're not *my* sister, my spicy little popover," Spense said, adding the cigar to his Groucho mimicry. "I've got a slick little robe I'd like to pop ya into ... and then over and out of."

"Hey, that's my sister you're calling a popover."

"All right," Kate said, laughing, "enough already. If you two are so fricking clever, how am I going to get my stuff and not be worried about being recognized? I'm beginning to feel like a prisoner."

"Right, right," Spense said, the wheels again turning. "Tell you what, let's borrow Lottie's boat. This is too conspicuous. We can take it to Treasure Cay and it has enough room for what you might want to haul back from Marsh Harbour."

"Lottie has a boat?" both MP and Kate spurted at the same time.

"You two are going to have to quit doing that. It's getting a bit queer. There's a lot about Lottie you two don't know. Have you seen her place?"

"No," Mick answered. "I do know it's in that gated area called Coconut Grove on the south end, though. I've wondered. Everything in there is kinda pricey."

"Yes, that's true. Lottie's story, however, is for another day. But she has a very nice Windsor craft that she keeps in

Coconut's private harbor. So, we'll requisition her Windsor … I'm guessing she'll want to accompany us, anyway. We'll dress you, Kate, in disguise. I've got a number of wigs."

"Wigs?" they once again sputtered at the same time. They all laughed, and Kate finished: "Just what are you doing with 'a number of wigs,' might I ask?"

"You might ask, but that's for another time as well."

Mick and Kate looked at each other, both thinking in what might have been sibling symmetry: "There's obviously more to Spense than we know."

"When will your friend be willing to have us visit to claim your possessions?" Spense asked.

"Oh, he never gets going too early. Late morning any day, I'd say."

"Tomorrow then?"

"Well, I can email him now. I'll come down to Cap'n Jack's at closing tonight and we'll make arrangements with Lottie," Kate said.

"Excellent," said Spense and handed his empty glass to Mick. "Another of these and I'll be incapacitated."

"Wait. I want to hear about the wigs," Kate teased.

Spense hobbled down the steps, somewhat sprightly for a seventy-something-year-old, and onto his cart, yelling, "For another time" and was off in a cloud of dust.

"This is great," Mick said to Kate. "I can email Barn. He's gonna be pissed it's been so long. And you can make arrangements with Sara. When was she planning on coming?"

"This weekend, if it is all right with you."

"Of course. Can she arrange things that quickly?"

"She flies all over. She'll have her SEC pilot drop her off in their jet in Miami and she'll take the puddle jumper to

CHAPTER 11

Marsh Harbour. We'll have to make sure we don't mention anything about Elbow Cay, just to be safe."

"Right. What about her family?"

"Doesn't have one."

"No husband? Kids?"

"Nope."

"What about you? My two questions a week never got me too far. I've been pretty patient about not asking you to divulge your secrets, but don't you think …"

"No kids; never a husband, only the bastard that's looking for me as a boyfriend."

Mick felt another instant pang of jealousy. Why, he had no idea, or no right, he realized. "So, this guy looking for you was really your boyfriend?"

"Well, more than a boyfriend. We were living together. Engaged, actually." Kate bit her lip and looked away.

Mick felt again, unreasonably, a stab of resentfulness. "What the … ?" was what came out, then: "I don't …"

Kate's eyes watered and she ran off the porch into the cottage, and he could hear her pad up the stairs, to her bedroom Mick assumed.

He just sat there. He tried to think. The thought prominent in his mind was something Kate had said: "I feel like a prisoner." He realized that they had to come up with something. This situation was interminable, so maybe it was inevitable that they faced this guy. It struck him they couldn't live every day wondering, worrying. Even if he was dispatched, as Spense might say, to Prince Edward Island or some other faraway place, the worry would always be there: Will he find us and what does he want? Might as well ask him. They were going to have to draw this villain to them and somehow deal with it, face it. But, a fiancé!

BACK TO THE ISLAND

He'd bring this up to Spense and Lottie tonight. He had an inkling Spense would concoct a plan. He hoped the emails were secure. A frickin' fiancé!

CHAPTER 12

DATE: Tuesday, Mar. 6, 2012, 2:05 p.m.

M: Hey, Barn. You there in yur cubicle? Wurkin on yur class notes for all those stunts who gets their knickers in an uproar over taxes?

Barn: Yeah, yeah. Shit, man, you OK? Why the hell haven't you been able to email? What's going on? Why can you now all of a sudden?

M: Sorry. I really am. I know I gave you a little info and then ... What the hell, my mail just plinked, or whatever that weird sound it makes, is that you?

Barn: Don't start this "Oh, I'm sorry" bullshit. I'm coming down there. Saturday, as a matter of fact. I'm flying in to Miami and taking Bahama Air to, what is it, Mush Harbor? I have a God blasted 3-hour layover in Fort Lauderdale, but it's all I could get. I won't get there until 6:00 PM. So pick me up.

M: Kate's sister Sara is coming down on Sat, too. Is that you plinking me again?

Barn: I don't care if your mom and dad are rising from the dead and landing in Mush Harbor and moving in with you. I'm coming.

M: I thought you had to wait until summer break?

Barn: It's interim. I only have 4 days. I'm coming. No sense in arguing about it.

M: I'm not arguing. I'm glad you're coming. It would take more than an email anyway to catch you up. It'll be interesting, I'm warning you. I'll see you at 6:00 at the airport.

Barn: OK. Sorry I'm so adamant. "Interesting" sounds good to a boring tax professor anyway. I've got to meet this chick, and what were you saying about a sister? Where do I meet you?

M: Slow down, will ya? I'm dying to meet the sister meself. Just come down here and join in on all the fun. Don't worry. It ain't a big airport. As a matter of fact, the last tax professor to take that puddle jumper to *Marsh* Harbour ... that's MARSH HarboUr, dumb ass ... shit his pants. You better be prepared. Better wear an extra pair of Depends.

Barn: Huh? What's that supposed to mean?

You're not going to answer are you?

Why? What might happen?

Shit.

M: Right!

Kate composed herself and came in at closing. Spense had picked up Mick so Kate could have Mick's cart. The first thing she spit out when she got there was that she had emailed Sara and would be arriving at Marsh Harbour Saturday at five thirty—a half-hour before Barney. So only one trip was needed to get them. Lottie had no problem with using her

CHAPTER 12

boat both days and was excited to be included. She would pick them up at Cap'n's dock in the harbor. They all agreed with Mick: they needed to devise a plan to outwit Kate's ex rather than hide and wait. No one was too happy with Kate for not wanting to give more information about herself but figured they could survive until the weekend when her sister would be there. In the meantime, they'd go to Treasure Cay tomorrow, Friday, early afternoon to get Kate's stuff.

Next morning, Kate slept in and Mick ran downstairs hoping to catch his young poet, but found only the folder on the floor of the porch. He opened it before sitting down and found no sketch but:

Loose Ends

I lost my father.
Not to death,
But to a distance,
—an anger, a hope, a puzzlement.
And I guess that is all there is left
To say after all these years. I doubt
That I could even remember quite how
He looks …

… but I do have a photograph.

And I must admit that there are still
Mornings when I awaken to the smell of
Him on my mind: as if when I go down
The stair, he will be waiting there, with
His cup of coffee and his newspaper
And his smile.
But when I open my eyes,

| 161

> There is just my room, and
> Just me—just ten or twelve years
> Different is all. And there is
> Another man in the kitchen, now. He
> Is married to my mother, but he is a
> Bit of a stranger to me.
>
> —H.S.

And a note: Is this what you wanted to know?

Mick wrote to her: No. I am sorry your real father left you. It seems you've been able to handle it all right. Tell me about this new father. Why is he a stranger to you? Did he adopt you? Tell me about him. Please. I like your poetry very much … and your drawings.

Mick spent the rest of the morning on his perch, writing. He was having trouble getting back into his novel *A Little Short*, so he decided to focus on *If I Had a Million Dollars*. This talk about people getting screwed by Wall Street got him thinking about the Boomers again: a reported 80% of them not having saved enough to retire on gave him an inspiration for the subtitle: "How to Achieve Financial Independence before Your Parents Do." He liked it.

Kate spent some time chuckling at Hiaasen. She was going into Jack's with Mick to listen to Spense after they picked up her stuff at both Mark's and her storage unit in Marsh Harbour, which was on the way. It was Friday night and Spense would be doing a long set. Mick came down and they made a list of songs to request … all, of course, made famous by dead singers or written by dead songwriters. Top of the list were "Poncho and Lefty," which they both loved, written by the late and great Townes Van Zandt, and Mick

CHAPTER 12

insisted on "Miss Otis Regrets," made famous by the Beatles but written by maybe his favorite songwriter, dead or alive, Cole Porter.

Spense always set up at the end of the dock, which was open to the air and cooler. It turned out he knew every song Kate requested, and he did an especially unique version of "Miss Otis Regrets." Kate loved it. Of course, because Kate was making requests, one very drunk newcomer started giving Spense shit for not doing his requests. Songs by live singers, of course. When he wouldn't shut up and started to get belligerent, a couple of crusty regulars escorted him to the door and heaved him out onto the cobblestones. When he came storming back in again in a drunken rage, the same two hooligans hauled him to the end of the wharf and tossed him in the bay. It must have sobered him up as he waded ashore and disappeared.

With Spense playing and it being a Friday night, the place was packed and so Kate helped serve for a while. It was a still, hot night and they had sent Ma home. At ninety-something, she had trouble handling the heat. Before she left, she had joined Spense in a version of "At Last" made famous by Etta James, who, unfortunately, had only made it available to Spense recently. The duet was a hit and they had gotten a standing ovation.

The afternoon had been fun and they had accomplished what they had set out to do. Mark had had all Kate's clothes all bagged up for her. There really wasn't that much. Everyone had liked Mark. He had a reputation as a character, probably much to do with his extraordinary beard. His French wife, Collette, was charming and quite the artist. Spense had set an appointment to return and peruse her work. Where he would hang anything he purchased was anyone's guess.

Lottie's boat was beautiful: a thirty-two-foot inboard runabout that had plenty of room for Kate's clothes as well as her stuff that had been in storage. There was definitely a need for some decorating in the cottage, and her stuff, although cheap and intended to be temporary, was more fashionable and would just enhance the already eclectic, happenchance design ... or lack of design.

Spense had brought quite the costume for Kate: a long, jet-black wig, a full-length Colombian multi-colored muumuu, and rhinestone-studded sunglasses right out of an old Hollywood movie. She was a riot and totally unrecognizable. So, all had gone well. They kept their eyes open for the big villain but hadn't seen him. Kate had shown them all the pictures she had of him, which had also been distributed to all the island boys. It had pained Mick as they had all ooh-ed and aah-ed at how handsome he had looked. But, to Mick, a closer look revealed the cold, calculating eyes of a predator. Kate had nothing to say about what her attraction had been, other than him being rich and a hunk, as Lottie had confirmed, to Mick's chagrin, and nobody had pressed her.

MICK ROSE right at daybreak on Saturday, the big day, to catch his young poet, assuming she would be dropping off another poem. The system was for her to leave the folder at the edge of the porch anchored with a large conch shell; Mick would put it back with his note in it, and it had disappeared each day. There was no folder yet, so she had not come by or arrived yet, if she was coming. So he went in and brewed a pot of coffee. As he carried a steaming cup out onto the porch, he saw her silently slink

CHAPTER 12

up to the steps. She hadn't seen or, probably, expected him and jumped when he said, "Buenos dias." She collected herself, quietly smiled up at him, looking embarrassed, and answered, "Good morning, sir."

"Would you like to come up on the porch for a moment? I'd like to ask you a couple things." He was immediately intrigued by both her appearance and her voice.

She stopped smiling and just stood there, looking intently at him. She seemed hesitant, so he walked down the steps and sat, patting the step beside him. She looked at the step, back at Mick, and then gingerly sat herself down. Her age was impossible to determine.

"Can I read your poem and then talk to you for a while?"

She nodded and handed him the folder. Above the poem was this drawing.

Mick swore he recognized the hand. It startled him. Below the familiar hand was:

BACK TO THE ISLAND

    so the tree
    stands on the edge
    silhouetting the dawn—
    an orange-red sky
    black against sky,
    tradition against the change and rebirth

    the tree—
    defiant, deep-rooted upon the past
    the sky—
    a hope of tomorrow, the promise
    of one more day.
    I stand between foundation—substance
    and something I can't even
    touch—intangible yet
    daring, laughing, soaring …
    I stand here with the wind and the
    Wind sings an old song

    we are torn between earth and sky.
      … day breaks.

    darkness and silence hide away.
    promise is kept. The tree I
    can still touch.

      —the day is here and here is now—
    standing on the edge of time.
      —H.S.

"Is this about your stepfather?"
She nodded.
"You wrote this all by yourself?"

CHAPTER 12

She squinted up at him. "Of course. Why do you ask?"

"Can I ask what the conflict is between you and your stepfather?" he continued, embarrassed by what he had asked. She just looked so young and fragile and innocent—like she didn't have it in her to write like this. He wished he could write like this.

She looked at him as if studying him. Her skin was a bright light brown: not dark enough for island native, but not white and just tanned, either. Her hair was in short braids, eyes almost colorless, like you could see yourself in them. Her body small, but not her mind, obviously. "I promised him never to tell anyone about our … conflict, as you call it."

Mick didn't know where to go with this. "Do you trust me?"

She smiled slightly, again studying him, his eyes. "I guess I must."

"Do I know your father?"

"You used to."

This drove him nuts. "From where?"

"Your youth."

His youth? He couldn't imagine. She was playing with him, obviously being evasive. "Does he have a conflict with you?"

"Hmm …" She seemed to make a decision. "He does things that I cannot determine whether they are good or bad. This is my conflict with him."

"Can I ask what he does that is bad?"

She looked away. Thought a moment. Looked back. "Have you heard all about the machines destroying the mangroves and the plan to blast the coral on the west side to try to make a harbor and a beach?"

"Yes, I have heard that from some young guys here on the island."

She smiled widely. Her smile conveyed a surprising vibrancy. "They are my friends. I know they are looking out for you and your senora."

Mick smiled. "My sister."

She looked at him oddly. "I don't think so. But, regardless, did you hear that all the machines were quieted?"

"Yes. They told me the engines all seized up. All of them."

"Well, my father did that."

"Your father?"

"Stepfather. He is now my father. My first father left, as you know; now my stepfather has adopted me."

"I was adopted by my father, too, you know."

She looked at him calmly, still studying him.

"How'd he do that to the machines?" Mick finally asked.

"This is my conflict. He put dirt and ground coral in the gas tanks. And he loosened some tires. One worker was hurt when the tire came off. I don't care about the machines, they are evil—what they are doing anyway—but innocent workers should not get hurt."

"But what they are doing is not innocent."

"They just need money. They are just doing what they are told."

"Yes … the universal soldier."

She smiled. "That's what my dad says. He says they do have a choice. They should not choose to do evil just because it pays. He says evil often pays well."

"What do you think he should do?"

She looked away again, down at the ground. After a long pause: "I don't know. Can I go now?"

Mick didn't want her to go. He had a thousand questions, and he was dying to find out who this ecoterrorist stepfather

CHAPTER 12

was. "Yes. Of course. Could you write me something more about your family? Maybe about your mother? You are a very talented writer, you know."

She looked up at him and smiled. "Thank you, sir."

"Call me Mick, OK?"

"OK, sir. Goodbye for now. Thank you."

"What is your name?"

She got up and, gliding away, yelled back, laughing, "Senorita."

Kate had gotten up, her time to smell the coffee brewing, and came downstairs to find Mick and the girl sitting on the front steps. She had quietly poured herself a cup and retreated to the living room. When Mick came back up to the porch, Kate joined him, bringing the pot of coffee with her. "So you finally caught her. How'd that go? Isn't she interesting?" She sat down and Mick handed her the new poem.

"Hmm," she said after reading it twice. "'The wind sings an old song.' Wow! 'Torn between earth and sky.' 'Tradition against the change and rebirth?' What does the tree represent?"

"Her stepfather."

"Do you know what she means?" Kate asked.

Mick told her what she had told him.

"So you think this is the guy behind all the sabotage going on at all the construction sites?"

"Sounds like it, at least here on Elbow."

"And you know him?"

"Knew him, I guess. I swear I recognized that big, massive hand," and a thought struck him like a bolt of electricity.

"What?" Kate asked, seeing his response to the jolt of memory.

"Nothing." Mick said. "It can't be ..."

"Can't be what?"

"Never mind."

"Hmm ... so what's her name?" Kate asked.

Mick looked at her and grinned. "She said it was Senorita. She referred to you as my Senora. When I reminded her that you were my sister, she said, 'I don't think so.' What do you make of that?"

Kate hiccupped, hesitated. "How interesting." Then after a pause: "Speaking of interesting, today should really be a zinger: Sara *and* Barney!"

"You're right there!" Mick affirmed heartedly. They both grinned, looking at each other, nodding, barely able to contain their excitement. Kate slipped over, sat on his lap sideways, and gave him a sisterly kiss on his cheek and hugged him.

Mick wondered why guys' minds and organs communicated the way they did. His cheek felt flushed, his heart started racing, and he tried to stop it there. "My sister, my sister" he kept saying to himself as he hugged her back. He was beginning to feel he could love her ... but not quite as a sister, yet. He hated himself as he let go and said, "I need another cup." She gave him another quick squeeze and got up ... just in time he realized, wondering, 'Are all men Neanderthals?'

Kate, grabbing his cup, said, "You haven't drank this one yet, fool! So, what's on the agenda today?"

"He grabbed the cup back, saying, "I'll heat this one up in the mike," thinking that sounded plausible. "I think I'll go up and do some writing," he said, afraid that his routine of the morning cup of java, muffin on the beach, and then writing up on his perch was gone with the wind.

"What ya workin' on?"

"*A Million Dollars*," he said.

CHAPTER 12

"Aren't we all? Think I'll grab a bite and get a run in on the beach. Why don't you heat your cup and I'll bring ya up a peanut and jelly toast?"

"Uh, OK, thanks," Mick said. "Peanut butter on one, jelly the other?"

"Natch," Kate answered. "That's the way I've always done it."

The way she's always done it, huh? Trivial, maybe, but definitely something in common. He knew he should be taking a run or walk on the beach as well. He was an avid believer in exercise. He had also usually done a bit of yoga, mostly stretching, mornings in the past … usually on the beach after his coffee and muffin. But with all the hell breaking loose today, he knew he had to get in some writing while he could. Not much would get done in the next few days. "Don't forget, Spense and Lottie will be here about three o'clock. I wonder what Barney and Sara will think of each other? Two detail-oriented number crunchers. Will they like each other or conflict … or both?"

"Why wouldn't they like each other?" Kate asked. "Everyone likes Sara. Barney sounds like a pretty good guy."

"He is. The same—everyone likes Barney, too. But …"

"But what?"

"When he gets his mind set on something, there's no changing it. We're an odd couple for best friends. Everything's black and white with him. I'm gray all the way."

"So, why are you best friends?"

Mick laughed. "I'm not sure. I've got other friends from grade school that are much more like me.

"Huh! What's Barney's real and last name?"

"McGannon. Patrick McGannon."

"That's right. You told me his name was Pat. Patrick in this case, I imagine? Another feckin' Irishman?"

Mick laughed. "Yup, and yup. An especially stubborn one in this case. My friends Jim and Jim and are from good Irish stock as well. We all went to the same Catholic grade school."

"So, why Barney as your best friend?"

"Well, he was the best man at my wedding, I guess, because he was my confidante. He's the one I always talked to, totally trustworthy and ... compassionate, I guess you'd say. A real good listener. I would have liked to have had four best men at my wedding: Jim, Jim, and Randy as well as Barney. They're all more like brothers. We go back to fourth grade, but it had to be Barney. When Martha got pregnant, he was the one I talked to about it."

"You *had* to get married?"

"No! I didn't *have* to get married. I *chose* to."

"OK. So, how old were you?"

"She was seventeen. I was nineteen."

"Kind of a horny sucker, aren't ya?"

If you only knew, Mick thought. "Yes, the scourge of the salacious and romantic Irish rascal."

"I'm surprised you've managed to keep your hands off Lottie. She's funny, nice, hot, and, apparently, rich." She seemed to say this like it was a taunt.

"Never was interested. Not my type." Mick was getting good at improvising convenient little lies. He didn't really know why he felt a compulsion to lie about Lottie, but he definitely didn't want to delve into explaining that relationship—or lack of now. He was getting the hankering to give it another shot, though, now that Mar ... Kate was not going to be an option.

"Right! She's just not interested in your white Irish ass." Kate had sniffed out that there was something there and felt

CHAPTER 12

plenty territorial. Lottie could pose a problem. She'd have to figure out how to keep him interested, but not too interested … until he knew the truth. A challenging balancing act she was blindly teetering into. Just like how they started.

"Well, it wouldn't be my *arse* she'd be interested in, would it?"

Kate looked in his eyes for a moment wondering what she could see there. "Well, you best get to your *Million Dollars*. I'll be up in a minute."

Mick was glad to leave this discussion. The one he was actually interested in was Marilyn … and she didn't exist anymore.

CHAPTER 13

THE AFTERNOON had heated up. Spense and Lottie arrived early, at two o'clock. They drove up in Spense's colossal cart, music blasting and laughing hysterically. "Get ready!" they both yelled up at the cottage. Mick peeked down from his perch and Kate walked out onto the porch. "We've decided to make a day out of it!" a shirtless Spense yelled loudly, totally out of character. "Lottie, my seductive little muse, has decided we shall cruise in her craft and grab a bite at Kippers on our journey to apprehend our new playmates. Jack has given us the night off so we can cut capers all day."

"C'mon, maties!" Lottie bellowed. "Get your bums in gear. The great mystique beckons." It was odd, Lottie seemed to have borrowed Spense's demeanor. It was totally out of character for her to say anything like maties, bums, or the great mystique beckons. She, indeed, was an interesting character. And she got much more interesting when she leapt out of the cart, Kate and Mick both realizing she was wearing a string bikini under a rather colorful and flimsy beach dress. Mick realized also that she was stoned. Music was blasting from the speakers in the cart and Spense danced up the steps. Mick also realized the reason he was out of character, being rarely shirtless and not usually boisterous, was that he was probably stoned as well.

Spense danced up to Kate and grabbed her around the waist with his right arm, holding her right hand in his left, and

CHAPTER 13

began to spin her around. Lottie looked up at Mick, lifted her shift, exposing the thong, and patted her well-tanned basically bare behind and yelled, "Get it movin', mon!"

Mick took a gulp of air, slid down the ladder, and ran down, finding Spense and Kate fallen on the settee. Kate looked up at Mick, laughing, with her arms spread and hands lifted in a "What's going on?"

Lottie wriggled up to Mick and, groin to groin, planted a decent smack right on the lips and handed him a joint. "Take a toke, mon, and pass it to sis. The vessel is stocked. Let's puff and get cruisin'!"

Spense stood, bowed to Kate, and said, "Thanks for the twirl, madam," and held out his hand and pulled her off the settee.

Mick took a puff, and still attached to Lottie at the hip, held it out expectantly to Kate, whose merriment turned noxious like a shade had been drawn. "I haven't smoked that stuff in ages." She scowled at Mick, grabbed the joint, and hissed, "But what the hell."

MICK SLID out of bed quietly so as not to wake Barney. Regardless of a queasy gut, thick head, and cotton mouth, he desperately wanted to talk to Senorita. The previous day had been riotous. The four of them smoked and drank on the Abaco Sea on their way to Kippers; they ate and drank at Kippers; they smoked and drank and chatted on the white sand beach below Kippers; they drank, Kate and Mick reeling off stories of Sara and Barney, on their way to Marsh Harbour. When they met Sara at the airport, they let her walk right past them, Sara not recognizing Kate in the disguise she had worn the day before. She had had giant hugs for all. She and Kate hugging multiple times. Mick had gotten a second round as well. She had looked as fabulous as Kate had described.

After meeting Barney, they had all drank and smoked on their way to Elbow Cay, and they drank, sans the smoke, at Cap'n Jacks. Mick, Kate, Lottie, and Spense, in spite of their stupor, had felt guilty leaving it up to Ma, Jack, Roland and two inexperienced island girls to handle a Saturday crowd. So they drank, laughed, and a little too gaily had helped serve food and drinks to the loyal patrons.

While Spense and Kate helped Mick and Lottie serve and tend bar, Barney and Sara sat together at a table at the end of the pier all night, nose to nose, arguing. Arguing and laughing. Barney, at five-foot-ten, appeared to be the same height as Sara, sitting erect at five-foot-six as he leaned intently into their discussion. The moniker, Barney, was bestowed on him from a grade school chum calling him "Barnyard" one day at recess. As a kid, his shoelaces were always untied, stains permanently on his shirt, whose tails seemed to just crawl out of his pants. He always looked a little disheveled, thus the name "Barnyard" stuck. Now, considered conservatively handsome, looking the part of a college professor, his short hair and mustache graying, he pretty much had a uniform: golf shirt—plain, nothing fancy—either clean, pressed jeans or khakis. Tonight, it being the tropics: pressed khaki shorts—with a belt—and Mick, in his role as fashion police, giving him shit for his penny loafers with white athletic socks. With Sara's flowered knit top and matching shorts, they looked like a match made in heaven. Although neither were obviously remarkable in appearance and choice of attire like Kate, Lottie, and Spense for obvious reasons, both looked like someone you'd simply like and want for a friend, and Sara, not skinny

CHAPTER 13

like Kate, looked very capable of a satisfying hug or imparting some quality TLC.

Kate and Mick took turns visiting at the table but were basically ignored, as if interloping on an unresolved, world-shattering issue being heatedly debated nose to nose under the tropical stars. Mick frequently stole a moment, in spite of the restaurant turmoil, and relished the sight of his best friend and new sister totally into each other, arguing but laughing. He knew he would like Sara, and like her he did.

Since Spense did not have his keyboard to mask his lack of vocal range, made worse by his current condition, he initiated a sing-along that broke out intermittently and randomly to "Let It Be, Let It Be." The only words most everyone knew were "let it be," so that was what it was … and nobody seemed to mind. Although a couple of patrons sober enough pointed out that all the Beatles weren't dead, and neither was Paul McCartney who had written it, Spense had confuted that John was the leader of the pack and he was dead, so had told them to "sod off!" To which a big, burly patron bellowed, "Let it be, let it be, words of wisdom: sod off!" The well-oiled crowd in Cap'n Jack's cracked up, and the entire sober harbor in the still of their boats was introduced to a new version of a song they were already sick of vibrating in their masts.

MICK STUMBLED downstairs to find "Senorita" sitting on the steps.

"You don't look so good, sir," she greeted him.

He sat next to her on the steps and greeted her with, "I'm not going to call you Senorita and you're not going to continue to call me sir. OK?"

"No," she responded.

"No, what?"

"No, sir." Mick studied her eyes. Was this her sense of humor or simply stubbornness? "For now I'm Senorita and I'm not comfortable calling you Mick, even Mr. Mick, MP or Mr. MP."

"How about Mr. Mulcahy?"

She smiled. "My stepfather, I guess I should just say father, said if I called you anything it should be Empy-headed." She grinned up at him and raised her eyebrows.

All right. Empy-headed went back to grade school, early grade school. He had changed to the parochial school in sixth grade and nobody there had called him that. So, this was someone in the public school from before sixth grade. That big hand Senorita had drawn had once been on his head, he was sure of it, holding him harmlessly away from striking distance. He was getting more and more sure of it. "Could you tell me your father's name?"

Instead of answering, she handed him and he read silently:

> When my civil discontent
> turns to mornings filled with
> "I don't care"
> find me marching toward the
> revolution
> shouting my convictions in the air
> —H.S.

"OK. Two things," Mick said. "One: I'm guessing the H stands for Heidi? Don't know why I think so, but I do. Two: does that mean you feel you should believe in what your stepfather—sorry, father—is doing?"

CHAPTER 13

"Your eyes are bloodshot," was her response.

"Yes," Mick confessed. "I had friends come to stay and we had a party."

"Looks like it," she said.

"Well?" Mick asked, through his headache and a sigh.

"Next time I'll bring one about my mother. As I'm guessing you'll be able to decipher, she's an island native with deep roots here. I have to go. Goodbye, sir. Thank you." And she wisped swiftly away, heading north.

He couldn't clear his head, so he decided to brew some coffee. He did a full pot, assuming that a lot would be consumed this morning.

Barney was the first to come down. "My God!" he said as he stumbled into the kitchen, also bleary-eyed. "You do that every night?"

Mick laughed. "God, no. That celebration yesterday was your and Sara's fault. No better way to break the ice than getting drunk and stoned."

"Don't blame it on me. I haven't had pot since you left."

"You and Sara seemed to hit it off."

"Well, yeah! Why not? But for twins, the McGennity girls don't seem too much alike. Sara seems so conservative and man, Kate. Well, she sure isn't conservative and can she hand out the shit, big time! And, Lottie. Man, she is really cute! Does she always dress that sexy? She seemed to show some interest in you, for some reason I wouldn't understand. Anything new going on?"

"Nothing much. And you always were good bait for shit," Mick said, changing the subject. "Give Kate an opening and she's merciless. Here, have a cup."

They walked out onto the porch. As usual a breeze was coming off the water and the sun had risen enough behind them to be illuminating the lighthouse in the morning glow. "Gosh. It really is beautiful here. I can see why you like it."

They heard the clanking of cups behind them, and both the McGennity girls shuffled out onto the porch, Kate in cutoff sweats and, still, one of Mick's T-shirts. Mick was afraid to look because she apparently didn't sleep in a bra, which was understandable, but didn't bother to put one on in the morning, which, to Mick, was not. Sara, a little too well-endowed to get away with it, fortunately, had one on under a powder blue gym suit. They might be twins, but they did indeed have different tastes. Sara was exactly the same height as Kate but more rounded, curvy, yet dressed moderately to hide it. It struck Mick that this was how Kate had dressed at Sears. "Jesus Christ, Mick, you do that to me again and I'll kill you," Kate greeted from behind bloodshot eyes. "Shit, man! Double jeopardy: booze and dope!"

Sara sat down, looked at everyone, tried a smile, and said nothing.

"Mornin'?" both Mick and Barney said tentatively.

All that came out from Sara was a hoarse croak. They had all piled on Spense's gas-powered buggy last night and sang—more like screamed—"Let It Be" all the way to the cottage from Cap'n Jack's, probably waking up the entire north end on their way. Sara, surprisingly, had been the most vocal and apparently was paying for her atypical exuberance this morning.

"My little sis has no voice left after her unusually spirited performance last night. You're going to have to debate yourself this morning, Mr. Barnyard."

"Little sis?" Mick questioned. "I thought you were twins?"

"I'm ten minutes older. I came out first, ready to face the world. My little sis is still the cautious one."

CHAPTER 13

Another hoarse scrape escaped Sara's lips and everyone laughed. "Later," she managed to grind out. And later, after several cups of coffee and bacon and eggs that Kate fried up, Sara's voice had returned and all were alert enough to think straight. "I hope Lottie and Spense made it back all right. Couldn't they have stayed here?" Sara asked, still a bit hoarse.

"That's happened before." Mick chuckled at the thought. "But we're a little short on sleeping accommodations, and there's little to get them in trouble between here and Hope Town and no such thing as a CWI on the island."

They all looked at him quizzically. "Carting While Intoxicated," he explained, and they all rolled their eyes.

"Well, where were they going to go?" Sara asked.

Mick walked over to the table on the porch where his computer always sat. "I'm not sure with those two. I'll email Spense. I'm hoping they just doried out to Spense's boat and that Lottie didn't try to take her Windsor down to Coconut Grove. Especially since it was low tide and it's tricky to get in that harbor sober and in daylight."

Soon they heard the *ping* of a text on Mick's phone, and Mick laughed as he read it. "It's from Lottie. They made it to the Plowed Mary, Spense's little vessel, and by the time the winch had gotten the dory up onto the deck, they both had passed out … in the dory. Spense was rolling around on the floor now hugging his knees, trying to get his spine back into shape. Lottie says she'll work on him and have him in satisfactory condition by lunch. We're supposed to be at the dock by one o'clock and they'll come in to pick us up for lunch on the boat and our tête-à-tête about Kate."

When Mick turned toward the three, they were all grinning. Sara spoke first: "Plowed Mary? Where'd that come from?"

Mick explained: "Apparently Spense's wife, Mary, liked to party—not that Spense doesn't—but when she died a few years ago and Spense had his yacht, schooner, ship, I don't know what to call it, you'll see it today ... named after her. We went by it last night when we went out and came into the harbor."

"Not that immense white futuristic thing?" Sara said.

"Yes, and when he had it built, he christened it the Plowed Mary in memory of his wife."

They all laughed but Barney, whose eyebrows were furrowed. "Do Spense and Lottie, uh, sleep together?" This helped confirm for Mick that all or most men—maybe not Spense—were Neanderthals, assuming, with any encounter between the sexes, the worst—or in their Neanderthal-ized brain—the best.

"I believe they sleep together, but not have sex," Kate explained patiently to an unconvinced Barney.

"But I thought she said she'd 'work on him.' Doesn't that mean a massage or something?"

"Of course," Kate said, a bit indignantly. "What's wrong with that? I've given Mick a shoulder and head rub. Matter of fact, I'd love one right now. And what's wrong with that?"

Sara looked at Kate. "Really?"

Mick cringed.

Barney scrunched his forehead, making him look even more Neanderthal. Kate, wanting to avoid the issue, said, "Well, you two go get ready. Mick and I will clean up. As Sara and Barney headed upstairs, Kate picked up the new poems, read them, slowly shaking her head. She looked over at Mick and crossed her eyes. Mick smiled, raised his eyebrows, and nodded.

When they got to the dock at one o'clock, they saw the dory heading in with just Lottie manning it, her hair flowing behind

CHAPTER 13

her in the breeze. Her typical beach cover-up was hiked up high on her thighs as she straddled the dory seat. The day was warming up. Mick wore his usual quick-dry trunks, T-shirt, and Crocs; Barney: belted dress shorts and his usual golf shirt and loafers. He must have been trying to be sexy, as he wasn't wearing his white sweat socks. Kate: swimsuit bottoms and a long sleeveless tee over her bikini top, and flip-flops—not apparently trying to look sexy, but succeeding; Sara: her pink workout shorts, a matching terry cloth top and pink tennis shoes, looked pleasantly plump and full of fluff.

"Hey, Mick. There's no Spense," Kate pointed out, looking out into the harbor. "It's not like him to let someone else operate the dory."

"OK. Just a damn minute, MP," demanded Barney. "I asked several times last night, what's the deal with 'Mick'?"

"You'll have to ask Kate," Mick replied. But Barney still got no answer as the dory pulled up.

"Where's Spense?" Mick yelled down to Lottie as she maneuvered up to the dock and held on as they climbed down the ladder. The tide was coming up, so they had only a couple rungs to manage.

"I think he's getting too old to pass out in dories," she said as they settled onto their seats. "I worked his back over pretty good, but he's hurting. Everybody settled? OK, hold on, we're off to Oz."

Spense was seated firmly in one of the burgundy-colored leathers, so Mick and Lottie had to give the tour. Even Barney, who was not known for his aesthetic attributes, was stunned by the affluence. Sara could not get over the incongruity of the intergalactic-looking exterior and classic, tasteful interior.

Finally they all sequestered cozily in the den/library, iced teas in tow thanks to Lottie. Spense, Barney, Sara, and Kate each had a chair; Lottie and Mick were together on the love seat.

"Well, here we are: the Plowed Mary Brain Trust, and finally we get the enduring tale of Kate on the run," Mick said.

"Here, here," Spense said, clapping his claws, and all followed suit.

"The floor is yours," Mick announced to Kate. "We've all waited long enough for this."

Kate and Sara looked at each other and shifted in their chairs. "As some of you know," Kate started, "Sara works for the SEC, the Security and Exchange Commission, remotely most of the time in Spokane, where we're from. For the previous year, before the Bahamas, I was in a contract position doing PR work for a big financial institution in New York. While there, I met Richard, an internal compliance officer for the same institution. Being in my forties, not having managed to save money like my sister, and Richard—a bachelor, very good looking, and financially well-off—made me feel safe in the Big Apple. So he proposed, I accepted, and we moved in together. It all happened way too fast.

"This institution I was doing work for is one of the biggies being investigated by the SEC and several other branches of the government. Sara contacted me and informed me that they were trying to build a case against them for fraud."

"Like what?" Mick interjected, always hot on this topic.

Sara spoke up. "I don't think we can, or should, get into the specifics."

"Just give us an inkling so we can get good and pissed," Mick said.

CHAPTER 13

Sara looked at the group and they all shrugged, Spense saying, "The suspense is almost intolerable. I believe we agree our lips are sealed?" Mick, Barney, and Lottie all nodded and were already on the edge of their seats, literally.

"Well, let's see. Some of it I can't tell you. I mean, there are people going to prison for insider trading. You've probably heard of that—using or letting out confidential trading information about companies that gives themselves or certain individuals an unfair advantage to trade their stock for profit. And there are speculators on Wall Street that were able to manipulate the market to their advantage. They're being prosecuted and going to prison. That stuff is blatantly illegal and they were audacious enough to assume they could get away with it but not smart enough to cover their tracks. Also, there are glaring conflicts of interest being uncovered, such as with the S&P—Standard and Poors. They rate the credit worthiness of the institutions that pay them, a conflict of interest, obviously opening the door to unethical practices. It's like a referee getting paid by whichever team wins. This may have been one of the first precedents where emails were used for evidence. If I remember it correctly, it was congressional investigators that unearthed an email sent internally within the S&P that said—I've got this one memorized: "Let's hope we are all wealthy and retired by the time this house of cards falters." They were arrogant, careless, and so got caught. We can prove through emails that they knew what they were doing was wrong.

"The big guys in the institutions like Richard's are even more arrogant but generally more careful and clandestine with their in-house communications. They're usually smart enough to hide their complicity, but the longer they get away with their corruption, the sloppier they get. They get cocky, think they're insulated and above it all. Kate was in the unusual position of having the opportunity to read and copy uncensored emails. With Richard's firm, one of the big ones we've been previously unable to find sufficient evidence to prosecute, there are billions of dollars invested that are just simply missing, unaccounted for. We can't trust bank accounting. It's like handing addicts a loan and asking them to keep track of where they spend it. When it's all gone, would you expect to believe their accounting of it? Some of the emails Kate was able to discover provide, hopefully, sufficient proof of actual complicity and, thus, fraud."

"Bastards!" Mick just couldn't help himself. "That missing money—our money!—is in somebody's pockets. These guys lost billions of our bank deposits, our money, money we thought was guaranteed, by making high-risk investments that failed, and then they receive golden parachutes —bonuses in the ten- to fifty-million dollar range. Probably to keep their mouths shut. Simply unbelievable! Just not acceptable!"

Sara smiled. "Yes. What I can tell you, though, to agitate your acrimony, is about the extent of leverage, which was a huge abuse … unethical for sure, but unfortunately, maybe not illegal, unless …"

"Like … ?" Mick prodded.

"Well, the average leverage …"

"Please explain leverage," Lottie interrupted.

"Debt, borrowing," Barney the professor answered. "Like a house: you may not have enough of your own cash to pay for it, so you borrow somebody else's cash. The more of your money you have in it, the more risk to you, like if you lose the house, you lose your own money. The more of somebody else's money, the more risk to them … you lose their money. That's leverage."

"But don't you just go to the bank to borrow the money?" Lottie asked.

"Yes," Mick said, "but it isn't the bank's money you're borrowing. It belongs to people who have entrusted their savings with the bank, expecting it to be safe."

"Oh, yeah. I think I see," Lottie said.

"The average leverage ratio with these big institutions," Sara continued, "was pretty close to 40:1. Meaning that for every dollar they invested of their money, they borrowed forty of ours. So, if a product rose by even 1%, their gain was 40%. A lot, *a lot* of profit was made, like Mick said. If the investment failed: no big deal—most of it wasn't their money. So this abuse of leverage didn't make any difference to them: *their* risk was low, *their* potential for gain, high. They thought they were just being smart. They knew how a system that very few people understood worked and used it to, in effect, risk our money for their gain. What we've got to do is stop letting them get away with it. To do that we've got to inflict personal pain: prison. What is at issue, legally, is whether or to what extent they knew, and so, misrepresented how risky that level of leverage was."

"Totally greedy shitheads!" Again, Mick. "They, the government or whatever, have got to separate deposit banking from investment banking once again." To Lottie: "See, people deposit their money in the bank because they believe it's safe and 'guaranteed' and they can get it if they want or need it."

"So, if the money's guaranteed, what's the problem?" Lottie asked.

"What money? The investment side took what should be these short-term, safe deposits—but low profit to the banks—and then takes not only this money but borrows even more against it and invests it in these longer-term, potentially more profitable but risky, complex investments. So when these investments failed, the banks wouldn't have the money to give back to their depositors if they requested it ... so the government had to bail them out because, as you've probably heard, they're 'too big to fail.'"

"No shit?" Lottie said. "This crap really goes on?"

"What about the 'selling short' shit?" Barney pointed out, and looked at Lottie. "That means they bet against their own investments. They would package a bunch of mortgages in what were called tranches and made tons of money by selling these as investments to individuals, but mostly to large institutional managers of retirement funds and nonprofit organizations. Many, too many, of the mortgages were very risky—subprime they're called—meaning they were made to people who were unlikely to be able to make their payments. So they also made money when these investments failed."

"What? They can do that?" Lottie exclaimed. "No way! That must be illegal."

"The assholes make a ton of money selling these products and also make money when they fail," Mick spit, getting heated, almost choleric.

"They can legally do this?" asked Spense, calmly.

"You've heard of hedging?" Everyone nodded except Lottie. "Hedging," Sara directed at Lottie, "is a balance of betting the market will go up but protecting yourself if it goes down. So, selling short, hedging, can on one hand mitigate risk but can certainly be unethical, depending on your knowledge of

CHAPTER 13

the investment risk and potential for loss. The practice itself is not illegal ... unless they had knowledge that they knew the investment was going to fail. That's what we now, with Kate's evidence, have proof of. I can't say much more, but some people at the top knew exactly what they were doing. They knew and understood the risk and that the products would fail. And if we can prove that they misrepresented to their sales force and the public, intentionally, what the risk was ... then there's fraud. 'Intentionally' being the key word, and hard to prove.

"None of the big honchos behind the debacle that almost caused our entire economy to fail—causing millions to lose savings, retirement funds, houses, and jobs—have been convicted, much less charged ... and won't, unless we have actual proof. And they can't just be fined. That accomplishes nothing. In their minds, they're getting away with it. They basically pay, not with their own money, but, in effect, our money that they've so cleverly manipulated into their own pockets. And then they think they're being smart, which they wouldn't be if it was illegal and provable. No. They have to be incarcerated to change the system of abuse. Their personal freedom must be at stake to keep them honest."

"So," Spense interjected quickly before Mick once again erupted, "how, exactly, is Kate involved and why is she in danger?"

"Well," Kate started, "I was around the condo a lot more than Richard. I rarely saw him, probably why we got along at the time. Our relationship was more like a series of first dates." She glanced at Mick, not looking thrilled that she was talking about this, or that he was shoulder to shoulder with Lottie on the 'love' seat, or that he was glaring at her.

Except at night! What? Like a series of one nighters? Mick thought, and then pushed the thought out of his mind. Why should he care?

"So, often, Richard," Kate continued, haltingly, "would leave his mail open, and after Sara clued me in on the apparent transgressions, I started looking at his emails."

"Uh-oh," Spense purred.

"Right," Sara said, taking over. "Richard, being a compliance officer, was privy to just about everything going on and *who* knew *what.* They figured nobody outside their exclusive group would ever see these emails. So Kate came across some that prove absolute and total complicity from the higher-ups in this institution that they knew the products were going to fail, allowed them to be sold, and made a fortune by cashing in their clients' money when they did fail. They win big; their clients lose big. These emails will go a long way, hopefully, in proving fraud and putting them away. When we build our case, Kate will be the star witness."

"That's almost out of the realm of believability," Spense said, shaking his head. "I more blame the system that allowed them to be able to do this than the buggers themselves. There always will be unscrupulous people in the world that will take advantage of people and do anything for money … and the bigger the payoff potential the easier to fall to, hopefully, a damning temptation. I have garnered a new respect for your newly discovered family, Mr. Mick."

"So why is Richard the one after you?" Mick asked Kate. "And you think he really wants to kill you?"

Sara answered: "He knows my involvement and has pressured me as to Kate's whereabouts and has let me know, in no uncertain terms, that he won't give up until he finds her. They obviously knew where I got the information, so if anybody

CHAPTER 13

gets brought down, he'll go down as hard and deep as any of them. He's also, obviously, not in good standing with guys in high places. The only way to redeem himself is to ensure Kate doesn't testify. I'm afraid he sees it as his ass or hers."

"I can see the higher-ups wanting you out of the picture, but do you really think this guy wants to kill you? And you thought you loved this guy?" Mick stood and started pacing the room.

Kate blanched as Mick lashed out. "I really can't imagine he wants to kill me, no. He's a fricking compliance officer, for Christ's sake. I don't know what he wants to do once he finds me, but I'm not anxious to find out … and what if he's not the only one looking for me?"

"What about witness protection?" Spense asked.

"We looked into it," Sara responded, "but there's a lot of red tape and, if you're getting to know Kate, you know she wouldn't agree to be sent to Timbuktu or some boring, out-of-the-way place."

"If I had to relocate, I wanted it to be somewhere I could live. I'd been here before—on Treasure Cay—that's how I knew Mark. I changed my name—Sara helping me with the documents—bought that little old van, got my job at Sears, and rented a little place. It's been longer than I anticipated; I didn't plan on staying here forever anyway. I just knew it was somewhere I could enjoy hiding out and feel safe, I thought."

"All right then," Spense said, struggling to get up. Mick walked over and gave him a hand. Once standing, he said, "Let's dispense, no pun intended, to the galley, have a bite, and devise a plan. We will not ensconce ourselves flaccidly waiting for this prick, pun intended, to find us."

Everyone groaned.

"But we'll devise a plan to bait this shark and reel him in, find out exactly what he wants."

As Sara and Kate stood, Sara first gave Kate a little hug and then grabbed Mick and ensconced him in a bear hug. He accepted happily, but leery of squeezing back with quite the same intensity. "Thank you, MP or Mitch or Mick. Glad to be your sister, whoever you are. I really feel Katie is in good hands, with you and your friends. I'm really happy and relieved."

Mick stammered an indistinguishable reply to the affirmative. Barney and Lottie looked like they felt left out. Spense hobbled out, smiling at the drama, and led them to the galley.

CHAPTER 14

SINCE EVERYTHING on the dawdling little island dwindled to a stop on Sundays, it took a while for things to pick up momentum again on Mondays. Mick and Kate took Barn and Sara to a late lunch at an upscale restaurant toward the south end, about a four-mile cart ride. It was the lodge and dining room of a small, upper-end resort with a well-known bar. The dining room overlooked the Atlantic. The drive there took them past the new road torn through the jungle to accommodate the machines beckoned to bastardize the west shore. They had made no attempt to mask their impropriety. Large piles of palms and ferns, lime, mango, mangrove, and star fruit trees were strewn everywhere. The rumor was the Mandelsungs and their investors had plans for a mega resort with casino, harbor, beach, and, down the road, a nine\-hole executive golf course ... and whatever else they could get away with, most likely. The west edge of the island was all jungle and mangroves with ancient coral lining the shore. This was the only part of Elbow not privately owned. It had been inaccessible by road due to the denseness of the jungle and mangrove lagoons, and by water due to pristine and, hopefully to remain, unspoiled coral reefs.

"Man, this looks like shit," Barney said, and if Barney noticed, it really looked like shit.

"How do they get away with this?" Sara asked. "Doesn't the government of the Bahamas care?"

"Money talks, I guess," Kate said.

"And when money talks, it lies," Mick said disgustedly. "Actually, money hires lawyers, and lawyers do the lying. They will speak of the assurance of bringing tax dollars to the islands. I imagine the government has been lured by the promise of money for education, which, if even true, may benefit Marsh Harbour, possibly, but more than likely places like Nassau, where the politicians, money, and power resides—certainly not Elbow Cay. And the promise of money for new, wide roads, which Elbow does not need or want, paved arteries spewing noise and exhaust that would destroy the quiet quaintness that the islanders hold dear and that actually attracts the part-timers and tourists to it. Think of the irony: the parasite kills what gives it life."

"How true," Sara replied. "On Wall Street as well. Leeching from an established system that's supposed to be the world's model until it no longer functions fairly and now is certainly no model for the world. Talk about irony! I hate to think of us humans here on earth as parasites, but some of us are doing a pretty fair impression."

Mick sped the cart away toward the restaurant.

They all had dinners of local fresh fish, passing the plates around and sharing. Barney, who generally put ketchup on just about everything he ate, tried to pour it on his snapper, but the girls wouldn't let him, Kate slugging him in the arm for the suggestion.

Mick had expounded several times on how outrageously remarkable it was that fate had brought them together, and several toasts were made to that affect. They all had good

CHAPTER 14

laughs over Kate's and MP's retelling of some of the Sears escapades, Sara and Barney having a hard time believing what dicks the A-hole brothers were. In his mind Mick was also trying to fathom that on top of running into his sister, that his old friend, Peewee, might also be on the island. If so, the stars were certainly in alignment. It struck him that if this happened in a story, it would hardly be believable. But, as they say, truth is stranger than fiction. It made him feel that coming to the Bahamas and Elbow Cay must certainly have been in his predestined flow toward some inevitable fate.

With Mick given the next two nights off at Jack's because of Sara and Barney's visit, and Lottie and Spense taking Tuesday night off, Barney was most likely going to get a memorable send-off. Therefore they returned fairly early. Mick and Kate went to bed, leaving Sara and Barney to lock horns and banter to their hearts' content.

Mick woke to Kate, who had slipped into the room, looking out his bedroom window. "She's down there. Want me to go?" she whispered so as not to wake Barney.

Mick slid out of bed, Kate whistling derisively at him in his boxer briefs. He ignored her and quickly pulled on a pair of shorts and a T-shirt and hurried down.

"Been here long?" he breathed as he settled beside her on the steps.

"No, sir. You look better today."

"Well, thanks," Mick said, grinning at her. "How are you?"

"I'm good, thank you."

"Whatcha got for me today?"

"Well, I mentioned I'd write something about my mother, and so I did."

She seemed a little off this morning. "OK, can I see it?"

BACK TO THE ISLAND

Heidi handed him a rather crumpled paper. He took it from her and paused before reading it, studying her. Then read:

Wounded Sparrow (Flight #1)

Mother
as we sit here, talking
about nothing specific
I keep my distance,

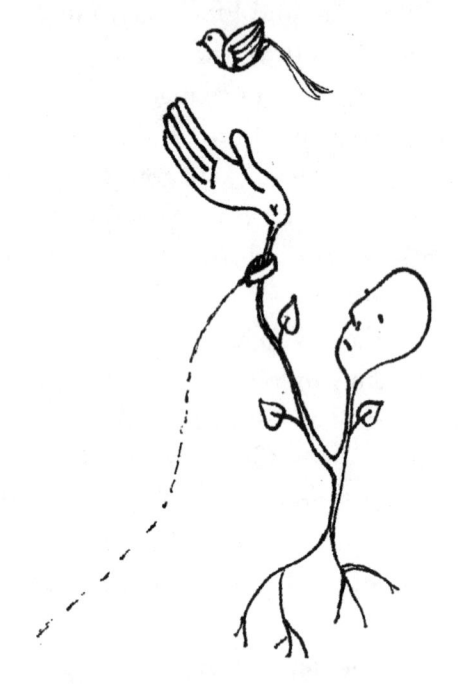

I am watching you.
and I almost ache to tell
you how it feels to be me
but something in your eyes
makes me believe that you would
never understand

CHAPTER 14

> or makes me certain that I might not want you to. And are there even words to tell you that last night I crawled myself into a tiny ball and cried until I could no longer breathe, then spent a crazy hour laughing because I needed to do something, but I didn't have any more tears.
> —H.S.

Mick felt like he had crawled under her skin when he read this. He looked up at her, again, noticing her nervousness. "What's the matter, hon?"

"I'm worried about my stepdad, sorry, my father."

"Why?"

"I heard him talking. I guess the development guys are going to dynamite or blast or something the coral reef to make a harbor and a beach, you know, there on the west side."

"Yes? And?"

"Well, I heard him say he's not going to let them do it. I don't know what he plans on doing, but I guess I'm worried about him—and others."

"Do you think I could meet your father? Would he maybe come here with you one day?"

She looked away, a little smirk on her face, and followed a few noisy gulls with her eyes. "Maybe. He said he liked you, even if you were a midget."

Mick was getting more certain about the identity of her father. Who else would joke about him being a midget? He was five-foot-six after all, only a midget to somebody pretty darn tall. "Is he a big man?"

She looked up. "Both my granddads were very big. So is he; he's the biggest. Too bad I don't have some of his genes, huh? My mother, as I am, is like a sparrow: small and tentative."

She, personally, didn't seem either to him. "So which of you is the sparrow in the sketch?"

She smiled broadly. "Maybe both? I must go."

"Wait! Tell me about … friends. You have friends?"

"Of course. I told you the boys watching out for you are my friends."

"Tell me about them?"

"We'll see. Bye, sir. Thank you." And she was off.

Mick looked at the poem again and by the time he was finished, realized he had smelled coffee. As he turned to go up onto the porch, Kate came out carrying two cups, and they sat side-by-side on the deck chairs.

"Whad'd you get today?"

Mick handed Kate the poem and watched her as she read it. Tears welled up in her eyes when she was done.

"What's the matter?" Mick stood and sat on the arm of her deck chair and put his arm around her shoulders.

"I don't know. She … I don't know why it makes me cry. She's so … precious. She speaks, really, for so many young women. I had these exact feelings with my mother, and here she's put those feelings down for me to relive. " She leaned her head against Mick's side.

"Her stepdad—she considers him her father now. I think I know who he is—he is going to try and stop them from blasting the coral reefs by where we were yesterday."

She sat back, alarmed, and looked up at him. "You know him? How? From where?"

CHAPTER 14

"I'm not positive it's him, but I'm pretty sure. If it's him, it's a guy I knew from third grade. We became really good friends, but when I changed schools, we kept in contact for quite a while but drifted apart eventually. I didn't know what had happened to him. He just kinda disappeared. I've never forgotten him and I think of him all the time. It would just be too weird if it's him."

"What gives you that idea? That *would* be way too weird."

"It's several things she has said."

"What about the blasting of the reefs? How's he going to stop it?"

"I don't know. God, I don't know what to think. I've heard of instances of ecoterrorism on other cays. It didn't do much good on some, like around Nassau. That's almost all developed."

"No shit!"

"Of course that was a long time ago. But this is now and closer to home. A few years ago, I guess, someone wanted to develop another big marina and harbor over by White Sound, you know, close to the south end. It was defeated, somehow, but it looks like there's more money behind this one, thanks, it seems, to our Ajax, Arthur, and their frickin' family. God, it's hard to imagine those two putzes being behind this. I guess it goes to show that money, unfortunately, is power.

"If her father's been involved at all, he might be more intent now. Messing with power is dangerous stuff."

"No shit, Lucille."

Mick laughed, having no idea how Lucille got involved, but said, "She's worried."

Just then they heard shuffling upstairs. Barney and Sara were apparently rising at the same time. "When did they go to bed?" Mick asked. "I didn't even feel Barn crawl in."

"I felt Sara slip in late, very late."

"Something going on there?"

Kate laughed. "Who knows? Here they come. Maybe we can tell."

MICK RAN next door, well, not next door exactly since next door was an empty lot filled with flowering bushes ... and picked up a couple of muffins at the bakery for Barney and himself to have with their coffee. He knew Kate and Sara, sharing at least one thing in common, would have yogurt and granola or at least some god-awful low fat thing. Both were in good shape, but Kate was right: Sara was rounder with considerably more curves—not at all fat like she had told him, maybe plump but firm, and pleasantly so—and definitely appealing. She was just smoother, softer—no hard edges like Kate. In the past Mick and Barn had not shared the same predilection toward women's bodies. Mick had thought he preferred lean, mean, and firm. Martha had been slim and small-breasted until she was pregnant and may have put on too much weight, and, though she had lost the baby weight fairly quickly after the first pregnancy, was never hard, muscular, like Kate. But Barney had always liked the curves, especially if the curves wound around well-rounded boobs, and Sara definitely qualified. Maybe Barney had something there. She sure was more satisfying to hug.

CHAPTER 15

NOT UNUSUAL for the Bahamas, it was a fine, bright, sunny day, the palms swaying soothingly to their own music. The season was warming as it reached for April. Being Barney's last full day, Mick decided to take him on the cart and show him the rest of the island. Kate and Sara demurred, saying they would take a run on the beach. The boys left, leaving Kate and Sara sipping their coffees on the porch.

The sisters talked about the similarities between Mick and Kate, Barney and Sara. Kate persisted in her strategy of keeping Mick interested and maintaining that the ruse wouldn't affect how he loved her; Sara balked at Kate's suggestion that she and Barney could develop a long-term relationship and questioned Kate's strategy with Mick. She insisted the situation was not fair to Mick. Kate countered with the argument that Sara, because of her position with the SEC, had the time and money to take time off and could work it out with Barney and still live in Spokane. Sara countered with how the presence of Hot Lottie being in the picture could disrupt Kate's strategy.

Both found themselves quiet, staring out at the lighthouse. Kate looked over and noticed Sara smirking. "Are you smiling at that huge phallus out there staring us in the face? Turn you on, sis?"

"Oh, shut up. Let's go take that run."

BACK TO THE ISLAND

They drained their coffees and went upstairs to change: Kate into her bikini, Sara into her lime-colored running outfit.

CHAPTER 16

BARNEY'S GOODBYE party got underway early. Spense and Lottie showed up at Mick's at four o'clock. Mick and Barney had just returned and had a head start as, while exploring Elbow Cay, they had encountered a few of the island spirits that haunted the various watering holes. Kate and Sara had run on the beach toward Hope Town and done some shopping—Sara in her lime-green jogging outfit, mortified that Kate wandered into stores in her bikini.

After just a few shops, Sara had convinced Kate that they should jog back to get ready for the affair. When back, while preparing themselves, the two razzed each other nostalgically: Kate giving Sara shit about always taking so long to prepare herself; Sara returning the shit by pointing out that maybe this time Kate should as well since Lottie would probably look like her usual seductive self; Kate telling her "so what," pretending she didn't care; Sara, of course, knowing she did.

Lottie, since they were on her boat when they visited Mark on Treasure Cay, had been appointed caretaker of Mark's batch of homemade "smash." Spense and Lottie had pulled up with a very large jar of the concoction sitting on the seat between them. As they carried it up onto the porch, Mick and Barney wobbled out to greet them, Mick eyeing the jar gleefully. Barney said warily: "What the heck is that?"

"That's our entertainment for the evening," explained Mick. "Gumbay Smash. Be cautious," he warned, laughing. "It goes down easy and carries a wallop. It's the islanders' drink of choice."

Lottie huffed up to Barney and unloaded the large jar of entertainment, saying, "Into the kitchen, my big, strong man." She then turned, wriggled into Mick, and laid a soft one, lips slightly parted, right on Mick's startled lips, saying coyly, "Ready to party?" Mick, not objecting to the titillating tease but still wondering "Why?" and "What's going on?" was intrigued but clueless as usual.

Kate and Sara came down into the kitchen right in the middle of Lottie's arousing greeting, Sara putting her hand on Kate's shoulder, Kate putting her hands on her hips. "Fireworks tonight!" Spense shouted. No one was sure exactly what he meant, but the discerning Spense, sensing with the 'smash' a good bash was on the way and picking up on the drama of what he thought a rather peculiar rivalry, thought the double entendre was in order.

Kate grabbed the glass basin from Barney and told him to help her pour some into a couple of large thermoses. Then she added limes, pineapple, and a little mashed mango to each for spice, à la her friend Mark.

They decided to start the party down on the part of the white sand ocean beach where it was wide and flat. The weather cooperated: it was, again, typically warm and sunny with the usual light breeze off the Atlantic. They all put on beach attire: Lottie in a bikini, skimpy but not string, looking like she had just walked out of a *Sports Illustrated Swimsuit Edition*; Kate, looking like a model for a workout magazine in a less tiny but tight, stretchy two-piece; and Sara, surprising to Mick,

CHAPTER 16

actually looked the best to him. She wore a simple, navy one-piece with a cute little skirt attached and so, maybe, in not trying so hard, succeeded in being the most fetching. Spense wore a brief Speedo, not looking bad at all for his age; Mick, his normal faded quick-dry cargo trunks; Barney, a shorter, tight, old-fashioned swimsuit and, instead of sandals or Crocs like the rest, he wore penny loafers sans the socks this time, fortunately. But Mick had to convince him he had to off the loafers and play barefoot.

Mick had brought a beach ball and, like children, they spent several hours playing a beach game in the sand, pausing to imbibe frequently. They formed a circle and for a while made a pretty fair attempt at keeping the beach ball in the air and off the sand using whatever body part they found convenient. To Kate's chagrin and the men's delight, both Lottie and Sara proved surprisingly adept at utilizing a couple interesting parts quite effectively. Eventually ball and body parts were all regularly rolling in the sand. The game denigrated into a free-for-all: if anyone managed to hit the ball up, everyone ran for it, smashing into and tackling each other—a rather raucous rumble in the sand.

Later, as the sun was setting behind the dunes, sweaty and encased in sand, they realized the thermoses were empty. By then none were feeling any pain, fortunately, or they would have all been in pain. Mitch suggested they head back for more "shmash." Lottie grabbed his hand and yelled, "Skinny-dipping first" and dragged Mick toward the waves. On the way, they threw off their suits, and all that could be seen in the twilight was two split orbs—one blanched and one bronzed—disappearing into the water.

"The hell with that!" Kate hooted and took off, top and bottoms peeled off and tossed. Spense looked at Sara and

Barney and shrugged a "what can you do?" and stripped off his Speedo, tossing it high in the air, giving a "whoop" and took off, one skinny, hairy ass bouncing into the dusk.

Sara looked at Barney. Barney looked at Sara. "I'll do it if you do," Sara said. That was all Barney needed to hear and after quaintly slipping out of their suits, not daring to look at each other, they trotted off toward the waves.

They all got out past the breaking waves and were bobbing around, all having fun except Barney, who was not a good swimmer and not terribly comfortable. Sara recognized this and stayed by him, assuring him that as long as he breathed he would stay afloat. The second issue was with Mick: First, Lottie came at him, splashing him in the face and then jumping on his back and playfully pushing his head under. Then, just as he came up, Kate leapt at him and not-so-playfully shoved his head under, holding it until he shook loose. He was not too drunk yet to realize that she might have been trying to drown him. So he swam over by Spense who was laughing hysterically. "Trouble in paradise?" he yelled at Mick and rode up and away on an incoming wave, aware that there was more to this brother-sister relationship than met the eye.

They all eventually washed up onto shore, Barney and Sara first to scramble to their suits and towels; Spense sauntering crookedly to collect his; Mick running, retrieving his quickly. Kate and Lottie were last. Kate not-so-playfully pushed Lottie from behind, knocking her to the sand. Lottie chased Kate, tackling her. Spense was the only one aware and wondering, as they continued wrestling and tackling each other, if an intervention was going to be necessary. Both had obviously drunk too much. Then they abruptly stopped and raced back into the water to re-rinse the sand off and emerged, surprisingly,

CHAPTER 16

holding hands—like twin sirens emerging from the deep, and, in no rush, casually roamed, picking up their suits, neither in any rush either to put them on.

The moon had begun to rise up out of the waves that appeared to roil on the horizon in the dimming light. Spense yelled to diffuse any tension, "My God! Three beautiful women, wet and naked in the moonlight. What more can a mortal ask for?" Barney sidled up to Sara, agreeing, although neither was any longer naked. Mick unbelievably decided to keep his distance from any naked women, especially two of the three possibly most frustratingly beautiful he had ever encountered, glowing naked in front of him in the moonlight—two being his SISTERS! The other, though, he felt no guilt ogling, thinking in his currently punch-addled brain: "She's absolutely gorgeous; why not give it another shot?"

They had all stumbled back to the cottage and managed to last, still into the smash, until early morning. Spense and Sara had taken the cart into Jack's and picked up some frozen pizzas, what might have saved their lives. At four, Barney and Sara said they were beat and were heading to bed, apparently together, to whoops of "don't be naughty," "don't do anything I wouldn't do," and "rock-a-bye-baby, in the treetop," yelled by Mick, that had everyone groaning.

"If Sara gets Barney, I'll settle for Mick," Lottie yelled. "Kate and Spense can have the settee."

Kate excused herself, saying she had to go to the bathroom. When Lottie grabbed Mick's hand he almost resisted; as wasted as he was, he was still aware enough to regard these sleeping arrangements with skepticism. He was surprised by Barney and Sara. He didn't really like the idea of Spense sleeping with Kate. Although he knew Spense was a consummate gentleman, both were drunker than skunks. And ... *and* what did Lottie have in mind? That thought was interrupted by Lottie grabbing his hand and hauling him up the stairs. When they reached Mick's bedroom, they found Kate, apparently passed out, on Mick's bed.

"Well," Lottie hissed, "looks like you're sleeping with your *sister*! Guess I'll settle in with Spense on the settee. Night, darlin'," and she stomped off after giving him a slap on the ass.

When Mick slipped gingerly into his bed, hugging the edge, his back to Kate, he heard a "darlin', my ass!" and then the scratchy snore he'd been listening to, previously from a safe distance.

When Mick abruptly came awake in the morning, he found the sun up enough to light the room and suddenly realized Kate was spooning him, with her arm thrown over his waist. He leapt out of bed before he became acquainted with anything more than the arm and tiptoed to the window to see if Senorita was still there. He saw her standing there looking up at him. He waved, put up one finger in a "just a moment," and realized, unlike Kate, he was still fully dressed, and stumbled downstairs after a pee and quick mouthwash.

She was sitting on the step waiting for him. There was no sign of Lottie or Spense. He came down and sat next to her and said, "Mornin'."

Without looking at him, she said, "Another party?"

He started, "Well, yeah, my friend is leav—" and then realized he was excusing himself apologetically to this young girl—well, not such a young girl—about his behavior. "Were there two people on the settee when you got here?"

"Yes, I'm afraid I woke them. They left. They said to have you say goodbye to a—Barney? How could you not hear their

CHAPTER 16

cart when they pulled away? I assumed that was what woke you. They looked almost as bad as you do."

"Well, thank you."

"My father drinks too much," she said, as if explaining.

"Is he a good drunk?" He couldn't believe he was asking her that. "I mean …"

"I know what you mean," she said. "He gets angry on occasion when drinking. Works himself up to a tither. Not at me and Mother. He's actually a very gentle giant. He gets mad at the world. He says the system sucks."

Mick smiled to himself. "Well, what do you have for me today?"

She said, "You wanted to know about my friends?"

"Yes."

"'History of My World' is about a boy and my best girlfriend growing up. She doesn't live here anymore. The second one is about the boy I thought I loved. You're a little late rising this morning. Those two on the porch … he looked a little old for her? Well, I've got to scat, sir."

"Scat?" Mick said and smiled.

She looked amused. "Yeah … scat. I love when words mean different things."

"Ever heard of a 'double entendre'?"

"I've read it. Is it when you say one thing but it means something else?"

"Yeah, kind of. Actually it means you mean two different things with one word or phrase, like you just used "scat.'"

"Like a metaphor?"

"Well, no. A metaphor is like using a tree to represent your father."

"I know. So give me an example."

"Hmm, they're hard enough to recognize much less come up with. Umm, I know: a friend of mine a while ago retired and he sent me an email of the motor home he and his wife were going to be traveling in. In the picture the name of the motor home showed on its side. It was called Endeavor. I sent him an email back saying: "Good luck in your Endeavor," meaning …"

"I get it. Pretty clever for an empy-headed midget," she said and sat there, smirking at him, eyebrows again raised in innuendo. "Now, like I said, I must scat. I'll be thinking about these double guys. Bye, sir."

"Wait, before you scat. Um, do you go to school? Or church?"

"OK, another endeavor for me, yes?" She looked up and said, "That woman is looking down at us again from your window. You sleep with her? Which, I believe, qualifies as a double entendre?"

"Yes … I mean, no. She's my sister. We just *sleep* together."

"You sleep with your sister?"

"Yes, SLEEP. No double entendre, see? All beds were taken last night. The reason we can sleep together is because we are brother and sister. See? *Sleep* and nothing else?" And two things hit Mick: one, she was fucking with him; and two, there were a lot of single entendres going on last night; he guessed that, ironically, though dangerously drunk, everyone was just *sleeping*.

"If you say so, sir. Bye." And the little gremlin was off.

Kate came down as Mick was reading "History of My World:"

1. The Memory

There was the moon. Shining down like an old friend, or maybe a lover from the past who knew all my secrets and knew that I hadn't

CHAPTER 16

really changed a bit. Even if I had gone through hell, I would not have changed. It just smiled at me knowingly. I half expected it to play some familiar song we might have called ours and offered me a drink and a warm body for the night. I might have accepted if it had been the real thing. We just sat there lusting at each other, sharing little tidbits of information that were common to both of us. I might have cried if it hadn't been so damned windy. I had drawn the conclusion that the wind was related to what I was feeling, and that being strong in the face of it signified something. Well anyway, I didn't cry.

2. The Beginning
It was the summer of nineteen-something. I was young. I believed in things. I never dreamed the world would change. It did. And I've been years behind the natural order ever since. I wanted to sit and dream, believe in things. It was the world that moved so fast.

I guess some things just happen that stop you inside a time, and that was the summer of my disenchantment, filled with wonder and frustration. The days were hot and dry. The nights were cool. The sky was filled with wind.

3. The Dune
"Hurry! You'll miss the cruise ship!"

Far in front of me danced a small figure of a friend who shared all my secrets—told and untold. The dune was alive that day, with sunlight and wind, friendship and laughter. We dreamed together, my friend and I, and the dune was the stage for our imagining.

It was early summer, and the freedom of those days was new. Maybe we were arrogant and secure in our passion for the open air, but we danced without regret or fear of what we were to become. We were enchanted. We were immortal. Most of all, we were young.

BACK TO THE ISLAND

"I'm coming! Wait up! Don't run so fast!"

I remember that she always ran and that she always ran faster. I was busy squinting at the sun and dreaming about a day a lot like that one. She wanted to hurry over the next rise to where she could see the ship slip through the break in the ragged coral of the reef and head out. I could see the stacks and the smoke drifting off over the horizon to the east. She was waiting for me at the top of the hill, panting and very self-satisfied.

"You ... almost ... missed it," she said between breathes. "Gawd ... isn't ... it ... just ... fa ... bulous!"

The ship was turning out to sea just as I reached the top. I didn't say anything, but I smiled. Without looking, she knew I agreed. We sat on the dune, picking at the grasses as we dreamily watched the ship cruise into a speck and then disappear into the other horizon, leaving its wake behind it. The sun was hot and wonderful. The sand was warm and grasses fresh. We were happy.

"Someday I'm going to be on that boat," she said. "I wonder where it's going, to what countries?"

I said I would like to see countrysides. Not the big cities, but the little ones. Be like John Steinbeck and write books. Then I said that I had read that Steinbeck lived in New York City.

She said she liked New York.

I knew she meant the movies she had seen about New York.

"I want the summer to last forever, don't you?"

I leaned my head back so that my face was full into the sun. I filled my lungs with as much air as they could hold. I said a breathless, "Yes, ma'am!" and stood to tear across the dune and through the grasses and run until I dropped. Together we zig-zagged across the sand. The wind through our hair pounded in our ears.

"Don't you wish you could fly?" she laughed as she ran.

CHAPTER 16

I always believed I might have if I could have run just one step faster. But she ran faster, not I.

4. The Tree

"Are you cold?"

The voice was strong and comforting as it reached with a blanket to embrace me and to guard me from the chill of the wind. He was strong. He made me feel warm. He was my first love.

It was a cool and windy summer night. The sky was clear and black and filled with stars. We might have counted all of them, if we had had the time. The moon was full and friendly in the sky. We might have reached up to touch it, if we could have untangled our arms from the blanket, and from each other.

"Here. Take a drink."

The wine he had was cheap and awful, but we were underage. We were sitting under the huge banyan tree that towered over the narrow beach. It was a scarred and ugly old beast of a tree. We liked it because it was old and we were not.

The air smelled of sweat and of a world that would not sleep. It was summer, and the lights from the town betrayed its summer underworld. The one that worshipped the sun in the day, the moon in the night, and did not rest until colder winds blew. It was a cool wind that night, not a cold one. It was the kind that brought bodies together, not the kind that was ruthless and biting cold; not the kind that separated people with sheets of icy rain.

We sat there, watching the sea glass carry the moon down. We hummed a quiet tune we both knew well. He kissed me. The wine tasted better on his lips.

"I want the summer to last forever, don't you?"

I held him closer so that I could hear his heart beating inside my ears. It was my heartbeat, too.

"I love you," I said. But it was a very short summer that year.

BACK TO THE ISLAND

5. Postscript
There was the moon. Shining down like an old friend or a lover from the past who knew all my secrets and knew that I hadn't really changed a bit. It was the summer of nineteen-something. The winds were aging and growing cold.

—H.S.

Kate sat next to Mick and he handed it to her. When she was done, she said, "'The winds were aging and growing cold.' My God, Mick! She's phenomenal! I think that's her best yet. I mean, it's perfect."

"It's remarkable! I may be partial, but I feel it's as good, poignant, as anything I've ever read. Look at this one. It's about a boy, or young man, she once loved. I don't know if he's the same as in 'History of My World.' It's confusing. In appearance she looks so young and innocent; it's hard to imagine her having had lovers, much less boyfriends. Yet in her writing, she's ageless. She could have had centuries of lovers. He handed Kate the poem:

> He spoke to me of shadows.—
> The ones that filled the night.
> That he had found in a lover's eyes.
> And the shadows within.
>
> I cried out with joy and laughter to
> Feel his words rumbling across
> My soul.
>
> And the shadows within me ached with
> The yearning to touch the one who
> Knew their secret.
> —H.S.

CHAPTER 16

When Kate finished he took it back. Kate didn't react. The "secret" line stung her. Could she be talking to her? Did she know? Was she implying she should tell Mick? She definitely "yearned" to touch him, for him to touch her.

He read aloud: "'And the shadows within me ached with the yearning to touch the one who knew their secret.' Amazing!" Mick proclaimed.

"Right!" Kate said, slowly nodding her head. "It is. She is. Truly. I'll get the coffee going. Think we'll need it?" Kate got up, put her hand on Mick's shoulder, leaned over, and kissed him on the forehead. "So are you. Thanks. I woke before you and realized how safe I felt in bed with you. Hope you weren't too uncomfortable?"

"Uh ... no, of course not," he lied once again. He had this longing to be close to her. He wished he could have just enjoyed the touch of her arm around him. He wished he could have turned and hugged her, assuring her that everything was going to be all right.

Barney and Sara, bleary-eyed from too little sleep and too much smash, crept down as soon as Kate got the coffee brewing. They had to get Barney to the eleven o'clock ferry to Marsh Harbour. His flight left at one. Both Kate and Mick perused the couple's faces, looking for any signs of guilt or turpitude. If they had any, they didn't show it. They headed out to the front porch, Barney a bit ridiculous in loafers, boxers, and a T-shirt; Sara, barefoot, looking cuddly in a cottony, conservative, knee-length opaque nightgown, only her cute, pleasantly chubby arms and calves exposed. As Kate poured coffee into Mick's mug, she whispered, "Sara's nightgown is on inside out. How do you suppose that happened?"

"Well, hmmm. Really? She was a little looped when they went to bed, so maybe ... she put it on that way? Or, maybe ... ?"

Mick frowned at the thought. "You get Sara's story and I'll get Barn's when I'm taking him to the airport. Do you think ... ?"

Kate shrugged, smirking. "I don't know. We'll see. Sara can't get a lie past me."

"Barney's a terrible liar. He's too darn honest. I'll get the truth out of him, too, I suspect, though he'll try to protect her honor."

"If there's any reason?" Kate said, and their eyes were locked, by something between affinity and wistfulness.

After they all had coffee and a light breakfast of toast, peanut butter, and jam, Barney went upstairs to pack. Mick, Kate, and Sara sat on the porch, absentmindedly sipping cold coffees and trying to make small talk. Finally Sara stood, smiled weakly, and headed upstairs.

"Where was Sara's mind, do you suppose?" Mick asked.

"Well, I'm guessing upstairs with Barney ... where I'm sure she is now," Kate answered after a pause.

"What, umm, do you suppose they're talking about?"

"Whaddya thunk, Sherlock?"

"What I mean is, well, you know what I mean. They seemed to connect. I've never seen Barn so attentive, and I've had plenty of experience observing. Usually the date, although he treats them well—don't get me wrong—but like they're an accessory. With Sara it seemed different."

"What'd he have to say about Sara?"

"He doesn't have to say anything. After a hundred first dates I don't have to ask, just observe, you know like ..."

"And so, what did you observe, Sherlock?"

CHAPTER 16

"Well, I'll ask him about it on the way to Marsh Harbour, but he did have one long-distance relationship before with a woman who traveled a lot. They always rendezvoused in Vancouver for some reason, but I don't think … no, I know … they never had any long-term plans. Just romantic liaisons that she apparently tired of. This, I can tell, is different."

"You mean to tell me you two didn't talk about his feelings toward Sara?"

"Umm, no, not really."

"Men!"

"What? I told you we didn't have to talk about it."

"So you guys have a crystal ball you don't tell us women about?"

"If you mean, 'What does he plan to do about the future of the relationship?' I said I would ask. But I already know the answer."

"Oh, that's right, I forgot you men are all clairvoyant as well. Sorry."

"What are you getting pissed about?" Mick said, getting defensive and a little pissed himself.

"Oh, nothing," Kate said with a sigh. "I'm just always amazed at men's lack of communication. Sorry. So what is Barney going to do?"

"First, we men don't have to overanalyze everything—talk about it, then discuss it some more. If he knew what he wanted to do, he would have brought it up, and we would have talked about it."

"So, you're saying he doesn't know what he wants to do with the relationship?"

"Right."

"So, he'll just forget about Sara?"

"No, no. He'll send her an email telling her how much fun he had and that they should come down here again and how concerned he is about you ... and me, probably."

"Then what?"

"He'll wait for Sara's response, and if she wants to pursue a relationship, I think he likes her well enough so he might go along with it."

"He'll leave it up to her?"

"Yah, pretty much. The Vancouver lady said meet me in Vancouver, and he met her. When she no longer acted interested, that was it."

"But, he didn't see any future in her, right? Isn't it different with Sara?"

"I'm not sure, really, and I'm guessing neither is he. With the Vancouver woman it was mostly the excitement of the rendezvous. It was nothing serious. It would probably be different with Sara."

"So, why wouldn't he pursue a relationship with her?"

"I'm pretty sure he might if she encouraged him."

"But that's the man's role. If she doesn't think he's interested, she's not going to encourage him."

Mick laughed sardonically, shaking his head. "Guess that's why there are so many lonely souls in the world. They are afraid to say the truth, expose how they really feel."

Kate started to respond, stopped, cleared her throat: "That just doesn't make sense!"

"Not to you and me, maybe. If you thought you loved someone, would you let them know? Or let them get away?"

Kate opened her mouth to speak and cleared her throat again, but nothing came out.

"When you say that's a 'man's role,' Mick said, "you know that's bullshit. It depends on the man *and* the woman. Could

CHAPTER 16

that be why two attractive, smart, wonderful people are still single?"

Kate bit the inside of her lip. "So, you wouldn't let Sara get away?"

"If she wasn't my sister and I felt about her like I think Barney does? Absolutely not. She's about as lovable as they come. But, as you know, I'm a cocky asshole who accepts rejection as a challenge. Probably why Barney has a lot more friends than I do—most of those cute young sweeties stay friends with him. But just occasional friends, from a safe distance."

"Like you and Lottie?"

Mick looked at Kate warily. Was that some kind of trick question? "Well, to be honest, I'm not sure about a safe distance on that one. She's been getting a little flirty-touchy lately. I don't know what's up with that."

"Oh? I haven't noticed." Kate's turn to lie. "If I weren't your sister, would you pursue me? You used to flirt with me."

Now he wasn't too stupid to realize that that *had* to be some kind of trick question. He'd like to say if she changed her name back to Marilyn and she wasn't his sister he'd be on her like a fly to sh— well, maybe a bee to honey might fly better. But, dammit, her name was Kate and she was his *sister*. "Well, now that I know you better, we'd probably kill each other. Both too much like our father the way it sounds." He wondered why Sara wasn't.

CHAPTER 17

THEY LOADED Barney's suitcases on the back of the cart. He always over-packed, which Mick thought was incongruous for a detail-oriented, apparently over-organized guy, and they headed into Hope Town to catch the ferry.

"So, get anything last night, big boy?" M asked nonchalantly as soon as they got under way, squinting into the dusty sunlight. After a couple minutes of no response, M looked over at Barney who appeared to be looking at the cottages, which M knew he had no interest in, as they passed them on their right. "Well?"

Not turning to M, but now staring straight ahead as if the answer to his question was also written on the windshield, finally: "Nahhh."

"Nah?" M said, laughing. "Why was her nightgown on inside out then?"

Barney looked at M, mouth open. "It was?"

"Yup. When did that occur? Before, during, or after?"

Barney looked away, shaking his head, laughing. "I meant I didn't g— Well," hesitantly, "now, don't tell her I said anything, M. Promise?"

"No way; I wouldn't," M said, thinking: He means to Sara, not Kate.

"Not even to Kate."

"You don't think Kate'll know what shenanigans you two were up to?"

CHAPTER 17

"You think they'd talk about it?"

"They're sisters, fool. Not only sisters, twins. Whaddya think?"

Barney grabbed at the sidebar as they rumbled over some ruts, raising even more dust. "Yeah, I suppose."

"Something tells me you didn't have sex. So … ?"

"All right. Yes, we messed around and the nightgown came off …"

"Yeah?" encouraged M.

"But we didn't do it."

Even though intellectually he enjoyed the idea of his sister and best friend liking each other, he was surprised that he felt relieved that they hadn't made whoopie. "Why not?"

Barney looked at M. "Number one, she's your sister."

"Personally, I think it'd be copasetic if you two fell in love." He didn't know if that was a lie or not. "So second … ?"

"Copasetic?"

"Fine, cool, more than OK, OK? So … ?"

"I think she would have done it. But she was drunk, and …"

"Yeah?"

"… and I really like her."

"Sooo … You don't make love to women you really like … unless they're sober and not naked?"

"Ehhh … you know what I mean."

"What? You'll only make love—or let me rephrase that—have sex with women you don't like?"

They hit the cobblestones at the edge of town and in a minute pulled up to the ferry dock. They boarded with the other passengers, lugging all Barney's shit, and not talking. They didn't say much as the ferry maneuvered out of the harbor into the Sea of Abaco. "M, man, it is really beautiful

| 221

here," Barney reaffirmed as they cruised past the lighthouse and turned toward Marsh Harbour. "You know Jim, Jim, George, and Randy want to come down, too."

"Why don't you guys figure out a time this summer, early summer before the hurricane season? That'd really be fun."

"Yeah, that's good. If you're still alive."

"Don't worry," M laughed. "Spense, Lottie, and the whole friggin' island, the way it sounds, have our backs."

"Spense is quite a guy. Weird looking, though. But I really liked him. And Lottie! God, is she cute. Don't tell me nothin's going on there? She sure seemed to be comin' on to you. You haven't told me much about you and her. You two have any history?"

"Well, if you remember," M took a deep breath and looked out at the almost transparent aqua stretching as far as the eye could see, "before I found out that Marilyn was Kate, and my sister, she's the one I had the hots for. Now I've just figured that I must have felt that connection, maybe, because she was my sister, which is a little weird. That means I was sexually attracted to my sister! Eeeew."

"Eeeew is right."

"Anyway, it's not the past but the future I may be interested in with Lottie. I don't remember if I told you, but there was this once ... she spent the night and in the morning did come on to me."

"Really?"

"Yes. But I couldn't do it."

"Couldn't do it? What do you mean?"

Mick glanced over to Barney, rolled his eyes, and looked back out toward Marsh Harbour coming into view. "It was like my erection stood up and pointed at me, yelling: 'What

CHAPTER 17

about Martha? What about Marilyn?' and then plopped back down again. I couldn't keep it up."

"No shit?"

Mick nodded at Barney with a look like he had just stepped in a pile of cow shit. "That ever happened to you?"

Barney returned the look. "Yeah, a couple of times."

"How about last night?"

Barney laughed. "It was weird. It was kinda like what you said, only my pecker didn't speak to me. You're so frickin' weird. I got turned on when we were kissing, and she got into it. But when the gown came off, something in my brain went: 'Nope. Not tonight. Not right.'"

"God, are we growing old … or just growing more slaves to our consciences?"

"Whaddya mean?"

"Well, as I think you know, I haven't slept with anyone since Martha died. Then 'Marilyn' pops into the picture and I start thinking … maybe she's someone I could actually make love to, not just an incidental lay, you know? So, I guess it wasn't the right time that morning for Lottie. Like it would have been a betrayal or something."

"So you see Lottie as just an 'incidental lay'? You're still weird, but I kinda like that one."

"I don't think so, no. That's maybe why my mind couldn't get into it. But now, I don't know. There is no Marilyn, and the more I get to know Lottie, the more I like her. She is really cool, besides the fact that she's feckin' gorgeous. With the first time, I was hung over. She had pulled out a joint, and she came onto me wearing my sweater, completely naked underneath and not hiding it. It was like she crawled right out of a *Playboy*."

"Shit, man. Sounds like it shoulda been fun."

"Look whose talkin'! Tell me it wouldn't have been 'fun' with Sara? I feel like I'm cheating on a dead wife and a woman who it turns out is my sister. How screwed up is that? And you won't sleep with a woman you like too much! Life'd be a lot more fun if we were just feckin' perverts."

Barney shook his head. "You're right there. But what if there really is a heaven? Gotta do the right thing, right? Just in case."

Mick was about as sure about there being a heaven as about what doing the *right* thing might be. He knew Barney went to mass every day when he could. He couldn't understand for the life of him why, but if it was right for Barn, that was fine. He wondered if the fear of not getting to heaven motivated himself. That's what the nuns and priests had told them all back in that Catholic school. But shit, man, if there ain't no heaven you could have been a happy-go lucky, fun-loving bastard all your life, and no big deal. "So, you going to pursue anything with Sara?" Mick asked as the ferry pulled up to the dock.

"I don't know. I don't know how we'd even see each other. It's probably best if we don't get any more involved."

"But you'd like to?"

"Well, yeah. But this is all too quick."

"Did you two talk about it?"

"Yeah, while I was packing."

"And?"

"Umm, we agreed to keep in touch. I'm actually more worried about you and Kate. You can email me now to keep me informed, right? Oh, and you're gonna have to email Jim, Jim, George, and Randy. They're kinda pissed. They want you to keep them informed about shit; you better."

CHAPTER 17

"I guess," Mick said as the ferry bumped the Marsh Harbour pier, and they lifted all Barney's shit onto the dock.

"Well, this was really fun. It's gonna make my cubicle seem a little boring."

"Oh, you'll get right back into that exciting tax stuff; just kiddin'. But you will get back into your students. I miss that, myself."

They caught a taxi to the airport. Both were unusually subdued and quiet. Barney worried about Mick and Kate; Mick wondering about Barney and Sara and Kate and Lottie and HS and Peewee … and Vernal. Vernal was in a very precarious spot: a mole in what could be a very dangerous hole. Did he see that?

When Mick got back, he found a note that Kate and Sara were on the beach by the rocks and that Mick could join them if he liked. Instead he decided to let them be alone for a while. He wanted to get back to working on *A Million Dollars* anyway. He headed up to his perch. It was sunny, warm not hot, and calm. There was usually a breeze up on his perch coming from one side or the other, but nothing today. He sat for a while, contemplating the horizon, thoughts running around in his head, bouncing off each other like arcade bumper cars. When placid, the Abaco, bottomed with bright white sand, was turquoise everywhere but where the reefs were. Most of the sea, surrounded and enclosed from the Atlantic by all the outer islands, was mostly only six to ten feet deep. And this clear day, from his perch, he could follow the now tranquil azure trail of the ferry almost all the way to Marsh Harbour.

Before he could get focused and settle into his writing, he heard Kate and Sara come in downstairs. Rather than try to get started writing, he figured he should go down and visit.

Sara only had a couple more days and she would be heading to DC or New York. Although very different from Kate, he was feeling closer and closer to her. She was much more likable than Kate. He assumed he could easily grow to love her. Kate was settling in his mind as his sister like a piece of a jigsaw puzzle fitting into place. What had him somewhat pleasantly muddled was that Sara's piece did not quite fit, yet.

The three sat on the porch and discussed where they were regarding Kate's state of affairs. Sara insisted that before she left she be involved in the planning about how things were to proceed: Were they going to lure Kate's pursuer to them? And if they did, what were they going to do to or with him? They decided to go into Cap'n's for a little while before it got busy, get a snack of conch fritters, and have a little powwow with Spense and Lottie, maybe set up a time for a longer discussion the next day.

The three of them plopped into Mick's cart and headed into Hope Town. Kate and Sara, being tired and a little stressed, hadn't planned on staying long after the little meeting, but Spense was in fine form, at his eclectic best, and they couldn't leave.

Early, the crowd had started chanting, "Dead Man, Dead Man," breaking up their little powwow. So they decided, quickly, to meet at Mick's place the next day for lunch and continued consultation. Spense then, already dressed in black, donned a black do-rag, of all things, and got his elaborate electronics to pound out the stirring bass beat from the start of the movie *Walk the Line*. He then growled like a constipated inmate a ramshackle rendition of "Folsom Prison" made famous by, of course, the late Johnny Cash. From there he crooned in a drunken slur, "That's Amore" à la Dean Martin; and like

CHAPTER 17

a transgendered, hard-drinkin' Janice Joplin "bluesed" his way through a rowdy "Heartbreaker," made famous by the oft-heartbroken queen of soul; on to Motown and a surprisingly sweet rendition of Marvin Gaye's "I Heard It through the Grapevine."

Kate and Sara ended up spending the night screaming in appreciation of the diverse character traits Spense had absorbed and the hilarity of his incongruous mix of genres. His almost beautifully misshapen face somehow captured the essence of the expired artists, his asymmetrical fingers delicately manipulating switches and toggles producing at times remarkably accurate resemblances of their music, other times only distant echoes. Lottie and Mick egged him on while keeping the crowd oiled. By eleven o'clock he hadn't taken a break. Lottie noticed how tired he was looking and slid up next to him by the mike. But he wouldn't quit or let her leave until they did a rather spicy duet of Hank Williams' "Why Don't You Love Me Like You Used to Do?" Lottie utilizing the mike stand to the crowd's delight. Then, because he was quitting early, he announced he would not end with the standard "Hit the Road, Jack" but a sentimental a capella version of Ral Donner's "You Don't Know What You Got Until You Lose It" dedicated to his late wife. When he finished, with a hoarse voice he yelled, "Everyone, have another on my Mary." Everyone cheered but Lottie, Mick, Kate, and Sara. The unnerving events of the day combined with the exhaustion and elation of the evening sent Kate and Sara out the door, wiping their eyes.

On Spense's way out, Lottie pulled him behind the bar with her and Mick as they were cleaning up, wrapped her arms around both, and kissed them. "God, what a life, guys. I love both of you fools," she said as she squeezed them.

CHAPTER 18

THE NEXT morning Mick got up before Kate and Sara. The sun had not risen above the dune at the back of the cottage and, although calm, it was cool on the porch in the early shade. He was huddled on the settee when Senorita arrived. "Well, would you like to sit up here on the porch for a change?" Mick asked her as she stood below the steps.

"Good morning, sir. No thank you."

"Well, I'd like you to meet my sister this morning."

"I've already met your sister, sir."

"Well, I mean I'd like the three of us to discuss something."

"Oh? What might that be, sir?"

"OK. For now, I'll come down there," and they sat side-by-side on the steps.

"Your friends, the boys, did they ever go to school, I mean high school?"

"Why do you ask?" Sitting on the steps, her head went only up to Mick's shoulders, so she was always looking up at him. He slid down a step so they were more at the same level.

She smiled. "Thank you, sir. Now I won't get a stiff neck."

Mick chuckled. "OK, listen. I'm guessing neither you nor your friends are in school now, correct?"

"That's correct," she said, a little reluctantly. "But I have been home schooled … and now, of course, you are officially my teacher."

CHAPTER 18

Mick couldn't help but smile at almost everything she said. "OK. I will do my best, or the best I can in the few minutes you allow me each morning."

"But you inspire me, sir."

"How do I do that?"

"Well, you ask me questions that I must think about, and I have to answer them."

"Who teaches you at home?"

"My grandfather got me writing, and my father would like to write, too. He wants things published in the local media and periodicals supporting his point of view. If he didn't encourage me, I wouldn't be here. My mother has taught me all the local history and myths and stories. My father is very informed on world history, geography, geology, although his view of politics is very slanted—not very objective, to say the least. But I read a lot. My mother is very adept at mathematics as well. She's island, but she grew up with a governess and was well-educated."

"Why doesn't your father have you write some articles? You're more than capable, you know?"

She shook her head, almost sadly. "He has asked, but as you know, we don't always agree."

"Hmm. I asked you before if your father would come and meet me."

"You've already met, sir."

"You could quit calling me sir. Mick would do, really. Would you call me Mick?"

"No, sir."

"Why not?"

She squinted at him. "You're my teacher. I call you 'sir' out of respect."

Mick smiled at her. "OK, you win. But I refuse to call you Senorita. So, what shall it be?"

"How about HS?"

"HS! You mean call you by your initials? That's a little strange, isn't it?"

"It's actually strange that you think it's strange, since you go by MP, or at least used to."

The smile, almost constant on his face, erupted into a laugh. "But it would appear I have to go by Mick now."

"Why, sir?"

"My sister Kate thinks MP is a stupid name. She's dubbed me Mick."

"A little presumptuous of her, wouldn't you say, sir? My father told me your name was MP, or M for short. I like it fine."

"OK, I'll call you HS. It's definitely an improvement over Senorita. How about you call me MP then?"

She thought for a while. "Mr. M. might be OK."

"OK, deal," Mick said. "Maybe when I'm no longer your teacher and we can just be friends, I can call you Heidi, I bet, and you can call me anything but Mr. or sir?"

"Unless we were betrothed, I'd always see you as my elder, sir. And, I suspect, always worthy of respect."

"OK," Mick sighed and shook his head, resigned to giving into the will of his student. He wondered where the betrothed reference came from. "But your father, can I meet him, again? He could come here, or I'd love to see where you live."

"He said he would come to visit, but I'm afraid there might be some conditions."

"Conditions? Like what?"

"Well, he held up the progress of the cancer, as he calls it, on the west side. But, they have repaired the machines, of

CHAPTER 18

course, and are preparing to continue their constr— I mean *des*truction. I believe he thinks you can help."

"So, what? He'll come talk to me if I promise to help him?"

"That would be the gist of it, sir."

"MP. Mr. M."

"OK, sir."

He couldn't help but laugh at her obstinacy. "All right. I'll agree to help if I can. When might he be able to come visit?"

"He'll come this afternoon if he believes you'll help."

"Hmm, how about he comes for lunch? If he'd be comfortable with other participants in the discussion. Kate, her sister Sara, and the two that you woke up that morning will be here, and, I do believe, they would be very willing to help as well. I thought you weren't in favor of your father's techniques?"

"I am unsure of what techniques are necessary, but I am in favor of putting an end to any decimation of our island and what little natural environment we have left."

"Hmph, OK. I agree with you there."

"And," she continued, "I believe Father feels that your friend's yacht could be very useful. So, I assume he'd be happy if your friends were there."

"And just how do you assume this? I thought your father was a stranger to you?"

She bit her lip. "Yes, an emotional stranger, because I'd call him an activist and I'm more of a ... what they say ... conscientious objector? But they have meetings at our place and he wants me to participate."

"Do you?"

"I listen."

"You don't say what you think?"

"No. They don't want to hear anything but action. My caution would have no takers. Father almost acts like this is one big comedy. No fear of a potentially tragic outcome."

"Are the boys, your friends, in on the meetings?"

"Yes. Of course. As are their fathers and some women. Father is aware of your circumstances with your sister as well. Most of the Bahamians on the island are. Father believes, I think he said, 'The renewal of your relationship could be mutually beneficial, as it was in the past.'"

"Is your father's name Todd?" MP was suddenly positive her father was his old friend Peewee. It had to be. But how weird it would be if it were true. Almost too weird.

"I call him Father." She smiled: "Mother calls him all kinds of names you wouldn't understand."

"Would one translate into 'Peewee'?"

She raised one eyebrow and before she had a chance to come up with a response, Kate walked onto the porch. "Morning, Mick. Sara's sleeping in." And looking at HS, she smiled the most affable morning smile she could muster and greeted her with a "Good morning."

"Morning," HS replied, self-consciously, looking down at the steps.

"Kate. Kate is my name."

"Yes, ma'am."

"What is your name?"

She didn't answer right away, shifting uncomfortably on the step. She looked at Kate for a moment, then answered quietly: "HS."

"HS, Kate and I have something we'd like to get your opinion about," MP said, daring to put a hand on her shoulder.

CHAPTER 18

HS looked at his hand, smiled at it, and then up at Kate. "My opinion?"

Kate walked down the steps and offered her hand. HS hesitated, then tentatively put out her hand and gingerly shook Kate's.

"Nice to know you. I hope you don't mind that Mick has shown me your writing. It's remarkable ... as are you, I suspect."

HS looked away shyly and didn't respond, her hand still in Kate's.

"Would you come up to the porch so we can talk?" Kate asked without letting go of HS's hand.

She looked up at Kate and, blushing, nodded her head. Kate held onto her hand and they walked up the steps, Mick following. When they were seated, Kate told HS that she was surprised Mick was able to carry on a conversation before he'd had any coffee. "He's not a morning person," she said.

"Could depend on what he's been up to the night before," HS said, and Mick and Kate laughed.

"Would you like a cup of coffee, miss?"

"Oh, no thank you."

"Don't drink coffee?" Kate asked.

"No, I don't."

"Tea?"

"Well, yes. I do drink tea."

"Then coffee for us; tea for you, it is," Kate said.

"Oh no, please. That's not necessary."

"Oh, yes it is," Kate replied. "We would hardly be comfortable drinking our coffee while you watch, cupless. Decaf?"

"Yes, please."

"Be back in a sec," and Kate disappeared into the kitchen.

"I think you'll like Kate if you give her a chance. Don't

hold it against her that she calls me Mick. You will discover that she's rather strong-willed."

"Nothing wrong with that," HS said.

"No," MP laughed. "I didn't believe you'd think so."

Kate returned with a tray: two coffees, a cup and tea bag, and two blueberry muffins. "Mick's a pastry freak," Kate informed HS. "I make him blueberry muffins because it reminds him of where he's from. If I have some at all, it's half. Want to share one?"

HS looked at it longingly and Kate could see she was torn between polite refusal and indelicate relish. "Here," Kate said, handing her the half muffin and a napkin. "Eat it or I'll be throwing it away anyway."

"Thank you, ma'am," she said, smiling at the muffin and nibbling at it immediately. "That'd be Minnesota?"

"Yup. Same place your father is from?" Mick snuck in.

No response. She focused on devouring the muffin.

"OK," Mick said, "Kate has an idea she'd like to bounce off of you."

"Mo-kay," HS answered, mouth full of muffin. Kate and Mick laughing again, HS looking embarrassed.

"Your friends," Kate started, "the ones I imagine you know are looking out for us …"

"Yes?"

"Well, since they're helping us, we'd like to help them."

"Oh? How?"

"I assume that the reason they don't go to school is because they don't like leaving the island? I'd like to teach—home school—them here."

HS paused and looked from Kate to MP. "If you read my answer today from your last question, you'll know why neither

CHAPTER 18

I nor my native friends would want to go to Marsh Harbour or anywhere else for school."

Mick had carried the folder with him up onto the porch. He held it up. "Mind if we read it now?"

Again, she hesitated. "You can read, 'Black Hole.' It's why I, and my friends, don't go to school. The second is in response to whether I go to church or not, really why I don't. But it's personal. I'd rather you read it after I left."

"No problem," Mick said and opened the folder. He read aloud:

Black Hole

You would have me fit, wouldn't you.
Into your mold.
As you sit there, pretending to have a face.
—H.S.

"Read it again, please," Kate said.

Mick read it again and then held up the sketch for Kate to see. Kate took the sketch from Mick and studied it. "You don't have a question mark after 'wouldn't you'," Mick stated.

"It's not really a question," HS replied.

"Who are the faces?" Kate asked.

"My father on the left. It is incongruous. He is big and strong, and, although he acts like his—is ecoterrorism the right phrase?—is all one big lark, he often weeps for me and the island, maybe often brought on by too much rum. My mother is on the right. She is the sad sparrow."

"The middle face is the system?" MP asked.

"Yes. You could say that. It's school, it's teachers, it's students, it's the church, any church. Yes, I guess you are right—it's the system."

"The system 'judges'?" Kate asked.

"Yes. I suppose it's hard not to judge," HS said. "My father, even. He judges me, tries not to, but if I don't endorse his actions, he thinks I don't care. My mother judges me because she thinks I may want to leave the island. Go out into the wicked world. I will say though, sir, I don't see you judging me. My father said you wouldn't." She then looked at Kate and smiled, not sadly, yet Kate's eyes were moist.

"You know you are very special?" Kate almost whispered.

HS didn't answer but stood up and said, "I have to go. Thank you for the tea. Sorry I didn't finish it." She smiled at Kate: "I'll take a blueberry muffin anytime. Maybe I can take one back someday for my father? Maybe it'll remind him of Minnesota and Empy-headed here?"

Mick wanted to laugh, to thank her for her subtle simplicity, her depth, her strength, but he found it surprised him that he was afraid to try to talk.

CHAPTER 18

"Bye." To Kate: "I'll talk to my friends. It's very kind of you to offer teaching them." To MP: "Expect my father at noon. He's quite excited to see you." And she was gone, leaving Mick and Kate wordlessly looking after her.

"We're meeting the father today?" Kate asked, her interest piqued.

"Yup. I can't wait. He's coming for lunch. Apparently we're striking some kind of deal. One that's 'mutually beneficial,' she said."

"Beneficial? For whom?"

"Us ... and him, I guess." Mick looked at the next poem. "I'm almost afraid to hear this one about religion," Kate said. "Well, here it is," and Mick read out loud:

> I am I, child of the cellar, waiting.
> Crouched in cobweb corners, waiting.
> Behind canned apricots and strawberry preserves.
> I am I, crouched knees bent to shoulders, hands
> over bare breasts, waiting,
> for proper clothes, waiting
> for Adam to descend and tell me it's all right
> that we've sinned.
> —H.S.

CHAPTER 19

SPENSE AND Lottie rumbled up, appearing gradually in the humid haze. It had clouded up, threatening rain, and the breeze had picked up, knocking coconuts out of the palms, sounding like firecrackers as they landed. Sara had slept late, but at midday, all three were nestled quietly on the porch reading.

"I hope you're all prepared to get your amygdalae alert and vigilant," Spense exhorted as he climbed the steps to the porch, Lottie right behind, rolling her eyes. Spense and Lottie hugged both Kate and Sara, who had stood, and Spense fisted Mick, who had remained seated. Lottie, on the other hand, leaned and, surprising Mick, kissed him on the lips and then sat on the arm of his chair, hand resting not uncomfortably on his shoulder.

"Amig … what?" Mick asked.

"Oh, God, please don't get him going," Lottie said laughing. "After my education on the way here about this organ or whatever the hell it is, I wasn't sure if I was going to be afraid of you two sisters and run, want to attack Mick or Kate, eat you out of house and home, drink all your smash, or …"

"Amygdala," Spense interrupted, drawing out a chair for Lottie and himself. "Google it sometime. It's our most amazing organ, controls us more than our morals and conscience, its function mostly unbeknownst to the general population."

CHAPTER 19

"I've heard of it," Sara said. "Doesn't it control almost all of our subconscious behavior, directly or indirectly?"

"You bet your amygdala it does," Spense said and plopped into a chair. "Now, let's figure out how to manipulate the amygdala of this fellow who's after our Kate. We either have to cause him to flight or fight, to run, or entice him into a trap from which he has no escape. I've grown quite fond of you, my dear. I intend on doing everything in my power to ensure no harm befalls you."

"Can't argue with that!" Mick said and Lottie affirmed.

"Oh my gosh!" Kate exclaimed. "I don't know how to thank you all. I really do feel like I've known you all for years, not just days. You are such good friends."

"That sentiment is reciprocated by all of us, I'm sure. Now, Lottie," the acutely cognizant Spense continued, "why don't you slide that magnificent tush of yours over here and into the chair I have appropriated and we'll get down to business."

"Hgggmm," Mick said, sounding like he was clearing his throat. "We're going to need another chair, that big one over there I'm assuming."

Spense and Lottie looked first at each other, then at Mick, brows raised. "Well, my good man, enlighten us. Is it some giant visiting us, a Paul Bunyan from your Minnesota northland, perhaps?" Spense mused.

"Close," Mick said.

Kate suddenly scampered to the edge of the porch, looking through the flowering bushes down the road toward the north end where the narrow, rutted road got even narrower. "I see someone coming. It's about noon, so it could be our man."

They all crowded the front of the porch and peered down the lane. "My God, look how big he is! He does look like Paul Bunyan," Lottie exclaimed.

| 239

BACK TO THE ISLAND

As he got closer, Spense whispered, "My Lord, look at the amplitude of that cranium. I sincerely hope he puts it to good use."

Mick strained to see if he recognized his old friend. The man sauntering toward them was indeed large, very large. His head was shaved, making it look even more prominent. He appeared to be tanned almost island brown. He wore khaki pants cut off just below the knee, huge calves bulging above what looked to be sandals. His shirt was white, sleeves rolled up to just below the elbow exposing heavily veined forearms, thick wrists, and huge hands swinging freely at his side. As he got closer, although he now sported a closely cut silver beard and sunglasses, Mick was sure he recognized him.

The behemoth, close to seven feet and looking like he topped three hundred pounds with no noticeable fat, stopped at the bottom of the steps, pulled off his sunglasses, and, as he used to do in fourth grade, stared up at the four of them as if he might reach up and mush them into little flesh balls. All but Mick stepped back into the porch. Then he beamed a giant's smile and bellowed, "MP, you haven't grown! Otherwise, how are you?"

MP started down the steps, grinning from ear to ear. "Peewee, I see you haven't shrunk." As MP reached the bottom step, Todd picked him up under his arms like a father holding his baby and said, "Long time. Give me a hug," and held MP like he was going to burp him.

The other three pulled up to the top of the steps and peered down at the scene, looking unsure if they should come any closer. Peewee set MP down on the steps and said, "Well, introduce me to the gang. I'm assuming the cute little one is Kate. You and me got some things to talk about," Peewee

CHAPTER 19

directed at Kate, Kate looking as if she were unsure if this was good or bad. "And although I don't frequent Cap'n Jack's, I have heard tell of a barmaid who, if a man looks her in the eye, will be enchanted and never be happy with another woman in his lifetime."

Lottie laughed a little nervously.

"And that delightful little miss must be the visiting twin? Aren't you the cutest little thing I've ever seen? And you, my very interesting-looking man, must be the owner of that monstrosity out there in the harbor. I hope, like me, big is better."

"Well, my most modest fellow, you are right on both counts, I hope," Spense tossed back at him. "It would appear you know a lot more about us than we know about you."

Peewee roared and started up the steps, grabbing Mick by the shoulders on the way. "On the island, there are no secrets. There are eyes and ears everywhere."

"Let's all have a seat," Mick said and pointed Peewee to the big chair as he pulled it over. As they all sat, Mick said, "As you've all figured by now, this is my old friend Todd Springer, father of my new friend ... " trying to trick Peewee into giving HS's name away.

Peewee smiled, "Oh, no. You'll have to get that from her."

"Hmm, well, Peewee, these are my sisters Kate, you were indeed correct, and her twin Sara McGennity; and, yes: enchanter, Lottie; and Commander Spense Redfern."

"Nice to meet you all. MP, you and I can catch up later. It is interesting that we both ended up here. My grandparents had a vacation place in the Nassau area before the Chinese turned it into the circus it is now. I'll have to hear what brought you down here, but for now I'd say let's get down to business."

| 241

Kate suddenly stood. "I have sandwiches and iced tea made. Should we eat something while we talk?"

"Why don't I give you why I'm here first? I believe my daughter has told you I'm hoping our meeting can be mutually beneficial. Then you'll have something else to chew on along with the sandwiches. And then we will discuss your dilemma, of which I already know quite a bit."

"The tea's made and glasses on a tray," Kate said. "Let me at least get these while we talk."

As Kate left, Spense asked: "So, Todd, where on the island do you live?"

Peewee looked calmly at Spense, large brown eyes unblinking. "I don't much talk about where I live. Sorry."

"Hmmm," Spense said, returning the look.

Todd turned to MP. "I'm guessing MP here might eventually get invited over. My daughter's rather taken with him."

"I imagine you know how special she is," MP said. "I'd love to come visit."

Peewee grinned. "She's a tough little nut, that I know. Thank you for taking time with her. She refers to you as Teacher." He looked up at Kate as she came out onto the porch with a tray of iced teas. "Speaking of teacher, I would like to thank you, too," he said as he took the tea, the glass looking like a child's in his massive hand, the same as the one in HS's sketch. "I've already talked to the boys' parents. They want me to check you out before they agree. Whaddya say, MP? She gonna be a good influence on the island boys?"

"Not sure, Peewee. She's certainly not a good influence on me."

"Oh, shut up," Kate yapped, laughing.

Peewee smiled. "Well, the boys will be all for it. They think you have a very nice *be*hind."

CHAPTER 19

"*Be*hind?" Kate asked, wondering. "Behind! You don't mean ... ?"

Again, Peewee roared his deep laugh. "As I've said, there are eyes and ears everywhere."

"Oh, God. I'm so embarrassed."

"No pun intended, I'm sure?" Spense slipped in, and all laughed.

"So, we'll make it happen. Those boys need it," Peewee said, getting serious. "We'll talk later. Now, down to business. I'm not sure what Heidi ..."

"Aha!" Mick exclaimed, interrupting. "I knew it!"

"Knew what?" Lottie asked.

"That her name was Heidi! All I knew from her was HS. But something told me it was Heidi."

"All right, understanding number one: you did not discover what her name was from me. She said she likes the synergism—gosh, what that kid comes up with—of MP and HS. So, not from me. Understood?"

"Agreed," MP answered. "I take it this is a strong-minded young lady."

"You have no idea. OK, next, I understand she mentioned to you the development on the west side?" Peewee leaned forward and perused them all. "Am I to assume everyone here is dependable, on the QT?"

"Yes," Mick responded. "You have my word on it. Heidi mentioned that you sabotaged the machinery?"

"Correct. But, naturally, the machines are back ... and now with guards—armed guards. According to Vernal, the Mandelsungs have installed surveillance cameras and even sound detectors."

"Vernal?" Kate asked. "Vernal from Sears?"

| 243

"Yes."

"But he's Haitian. I thought the Bahamians hated the Haitians?" Kate said.

"Sure, the lazy, good-for-nothing Bahamians who can't hold a job hate them because they work hard. But they are just as strong against destruction of the islands as we are."

"I knew Vernal was kind of an organizer among the Haitians," Kate said. "I also guessed he was spying on Ajax, but I didn't know what for."

"He's our main mole in the Mandelsung group. He lurks, listens, looks, and passes on information."

"So, Ajax and Arthur *are* behind the development?" Mick asked. "They seem like such dimwits, and do they really have the resources?"

"Their family does," Peewee said. "Old money … all the way back several generations to England. They're also backed by the Chinese—lotsa moola there. Ajax and Arthur certainly aren't the kingpins of the operation but are the local assholes here in the Abacos. And, they are major assholes. They have screwed over many an islander, Bahamian and Haitian alike. There had been for years a little settlement of poor Haitians squatting on a little island of solid ground in the mangroves near the west side, doin' no harm. They work here on Elbow, providing labor that's needed, but can't afford to rent, much less buy. They had little shelters built of palms and bamboo mostly. This Mandelsung group and their hired thugs came in and drove them out—men, women, and kids beaten with clubs and rifle butts, their little homes destroyed. I figured that these Haitians might not have been able to stay there squatting forever, but it was the way they went about it. They think they're above the law. They make their own rules. They

CHAPTER 19

think they're some kind of royalty and their shit don't stink, but it does. They must be stopped."

"No argument from me. Believe me, I know they're assholes. So, Heidi—HS—said you wanted our help?" Mick asked.

"Yes, on several levels if you would. Nothing dangerous, of course. First, MP, we'd like to utilize the power of your pen. Get editorials exposing the potential fallout from these developments, especially this development. Through my—our—contacts with various periodicals throughout the islands, I could get articles printed supporting our cause. Our government, like almost all governments, faces debt and increasing deficits. Their vision becomes shortsighted when they hear promises of tax revenue, increased tourism, money for schools, programs for the disadvantaged, you know: progress. Of course there are bribes, pockets get padded, and if any of this does get back to the Bahamas, little, if any, will reach Elbow Cay. Here we have no real poverty, our little elementary school is perfect for the island, and we don't want bigger roads, bigger cars. With a cay only six miles long and not more than a half mile at its widest, carts, for most, do fine. And on this north end no cars are allowed, as you know. Would you want your little lane here widened with cars roaring past your front porch?"

"God, no," Mick said. "That would change the whole way of existence here."

"Exactly our feeling. The thing that attracts the resorters and tourists back every year is the slow, leisurely pace. We don't even have a real policeman. We can pretty much self-police; we literally have no crime. If we allow this to happen, the floodgates would be opened. We could start to become a mini-Nassau with gambling, crime, murder. Then private owners would sell and more development would happen; the entire flavor of the island would change. Us, the real Elbow inhabitants, would be driven out to make more room for ..."

"Guess you're not just a pretty face, Mick," Kate interrupted, referring to Mick's previous parasite diatribe.

"Mick?" Peewee questioned, frowning.

"For later." Kate chuckled. "Anyway, MP pointed out the irony last night when we stopped by their new road, which looked awful, that 'the parasite destroys what gives it life'"

"Aha!" Peewee said, slapping his knee. "Exactly! And exactly why you could help us penning some of your wit and wisdom."

"Not sure about 'wit and wisdom,'" Mick said, "but you betcha, I'm in. I'm not so sure HS couldn't contribute herself. She's a great writer, you realize?

"She mentioned you might have use for Spense's yacht?" Mick slipped in quickly, skipping past the "HS contributing" reference, assuming it might be a trite controversial. He just had to throw it out there, he couldn't help himself.

"Oh?" Spense said, having been unusually quiet. "How might I be of assistance?"

"Well," started Peewee, "two ways, actually. First as a distraction. We need to somehow get rid of the explosives they have brought in and have stored somewhere at the site. Have you seen what they've done? They've taken bulldozers and earth movers and are just pushing the trees, everything, back into the mangroves to clear for construction. It's a mess. It's a huge wound, an open sore on our island, and it's only the beginning! If we don't do something, the cancer will spread. We heard from Vernal that the next stage was to start blasting for a beach, a harbor, and to get boat access for construction. And, of course, the earthmovers and other machinery have been repaired—don't know if you're familiar with what we've

CHAPTER 19

done so far. I assume, being MP's friends, that this information is safe?"

"Yes, you assume correctly, and, yes, we are appreciative of and have been apprised of your effective efforts thus far," Spense assured him.

"Well, somewhat effective. We need to disable these machines somehow again, hopefully permanently this time."

"So ... a distraction?" Spense asked.

"Yes. We have two problems: One, the armed guards. Two, the sound and movement detectors. We're not sure yet what we can do about these. But the easiest approach to get at the machines and explosives would be by water. At high tide on a calm night, it would be possible for some of our swimmers to get ashore. There are paths through the coral. We would have the element of surprise, as they look at the coral reefs and think they're impenetrable, so they will be concentrating on protecting the road access."

"OK?" Spense's interest was obviously piqued.

"But we need a distraction, a diversion to gain time to do what we need to do. We don't want to hurt the guards. They are not from Elbow, but other islands—misguided islanders—but islanders just trying to make a buck. One was injured because of something I did, and I feel very bad about it."

"So what are you thinking?" Mick asked. "What kind of distraction?"

Peewee smiled sheepishly. "Don't really know. I could use some help on this one. The boat alone is a distraction." Everyone laughed slightly, nodding. "But I thought you might have some ideas."

Spense suddenly stood and started pacing, hand to chin as usual. "Well, actually the detectors are easy. I have sonar and other devices to disable these, remotely, or at least render them moot. The distraction, hmm, I'll think more about that, but I have a sound and light show I occasionally do on my travels. That would be at least a minor distraction and loud and bright enough to certainly cause confusion. Of course you need the cover of dark. We could try to do something, however, to draw the guards away from the shore where the explosives and machines are, I assume? This will require some more thought, contemplation. But, no worry. I'll figure it out."

"Won't they just get more explosives and repair any disabled machinery again?" Kate asked.

"As I said, last time the ground coral just clogged the filters. This time we'll use sugar. That should put them out of commission pretty permanently. We'll see who has the most perseverance," Peewee said.

"And money?" put in Lottie.

Peewee looked at Lottie, smiling. "That's their problem, not ours. We have no money, just determination"

Peewee turned to Mick. "I can't wait for our little conversation. We've got a lot to catch up on. So, I believe we agreed to 'mutually' beneficial? Let's see what we can do to help your sister here."

I'm not his SISTER! Kate wanted to scream, but in a rare display of discipline, bit her tongue. They spent the next hour eating the sandwiches and explaining Kate's predicament. They pointed out that although the guy could be running around the globe chasing Spense's VPN, virtual personal network, that they now wanted to lure him here to Elbow Cay and deal with him on their own terms.

Peewee ensured them that this guy would be intercepted at any attempt to get on the island unescorted. If he ferried

CHAPTER 19

over or used any of the harbors, he would be discovered. Plus, there was no harbor on the east, ocean-side of the island. He would have to moor way out in the Atlantic, and that would be very difficult, even if someone knew what they were doing, to get any kind of even small craft over the underwater reefs and handle the breakers. And even if he did try, it would be very conspicuous and the islanders would be aware of it.

They broke up the meeting deciding they would discuss further the diversion and how to attract this Richard to Elbow Cay. Peewee promised Richard would not be hurt, at least badly, guaranteeing, however, he would be accosted if he ventured uninvited onto the island.

Sara, who had been mostly silent throughout the entire discussion, broke down in tears after everyone left. Totally stressed and worried about her sister, she excused herself, saying that she had to go lie down. Tonight was Sara's last night, and Mick and Kate, left on the porch, discussed how to spend it.

"I don't know who's more stressed, me or Sara," Kate said, sighing. She then sat on the porch floor, wormed her back against Mick's chair between his feet, and ordered: "My shoulders and neck are really tight. Give me a little rub, would ya?"

Mick had made it this far without reciprocating. He figured neck and shoulders he could handle—until she pulled off her T-shirt. She was hunched over, hugging herself, so really, nothing he shouldn't see was visible. But, as he had tried to convince Barney one time, nothing stirred him like a bare shoulder, and at this moment, there were two, along with a tanned, shapely, naked, bare back. He was just convincing himself that really, she could just have a one-piece swimming suit on with a low back, when she said, muffled with her chin tucked respectfully between her arms, "What are you doing? Just rub my shoulders, you moron!"

So he gritted his teeth, wishing he could enjoy this, and dug in.

"OW! Take it easy, will ya? That hurts."

"Sorry." He was a moron. His sister was in trouble, tense, and hurting. Why shouldn't he be able to help? He relaxed and focused on gently rubbing the top of her shoulders and inside the shoulder blades where he liked it.

"God, that feels good. That's more like it."

He found, delightfully, that this did not unduly unnerve him ... if he didn't think of the bare breasts lingering close by. He noticed, happily, that her muscles had been tight and he could feel them relaxing under his touch. He was proud of himself. He *could* think of Kate as a sister, not a carnal object. Why not, for Christ's sake? He could love her as a sister, and what's wrong with a little TLC with a person you love—as a sister?

"Get my neck a little. That feels great, Mick." And it did to him, too.

WHEN SARA got up, she found Kate snoozing in the hammock and Mick reading in one of the deck chairs. They both roused as Sara stepped onto the porch. The day had turned calm and clear, warm now with the breeze lightly massaging the palms, so they decided that all three of them would take a walk on the beach. It was a perfect day for Sara's last.

Mostly they slowly strolled, sometimes they found themselves with arms around each other, sometimes all three holding hands. One time Sara startled Mick after he had made one of his stupid remarks by suddenly grabbing him and trying to toss him into the waves. When he fought it with a man's inane machismo, Kate ended it by running at them and pushing a

CHAPTER 19

bit more forcibly than Sara and all three ended up laughing and choking in the water, Sara on top of Mick, Kate on top of Sara. It felt good to Mick, who had been an only child, to have sisters, a family; and to Sara, who had never had a brother or a casual, easy relationship with a man. Kate, on the other hand, was feeling less and less "sisterly."

Mick had the night off, and they knew Spense and Lottie would expect them at Cap'n Jack's, but neither of them wanted to drink anything and, despite their naps, both Sara and Kate were worn out. So Mick texted both Spense and Lottie and suggested they meet at the harbor in the morning. Lottie had insisted on taking them into Marsh Harbour in her Windsor for Sara's flight to Miami in the morning. Goodbyes would be tomorrow.

"OK, I'm just not comfortable leaving," Sara had pronounced when they settled on the porch after returning from their beach walk. The day had cooled a bit into early evening and the sun was setting behind the lighthouse. Sara, for this occasion, had slipped into a plum-colored velour workout suit and sat on the settee with a blanket pulled up, although it wasn't particularly cold. Sara had a soft, savory voice and always spoke like she had considered for several days what she was going to say, much unlike her twin, who frequently didn't appear to think about what she was going to say until after it was said. "Mick, I'm just getting to know you and here I am leaving. I was so worried about Kate, but, I must admit, I feel much better now. We've been so fortunate to have found you, and then your friends have been great. Of course, I'm still very concerned about Richard and what his intentions are."

"With Spense, Lottie, and especially Peewee and the islanders behind us, I'd worry more about Richard if I were

Richard," Mick said, still in a deck chair and gently swinging Kate, who was also bundled up, in the hammock next to him. "Since you work remotely, couldn't you work from down here? I don't want you to leave either. It's been so nice having the good twin around rather than just the evil one."

"Hey, shut up!" Kate yelled, pretending petulance.

"See what I mean? Sara has not hollered at me once and I bet would never yell at me to shut up!"

"You two are starting to act like a real brother and sister. Right, Kate?"

Kate peeked up and gave Sara a dirty look and answered bitingly: "Right, Sara. Whatever!"

"What was that about?" Mick asked, puzzled at the first sign of friction he had noticed between his sisters—not that he would have likely noticed had there been any before anyway.

"Ne—e—ver mind," Kate said as she laid back and inadvertently placed her hand on Mick's where he was rocking her.

Mick registered that he felt no compulsion to pull his hand away. Physical contact with his sister was beginning to feel natural, comfortable.

"No, I have to get back," Sara said, heaving a big sigh. "I don't know where this case is going to go against Richard's firm, but I'd like to speed it along, which means meetings and more meetings."

"Where would the meetings be?" Mick asked.

"Oh, New York and Washington DC mostly." After a pause: "How do you feel toward Lottie? I've noticed her acting pretty cozy toward you?" Again Kate tilted her head up and she and Sara held eyes for a minute.

"Well, something almost happened between us, but I thought we had agreed since we were working together, nothing was going to."

CHAPTER 19

Again, Kate's head popped up and she removed her hand from Mick's. "What do you mean? What almost happened?"

Mick stopped swinging the hammock, sensing something he didn't understand in Kate's voice. "None of your business, little sis," he answered, trying to sound like he was joking.

Kate swung herself around, knocking Mick's hand away and sitting sideways in the hammock.

"Well, it's probably a good idea not to get involved with someone in the workplace," Sara said, frowning a warning at her sister. "It's against the rules in my line of business."

"Uhhh, not many rules in my line of work. Actually, I'm thinking I'm gonna cut back on my hours. Now that you and Barney will be gone, I've got to get back to my writing, and it looks like Peewee's gonna keep me busy, too. I've never been to Lottie's place, but I'm going over there to discuss how she feels about me working less."

"Oh? When?" Kate's question was thrown at him like a dart.

"That Peewee fella is quite a character," Sara said, rearranging the topic. "I'm certainly glad he's on our side. Please be careful helping him, though. He acts like it's all a big lark. It sounds to me like it could be dangerous. Be careful."

Kate swung off the hammock and tramped into the kitchen.

Both Mick and Sara watched Kate disappear. "What about Barney?" Mick asked Sara after a tense moment. "I couldn't help but notice you two didn't have the warmest parting. Not that I saw anything wrong, but it looked like you two had hit it off."

Sara laid back, putting her hands behind her head and didn't say anything for a while. Mick waited, wondering what that meant. "He's a great guy ..."

"But ... ?"

"Well, I imagine you two talked about us?"

"Yes. But, honest, he didn't want to. He made me promise I wouldn't say anything to you … or even to Kate … not that, apparently, there was that much to talk about."

Sara jerked upright and looked hard at Mick. "You're referring to last night? So, you know about that?"

Mick gulped. That obviously wasn't what she had meant. "Crap! I pulled it out of Barney, honest. He didn't want to tell me. As a matter of fact he made me promise not to let you know we had talked about it. But, sis," Mick grinned guiltily, "when did you realize that your nighty was on inside out?"

Sara slowly shook her head, smiling sheepishly. "You don't think my sweet twin would let that slide? Oh, no. She just, obviously, hadn't told me you two conspired against me. I am embarrassed, you realize? You do know nothing happened? You are aware it's different for a woman than it is for a guy? He was, fortunately, a gentleman. I was intoxicated and that's when mistakes happen, naturally. It might not be a big deal for a guy to get naked with a woman, but it is for a woman; at least it is for me."

Mick felt horrible. This was about something between his best friend and the last woman in the world he'd want to alienate, and he had stupidly said something flippant: "not much to talk about!" He knew he had accomplished his first major faux pas with this sister. "Sorry, sis. You'll learn I'm a dumbshit. I guess I was focusing more on the fact that Barney was noble. You may not have any idea how difficult it is for a guy … I mean, my God, in bed with a gorgeous woman, naked it sounds, and … one I'm sure he really likes … and not do anything? I mean, the man was totally righteous. Of course, being the friend he is, the fact that you're my sister had a lot to do with the lack of … incident."

CHAPTER 19

"'Incident,' eh? Nice euphemism."

"Eh?" Mick said, grinning.

"Eh, what?" Sara responded, frowning.

"Never mind."

"Well, thank you, I guess. I'm still a virgin, thanks to you," Sara said, somewhere between sarcasm and cynicism, and quickly: "You really think I'm gorgeous?"

"Yeah. Who in the hell wouldn't? The most gorgeous virgin I know."

"I should have known you wouldn't let that one go! You don't have much of a filter do you?"

He couldn't tell if she was playing or getting pissed. But he could detect a smittering of a smile, so he went with play. "A filter?"

"Yes, a filter that separates appropriate from inappropriate, insult from injury."

Mick's smile faded fast. "Holy cats, sis. I didn't intend insult or injury."

"Actually," she said, scrunching up her nose, "I think it's rather fun to see just how many steps over the line you think you can get away with. I'm afraid you can probably take as many as you like with me. I find it rather refreshing. Most of my interactions with men are formal, calculated almost. Somehow I don't think you could insult me even if you tried."

Mick sighed with what he thought was relief, but it got stuck in his throat. "Well then," he managed, clearing his throat, "we've got nothing to worry about. There's absolutely no way in hell I'd intentionally ever try to insult or injure you, and something tells me I've got nothin' to worry about from your end. Even an occasional fart would be OK, but somethin' also tells me that ain't gonna happen either."

"The line! I will always remind you, regardless, that there is, indeed, a line." She drained her beer and suddenly whipped her head from side to side. Her hair, about shoulder length and generally neatly styled close, was suddenly loose and flayed rather wildly around her face, narrowing it. This had a startling effect on Mick. It altered her demeanor remarkably. She went from conservative and cute to really quite random and ... sexy, he realized. This unnerved him for some reason.

"Your friend Barney seems acutely aware of where the line is. I haven't heard an uncouth remark from him, the consummate gentleman, unlike someone else I can think of."

"He's indisputably a gentleman." Mick oddly felt a tinge of resentment, competitiveness. "His problem is who'll put up with his obstinacy."

"There's certainly that, but we seemed to agree to disagree."

Hmm, Mick thought, wondering what that really meant or implied. "Well, right, yeah, you guys seemed to hit it off in spite of ... whatever. Anyway, how cool for me: my best friend and new sister." He wanted to feel he meant what he said, but it sounded insincere, even to him.

"I don't know. He's a great guy, but ..."

"But ... ?"

"I've had a little heartbreak ... and I don't want to hurt him."

"You two are a lot alike."

"Maybe too much? What happened to opposites attract?" Sara asked, not expecting an answer.

Kate clomped back onto the porch, right on cue. "You grill or are you as helpless there as in the kitchen?"

Mick and Sara looked at each other, Mick miffed by the interruption and blatant display of distemper, yet clueless, naturally, as to its cause. Sara, of course, understood Kate's

CHAPTER 19

irritation. "I love grilling," Sara said. "Mick, why don't you grab the brats and I could handle one last beer."

"It's a gas grill. I might be able to handle turning on the gas and lighting it."

"Kate 'n' I'll get it started. Go ahead and get the brats and beer."

As with Barney's departure, the mood was a little somber over dinner—Barney hadn't wanted to leave and no one had wanted him to; and Sara didn't want to go, and Kate and Mick didn't want her to. After dinner, they spent the rest of the evening bundled up on the porch. The wind had picked up earlier but died late, and the harbor was pretty as the boat lights slowly burnt into the dusk, reflecting off the calm water. The lighthouse started its endless swivel. They spent most of their time catching up on history: Kate and Sara telling tales of their love of the mountains, Mick his love of northern Minnesota lakes. There was a lot of history to catch up on and, they hoped, a lot to look forward to.

The next day was sober but anything but somber—to start. HS was forewarned to take the day off. The sun was bright as it rose, but an odd shade of yellow. They could see a storm brewing out over the Abaco to the west. The Sea of Abaco was wild out on the horizon. Fortunately, Lottie's Windsor Craft was a 40 hardtop, translating into forty-two-feet long, a twelve-foot beam with an enclosed cabin so, even though the ferry had cancelled their excursion to Marsh Harbour in fear of what might be coming, they bounded along safe and sound for a while. Soon it started to rain, but it was a cozy little party in the cabin. Spense and Lottie were maybe a little too buoyant in an attempt to calm Sara's nerves, which were already raw, with her leaving her sister—if the plane was able to fly out in the storm.

The wind and rain had increased and, by the time they got docked and to the taxi, they were all wet and chilled. The rain continued, but the wind abated enough for the private SEC jet to get off. There had been hugs all around, and Spense and Lottie remained upbeat, almost effusive, intuiting the emotion that was going to be spilled between Kate and Sara. And sure enough, at the final hug, Kate and Sara broke down. Mick, who had remained relatively calm, nearly fell apart himself—for Kate, for Sara who he did not want to say goodbye to, and for himself.

As always when living away, no matter how beautiful it is or how exciting, when you are reminded of home, you start missing family, friends, a promising spring breeze, the bittersweet crispness of fall, even the wonderful cold bite of a blizzard. It's hard and lonely at times. So, Barney having left and Sara now gone, loneliness was bound to be an emotion Mick and Kate would be sharing for a while; at least they would be sharing it together, Mick thought. Misery does, indeed, need as well as love company.

CHAPTER 20

THE RIDE back was tense. The release of emotions wore everyone out. Spense and Lottie were no longer cheerful. It felt like the party was over. Sara and Barney had made an impression, leaving their visit seem almost like it had been an Irish wake. Lottie handled the rough seas masterfully. Spense, a seasoned seaman, quietly enjoyed the turbulent ride. Mick and Kate allowed themselves to be tossed around in the cabin like rag dolls, almost limp in the melancholy of loss.

After dropping Mick and Kate off, Lottie decided to dock for the night in the relative calm of Hope Town Harbor and spend the night on Spense's yacht rather than try to maneuver into her little harbor. She had told Mick if the weather improved, they could ride to her place in the Windsor the next day and she'd drive him home in her jeep after dinner.

Mick and Kate, cold and wet, hunkered down in the cart for the chilly ride back to the cottage. Kate headed upstairs when they got back, saying she was going to take a hot bath. After, she disappeared into her room. When Mick knocked later to see if she was interested in anything to eat, she didn't answer.

Mick had been unable to find any motivation to write or even read, so he had gone to bed almost before it was dark. He had lain silently in bed listening for Kate in her room. He hadn't heard any crying, but neither did he hear the raspy breathing signaling she was asleep. Should he offer consolation?

Would she want to commiserate? He started, instead, to focus on the sound of the wind swirling and the rain slapping and he fell asleep, fitfully, waking and wondering intermittently.

He woke before daylight. He lay there. Still no sound from Kate's room. No wind, no rain, but he could feel cool, damp air drifting in through the window. Hopefully the storm had passed. He wondered if HS would come after such violent weather. He went down in the dark, put on the habitual pot of coffee, and looked to see if there were any blueberry muffins left. Finding none, he poured himself a cup, slipped on a sweater, and walked out onto the porch.

"Good morning, sir," came from the dark below him.

Although spoken in her cottony, delicate voice, it startled him and he jerked, spilling his coffee. "My gosh. You absolutely scared the sh— crap out of me."

"Sorry, sir. If we're ever to be friends, as you say, you can say 'shit' in front of me. I am almost twenty, a bona fide adult in my world."

"What are you doing here so early in the dark?"

She walked up the steps onto the porch, surprising him. "I'll take a blanket and sit on the porch this morning, if OK with you, sir?"

Once again, he couldn't help but smile at her words. Everything she said came out so … graceful, almost refined. "There's an afghan on the settee. Grab it and sit over here on this chair. I'll go in to warm up my coffee."

He disappeared into the kitchen to heat his coffee and a cup of water for tea. He knew she would refuse if he asked. As he came back out, she had her feet pulled up under her in the Adirondacks chair and was entirely wrapped in the afghan. In the thin light now on the porch, it was almost as

CHAPTER 20

if a filter had been put over his eyes, like on a lens to soften the image. He had always thought of her as a cute young girl or, now, a woman. This morning, with her features faint and silky in the half-light, she looked pretty, beautiful. Maybe her telling him that she was almost twenty made him realize that in spite of her fragile figure, she was a woman. Her hair, which was usually combed back, was hanging loose and it provided the perfect frame for her fine-boned face. In the predawn under glow, she could have been ten or forty and sitting for a portrait.

"Why are you standing there holding my tea and your coffee, sir? Thank you for knowing that I would have refused the tea. It will feel good this morning. Don't s'pose you have another muffin? We don't get those around our place."

His smile turned to a wide grin. "Sorry, I already searched for a muffin, but no luck."

"Well, the tea will be nice … if you're going to give it to me."

The grin was now a laugh. "Sorry. You look quite beautiful this morning," he told her as he handed her the cup.

Since she didn't answer but seemed intent on playing with the tea bag, he assumed he had embarrassed her. "Since you're so early today, could we take a little time and talk about your writing?"

She looked up from her tea cup and smiled that quiet smile of hers. "Yes. I was hoping you had time. But I certainly didn't expect you to be up so early. I was actually hoping to catch your *sister*."

"Oh? How come?"

"Well, I wanted to talk to her about her proposal to teach the island boys, and what I wrote for today is for her. You didn't give me an assignment last time. I know she must be feeling down with her sister leaving yesterday."

"Oh, you remembered that?"

"Of course. We women are more aware of and sensitive to feelings than you men are, I'm afraid."

"You 'women,' huh?"

"You don't think of me as a woman?"

"To be honest, I don't know what to think of you. You're an anachronism to me."

"Hmmm, anachronism. When I've seen that word, it seems like they mean an irony? Is that good?"

"It's neither good nor bad. It's not a judgment. I mean it in a good sense, though, like you're timeless. You seem young, innocent on one hand, and wise, mature on the other. A mystery."

"A mystery? I'll take that as a compliment, sir."

"Speaking of ironies: I've been thinking of ways to assist you in your writing, since I understand I am your teacher. You also have a very anachronistic style of writing that's … instinctive, I guess I'd say."

"You're going to have to explain that one to me, sir."

"Well, like you, your style seems simplistic on one hand and yet universal in its meaning on the other. So is your art. And I'm not able to suggest improvements. You're already an artist. I'm actually trying to find the artist in myself, without much luck I might add."

"Just inspiring me, sir, makes you an artist."

MP found himself caught in an incongruous web of emotions every time he talked to her. Everything she said made him smile, yet he was always a little choked up as well. "Well, thank you, HS. What I might suggest is to have you write a

CHAPTER 20

daily journal to help you get even more inspiration for your writing."

"Yes, sir. I do keep a ... well, journal, I suppose. It is where I find shelter from my insanity."

Holy shit! Shelter from her insanity? Mick decided to think about that one. "Well, how about I try to give you ideas that you might not consider otherwise?"

"Sure, sir. Like what?"

"Well, like looking for ironies, for example, and writing them down."

"OK. Could you give me an example, please?"

"Well, take for instance the developers of the west side of the island. They think that by developing a big tourist attraction, more visitors will come to the island, yet the reason visitors come to the island is for the peace, tranquility, and escape from 'progress.'"

"It reminds me of what that baseball guy, Yogi Berry or something, said: 'That restaurant is so popular, nobody goes there anymore.' Yes, I've thought about progress. I don't want to be opposed to progress. It is inevitable and there's no sense in fighting it. But if their idea of progress is that every bird sings the same song, that may look like progress, but it's actually regression. All these developments look the same: little boxes piled one on top of another with a 'garden view' or 'ocean view.' Think how terrible it would be if we woke up one day and every bird's whistle was the same."

Holy shit, MP thought again. And I'm trying to help her? It's much more like she's my teacher. How in the hell did she know about Yogi Berra? Probably Peewee.

"But you're right, I do see the irony. So I could write one day about trivial daily ironies, like: 'the more you hurry, the longer it takes you.' Or 'the less a person explains, the more he says.' Or one I've experienced in my brief, simple life: 'The harder you love somebody, the more you drive them away'—rather like the trite cliché about squeezing a handful of sand."

Was he seeing a cynical side of her he'd never noticed before? He was constantly surprised by women, this little one being such a tantalizing mystery, maybe the surprise of all his surprises.

"Sorry, sir," she added quietly. "I just haven't had much luck in my relationships in this small corner of the world, and the irony there is that although I love the Abaco horizon, if I don't expand on that horizon, will the sunsets all start to look the same?"

"Umm," Mick couldn't think of a response that wouldn't have been inadequate.

"But," she said, apparently sensing she needed to fortify his efforts, "I saw a film the other day of students in France protesting the lack of jobs in their poor economy and their inability to find employment. Many had spiked or colored hair, conspicuous tattoos, unorthodox clothing. What kind of jobs did they think they were going to get? Who'd hire them? There's an irony right up your alley, I'd guess. I'll write something about that one. What do you think, sir?"

Well, Mick was no longer smiling and he had no idea what to think. Of course, she was right. But where did that sardonic, scornful vitriol in this darling island-raised young woman come from? It surprised him. Fortunately, he was saved by Kate's sudden appearance.

"Good morning, you two." Mick realized the day had dawned, a little muggy, still cool, but sunny and calm.

"Did you have a bad night's sleep last night, ma'am?"

CHAPTER 20

"Kate," Kate said. "Please call me Kate. Do I look that bad?"

"Oh, no, ma'am. I just guessed you'd be sad with your sister leaving yesterday."

"So I look sad?"

HS handed Mick her empty cup. "I have something in the folder for you, ma'am."

"Kate," Kate said again.

"I was hoping to find you up early this morning to discuss with you what you wanted to do with the boys. Would it work out if I sent a couple around after lunch, say one o'clock? I do need to go now."

"Well, yes. That's fine."

"Just talk to them and see what you think. I guarantee—well, I should say my father guarantees—they'll be good. They've not been the most ideal students in the past. But they respect my father and will do what he says."

"I hope I earn their respect," Kate answered.

"Oh, when they realize you're simply trying to help them, you will. Don't worry. Again, thank you, and I'm sorry your sister had to leave. Bye," and she slipped away.

Kate turned and walked back into the kitchen.

"You want me to wait to read the newest?" Mick yelled. "It's meant for you after all. It's pretty obvious her writing is no mistake. And the sketch makes me very curious about whatever she wrote."

There was no answer. Kate walked back out. "I'm just getting myself some coffee, for crying out loud. Here, hand me the folder." She grabbed it, sat down, and read the poem silently to herself and studied the sketch. "Well, that is remarkably insightful. It's exactly how I feel."

Mick took the folder from Kate and read to himself:

> There are raw days
> that make me cringe and
> hide away. And there are
> chilling people who cut and
> bruise with sharp-edged
> words and cold, hard eyes.
> These are times when I
> feel too fragile to go out
> into the world:
> When friends hurt
> and hate hurts
> and goodbyes hurt
>
> —H.S.

Mick read it over several times, trying to figure out what Kate meant by, "It's exactly how I feel." He supposed yesterday qualified as a raw day here in the tropics. But who are the chilling people? Who said anything cruel? What friends hurt? Me? And 'hate hurts'? Was she thinking about Richard? Or himself, he considered from the way she was acting? He was hoping it was a temporary despondency due to saying goodbye to Sara. And, if it was insightful, how could that little island hobgoblin know how she felt?

Finally: "Were you upset with me yesterday?" he asked her.

No answer.

"Did Lottie or Spense say something to hurt you?"

She looked like she might cry.

"Sorry. We don't have to talk about it now. I just don't understand."

"Of course not. You wouldn't."

CHAPTER 20

This pissed him off. "Look. I feel bad Sara left. I feel bad Barney left. It was nice of Lottie to take us to Marsh Harbour in that kind of weather. The ferry wasn't even running. If it weren't for them, Sara wouldn't have made her plane. I just don't get it."

"Look," Kate said on the verge of temper and tears, "I know they were acting all chipper to cheer me up. I just wasn't in the mood to be cheerful, OK?"

"I can understand that, but ... what'd I do?"

"Nothing. Just leave it. Don't you know what 'too fragile' means? Aren't you supposed to be meeting Lottie the Hottie?"

"Lottie the Hottie? Jesus, she's your friend, too. If you don't want me to leave, I won't."

"No, I want you to go."

"Oh, thanks."

"Look, I really just want to be left alone, OK? Goodbye." And she hurried off the porch. Mick heard her cup rattle in the sink and she stomped up the stairs and her door slammed shut.

OK, now what to do? He wanted to hug her, maybe spend the day sulking and commiserating. Maybe lie around and watch a movie. But the way she said 'goodbye,' he knew she meant it.

THE DAY was starting to warm up nicely, the sun taking over. He emailed Lottie and she emailed back saying she'd pick him up at the Cap'n's dock in her Windsor Craft. "Why not make a day of it?" she had said. "We both have the day off; let's make use of it." So they skipped across the Sea of Abaco to Nippers, once again—the trendy, popular bar on the small cay where Spense sometimes played—and had lunch and a few drinks.

BACK TO THE ISLAND

On the way back Lottie pulled out a joint. It wasn't until after the second puff Mick noticed how clear the air and deep blue the sky, a few wisps of clouds playing here and there; the amazing expanse of aqua appearing in front of him as if lit from below; the effortless plane of the Windsor as it sliced the waves; and the absolutely gorgeous woman next to him, her slender fingers wrapped easily around the wheel. In the sun, her freckles came alive and her cheeks and shoulders took on a light blushing, her hair turned a deeper red. In the angle of the afternoon sun, her beach dress, tantalizingly slid off one shoulder, lost its opaqueness. He could see the lightness of the tender swell above her swimming top, the roundness of her paler bottom, the silhouette and shape of her legs. The thong, her exposed shoulder, her auburn hair curling around her face in the backdraft of the wind, her beach dress blown tight against her thighs forming a rather delicious delta; everything about the moment and her became almost unbearably exciting and enticing.

He leaned in and kissed her on the ear, bit her lobe gently. She immediately stopped the boat, letting it drift in calm, open water, turned, cuddled comfortably into him, and kissed him on the mouth. He let her nibble his lips without returning the kiss. He slowly spread them and her tongue touched his. First a flick, then both tongues entangled like wrestling to capture a cherry in warm sluice. Wrapped tight in a full embrace, she writhed against him, sliding her hand beneath his suit in the back and tantalizingly slipping it around to the front. This was more than he could handle. He whipped her dress off over her head. As he untied her bikini top, they stumbled, still trying to embrace, into the cuddy. This time he had no trouble getting it up, keeping it up, and losing it

CHAPTER 20

in a sensationally sensual release. She didn't seem to mind.

They went to her place in Coconut Grove: a small, for Coconut Grove, cute stucco red-tiled villa on a little hill surrounded by palm trees and flowering bushes. They showered together and she pushed him against the shower wall and, once again, he had no problem getting it up, and she got it down ecstatically in by far the best oral sex he had ever had.

In the kitchen, Lottie started cooking dinner, adorning herself in only an oversized dress shirt which she had not bothered to button, causing his hormones to rage. Figuring it only fair play, he arranged her on the chopping block island and returned the favor—the only time he had given a woman oral sex other than his wife. She came dramatically and shamelessly, her back arched and arms gripping the edge of the island, pots and pans having clattered to the floor. Her breathy wail as she climaxed, the only sound to Mick surpassing in beauty that of loons.

After dinner, Lottie asked if he wanted to settle in and watch a movie. Although the thought of cuddling on the couch was tempting, he apologized and told her that Kate had been really down after Sara left and he felt he should get back and check on her.

"You sure?" she cooed, as she pushed him onto the couch and straddled him, thighs spread, facing him on the cushions. She had changed out of the now food-stained, oversized dress shirt to an undersized, semi-sheer beach dress—no suit, or anything, under this time. He was still in his swim suit. Rather than kiss him, she started biting his lips and flicking her tongue. She stretched, pulling up her shift, and slid her breasts against his face. When he didn't respond, she grabbed his hair in both hands, directing his mouth to her nipples.

Although his heart was racing, driving out blood wildly, all of it seemed to go to his head, and he felt his face first flush then feel like it would burst. He wrapped his arms around her and stood up, Lottie sliding down his body until her toes tickled the floor.

"Well, it doesn't feel like your gentleman down there is interested?"

True, his "gentleman" had not stood up before he did. A sign, he assumed, that it was a good time to call it a night. He gave her a brief, firm attempt at a parting kiss, holding it for a second, and put his hands on her shoulders. "This is the most fun I've had in a long, long time," he told her. "Thank you."

"We never made it to the bedroom," she teased, running her tongue from his chin to his upper lip. "Don't you want to check out my bed?"

"Lord, you do make it difficult to leave."

"That's the idea, Romeo. This is also the most fun I've had in a long, long time. My only sleeping partner on Elbow Cay has been Spense, and his gentleman can no longer tip his hat."

"Oh, and how do you know that?"

"He told me, whatcha think? What? You jealous of Spense?"

He laughed and held her away. "Well, yes, I am. But it has nothing to do with sex or sleeping. I've never had a ride in your jeep. I really want to check on Kate. Ready?"

"You think I should go like this?"

"Uh, no, as a matter of fact."

"Afraid Kate'll see me?"

He hadn't thought of that. But, no, he would get dropped off in Hope Town and guide his cart as guilelessly as possible back to Kate. But, what difference should it make if Kate knew about the day? Why should he feel any guile or guilt? He was

CHAPTER 20

beginning to sense Kate resented "Hot Lottie." Why? And why did he actually feel guilty? But he did. Not about Lottie; she was a big girl, and the passion had been totally consensual and reciprocal. "It's not Kate I'm worried about," he lied.

"Yet, you're leaving?" She wriggled back onto him. "Then, I guess I'd better change." She lifted her shift up over her head, removing it this time. He could feel her nipples hardening against his bare chest as she wormed back into him, tickling the back of his neck. Now, both sweaty, she slid slightly up and down. He tried not think about what the breasts were doing. But then she started a gentle grind, reminding him of another of her attributes. He still resisted; she slowly licked his lips, tongue lingering, entering, until his gentleman was duly impressed, stood up, and informed him: "Hey, it doesn't look like we're leaving."

An interesting hour later, they were in Lottie's Wrangler breezing through the evening toward Hope Town. It was a balmy night and the palms on the side of the road swayed like drunken traffic cops as they passed, either waving them on or hailing a warning.

After being dropped off at the pier and being given a parting kiss, he slowly wandered to his cart, maneuvered it over the cobblestones and through the shifting shadows on the quiet lane, to the cottage, parking the cart in the back. When he walked in the back, he noticed the glow of a light out on the porch. He kicked off his shoes and padded out to the porch to find Kate on the settee, book in lap, eyes closed. Was it guilt he was feeling? It was something. If guilt, why?

He could tell from her breathing that she wasn't asleep. "How you doin', hon? Feeling better?"

She opened her eyes. "Bet you are."

OK. Now what? Do you ask what she means? Didn't seem like a good idea. Can't really say: Yeah, I feel great: got a blow job and laid twice. But then, if she wanted this open relationship, why shouldn't he be comfortable sharing? Some instinct camping near his amygdala directed him to flight rather than fight. But leaving without a response seemed like an admission of something, some behavior he couldn't confess to: "Bless me, Kate, for I have sinned." It was actually confession that caused him to leave the Catholic faith. When Martha had gotten pregnant before they were married, he felt he had committed no sin and didn't feel it was anybody else's job to judge him. He tried to convince himself that he felt no compulsion to judge himself tonight.

"Why are you just standing there? Did you have fun?" The tone of her voice did not match the words. She said "have fun" like it was something you would do in purgatory.

"Yeah. We did have fun. It was a nice distraction before we get back to our problems."

"Distraction?"

"Well, yeah, I guess."

"What did you do all day?"

"Uh, nothing."

"Nothing, eh?"

OK, stupid. That's exactly what a teenage kid responds when he's been drinking Slow Gin or looking at a *Playboy* when confronted by his parents. "OK, we went to Kippers, had a drink and a bite. Cruised around the Abaco. Went to her place: it's really cool. A little stucco villa, white with red tile roof, on the top of the south end hill on the Coconut Grove harbor."

"Nice bedroom?"

"Then we had dinner …"

CHAPTER 20

"Skipped the bedroom?"

It was coming down to how to tell the truth—although maybe a 'convenient truth.' But he had learned lying eventually came back to bite you. So, what's he say: that she not only had a good bedroom but cuddy, shower, and cutting block as well?

"Well?"

"There are two bedrooms, as a matter of fact. They were both very nice, so was the kitchen, living room …"

"Nice master, or should I say 'mistress' bedroom?"

What the shit? He decided to screw it and be blunt. "What are you doing?" he said and sat on the corner of the settee. "You sound like you're jealous of Lottie."

"What do I have to be jealous of Lottie for?"

OK. She was going to be better than him at this game. Probably a game he was predestined to lose from the kick off. "I don't know. Sorry. I think I'll head up to the perch. I haven't had any time to write. I need to get caught up."

"Could have had all day today."

He wasn't going to bite. "Spense and Lottie are coming over before work tomorrow afternoon to discuss our plan. I wanted to take the kayak and check something out in the morning. Maybe we could get a tandem … for two …"

"I know what a 'tandem' is."

"All right." He had seen inklings of this side of her. He supposed her mood would improve with a night's sleep and then the prospect of forming a plan so she wouldn't feel like hidden prey. The pressure of the unknown was probably getting to her. "Well, if you want, I can call and have a tandem brought to the harbor and we can go out together, or you can have your own. Most of the rentals are tandem, but I'm sure I can get a single if you want. That is, if you want to go?"

"Sure. Why not?" Kate answered and rolled over on the settee and closed her eyes.

Mick headed up to his perch, initially intent on writing something, but made a detour when he passed his bedroom and headed to bed. He knew he was never going to be able to focus tonight ... on anything. He might as well disappear into the obscurity of sleep, the shallow sleep of guilt as it turned out.

DATE: Tuesday, Mar. 9, 2012, 10:00 p.m.
Kate: Sara? You there? I know it's late, but I haven't heard anything from you lately, so I thought I'd check.

Sara: Hi, hon. Yup, I'm up. Just got to my room. I'm in DC. Good timing. They flew me directly from Miami to Washington for some meetings. One of the senators wasn't too happy with me for being down there. I was tired, and I can't believe I did it, but I told him "tough shit." Can you believe it? A senator! Some of these guys can be real assholes. Their agenda is the only agenda. And it's all for show, anyway. It's hard to know who's in bed with Wall Street and who you can trust. Money and politics make abominable bed partners. It would be nice if ethics and politics at least got together for a cocktail one in a while, but the more time I spend here in Washington, the more I realize ethics and politics is a contradiction in terms. So, sorry I hadn't gotten back to you yet. I've been under the gun and my little retort got me into hot water. (Sorry for mixing my metaphors.) It's what I get for spending time with you. You start to rub off on me.

CHAPTER 20

Kate: What? I mix my metaphors?

Sara: Very funny. It's the hot water part I'm talking about. Speaking of that, how are things down there?

Kate: Well, I guess we're having a planning session tomorrow afternoon.

Sara: You're the prime topic of conversation up here. Most of the committee believes our case for fraud would hold up with your testimony backing the source of the emails. BUT, this is really weird. The senator I got in trouble with, he asked if I was visiting you on Prince Edward Island! Where did he get that idea? Isn't that where Spense said he has his dish or whatever pointed? Where the satellite sends his server?

Kate: No shit! That can't be a coincidence. He must be talking to Richard or somebody.

Sara: I know. As I said, you don't know who you can trust. I was able to avoid answering him. And then I have a message from Richard saying he wants to talk to me.

Kate: Shit. What are you going do?

Sara: Talk to him, I suppose. You'll have to contact me after your meeting and tell me what you decide—before I talk to him. How's Mick? Gosh, Kate, I really liked him—brother or no.

Kate: I've been a bitch, Sara. He spent the day yesterday with Lottie. When he got home last night, I could tell he had slept with her. The fool is an open book.

Sara: Oh, Katie. Why don't you just tell him?

Kate: It's too late now.

Sara: What do you mean? Of course it's not too late.

Kate: I think it is. Anyway, I'll think about it. OK if I call you now?

Sara: You won't get me during the day, so you can leave a message. I've got my cell, and the prepaid still has more time. So you can call me on either in the evening, although I'm frequently in meetings or out. It might be best if you just e me. I get those on my phone, you know. Or just text me when to call you.

Kate: I will. I'll either send you an e or if I call, when most likely might you be available?

Sara: God, there's no way of telling. Like I said, just leave a message. If I'm not available I'll get back to you. Kate, hon, don't let this ruin your relationship with Mick. He doesn't deserve it. I hate to say it, but you made your own bed with this one, and it's not his fault he's not in it.

Kate: Oh, fine. You've got to slap on me one of those stupid double entendres the fool's been going on and on about lately. Ouch!

Sara: You're not mad?

Kate: Not at you.

Sara: Or Mick?

Kate: No, yes, I don't know. Later.

A seagull screeched outside the window and Mick sat up, alarmed and now irritably wide awake. The dream he was in hadn't made sense but it was ominous. Something bad was going to happen to someone, somewhere. It dawned on him that Kate was supposed to meet with the island boys yesterday,

CHAPTER 20

and in the daze of his diversion yesterday, he had forgotten about it. Was that why she was so uptight? Then, that it was morning dawned on him. He went to the window and looked down. It was still early and the morning dim yet. HS was not there and he wondered if Kate might be awake. He felt terribly guilty for not asking her about the boys last night.

He had a chill so he wrapped his sweater around himself and crept over to her door. Just as he leaned, putting his ear against the door to see what he could hear, Kate opened it. He left his head there, trying to be funny, but immediately regretted it as all he could see was the hem of an undershirt and two bare legs. "Sorry I was such a bitch yesterday," she said through a yawn and hugged him before he could lift his head.

Knowing her untethered breasts were bookends for his skull, he pulled free and held her away. "I'm sorry. I completely forgot to ask you about the boys coming over yesterday. How did it go?"

She leaned back into him and gave him a little squeeze, laying the side of her face against his shoulder. "Just hold me for a minute, OK? I really am sorry about yesterday."

He was proud of himself. Surprisingly the only thing aroused was his curiosity. "So, sis, how did it go?"

She stood back and grabbed his hands. He kept his eyes directed at her eyes. "I just *talked* with some of them yesterday. Tomorrow we have our first class. Let me get dressed and let's go downstairs. Get the coffee started, I'll make muffins, and we'll sit on the porch. We've got a lot to talk about."

When he got down into the kitchen, Mick peeked out onto the porch, and sure enough, HS was there, sitting on the steps with a blanket-like thing wrapped around her. "Morning. Be right out," he yelled.

"Sorry, do you mind finishing up the coffee and doing up a cup of tea for Senorita?" he asked Kate as she hit the bottom of the stairs.

"Mick, *we* need to talk," she whispered, seeming irritated HS was there. "Oh, go ahead on out. I'll bring coffee and tea."

"Porch or steps this morning?" he asked Heidi as he walked out.

She smiled up at him. "The porch; why not?"

As they settled into the deck chairs, he noticed the blanket was more like a square poncho. "So, wrapped in your own warmth this morning, huh? Is it a poncho?"

She pulled her legs up under herself and with her arms tucked under the blanket she looked like a teepee with a head. "Actually it's called a ruana. It's not much more than a blanket with a slit for my head. But they're cool … ha, ha. On a chilly morning like this, I put it on and it does keep me warm. When the day warms I can fold it and throw it over my shoulder. Works good."

"Are they common here in the Bahamas? I've never seen one."

She smiled her demure little smile again, like she knew secrets about the sea. "No. I doubt anyone else would have one. My mother brought it back from South America. She said Bogota, where she was, was over eight thousand feet and so could be very cold in the morning but hot by midday because of its proximity to the equator. So, very practical they are."

"Indeed," Mick said, playing off her quaint, almost formal mannerisms.

Kate walked out and handed Mick his mug and HS her cup and saucer. "Good morning, miss," Kate greeted, knowing HS would call her ma'am.

"Good morning, ma'am. I hear you met the island boys yesterday."

CHAPTER 20

"Yes. There were seven of them."

"That's all you're going to get, I'm afraid. There are a couple: one—too proud, another—too ignorant to think you could teach them anything. The ignorant one is Harvey, the one you may have seen with the broad face. He's very insecure. I don't trust him. The other is small and very proud. Oddly, he's the leader of the pack. That's Rashi."

"Oh, yeah. I've noticed him, I think," Mick said. "He seemed like the sharpest one. I'm surprised he's not interested."

"He's actually my best friend in the group. He is, what I suppose you'd say, the wisest, most street smart. But he has trouble with reading, and his writing skills are poor."

"Maybe he has a learning disability," Kate suggested.

"Yes, I'm sure. But he's very embarrassed by it."

"He sounds like your stepfather," Mick said.

"You can call him my father, sir. He is now. But yes, exactly. That's why my father would like you to do his writing for him. He knows what needs to be said but can't formulate the words. He has dis—"

"Dyslexia?" Kate said.

"Yes. That's what he said."

"You know your father was the smartest kid I knew back then. But he did poorly in school."

"Yes. I know the story. That's why he rails on about the school system so much. Says they don't understand reality and teach a lot of, excuse me, bullshit."

Both Kate and Mick laughed. "Bullshit" sounded so incongruous coming through her delicate lips, although HS did not laugh.

"I really liked him in grade school. He saved my ass several times."

"Oh? He just said you were nice to everyone unless they crossed you, and then you had a bad temper. He said you were otherwise pretty smart but that he taught you a lesson about your temper."

"Ha! That he did. That he did."

"The boys told you where you would be teaching them?" HS asked Kate.

"Uh, yes, they did. They didn't want to have class here but at their clubhouse? That they would stop by and get me to bring me there?"

"Yes, that's their special place. It's actually an honor that they're letting you go there. I've never seen it … well, I've seen it, but I've never been inside. It's well hidden. No girls are allowed."

"Why me then? And why there?"

"You'll have to be considered androgynous: their 'teacher.' I don't think they want it to be common knowledge that they're in 'school'!"

"They're embarrassed?"

"Well, not embarrassed exactly, but they have what they believe is a reputation to maintain. You'd best not be telling anyone."

"Hmmm, OK, I won't."

"Well, what do you have for us today?" Mick asked her.

Kate excused herself to get Mick more coffee and HS more hot water and a fresh tea bag, and then disappeared inside.

"If you recall, you requested that I take note of double entendres. In thinking about this, I suspect the most prominent use is in sexual innuendoes? Implying one thing but solicitously meaning another. Maybe a way to flirt?"

Mick, once again, realized he was always caught a little off guard by her innocent yet sophisticated perceptions and so, almost constantly grinning, replied, "Yes. I'd say you're right."

CHAPTER 20

"Do you know the Traveling Wilburys?"

Mick nodded. "Sure. Love 'em."

"Me too. You know the song 'Dirty World'?"

"Yeah, it's one by Dylan ..."

"Yes. I believe those are all a bunch of double entendres."

"Hmmm, like what?" He knew he shouldn't have been, but he was surprised: that she even knew the song, and although he couldn't remember exactly, he loved what Dylan had done with the words and so, he was guessing she was going to re-create them here for him.

"I particularly like, 'You don't need no wax job, you're smooth enough for me. If you need your oil changed, I'll do it for you free. Oh, baby, the pleasure'd be all mine if you ...'" She looked up into her eyelids. "Let's see, something like, 'If you let me drive your pickup truck and park it where the sun don't shine.' I think that's it. That's where I had gotten the idea for mine. And then he does several: 'I love your fuel injection. I love your five-speed gear box. I love your parts and service' and others. I'd guess these would qualify?"

By the time she was done, Mick was shaking with laughter. She had tried to use a pseudo sexy tone to say the lines and it was hilarious coming from the head at the top of a tent. "Yup, you're right. They qualify."

"So I found this old entry in my diary that I had jotted down one rainy night, back when I thought I was in love. I believe it qualifies as well."

"Well, shall we read it?"

"No. I'd rather you waited until I've gone. Do you have any suggestions before I go?"

"You know, what I am really impressed with is your way of saying so much with so few words."

"Like what, sir?"

BACK TO THE ISLAND

"Well, have you ever heard of William Carlos Williams?"

"No, sir."

"He wrote a poem that I've always loved. It's short and so I know it by heart. The title is: 'This is Just to Say.' It goes:

> This is Just to Say
> I have eaten
> the plums
> that were in the ice box
>
> and which
> you were probably
> Saving
> for breakfast
>
> Forgive me
> they were delicious
> so sweet
> and so cold.

"On the surface it appears trite and meaningless. But it's like an allegory for so many things. Or like a song, 'Back to the Island,' by Leon Russell. He meets a woman, like in a city somewhere, and he breaks up with her because 'I just had to go back to the island.' We all have our island, you know? Some person, thing, place, or comfort we need, must return to."

"Oh, yes. I know. My mother, for instance: literally and figuratively. Yet here I am, as you know from 'History of My World,' feeling I must leave my island."

"Yes. I understand. The danger is, I suppose, if you can't get back if you need to … or, if you do, the island, literally and figuratively, isn't the same."

CHAPTER 20

"It will be if Peewee has his way. I must be leaving. I really enjoyed your 'plum' poem. I'll see what I can do. Bye, sir. Thank your, well, Kate, for me. She seemed a bit off this morning, but I do like her. She is lovely and tries to be understanding. So, I apologize. Admittedly, I didn't want to share my morning time with you with anyone else either. I've realized something in myself and other women: we tend to be territorial. I don't know why she should be with me. I'm not a threat, am I, sir? Bye now."

What the hell? Mick thought. Just what did she mean by that? Have I just been mentored by that little ragamuffin?

"SO, YOU'VE kayaked before?" Mick asked Kate as he pushed them out into the harbor and jumped into the back of a bright red tandem he had rented for the day.

"I told you, Bozo, I am the athletic one. Of course I have. Where we grew up there were tons of lakes and rivers. Dad, your dad, got us a cabin on a little lake—Rose Lake—in the Coeur d'Alene area of Idaho, not too far from Spokane. We kayaked all the time. Of course, if it was with Sara, we went tandem, and I, see, was the one in the back."

"You wanna switch?"

"No, I'll bow, no pun intended, to tradition. Allow you to be the man."

"Hey, pretty quick there. We can alternate. I don't care."

"Just giving you shit, bro! You're the one who knows where we're going anyway. By the way, where are we headed?"

"We'll head out of the harbor and down the west side of the north end."

"By where we are—our cottage I mean?" Kate asked, pulling off her T-shirt, leaving her wearing a white sports bra—thank

God—long canvas khaki-colored quick-dry pants, and Tevas. The perfect kayaking outfit, as long as it stayed dry.

His wife Martha had been relatively small-breasted like Kate, and so could also get by both braless and exposed sports bra. No problem, until one day when MP and Martha had been on a bike ride up in northern Minnesota on a hot day. They had stopped by a beach and dove in to cool off. When they walked out of the water, Martha might as well not have had a bra on at all. It had been totally transparent. MP had almost peed, then decided to do something else with it. They *were* alone on the beach and, it being their first year of marriage, had headed right back into the water. But ... that had been his wife, they were married, they were in love, and so his reaction to the see-through bra was totally understandable ... and acceptable. *But*, this was his sister, and she would not be getting wet. He was almost surprised but relieved for sure that at least she was wearing a bra of any sort. He simply didn't understand her compulsion to always assail convention ... or whatever it was she was doing.

Kate turned and looked at him. He had quit paddling. "So, you want to be in the back so I don't know that you aren't paddling, eh? Is that it?"

"Eh?" he said, mocking her. Mick whipped off his shirt as well. It was becoming a typical day in the tropics, maybe a little warm for March: blue sky, blue water, and only a light breeze, so easy paddling. "Might as well get some sun, too," he said. "Let's swing by Spense's boat on the way out. Say 'hi.'"

"You want to stop?"

"Naw. Just yell hello if we see him. We don't have time to stop."

CHAPTER 20

As they came around a vintage Hatteras, they paddled between two of the largest yachts: Spense's and a sleek sailing yacht with the name "Tosca III" on the side. "See him?" Mick yelled to Kate.

"Shhh," Kate hoarse-whispered and pointed up toward the mast of Spense's yacht. "Look! Do you see him?"

"No," Mick said as he steered behind the Plowed Mary. For the first time he noticed the make of the vessel, Oyster, plated in gold on the port side. "Where?"

"Shhh," Kate whispered again, her hand on the side of her mouth directing her voice back to Mick. "Look at the mast, near the bottom. He's hanging there, from the boom, or whatever it's called, upside down."

"Oh, oh, oh yeah. No shit. He is," Mick said, shading his eyes.

"What the hell?" Kate said. "He think he's a bat or something?"

Mick laughed.

"Shhh, he'll hear you," Kate said.

"So what?"

"Because, I mean, what the hell's he doing?"

"Well, I doubt he thinks he's a bat."

"Oh shut up, fool. Just tell me what he's doing."

"He's probably stretching his back."

"What? By hanging upside down like a frickin' vampire?"

Now Mick's turn to shush her. He steered them by and headed out of the harbor.

"What do you suppose his neighbors think ... on the other boats?"

"You're nuts," Mick chided. "Shut up before he hears you."

"What? He has special bat hearing? Don't tell me I'll come up to your perch one night and find you hanging there?"

"I don't know, maybe … who knows? You're the fool. Now turn around and paddle, will ya before I bite your neck."

When they cleared the harbor, they turned right out of the channel and cut between a little island completely encompassed by a large pink stucco villa, and the point. The tide was low, just coming in, and it got so shallow they had to get out and walk the kayak over a sand bar.

"Is it like this all along this side of the island?" Kate asked.

"Pretty much. It's all sand and kind of gets a little deeper in some places but shallow in most."

"So, why we going here?"

"Well, when we get down by our place and beyond, the cottages have some docks. They're longer than hell, but there are obviously ways for a boat to get in and out. So, I want to check the accesses. I think it has to be high tide for a motorized boat to get into shore … or out."

"So, you're thinking of Richard?"

"Yeah, of course. These are all private places along here. They're not islanders."

"They're not?"

"Well, they're more like permanent resorters. Most, if any, don't live here year round, but they're back every season. Some rent out their places."

"So you're wondering how or if Richard would be seen if he came ashore along here."

"Exactly. Hey, you got a Kleenex? Paddle hard for a sec, we're going over another bar."

"OK. No, why in the world would I have a Kleenex?"

"Doesn't your nose run when you exert yourself?" Mick said, and he launched a green glob that plopped into the water and floated awhile before it sank.

CHAPTER 20

"Gross! Guys are so gross."

"What? Watch this ..." and he pressed his left nostril closed and blew ... or tried to blow snot out of his right, resulting in a green sticky mess stuck in his mustache.

"Oh, cool move," Kate said laughing. "Totally disgusting. Now for your next trick, I suppose you clean it off with a swish of the tongue?"

"If I'm hungry."

"Gross! Gross!"

"What, would you rather swallow someone else's spit or snot?"

"Would you wipe that booger off before it is in your mouth or I'm never kissing you again."

"Good idea. I'll just leave it there and then I don't have to stress over my sister kissing me on the lips. Well, what is it: saliva or snot?"

"It's a stupid question, but obviously saliva is more palatable than snot, you dumb shit."

"Oooh, good one: how 'bout snot or shit?"

"My God! How old are you?"

"Hey," Mick said, "this is the kind of earth-shattering conversation brothers have all the time ... you know, solving all the indelicate little mysteries in the universe. So, why not brother-sister?"

"Since you didn't have a brother, these must be conversations you've had with yourself, which is very interesting. By the way, in case you haven't noticed, being lost in such deep thoughts and all, we're not moving."

"OK, turn around and paddle hard. Hey, look at that starfish!"

"Where?" Kate yelled. "Oh, cool. My God, it's huge ... and red!"

"Aren't they great? But we'd better paddle hard. If we have to get in the water, it'll attack."

"What?" Kate screamed, holding the paddle out of the water as if it were in danger.

"Yeah. I've heard of some that jump right into boats and latch onto you."

Kate froze for a moment, then: "You're so full of shit. I'm climbing in to get a good look. Man, it's bright red, must be a foot in diameter."

She slipped out of the kayak. The water was only about a foot and a half deep or less, and when Kate squatted to get a good look, Mick yelled, loudly: "Look out!"

Kate sprang back, tried to jump backward back into the kayak, and went right over the other side, heels over head.

Mick was laughing hysterically until Kate stood up coughing and choking and, like preserved neatly in Saran Wrap, to his horror, were two small, round nubbies each with a dark eye staring directly at him.

"Ahhh, Kate! Your …" he started to say as she calmly flipped the kayak, sending Mick mouth-first into the water. He came up choking, refusing to look at her. While still coughing up saltwater, saliva, and boogers, he was attacked from behind and driven, once again, yapper-first, back into the water. Once again, he emerged coughing and spitting out a fairly large serving of the salty sea.

When Kate persisted in her unsisterly assault by leeching onto his back, trying once again to dunk him, Mick held his nose and pushed over backward, pinning Kate between his back and the sandy bottom. When he rolled and tried to stand, he found her still latched onto his back, her legs and arms wrapped around him like an octopus. So he grabbed her head over his shoulder and dove forward, flipping her onto her back into the water, unlatching her. When they lifted up

CHAPTER 20

their heads, kneeling, they went forehead to forehead and, both breathing hard, still coughing and spitting, started to laugh as best they could, and Mick forgot for a moment that he couldn't look at her ... until she stood up. Once again, he squawked an "Ahhh ..." and dove back under the water.

When he again surfaced, he sloshed toward the kayak, his back to Kate.

"What's the matter? Can't handle your sister in a little friendly fracas?"

"The fracas isn't the problem. Kate, look at yourself!"

"What? You mean my little boobies showing through my sports bra? Big deal!"

"It is a big deal," Mick whined.

"I'm your sister. If this were, like, Lottie, it would be a big deal, two big deals as a matter of fact. Christ, we've seen each other naked, for crying out loud. It's totally natural to be naked. Why are you so hung up about it?"

How could he explain to his sister that he was attracted to her? His *sister* for shit's sake. "I'm sorry," he said, almost in a pout, "but I am just not comfortable with your nipples staring at me."

"Well, don't stare back then. Want me to put my T-shirt back on, wuss?"

He was confused. 'At sea,' he thought, indulging himself with his own double entendre. He was aware of the contradiction: of his imparting to the world his "go with the flow" philosophy yet his conflict with this "open" relationship with his sister ... and he *would* like to be agreeable to an unconditional brother-sister relationship. Logically, Kate was right. If they were brother-sister and so nothing sexual between them, why not be free and easy with each other? Why not provide

TLC when needed? What was wrong with an inadvertent see-through sports bra? Yeah, what was the big deal? But two things bothered him: one, was the seeing-eye sports bra really inadvertent? And two, he was afraid.

When he had first met her, he had found the unintentional slit and exposed skin extremely stirring, but that was before he knew she was his sister. He was afraid: he had loved hugging her that first night at his place, felt a deep satisfaction with her falling asleep in his arms. But, then an almost electric impulse that time—the fear of pleasure—when he awoke with her arm around him, spooning, an impulse so strong that it had shot him out of the bed. He was afraid he wanted her to kiss him, that he wanted to kiss her. Afraid that when he was kissing Lottie, he really was wishing it was Kate … well, Marilyn actually. Had Kate taken the place of Martha in his fucked-up psyche? He had this, maybe irrational, fear of desiring Kate because he was afraid he already had.

"Well? And what are you frowning at, goofball?"

"Uh, look, I don't care. I'll be looking at your back anyway. We better get going because we gotta be back for the meeting."

"Aye, aye, Skipper. Let's get under way," and they climbed back into the kayak.

After paddling for just a few more minutes, the hills behind the shore on their right started to rise and Mick's … and Kate's … cottage came into view. "Thar she blows!" Mick hollered.

"Thar what blows, Cap'n?" Almost everything she said sounded sarcastic.

"Our place is showing just above that low-slung white place with the British flag flapping in the wind."

"Oh, cool!" Kate exclaimed. "Look at how your perch is sticking up over all the palms. Hey, you know, we've got a view of this part of the shoreline from your perch."

CHAPTER 20

"Yeah, of course, but only this stretch. And, what does that matter? What are the odds, *if* your Richard decides to come ashore here, that we'd be on the perch watching?"

"But what's up on top of the hill where the rock starts, farther up from your place? That'd give a view of the whole north end it looks like. And it's not *my* Richard, peckerhead."

"Don't know what's up there," Mick said. "It's pretty inaccessible."

"Look how cool your place looks, bro."

"Yup."

"You plan on staying here permanently?"

"Dunno." The bottom of the kayak started catching against the sand and he had to push with his paddle to guide the kayak farther out from shore.

"Would you consider moving back to the States?" she asked, helping him by pushing with her paddle as well.

"What about you?" Mick countered.

"I don't know. I guess when I go back to get all this cleared up, whatever happens, I'll probably stay."

"Where?"

"Where?" Kate asked. "You mean New York or Spokane?"

"Yeah."

"Spokane. At least that's where Sara will be, most of the time."

"What about where I am?" Mick ventured. It suddenly struck him: he had been so wrapped up in Kate moving in, Barney, Sara, Richard, HS, Peewee … that he hadn't had time to think that much about the future, especially the near future, without Kate in it.

"Tell me again why *you're* down here?" Kate asked him. "Escaping from, hiding from—what? God, you almost sound like me."

Mick laughed. "I guess it does. I don't know. When Martha and our baby died, their death and then just about everything started to leave such a bitter taste in my mouth. Everything started to really bother me. We are fricking destroying our planet. No, let me correct myself, the planet will survive; we're destroying ourselves. I felt I didn't want to be a part of it. I don't want to feel like a goddamn parasite."

"How is living down here any different?"

Mick laughed again, only a cynical laugh this time. "I felt the common denominator here, in a small little island nation on an even smaller little cay, was not money. When money is the bottom line—the raison d'etre, the end purpose—decisions are likely made for the wrong reason: it's about 'profit' not 'right or wrong,' and the two are rarely in synch."

"I don't disagree. As a matter of fact, I don't like to admit it, but I agree with you. Obviously, if I didn't, why would I be hiding out here, afraid, when all I want to do is the right thing? It would be a lot simpler to say screw it—this is the nature of humankind. No matter what I do, it ain't gonna change it. As a matter of fact, I could have probably gotten a pretty nice payoff to keep my mouth shut. Maybe that's all Richard wants ... is to buy me off."

Mick hadn't really thought about it: here he was feeling all righteous and altruistic about writing *A Million Dollars*—a simple little tome for youthful good Samaritans—definitely good, but Kate was really putting it on the line. "I haven't actually come out and told you this, hon, but I am really proud of you." And in this kayak on this sea with the tide coming in, the breeze blowing, the sun at their backs, he realized that: sister, half-sister, conventional or un, they were for the lack of a better word, now "soul mates" and that he was learning

CHAPTER 20

to love this chaotic spirit. "Think you could live in the land of the loons on a lake in the woods of northern Minnesota?" he asked her.

"Proud of me for being a fool? Oh well, thanks, I guess. Why are you asking me about the woods? And you mean land of the mosquitoes? Who would live there?"

Me, MP thought. Us, Mick dismissed, realizing it appeared that it would not be happening. And why would it matter if his sister lived with him or not? He resolved right there and then that self-preservation required that he face it: there was no Marilyn. Kate was his sister. "Guess I'll just hang here and go with the flow," he told her. "Speaking of the flow, the tide has come in quite a bit. We're floating free now, so let's go check out the access to those docks ahead."

They made it the two or three miles to the rock and coral at the north end that barred the way. They counted a dozen docks with small boat access. At low tide, a light boat, drafting little, with motor tilted up might make it to dockage. It was all pure white sand, but the bottom undulated due to wave action and so would be easy to get hung up. At high tide, although still rather shallow, small crafts could, and do, get out ... and in.

The wind came up, and although more brisk now from the north, helped blow them home. If they both held their paddles horizontally across the gunnels so the wind caught the blades, they got a good lift and could almost lay back and sail in. Although they had chatted almost all the way out, they were quiet on the way back. Mick assumed Kate was thinking ahead to the meeting. Kate assumed Mick was thinking the same. Both were wrong.

BACK TO THE ISLAND

AFTER DROPPING off the kayak, Mick remembered on the cart ride back that he had not read HS's newest. So, when he got back to the cottage, he headed straight to the porch and waggled the folder in front of Kate. "I waited to read this with you."

"Oh, HS's? Why wait for me?"

"Well, I'm almost afraid to read it."

"Huh? Why?"

"I believe it's a sexual double entendre."

"Really?" Kate said surprised. "What gives you that idea?"

"Because she asked me if double-e's aren't usually sexual … ways to flirt."

"Hmmm, you think she's flirting with you? Just read it to me, chickenshit."

"OK, here goes:

> **Yesterdays and Nevermores**
>
> It's raining now.
> The kind of monotonous,
> dancing rain that lovers
> must sit and listen to, as
> it draws them together
> closer to each other
> deeper into the dark.
>
> —H.S.

Kate raised her eyebrows and smiled at Mick.

"Does she mean what I think she means?" Mick asked and read it again to himself. "She said she got the idea from the Traveling Wilburys' song 'Dirty World.'"

"Oh, I love that song. 'I love your high-speed gearbox. I love your power steering.' What line?"

CHAPTER 20

"'If you let me drive…'"

"'… your pickup truck and park it where the sun don't shine' or something like that. Yup: 'closer to each other, deeper into the dark.' 'Where the sun don't shine.' She's fun," Kate exclaimed, excited.

"But that's pretty frickin' intimate, if that's what she means. What would Peewee say—it's his daughter?"

"But not his 'little girl.' I think she wants you to know she's grown up—an adult. It's a pretty sophisticated double entendre, really."

"Well, yeah, right. I can see why she didn't want me to read it with her there, though. I mean … she's having sex, right?"

Kate punched him in the arm. "Maybe, but not necessarily, dufus. It's poetry. It's fiction. It's really beautiful. C'mon, 'The kind of monotonous dancing.' Shit. '*Dancing rain that lovers must sit and listen to!*' I want to be there now, in love. You?"

And then a slow rain started. This is way too melodramatic, Mick said to himself, listening to the soft patter on the palm leaves and bushes. If this were a novel, the readers would say: Bullshit. That's way over the edge: you just happen to meet an old friend and run into a long-lost sister on a little outer island in the Bahamas? And now a slow, probably "monotonous dancing rain that lovers must sit and listen to" begins? And then, suppose she melodramatically turned abruptly and ran up the stairs, upset by the concurrence of events? Way too histrionic! Way too unbelievable!

"Yesterdays and Nevermores." He didn't like the sound of that title; way too sinister, melodramatic, overly sentimental but, God blast it, way too real.

CHAPTER 21

MICK MADE some sandwiches for them to have before the meeting. He called up to Kate who didn't respond but came down in a few minutes. Something looked different about her. While they were eating their sandwiches, Mick realized she had put eye makeup on, which he thought was weird. If she ever wore makeup, it was awfully subtle. Why now for a meeting with Spense and Lottie?

They were just finishing a quiet lunch when they heard Spense's cart coming, the engine surging as it maneuvered over the ruts. Mick suddenly realized he hadn't seen, emailed, or talked to Lottie since their rather consummate, almost exhaustive, date the day before. The memory stirred that incongruous feeling one gets deep in the groin when excited, or was it fear? Like on a wild ride at the fair? Or when you see someone get hurt. How should he act toward her? He really wasn't comfortable with even Spense knowing what had transpired. For sure he wasn't comfortable with Kate knowing. Would Lottie have told Spense? Would Spense say anything? How would Lottie react? How would she expect him to act? The day definitely had been … orgasmic, but, to him, intimate, clandestine. Having been married so young, he had had no experience with casual sex and thus the morning, or day, after. Was this "casual" to Lottie? He realized he had not thought about it today, had pushed yesterday out of his

CHAPTER 21

mind. Was it even casual to him? Should he act blasé? Cool? Clandestine? Loving? Did he love Lottie or just *want* her? What about her? Why did she seem to want him? Because he was simply available and, now, able? Not a huge selection of suitable, available men here on this little island. He watched with trepidation as they drove up and parked by the bushes just off the road in front of the cottage.

Mick and Kate walked to the edge of the porch and looked down at the two as they climbed out of the cart. "Prepared to deliberate, are we?" Spense called up to them. He and Lottie came up on the porch, Spense kissing Kate on the cheek while simply putting a hand on Mick's shoulder. Lottie came behind, hugged Kate, and sat down, ignoring Mick.

Mick, feeling awkward as hell, walked behind Lottie and placed his hands on her shoulders, leaned over, and kissed her on the forehead. "Hi, darling," was all she said. Fortunately, she was dressed, for Lottie, rather conservatively: sandals, shorts, and a modest cotton top all browns and tans. Kate, sporting her eye shadow and liner, was barefoot in shorts and, rather than her standard T-shirt, had on a thin, gauzy blouse Mick hadn't seen before, unbuttoned quite a ways. Out of fear, he avoided noticing if there was any cleavage, which was pretty much nonexistent anyway, or whether she sported a bra or not. But he couldn't help but notice she looked pretty damn fetching. He wondered what was up with that. Spense, on the other hand, could have been a Tibetan monk or Richie Haven's brother attired in a colorful, East Indian–looking robe and turbanesque chapeau. No one even seemed surprised at the odd attire. It fit his personality to a T.

For a couple of hours they sat, tête-à-tête, deliberating intently, focused on the issue of Kate and Richard. They considered continuing to, apparently, sending him on wild goose chases. Spense said he could "persist in altering the location of his server." But, they decided, as previously discussed, that this would be just deferring the inevitable. All agreed in the end that they might just as well lead or invite him to them, the sooner the better, and deal with him as much as possible on their own terms. The issue they got stuck on was how to ensure it was on their terms and that it was, indeed, Richard they would be dealing with, not someone possibly more sinister, like a senator or his hired guns. They all agreed, tentatively, that with hard evidence—the emails—already in the hands of officials, it was unlikely that they wanted to eliminate Kate, which would have to appear awfully suspicious. But, instead, they would want to negotiate, somehow or another, assuming that since Richard had been Kate's fiancé he had the best chance of success in deterring her from testifying. Mick wondered if they even needed Kate's testimony. He guessed they must or why the fuss?

Mick argued that they couldn't just lead him to Elbow Cay, as he felt the areas like the west side of the north end, where he and Kate had just kayaked, could provide access without detection. Not that the islanders wouldn't be vigilant, but that he and Kate would feel like sitting ducks and vulnerable.

"Sitting ducks?" Spense squawked. "That must be one from your northern habitat? A bit provincial, but it works. I agree."

"Why don't we set up an intermediary?" Mick suggested.

They all looked at him, eyebrows raised. "Like Peewee or one of the islanders?" Kate asked. "It probably shouldn't be one of us."

"I believe it should be one of us or, at least, someone who has a stake in this," Spense suggested. "I believe our compatriot, Peewee, could handle security quite adequately."

CHAPTER 21

"You think Richard would just walk right into this?" Mick questioned.

"Does he have a choice?" Lottie asked.

"Richard is very cautious. Remember he was in frickin' 'compliance' at a large firm. But, regardless of what measures he might make to safeguard himself, I feel we would be safer if he were escorted here." Kate looked at Mick. "Don't you think?"

They all sat silent for a moment. "It's probably as good as we could hope for, I guess," Mick finally said. "I'll talk to Peewee. See what he says. He'll probably feel, if I know him, that he's the best person to either bring this to Vernal or do the escorting himself."

"Speaking of Peewee, I've been thinking about how my 'Proud Mary' might assist in his next ecoterrorism venture," Spense said. "Why don't we take a break? Don't know about anyone else, but I must tend to my bladder."

"Well, while you tend to your bladder, I'm gonna pee, and not in any frickin' closet," Kate, reliably indelicate as usual, pronounced, and all had the first laugh in a while. "Mick, why don't you get some refreshments for us?"

"Drinks?" Mick asked.

"Let's stick with iced tea until we're done. We'd best stay on task," Spense yelled as he headed for the water closet, as he called it. And Kate headed to the upstairs bathroom.

Lottie followed Mick into the kitchen, wrapped her arms around him from behind, and whispered in his ear, "Miss me?"

Since it was only the day after, Mick assumed it wasn't "her" she was asking if he missed. When she kissed his ear and nibbled on his lobe, he knew what she was referring to. He appreciated that Lottie had not come into his home all sloppy and emotional. She was cool and, he was learning, thoughtful and considerate, nice and funny, and alluring, almost intoxicating. But? But now what were her expectations? *Her* intentions? And, *now*, more importantly, what were his intentions? Now how should he answer: "Do you miss me?"

He turned around, gave her a gentle kiss on the lips, said "Nahh," and broke away to pour the glasses of tea. He was getting pretty good at lying by telling the truth. He wondered if there was a word for that.

Kate came hopping down the stairs the same time Spense exited the first floor bathroom. "Well, let's get back to it," Spense said. "Three of us have to assist Jack and Ma in providing the means to happiness for all the patrons of the Cap'n's in a short while." They each grabbed a glass and settled in the same chairs on the porch.

For the next hour Spense outlined his plan of diversion and attack: he would moor the Plowed Mary offshore of the development site, carrying the men who were to swim ashore. He would drop them off short of the site and they would swim ashore in the dark, pushing something like darker-colored inflatable rafts ahead of them. He would then do his thing: his sound and light show. This should not only be a distraction and cause confusion, but for sure disable the sound detectors and most likely the motion detectors they had. Spense would have provided Peewee and his other cohorts on land with walkie-talkies and small remote amplifiers. Although it was a good quarter of a mile from the main road to the site, they would go as far into the mangroves as they needed, and amplify their voices like in a conversation, hopefully making it appear they were almost on top of the guards, but actually far enough away that they couldn't be hit in case the guards decided to fire on them.

CHAPTER 21

With the guards occupied searching the jungle, away from the shore, the swimmers would come ashore, with some working on disabling the machines, which should be relatively quick and quiet. While that was being done, the others would hopefully be able to load at least some of the explosives in the rafts. They would then transport them to Mary. Of course, neither Spense, nor anyone else, had any idea how many explosives there were and if they could get at them. Maybe Vernal could discover if the explosives were under lock and key and how they might be accessed. It concerned them all a bit what plans Peewee might have for the pilfered munitions.

When both deeds were accomplished and the swimmers were back, Spense would cease with the fireworks and instead send flares over the guards' heads, illuminating them, which could or could not be important, but should continue to divert their attention as Peewee retreated.

Mick had brought up three issues: first, if there were too many explosives to transport, which seemed likely, what would they do about the rest? Maybe they could do more than one trip, but with the guards, as well as the elements—especially the wily wind—that might not be possible. Second, could flares fired into the jungle cause a fire? And third, might they illuminate Peewee and his gang as well as the guards?

Spense guaranteed that if the flares burst in the air, by the time they burned out and landed, they would not ignite the undergrowth, especially since it was a mangrove swamp; and if Peewee didn't try to get too close to the site, they could easily remain concealed, in spite of the flares. Although in response to any remaining explosives, he agreed Peewee might have his own agenda.

BACK TO THE ISLAND

They decided they would meet with Peewee the next day, if he could, and see how soon he would want to proceed, if he indeed liked the plan. Spense would be ready to go tomorrow night, as he assumed Peewee would consider time to be of the essence. All three would arrange for tomorrow night off, in case. Kate said she would email Sara when they knew exactly what the plan was and then Sara and Richard would meet in New York to set up the meeting in the Bahamas. Then they would draw Richard to them. Exhausted by apprehension, three of them headed into Cap'n Jack's, leaving Kate alone to her own thoughts.

Shit was definitely going to be happening … soon.

Kate emailed Sara after the trio left. She clued her in on the pending excitement, and told her to go ahead and arrange to meet with Richard when she was in New York and gauge his intentions regarding Kate. If his intentions were to simply meet with Kate, to have him email Kate when he would plan to come and she'd make the arrangements to meet him at the Marsh Harbour airport. Of course there was no way of ascertaining his true intentions, but Kate felt comfortable with her security force in Hope Town. Although worried about Kate having to face Richard, Sara agreed that it was better to arrange a meeting and that the precautions they were planning sounded safe, although it still concerned her about the senator's involvement. She hadn't found out anything more about the connection between Richard and the senator but had put out feelers. In her position with the SEC, a lot of people were very willing to provide favors, which probably meant they had something to hide, but then, she pointed out to Kate, who doesn't in banking and politics?

CHAPTER 21

She told Kate she would love to be there for the ecoterrorism adventure, that it was right out of a novel or movie. She had had only the one email from Barney telling her how much fun he'd had. She'd responded with the same sentiment. No, he hadn't responded back and, no, she hadn't contacted him again, either. When Kate started to rail on her for being so passive and not proactive, Sara brought up her *sisterly* relationship with Mick and that put an end to their little row. They signed off not angry with each other, but both with themselves.

MICK WOKE covered in a layer of sweat. It was the first really hot and humid night, a harbinger of the tropical summer searing its way up from the equator. He peeked down and saw HS sitting on the steps, barefoot in a fairly skimpy halter and rather short shorts. As he slipped by Kate's room, he could see she had had a hot night as well, naturally. She had taken to leaving her door open, Mick figured, to get some breeze from the sea side of the cottage, and was sprawled on the bed, face down. Her T-shirt had hiked up over her hips leaving, thank goodness, bright red undies glowing in the early light. She either had had the foresight to turn her overhead fan on or had woken in the night and switched it on. Mick's room, being at the front of the cottage, seaside, would normally get more of a breeze than Kate's, which was at the rear with the dune partially blocking any breeze coming off the Atlantic. That's why MP had felt it essential to build his perch: for the view and breezes. There was no breeze this morning from either direction.

Mick came down and leaned out onto the porch: "Morning, HS. Why don't you come on up and have a chair. I'll put on some coffee and water." He knew she wouldn't come up onto the porch unless he asked her.

"OK. Good morning, sir. How about some iced tea this morning? It's a hot one." She picked up her satchel and headed up onto the porch.

He came out and handed her a sweating glass of tea and went back in to pour himself a cup of caffeine. When he came back out she handed him the folder. "Here. My attempt at a plum poem, sir."

"Attempt? Most of your writings are plum poems. You're a master at it."

"Well, thank you, sir. But I don't think this one is very good."

Mick opened the folder and read:

> If I fell when I tried,
> Would you laugh if I cried?
>
> —H.S.

He read it over to himself several times. He wasn't sure what to think of it. He definitely liked it. It was simple, clean, and uncomplicated as could be, and he immediately could relate it to events in his life. The big one that jumped right out at him was how he felt about moving forward after his wife and child had died. "Why don't you like it?" he asked her.

"I like it. I'm just not sure it's a strong enough analogy to be universal … for other people to relate it to their lives."

Well, she sure knew what a plum poem was supposed to do. This one was about as simple and brief as a poem could be, yet definitely unearthed analogous truths. "I did, immediately, and as I think more about it, other things in my life pop into my mind as well, especially how I felt when my wife and baby died."

CHAPTER 21

"I'm sorry, sir. What a terrible loss for you. I hate to say that you finding my meager little plum a metaphor for misery is good. I guess we do grow from and out of sorrow. But I'm guessing you're a little partial as to whether it's good or not."

"Partiality has nothing to do with it. It would have conjured up images of past events in my life whether you or a stranger had written it."

"So you don't think we're still strangers, sir?"

"Only if you keep calling me sir."

She laughed. It was maybe the first time he had heard her laugh. She smiled often, but didn't laugh; of course this could be more a reflection on him than of her. Her laugh was fun, but not a young girl's. She reached for the tea and took a sip. He took advantage and studied her appearance for the first time this morning. He had never really noticed anything about her figure before except that she was petite. She had always dressed conservatively with long pants and loose top, high at the neck. Not this morning.

Her legs he noticed were delicate, but shapely, not thin. Her midriff was tight but again not skinny: no bones showing, just a small circular scar exposed below her halter. Her arms also managed to look delicate without being thin. It was a woman's, not a child's, body. Her halter was meager enough to demonstrate cleavage. She was diminutive maybe, but fully developed and well-proportioned. Suddenly he noticed that from just beneath her neck and running down disappearing into her halter was a long but not conspicuous scar. When he looked up to her face, he realized she had caught him detecting the scar. She had her hair pulled over to one side and pinned back on the other. Although cliché, he felt she looked like a flower, but oddly, one that had blossomed too early or out of season.

She smiled rather sadly. "Since we are no longer strangers, I'll tell you about my nemesis which, unfortunately, is my own heart."

He swallowed hard.

"I was born with a heart murmur—two, actually. Both my aortic and mitro valves didn't operate properly. They tried to repair them, but that didn't work, so I now have two artificial valves."

"But that's OK, isn't it?" Mick managed to say.

"The valves should be fine. But the leakage has caused my heart to be abnormal. One chamber is larger than the other."

"That's not OK?"

She smiled, a flavorless smile this time. "Maybe not."

He had a difficult time asking, afraid of her response. "Does this affect your life expectancy?"

"Maybe," she said again. "Anyway, it leads me to the philosophy of living life like a river."

Who the hell did she think she was—Hermann Hesse or something, reminiscent of the novel *Siddhartha*? For some reason he felt angry.

"You know: follow the path of least resistance," she said.

"Meaning?"

"Meaning if I don't try, maybe I won't fall."

He knew she was referring to her poem, but what the hell was she implying? "You mean ... it sounds like you're saying you're giving up?"

"Oh no, not at all, sir. But like a river I have a destination, maybe unknown, but nevertheless it ends somewhere, either blocked or diminished."

"But doesn't a river go on forever, HS? From a mountain to a creek into a stream to a river to the sea."

"Nice illusion, Mr. MP. But it ends somewhere. It's the basis for my problems with my father. He seems to look for

CHAPTER 21

resistance and tries to conquer it by force. I am really worried about him and my friends and now you, it would seem. I know you believe in going with flow. Isn't that the same as following the path of least resistance?"

"So, you mean to *not* attempt to stem progress, like the development on the west side?"

"Exactly, sir. I think it's my father's tragic flaw. He lives life like it's an obstacle to be overcome. Some day one of those obstacles may overcome him, like this one. I just have a bad feeling about it."

"But ... yes, but ... OK, I'm gonna ramble for a while. I believe going with the flow means that if fate presents something to you, enters it into your life, you don't say: 'Oh, I wasn't *planning* on that leading me ... let's say ... to what I might have thought was 'my destination.' So, then, you don't go with it. But, like with Kate: I wanted a room with a view, so I decided to build my perch up there—I'll show it to you later if you like—so I needed tools; my dad had always bought tools from Sears, so when I saw Sears, I went in. Fate walked me by the women's department. I needed a job, but I ran into an obstacle: they weren't hiring. Then fate walked me by the shoe department and presented me with this woman that immediately made an impression on me. So, rather than leave, I asked her about the job. She obviously felt fate had presented something to her and so she overcame the obstacle, Ajax, by offering me the job. So, rather than like a river with a dam in the way, I didn't just say, 'Oh shit, this must be the end of the line,' I went with the flow: over the dam or around it or whatever. If I had said to myself: 'Oh well, it would have been nice to have this job and it would have been nice to meet this intriguing

307

woman, but the path of least resistance was to stop, leave. I never would have met my sister."

"Your sister?"

"Yes—Kate. My sister."

"Very interesting, sir. I hope you're right. I understand. That development is an obstacle in my father's pursuit of what he perceives as his destiny. And fate, by bringing you here, has presented to me the means by which I, the wounded sparrow, can fly from nest."

"What do you mean by that?"

"It was almost comforting to think of the ocean as an impassable dam and the path of least resistance was to turn back and be content in the refuge of my nest. I felt fate put me on an island to keep me here. But because of you, I see I must leave the island."

"Wait, err," Mick stammered. "What did I do? Why do you need to leave the island?"

"Aren't you contradicting yourself with that question, sir?"

"Why me? What have I done to make you think you need to leave your home?"

"You gave me confidence, Mr. MP. Helped me to realize that maybe I will need or want to come 'back to the island' but I won't know that or ever be able to 'come back' if I don't leave."

Mick didn't know what to say or what to do. He felt so protective of her. He imagined Peewee did as well. She referred to herself as a "wounded sparrow." Could she fly and survive if she left the nest?

HS stood, and when she turned noticed Kate: "Oh, good morning, ma'am. I didn't see you there."

Kate, who had been silently leaning against the porch door jam, simply returned the smile but didn't say anything.

CHAPTER 21

"I'll take you up on your offer of a tour another time, sir. I really should be going," and she walked down the steps.

"Oh, HS, are you going to see your father this morning?" Mick stood and leaned on the porch railing.

"Why do you ask?"

"Well, we'd like to meet with him today, when he's able, if he's able," Mick said.

HS looked at him with what was best described as a "shit-eating grin" and flaunted what appeared to be a smart phone. "I'll call him and see. We're more connected on this backward island than you might think. When do you want him to come? I know he's anxious to talk again."

"I'm meeting with the boys today at one o'clock," Kate said. "So, before or after if possible."

"Spense and Lottie are available anytime. They both could be here within an hour," Mick told her.

She called Peewee. He agreed to be there within an hour himself. After standing and starting down the steps, HS stopped: "I almost forgot, Mr. MP. My mother and I would like to have you over for brunch tomorrow. Are you available? I thought after our morning session, if there is one, we could head over to our place, together. It's not easy to find." She looked at Kate. "Sorry, Miss Kate"

Kate clapped her hands lightly. "All right, progress!" she exclaimed at HS calling her Kate.

"I'd like to invite you, too, but Mr. MP is a special case. No one but islanders, and then not all of them, know where we live. Most, due to my father's reputation—more to do with his size and frightful stare than anything—feel it best to leave us to our privacy. I, of course, would have no problem trusting you, but my father …"

[309

"No problem," Kate answered.

"Maybe another time?" HS said, sounding and looking remorseful.

"Don't worry. Thank you."

"You're on!" Mick said, feeling like he'd just been invited to the White House.

"I think you'll be pleasantly surprised," HS told him.

"Anything with you is a surprise, so I won't be surprised if I'm surprised."

She laughed for the second time that morning. "OK, good. Bye, sir. Bye, Miss Kate."

Both said goodbye to her, and Kate turned to Mick and gave him a hug, kissing him on the cheek when Mick turned his head. "Quite the conversation this morning."

He held her away by the shoulders for two reasons, the second being to ask her: "You heard our conversation? How much?"

"Just about everything, I think," Kate said. "I was going to come out to say hello but stopped just inside the doorway. Sorry for eavesdropping. I didn't want to interrupt, but I couldn't leave either."

"Well, shitdamn. So, what do I, we … you heard about her heart? I don't know what …"

"I know. I don't even want to think about it. We'll have to talk later. Now, why don't you let Spense know about the meeting? Do you suppose Lottie'll want to come?" Kate intimated, hoping, but knowing the answer.

"What? You crazy? She'd kill me if I didn't let her know," Mick answered, wondering why Kate had even considered that.

"Well, then, let 'em both know. I need to borrow the cart."

"Sure, but what for now?"

CHAPTER 21

"I need to go to the library to get something for my 'class.'"

"OK, hurry back."

Kate, Spense, Lottie, and Peewee all arrived at the same time, forty minutes later. Peewee gave MP another bear hug. Everyone else sat down quickly. Although they all assumed he was a gentle giant, they took note of how he hefted MP like he was his cub and decided to establish residency firmly in a chair and take a rain check, just in case. He had looked like he wanted to hug them all.

They decided to talk about Kate's situation first. Peewee reaffirmed that he was confident that if anyone even looked like they were making a furtive attempt at coming ashore, they would be seen. He didn't elaborate on why, but he liked the idea of an intermediary escorting Richard or whomever to Hope Town. He said he was glad to do it. When they brought up alternatives like Vernal, they got the flesh ball stare and the subject was dropped.

Having apparently solved the Kate problem, they could tell his mind was on something he considered more urgent … and imminent. So, Spense outlined his plan. When he was finished, Peewee roared, as usual, his approval and said, "Great minds think alike." Peewee said they already had black rubber rafts appropriated to maneuver ashore to remove the explosives. Vernal had heard that they were being stored in the container of an eight-wheeler that had been brought over on a barge to Hope Town, that it was only padlocked and so easy to break into. Peewee said that had been confirmed by several of the island boys who had seen a large trailer dropped off and then transported to the site. They figured it probably contained the explosives. They had already planned, this time, on filling all the gas tanks with sugar.

What he hadn't been able to come up with was an effective plan for the diversion. You could tell he wanted to hug Spense, whom he referred to as 'Kimoto Man.' Whether it had something to do with the elaborate robe or he misspoke "kimono" or he thought Spense looked like a dragon—komodo—or both, he wasn't sure, but the moniker worked, the way Spense looked. He told Spense he was a gentleman and a scholar and asked when this could all happen. When they told him that they had taken the night off and if he was ready they were ready, he abruptly stood. "We're prepared," he answered.

The rafts were all hidden and floating a ways up the creek that ran into the mangroves at the end of the harbor opposite the mouth. They would pull the rafts by motorboat to Spense's yacht. He had figured he would leave ten swimmers, two to each raft, with Spense: enough to do the job, but not too many that might be easier to detect. He could bring as many men as needed to provide the diversion from the road side. Spense suggested a half dozen might be best. Again, sufficient to provide the amplified voices, but the fewer the less chance of problems. Peewee asked why not use the road they had ripped through the mangroves as access. Spense told him he had considered that, but they might be too exposed, and not knowing what safeguards the Mandelsungs had put in place to protect themselves, the jungle with mangrove swamps, familiar to the islanders but not the guards, should be the safest.

Peewee reached down and picked up Spense under the arms and held him above his head gleefully, like he was a toddler. At first, there were three gasps, but then they all cracked up. The image was right out of *Gulliver's Travels* or *Lord of the Rings* or some other fantasy: a giant suspending a

CHAPTER 21

twisted magician who wasn't sharing, however, in the mirth of his audience.

When Peewee set him down, Spense's legs almost buckled. He composed himself, smoothing his robe with his hands, cleared his throat, and told Peewee: "I appreciate your enthusiasm, but if tonight is a success, as I assume, may I preface the evening's adventures with 'once is enough?' My gracious, man, you are a Goliath."

"Sorry, little Kamoto Man, but I just couldn't help myself. I'll celebrate tonight with one of the ladies instead." Kate and Lottie's smiles turned into shivers and they pointed at each other and, laughing, yelled: "Her!"

This ended the meeting rather comically, Peewee planning to come get the audio equipment that afternoon from Spense at his boat, and agreeing to a timetable: the rafts and men would be at Spense's at ten that evening. The swimmers and mangrove marchers would be in place before midnight, and then the fun would commence.

After waving Spense and Lottie off, Kate turned to Mick, heaved a huge sigh, and said, "I want to talk about HS, but first, my God, it feels like there's rebar running down my spine ... you?"

Mick rolled his shoulders and had to admit that besides rebar, it felt like a load of cement had hardened around them.

"No shit," Kate said and sat in one of the deck chairs. "Here, sit down on the floor and I'll give you a shoulder rub."

He reluctantly sat between her feet. She reached down, grabbed his T-shirt, and whipped it up over his head, forcing his hands up as if being arrested, which is what he figured he should be because he didn't want to reciprocate, knowing damn well she would be whipping off her own T-shirt.

"Eww. Nice essence emitting from those pits, man. When's the last time you showered? I've heard of musk, but that smells like it's coming from a musk ox. Man!"

"Well, we don't …"

"Ah, shut up, will ya. I'm just kidding … sort of."

"You said you heard my conversation with Heidi?"

"Did you hear me? I said 'shut up.' Just relax and enjoy this, will ya?" She then started rubbing her fingers through his hair and the tension lifted like a morning fog. She rubbed hard with her fingertips first, then ran her fingers from the base of his neck all the way to his forehead. It felt like feckin' heaven. Then she got to his shoulders and shoulder blades and he felt like he was melting, which he almost was. "Damn, it's so hot, we don't even need oil, there's a light coating of sweat and my fingers just glide." And glide they did and he blissfully relaxed, until: "OK, my turn."

They traded places, Mick with his standard trepidation, and sure as shit, off flew her T-shirt and, sure as shit, no bra! He closed his eyes as she situated herself between his feet. He started with her head, the same as he had received. But, where he had suffered his bliss in secrecy, Kate ooh'd and ahh'd and moaned, leaving Mick to completely tense up, almost negating the good Kate had done.

After about the same amount of time she had spent on him, she stood up and turned, saying, "God. Thank you. That was great," to find him staring down with his eyes clenched tightly shut. "My God! You're afraid to look at me, again! Open your eyes!" she demanded.

"No," he retorted adamantly.

"I bet there isn't a red-blooded male in the universe that wouldn't enjoy looking at me … any naked woman probably."

CHAPTER 21

"'Red-necked' male, you mean, if the naked woman is his sister."

"Will you just look at me and get over this hang-up, this modesty bullshit. I'm your sister. A woman's body is the most painted and photographed object in history. You should be proud that your sister has a good body. Aren't you proud?"

"Yes."

"Then open your frickin' eyes and look at it."

"No."

He could tell she had slid off her shorts. "Look. Here's just a simple little butt. Yes, it's a nice butt. Aren't you glad your sister has a nice butt?" And, apparently, her underpants as well.

"Yes."

"So, look at it!"

"No."

"OK, dammit," and she moved across the porch and came back. "I'm taking a picture of my ass with my phone."

He jerked his head up but didn't open his eyes.

"And here's a picture of my little boobies. They're no big deal. And here's my midriff and belly button with a little bushy bulb below. A curly little brunette, not a *burning* bush, by the way. You know anyone with a red bush? Huh, Romeo? Look. I'm in good shape; it's a nice bod. Aren't you proud? Here's my legs. You used to think I had nice legs. Do you still think I have nice legs?"

"Yes."

"You're not going to open your eyes?"

"No."

"Well, I'm going to print these out and hang 'em in …"

"No, you're not."

"Not what?"

"Hanging them anywhere."

"Oh, yes I am. I'd say ... in the bathroom. Upstairs. You don't have any pictures in there anyway. It'll be art on the wall."

"It'll be trash in the garbage."

"I'm not going to leave until you open your eyes."

He opened them.

"What are you looking at?"

"Your feet."

"Aaaah ... they're naked!"

"Very funny."

She took a picture of her feet. "There, now we have my feet as well. Are they nice feet, Mr. Shoe-dog, pediatribe par excellance, or whatever?"

"They're skinny."

"Ohhh. I suppose Lottie's are prettier?"

"Never noticed her feet." He couldn't believe he had said that, so he added quickly: "Your sister has sweet feet."

"I thought they were pudgy."

"Who told you that? Not me."

"Can you look at my knees? Is that OK?"

"No."

"Why the hell not?"

He didn't answer but just sat there staring at her feet, now smiling. They were long, veiny, and skinny.

"Ahhhrgg," Kate screamed. "Well, I'm going to jump in the ocean to cool off."

"Naked?" he asked.

"I just might."

"If you put on a suit, I'll go with you," he told her, still smiling smugly, looking at where her toes used to be. He had no idea why he was enjoying this, but he was.

CHAPTER 21

"All right you anal asshole!" she said, gritting her teeth.

As she walked away, he quipped, "A little redundant, aren't we?" and as he opened his eyes he caught a snippet of her cute little buns as they disappeared around the corner.

Suddenly she peeked back out at him and yelled "Aha! Gotcha, you pervert!" and padded up the stairs.

For some reason he felt proud of himself, self-satisfied. He found he was still smiling as he sat back and noticed a mild breeze had started up, heading in off the Abaco.

They raced to the beach, pushing and trying to trip each other all the way like little kids. When they returned after a quick dip, during which Kate had kept her suit on—thank goodness, there were other people on the beach—she went upstairs to change for her class. Mick made sandwiches for them. While eating, they finally faced up to the fact that they had to discuss the conversation between Mick and HS that morning. "So, what did you hear?" Mick asked Kate.

"Pretty much the whole thing, I think," Kate responded. "'Going with the flow,' 'path of least resistance,' very interesting."

"Leaving the island? Her 'abnormal' heart!"

"What did she write for today?" Kate asked to avoid talking about her heart.

"If I fell when I tried, would you laugh if I cried?" Mick said to Kate.

"What? Of course not. Well, maybe. Tried what? Why'd you ask me that? It sounds more like something HS would ask."

Mick just raised his eyebrows.

"Oh, oh. Shit. That's it? That's all?"

"Well, you know it's supposed to be a 'plum poem,' like the one I showed you: 'This Is Just to Say … ' The challenge was to say as much as possible in as few words as possible.

"Well, shit, yeah. Think about this and her heart?"

"I know, I know. But I don't want to."

"Me either. I'm just going to assume its fine. She'll outlive me."

"What about her leaving the island?" Mick asked.

"Well, I guess the poem might be more about that. I'd say with her mind and fortitude, she'd have to spread her wings, wounded or not. Find out what's out there. She's a strong young woman, no sparrow in my mind. She'll be all right."

"But, what if her heart's not? She did refer to herself as a 'wounded' sparrow. If she fell when she tried, I certainly wouldn't be laughing."

"I don't want to talk about it," Kate said. "But …"

Just then a gaggle of young men appeared in front of the cottage. "Hello, ma'am," a tall skinny one with dreads said. "We're here to get you for our schoolin'."

Kate stood, swallowed her last bite, and said to Mick, "I've also got to tell you what the realtor at Sotheby's told me. Later."

"Hi, guys. I'm ready. Let me grab a folder and we'll be on our way." She walked down the steps and was immediately surrounded by a motley crew of island boys. He watched them head north on the narrow sandy road. He could see her mouth moving and heard the guys laugh. He felt like his heart was fibrillating. "That's my sister," he said aloud to himself. He was feeling, in spite of his previous discomposure, that he was coming to grips with this notion, finally.

Mick went up to his perch to try to write, but his mind would continue to flitter to the coming events of the evening and what could go wrong. He was secure in his desire to be part of it, but it all seemed a little flippant, like the—what could be a dangerous ordeal—was just a little lark. He knew

CHAPTER 21

they had to act before more damage was done, but what they were doing with pyrotechnics, amplified sound, almost seemed like farce, comedy—hopefully not a comedy of errors. He had a feeling of foreboding he could not get out of his mind.

When he heard Kate come back, he went down without having written a word to see how the class went. He found her standing there, waiting for him, percolating with excitement like she'd just thrown back a couple double espressos. "Well, how'd it go?" Mick asked her.

"Great, Mick! They're really cool. Their hideout or clubhouse or whatever is fantastic. It's an old abandoned house up on the cliff just down the road to the north. It's like your perch, only higher and nearer the end where we were looking in the kayak, where the island tapers, so a panoramic view of both the Abaco and Atlantic." She took a breath and slowed her sprint a bit: "It's why they saw us skinny dipping and why they think they would see any boats coming ashore—even where we kayaked—along the entire shoreline."

"Yeah, but they're not there all the time, and how the hell could they see us well enough to establish that you had a quality behind?"

"They have telescopes and binoculars, bonehead. They can see us, even though we can't see them up there. They can see the harbor and a lot of Hope Town, too. Some of them sleep there, I could tell. There's bunks and stuff. I'm not so sure some of 'em aren't homeless. Most of them still live with their parents, though, the way it sounds."

"How do you get there? Heidi made it sound like it's hard to find."

"Oh, it is. There's only a trail that winds up through the brush, and at one point you have to climb a rope ladder to get up a cliff."

"A cliff. No shit! How high?"

"It's only like ten to twelve feet, but without the ladder you couldn't climb it. They have a system to pull it up when they're gone. God, what a fun spot. It isn't really rock up there, it's mostly like petrified coral or something, and that's what the house is made out of. It's cooler than shit, Mick."

"How'd the class go?"

"Well, some of 'em talk in kind of a slang, a creole that's almost impossible to understand, but when they read, their English is pretty good, kind of a British English. It's weird."

"How did they read?"

"Some really good. They're not dumb. But some labored, read real slow. They said Rashi, the little guy, can't read or write at all. But he's like their leader, so he must have a learning disability, you know, like we talked to Heidi about. He hung around outside the door listening in, though. I'm gonna work on him."

"Why don't you have Peewee talk to him?" Mick suggested.

"I think he already did from what Heidi implied."

"Wasn't there another guy who wasn't going to show up?"

"Yeah. Harvey. They said I wouldn't want him there. They said he was OK now but could be trouble, whatever that means."

"Hmmm, I guess there's always someone screwed up. There was almost always someone in each class when I was teaching. Usually, if not always, it was because of the frickin' parents."

"I suppose. Anyway, I think this'll really be fun."

Mick noticed her eyes had a sparkle, like when they had first met at Sears. It had seemed "Marilyn's" energy level, spunk, effervescence, had fizzled, dulled. Although "Kate's" behavior was still unpredictable and he could sense she was always at the verge of some random, probably irreverent act, of

CHAPTER 21

late she had become somewhat despondent and disagreeable. The merriment, which had always sizzled in Marilyn's eyes, had turned more to melancholy in Kate's. But today her eyes were alive. The sullen Kate had suddenly revisited the sassy, sanguine Marilyn. He so much wanted to hug this version of Kate, kiss this lovely woman. He felt he needed to express this surge of pride, regard, he felt for his sister, but he could think of no appropriate, befitting way to do so.

CHAPTER 22

AT NINE o'clock Mick and Kate headed into Hope Town. Both were tense. Spense was there at the pier to pick them up in the dory to convey them to the Plowed Mary. At 9:45 Peewee and the ten swimmers—eight fellow islanders and two Haitians—arrived with the rafts. The five black vinyl rafts were each the size of a lifeboat, maybe four feet wide by about seven feet long, and had been lashed together. The only cargo, in one of the rafts, was sufficient sugar to pour into the gas tanks of the "machines of mass destruction." While the ground coral had only clogged the filters, the finer sugar granules would sperm their way deep into the vaginas of the engines and disable them permanently. They were all then tied to the rear of Mary, meaning a slow, four-mile cruise out the channel and south to the west-side development site. Spense had already given three radio transmitters, modern day walkie-talkies with amplifiers, to Peewee. He gave another one to Angus, one of the swimmers, and the last one was for them on the Plowed Mary. That would enable them all to be in contact with each other throughout the venture. The swimmers were all small, lean, dark-skinned islanders. Peewee, with two of his men and two Haitians, would be driving to meet Vernal and his men at the entrance to the new road the developers had cleared through the jungle and then approaching through the mangroves.

CHAPTER 22

Angus told them it wouldn't take Peewee long to drive to the new road. A high, electric gate had been installed at the entrance. Vernal had heard that the wetlands on either side of the gate also had an electric charge dispersed into them. So Peewee and his men would navigate into the mangroves toward the site a ways away from the gate and the new road. They had contemplated veering back to this road a distance down the road from the gate to make their approach easier. But it had been decided that they would then be more exposed, thus vulnerable, as Spense had suggested, and Vernal wasn't sure they didn't have some other types of security devices on the road. So, Peewee figured maybe a half hour to navigate far enough through the mangrove swamps to be close enough to the site for their amplified voices to be heard by the guards.

Spense estimated it would take the Mary about a half hour to exit the harbor and reach the drop-off spot for the swimmers, and another half hour for them to get underway and swim the rafts ashore. In the meantime, Lottie, who had been designated skipper, would get Mary in position. Mick and Kate would ready the mortars, like miniature cannons, for the pyrotechnics. Spense would prepare the equipment to blast the sound and assist with the fireworks. They would wait for Peewee to let them know when he was in position. If there was a problem with the transmitters, Spense and the Monkey Wrench Gang, as he had dubbed them—a reference to Edward Abbey's great ecoterrorism novel—would start the show at eleven thirty, regardless.

At ten thirty they dropped off the swimmers. It had appeared the elements would be gracious: no moon, high tide as they already knew, and little wind. With black rafts and only dark faces showing above the water, they were near to invisible. Each raft would be pushed by two swimmers. The rafts drafted little, and each swimmer was experienced with the shallow reefs, having snorkeled and dove among them all their lives. The only problem would be if a strong wind came up, blowing in. Even with two swimmers per raft, a strong wind would make it difficult to swim the rafts, especially if loaded with explosives, back to the Mary.

After dropping them off, they cruised slowly to about two hundred yards off shore—close enough for the fireworks and flares, yet far enough that it shouldn't be in range of the 9mm Uzi submachine guns Vernal had said the guards should be using. The Uzis were outdated, had a short range, and reportedly had no optics. So they figured two hundred yards should be a safe distance. As they anchored, a light wind started to blow in. The swimmers and rafts were invisible in the dark night as they had drifted off, the breeze behind them.

At 11:10 Peewee let them know he and his group were set up on a little tuft of solid land in the mangroves.

At 11:20 the swimmers transmitted that they were all inside the reef at the shore and were ready to go. They would wait until Spense commenced with the show. Spense had decided to blast "The Battle of New Orleans" loud enough to disrupt any sound sensors, and the flares and pyrotechnics initially would be lighting the site and exposing the guards. The swimmers were to navigate the rafts as close to the site as possible while staying out of the light in the shade of the shore trees. Then, Spense and Kate would shoot the flares and fireworks over the guards' heads into the mangroves, hoping to draw the guards down the road, away from the shore, into the swamp in search of the amplified voices. In Mick's mind, "hoping" was the key word.

CHAPTER 22

At eleven thirty Johnny Horton's "In 1814 we took a little trip" filled the sky, rebounding off the water and palms on shore. Simultaneously, a flare burst above the site. Illuminated were four guards standing, facing the water. Lottie, on the bridge with a high powered telescope, called down that they all were holding some sort of machine gun–looking weapons, up and aimed, as if they were expecting company from the water. The sound and lightshow appeared to do nothing to confuse or even surprise them. They just kept sweeping their weapons back and forth facing the water.

"Somethin' ain't right," Mick, who had field glasses, said to Spense and Kate who were busy loading mortars. His heart started pounding; obviously something was awry already. "Peewee, are you guys amping your voices?" he yelled into the radio.

"Sure are, MP. Why?"

"The guards are paying no attention to you guys. You sure they can hear you?"

"I believe we got a problem, MP." Peewee's voice was grim, deadpan.

"What's up?" Mick asked. He could hardly hear with his heart pounding in his ears. The dread he woke up with was coming to bear.

"Vernal never showed. His two guys are here. Said Vernal never came to meet them in Marsh Harbour, and he didn't answer his phone."

"Did they go look for him?"

"They didn't have time. They wanted to show up here on time. This isn't like Vernal. Vernal is as dependable as they come. You say the guards are paying no attention to the sound of our voices? Maybe they can't hear us over the 'Battle of New Orleans' blaring at a million decibels."

"OK. We'll stop the music. Angus, where are you guys?"

"We as close to the site without being seen."

"Oh. Stay put. We'll cut the sound for a minute but keep the lights coming. See what they do."

The sudden silence seemed louder than the music had been. When a couple skyrockets illuminated the shore, the guards still didn't pay any attention to the voices coming from behind them that were now even skipping across the water to the Mary. "Angus, push a raft just out of the shadows at the next skyrocket," Mick told them. "Let's see what happens."

When the sky lit up again, Mick could see the raft through the glasses. As the front edge of the raft appeared in the light, without hesitation all four guards opened fire, like they were expecting the raft. The front end of the raft started to deflate as it disappeared back into the shadows.

"Angus, are you all right?" Mick yelled into his mouthpiece.

A ramble of unintelligible creole erupted in their ears.

"English, Angus! I can't even understand that gibberish," Peewee reproved.

"Yeoh, mon! Sheet!" Angus's excited speech burst back now in his island lilt.

"No one's hurt?" Mick asked again, afraid of the answer.

"We all right, but sheet, man. Dot just open up like he knows we was here."

"Peewee, what you thinking?" Mick asked. "Peewee … ?"

"I'm thinking. I'm thinking."

"I know how important this is to you, but we don't want anyone killed. I think we should abort." Mick looked over at Spense and Kate who both just looked back, eyes wide.

"Abort?" Peewee said sarcastically. "I think you've been watching too many movies, MP."

CHAPTER 22

"OK: desist, stop, cease, quit!" Mick yelled, near panic.

"Angus, you guys back off to where you can get back to the boat. It would appear they were expecting us," Peewee ordered. "Mick, why don't you fire some flares over the guards' heads into the mangroves. We'll come closer and turn up our amps. See what they do."

"OK, I guess," Mick replied. "But why?"

"Just do it, OK." It wasn't a question.

Spense shrugged at Mick when he told him, turned, and fired a flare over the guards' heads above the jungle. The amplified voices filled the night, loud even at the Mary. One guard turned, faced the jungle, and fired several rounds randomly in the direction of the voices.

"You OK, Peewee?" Mick shouted into the mouthpiece.

"No. You have any idea what you're doing to our eardrums, little guy? Don't worry. We're covered. We're nowhere near in range."

"Do we have to worry about starting the jungle on fire?" Mick asked a little less loudly. He knew that was dumb, but he had no idea what else to say or do.

He could hear Peewee laugh. "It's a mangrove swamp. Napalm couldn't start a fire in here. MP, I'm sending my men around farther on the right. They'll keep talkin'. I'm going to cross the road and come in from the other side. Why don't you start the music again? In case they do have some kind of sound sensors."

"Come in? To where? What're you doing? I thought we're gonna stop?" Mick said.

"There's no 'I' in stop," Peewee tossed back, blithely.

"What's that supposed to mean?" Mick yelled again getting angry.

"You're gonna have to stop that shoutin', MP. You're giving me a headache."

"Well, if you're saying what I think you're saying, let me point out there's an 'I' in desist, abstain, avoid, yield, relinquish, resign …"

Peewee laughed again. "There's my wordsmith. I can't wait to see your coverage of this event. I'm crossing the road now."

"Coverage! Peewee, you're nuts. It's too dangerous now. We've apparently lost the element of surprise. They're prepared for us."

"So, we'll package up a new surprise. You might as well save your voice, MP, and my eardrums. They've obviously gotten to Vernal somehow. I'm not leaving knowing they'll be starting their shit up again tomorrow. Angus?"

"Yes, Mr. T?"

"I want you to have all but you and one other man take the rafts, except the one with sugar, and swim them back out beyond the reefs to the boat."

"OK, we will. The wind blowin' pretty strong. It going to be tough to push da rafts."

"Do what you can," Peewee said. "The rafts are expendable. You're not. Just be sure the guys are out and away?"

"Yes, sir."

"Then, when we clear the area of guards, you and whoever get all that sugar into the gas tanks of those vehicles."

"Yes, sir."

"Just how do you expect to clear the area of guards, and what do you plan on doing about the explosives all by yourself, Peewee?" Mick asked hoarsely, trying to remain calm and not lose his composure. Every time he looked over at Spense and Kate they just stared back, wide-eyed.

CHAPTER 22

"What I planned on before we got the idea to confiscate the stuff—like I said: explode or burn them."

"Wait," Mick said. "Spense is putting this on speaker."

"Hello there, Peewee my man. It's Spense."

"I'm guessing that twisted little mind of yours has a plan," Peewee wheezed as he wound his way through the mangroves.

"Well, even though my vote would be for all of us to get the hell out of here before we end up dead or incarcerated, the little that I know about you informs me that you're not going to desist, yield, or whatever. So, yes, I've got a suggestion. How close are you to the site?"

"Not sure. Why don't you fire a flare right over the site? I'll get my bearings and then, if you can see, tell me which way the door to the trailer opens."

"It sounds like our two minds are navigating the same channels," Spense said. "What are you contemplating?"

"Spense, tell me what'd happened if you shot a flare into that trailer full of … Vernal said it was Semtex and maybe some ammonium nitrate and something called Dexpan, and maybe some TNT dynamite?"

"Exactly what I was thinking. I'm not an expert, but plastic explosives should only burn, not explode, if set on fire by a flare. Ammonium nitrate—I'm not sure, but I don't see a flare causing a major explosion. I think that'd all just burn. I've heard of Dexpan. It's been used for underwater demolition on some of the development sites I've seen on other islands. It's a nonexplosive out of water, I believe. I assume it would just burn also. Of course, you know about TNT. Depending on how much they have, there would be an explosion, definitely. I wouldn't suggest you linger too long. Better get those guards out of there, somehow, as well."

"How good are you at aiming that flare gun?" Peewee asked.

"Good enough. I'd guess that if the trailer opens toward the water, I can get one in … if it's open."

"Well, let loose with a flare and we'll talk."

As the flare illuminated the site, Peewee realized he was closer than he thought. He could see that the trailer, situated on his side of the almost four-acre cleared site area, had the hitch facing toward the jungle, which meant the door, though closed, was facing the water. "You see what I see?" Pewee asked.

"Yes. You have some contrivance, I assume, to get it open?" Spense asked.

"Sure, my teeth," Peewee answered.

Spense, Mick, and Kate all looked at each other, not sure if he was serious or joking. Mick, feeling a little dazed and disconcerted, asked Spense if he was seriously considering what he just said they were supposed to attempt to do with the flares. Spense shrugged; Kate just stared, still wide-eyed but for some reason smiling.

"Your teeth, eh?" Kate yelled into the mike.

"Could do, Sweetie," Peewee quipped, "but I think I'll use this little crow bar I had the foresight to bring along, instead. So, think you can keep them distracted while I break this wee lock?"

Mick, exasperated, spit into the mike: "How do you 'contrive' to get the guards out safely and give Angus the time to 'safely' dump a load of sugar into each vehicle? I suspect a trailer-full of explosives may create a mighty big frickin' wind!"

"The same way I plan on telling my boys here in this frickin' swamp to beat ass: a loud, amplified voice telling them to shake their asses out of here if they don't want to get them blown to bits."

CHAPTER 22

"What if they don't listen? My God, Peewee, everyone could be blown to bits!"

"Hmm, Spense, how about some near misses at the cock suckers—excuse my French, little lady? Think that'll set the fear of hell fire in 'em? Maybe they'll take off runnin' if some pretty little missiles part their hair."

"You got it, my superlative saboteur," Spense answered, not willing to argue with the determined crazy man. "I wonder, will a flare from this distance injure a man? What about a firework?"

"If you hit one, just don't hit 'em in the head … if you can help it."

"OK, I guess. We'll do our best. Give us a couple of minutes and I think we'll garner their attention." Spense called up to Lottie, who was standing up on the bridge, hands on hips, shaking her head disgustingly: "Hold us as steady as you can, my dear."

"You better hurry," Lottie called down. "You're all insane, you know. The winds comin' up and even this monster will be listing, so good luck."

Spense and Kate, who now had determined scowls on their faces, loaded the mortars. "Do we aim at 'em low or over their heads?" Kate asked.

"I'd say start over their heads until you get the range, then powder their behinds if we have to," Spense said.

The first two aerial shells burst right over the guards' heads and all four of them hit the ground. Spense then fired some ground spinners right at them and Kate, almost simultaneously, a flare. The spinners got them up and hopping as they randomly whirled around them, bouncing off their legs. The flare was a near miss and sent them scurrying to the massive graders and machines for cover. The second barrage of rockets—a Comet and Mad Dog—ricocheted around the huge machines. They heard a scream, assuming one of them had gotten hit. In the flashes and moving shadows Lottie could see Peewee had climbed up on the back of the trailer. Spense fired a batch of Parachutes over the machines, illuminating the machines and the crouching guards only, leaving Peewee in dark shadows.

"It's open," Peewee announced. "Fire a flare near the trailer to get your range and let them see the opened end of the trailer. That should give them an idea of our intentions. If they have any common sense, maybe they'll get the hell out of here."

"It sounded like one of the guards was hit," Mick told Peewee.

There was a long pause. "A firework's not going to kill anybody. Spense, send that flare."

Spense fired a flare that landed on top of the trailer.

"Holy shit, mama!" Peewee, this time, yelled into his mouthpiece.

"Sorry," Spense said. "A little too close for comfort?"

"No shit, Spenser!" Peewee's voice then boomed into the sudden darkness: "Everyone, run for your lives. The next one goes into the trailer and this whole place goes up!"

Spense fired another flare over the machines and three guards took off running out the road, one limping. But the one left walked out defiantly and shot several rounds toward the trailer.

"You OK?" Mick yelled to Peewee.

"No," Peewee answered. "My eardrums are damaged."

"Sorry," Mick said more softly. "Are you hit?"

"Don't worry; I'm OK. I've got cover behind the trailer. But you better show that macho idiot that we mean business.

CHAPTER 22

Fire a rocket at the son of a bitch; get macho man moving. Once he's gone, I'll help Angus."

"What if I buffet the buffoon?" Spense asked.

"OK, shoot a smaller rocket or something, but what are the odds you'll hit him? Maybe first shoot a flare toward the trailer ... a little less close, if you don't mind, to remind him we're serious. If he's not a complete idiot, maybe he'll take off."

Immediately a flare flew and bounced off the side of the trailer.

"Did I hear that flare hit something?" Peewee asked.

"Nah, just your imagination," Mick joked, finally accepting the inevitable and figuring he might as well enjoy himself since Peewee was not going to back off until the deed was done.

Again, Peewee's voice boomed into the night: "The next one is in the trailer. Run for your lives!"

And immediately, a rocket whizzed toward the guard who was holding his ground, looking at the trailer but not firing anymore. He apparently heard the rocket, turned, and froze as the rocket twisted and spun, nailing him right in the midsection. He immediately buckled and fell to the ground.

"Uh-oh," Spense said.

"Uh-oh what?" Peewee asked.

"I fear I have hit the miscreant."

"'Miscreant'?" Peewee exclaimed. "Where you get words like that?"

"Genetic. I was born with a propensity for presumption. But the man is not moving. What do you want to do?"

"What I'd like to do is leave him there as a warning message, but hold off and I'll go check on him."

Peewee ran in the dark to where the guard lay. He was alive and started to writhe on the ground. Peewee grabbed a piece of wire and tied his hands and feet together. He picked up the Uzi in case the other guards might return.

"Angus, get your ass and the sugar over here. Hurry! Spense, give me a flare down the road. Make sure those suckers haven't changed their minds about runnin'."

No guards were visible in the eerie light of the flare, so they either had scampered away or ducked off the road. Angus and his accomplice were hauling the sacks of sugar as fast as they could. Peewee started prying all the gas caps off the various machines: graders, earth movers, front loaders, trenchers, bobcats. Spense fired another flare, high, to illuminate as much as possible of the site and road, but the only guard visible was the one tied on the ground.

When Angus and the Haitian were done pouring the sugar into the gas tanks, the two swimmers, along with Peewee, headed back to the water and the raft, each with an armful of explosives Peewee had carried to them. Peewee headed over to the guard. "Give us another flare," Peewee requested.

When the flare burst, they could see Peewee bent over the guard. "How is he?" MP asked.

"He's gonna have a good bruise and nice sunburn on his front side; nothin' a little ice and aloe won't take care of. I'm gonna haul him out of here, down the road a ways. Did you see anybody down there?"

"No," Mick said. "But they could be hiding somewhere off the road. Be careful."

"This fat ass will make a good shield. They'd have to shoot through him to get me, and I got the Uzi. Don't worry, little guy. Why don't you shoot a rocket straight down the road just in case they have decided to get brave?"

In a few seconds a multicolored rocket slithered over him and bounded down the road in an incongruously lovely

CHAPTER 22

display of color in the dark night. "Nice shooting for an old fart, Spense."

"Not me, I fear to say. That's our straight shooter, Kate."

"I'm impressed, li'l sister. There's apparently more to you than meets the eye. I'll have to thank you properly when we return," Peewee said.

"I'm not sure what you've got in mind, but let's just make sure we all do return," Kate begged. "Now, get the hell out of there, and Spense and I will rid the world of the explosives." She looked at Mick and Spense. "I can't believe we're doing this!"

"You're on," Peewee responded. "Spense, light us that road one more time and I'm outta here." When the flare illuminated the road, they could see Peewee had untied the guard's legs and was leading him down the road. "Give me five and I'll be out of harm's way." They could hear Peewee's breathing and the guard's muttering as they hurried away. When all fell back into darkness, all three of them stared at the walkie-talkie in Mick's hand, like they could see Peewee and the guard in the transistor.

Just as Spense and Kate were ready to let fly, they heard several rounds of rapid submachine gun fire coming from the jungle. "Goddamnit," screeched out of the mike. Then Peewee's strained voice: "Blow the shit up! Blow it!" Then a pause and more gunfire.

Mick, Spense, and Kate looked at each other. "Peewee! What happened?" Mick yelled into the walkie-talkie. "Peewee?" No response. "Peewee? What do we do?" Mick implored the others.

"What the hell happened?" Lottie yelled down from the bridge. "I couldn't see anything."

Mick looked up at her and shrugged. "What we gonna do?" he repeated.

[335

"We have to blow it," Spense said. "Regardless."

"What if he's not safe?" Kate wailed.

"I'd guess we're not safe if we don't," Spense said. "You want to argue with Peewee?"

"What if there's no one to argue with?" Kate asked sarcastically.

"Personally, I'm not willing to take that chance," Spense answered. "Take aim … and fire." Spense's flare hit below the trailer and bounced under it. Kate's aerial shell flew over the trailer and burst at the far edge of the clearing.

"I'm low; you're high. Go again," Spense said, his voice trembling. The next flare hit the top edge of the trailer; Kate's shell was right on and went into the open end.

It burst, and multicolored light bounced around in the trailer. They all waited in anticipation. "I can't see anything. What do you see, Lottie?" Mick hollered up.

"It looked like something was burning, but now I don't see anything," Lottie yelled back down from her higher vantage point. "But good shootin', you guys. It'll go up, I bet, if you hit it again."

"Again," Spense said. "This time launch some ground spinners. They should stay lit longer." Spense's flare went directly into the black hole this time. Kate's spinners missed low and lit up the area as they twirled around the trailer. Light glowed from inside the trailer. "Again!" Spense yelled. They both now had the range, made easier by the light from the spinners. Kate's Mad Dog and Spense's flare both burst inside the trailer. Suddenly a vivid, intense, translucent glare emanated out the door of the trailer. It was almost other-worldly. There was no sound at first, but a brilliant, blinding effervescence shooting out of the opening at the end of the trailer. Then before they

CHAPTER 22

could blink, they were blinded by an overwhelming flash ... before any sound. By the time the deafening roar reached them, the trailer had dissipated into a million particles and the boom rolled past them in an intense wave of sound and heat deflecting and reverberating off the trees, water, and it seemed, the stars.

They had all instinctively ducked at the eruption of light, then sound, then heat. When they looked up at the site, there no longer was a trailer, only a glowing mass of unearthly light emanating into the sky, illuminating the jungle, creating sinister moving, swaying shadows.

CHAPTER 23

MICK WOKE abruptly in a cold sweat, twisted up in his sheets. Again, he couldn't make sense of what he had been dreaming about, but whatever it was had his heart pounding. He looked at the clock: ten a.m. He got up, confused, wandered around the room, and ended up at the window facing the Abaco. He could see the sun had lit the lighthouse, the red and white stripes bright and clear, but Mick couldn't clear his head. Last night seemed like a hallucination. What was he supposed to do this morning? He knew there was something, but his brain was scrabble. Shit! It was supposed to be brunch at Heidi's. And Peewee! Damn! His mind must be rejecting the occurrence of last night. What about Peewee? Like pulling in a fish, he reeled in the recollection of last night's events.

They had picked up the swimmers and the rafts, including Angus and his companion. Everything was fine with the swimmers. It had been difficult for them to get the rafts back, especially the half-deflated one, as the wind had picked up, blowing in. Then they had cruised slowly back to the harbor, nobody talking, nobody knowing what to say, nobody wanting to think. They had moored the Mary, dropped off the swimmers with the rafts, doried in, piled into Lottie's jeep, and hauled down to the road that led to the site ... but no one was there. They all had stood at the gate for a while, just staring off. It had been eerie: a deathly silence with the

CHAPTER 23

unearthly radiance still dancing in the distance like a too luminous, sinister aurora borealis.

Mick peeked into Kate's room. She lay flat on her stomach with her clothes still on from the night before. They had both walked into their rooms without a word. Mick had lain on the bed, fully clothed as well, and had immediately fallen asleep. Kate had apparently done the same.

He walked downstairs like a zombie and began the morning ritual: put the coffee on and walked out onto the porch. But when he began his breathing—good air in, bad air out—he started hyperventilating. He leaned on the railing for support and for several minutes could not catch his breath. He started taking slower, shallow breaths and gradually came out of it. He couldn't remember what time HS had said for brunch, or even if, after last night, there was to be a brunch, much less a father. He seemed to recall that she had said that after their morning session, they'd head out. So, then, why wasn't she here? She'd never been this late before. Was it because it was supposed to be a brunch? Or … he didn't want to consider the alternative.

Why hadn't Peewee answered last night? Gunfire and then no response? No one had even wanted to talk about or consider why last night. The entire ordeal still seemed like a horrible phantasm: rockets, flares, the Battle of New Orleans, Uzis, topped off with what a miniature nuclear ignition might look like. He figured they were all in a state of shock, maybe denial. What would the authorities do? How would everything be explained? Although there was no real police presence on Elbow, wouldn't the police in Marsh Harbour or even Nassau get involved? The script for the evening could have been written by Lewis Carroll. Would Peewee climb out of the rabbit hole?

| 339

He hadn't heard Kate come down, but suddenly her arms were around him and she laid her head against his back. He covered her hands with his own, and both stood speechless for several minutes. Then Kate almost whispered, "Do you think Peewee is all right?"

He didn't answer. In his heart he felt Peewee had to be all right. But was this just unrealistic wishful thinking? Then, Mick saw HS coming down the road from the north. His body stiffened and Kate felt it and looked up, seeing her as well. They both stood there, silently, Kate hugging Mick harder as HS walked up.

She stopped at the bottom of the steps, looking up at them quizzically. "Busy night last night I understand," she said calmly, caustically.

OK, they both thought. If the authorities had visited, if something was wrong with Peewee, she wouldn't be this unruffled, unemotional ... or would she? She was so strange, pleasantly strange maybe, but definitely difficult to read. They both knew she didn't really approve of their and especially her father's antics last night. Was this her means of vindication?

Mick and Kate stood their ground and just looked at her expectantly. Finally, the corner of her mouth curled into what was almost a smile. "If your concern is about my father, he's fine. You have to learn not to worry about him. He does what he does, always like he's in some absurd comedy, and seems destined to enter and exit laughing."

Kate let go of Mick and told HS: "Heidi, please come up and sit down and tell us what happened last night. We heard gunshots and then lost contact with your father. We went back and couldn't find him. We were worried sick."

CHAPTER 23

HS came up onto the porch, carrying the folder, and sat in a deck chair. "No coffee cups this morning? I repeat: it does no good to worry about your Peewee. Mother and I have quit. My 'plum' today explains why we cannot worry. Want to read it?"

"No ... I mean yes," Mick sputtered. "But what happened last night ... to your father?"

She pulled her feet up, hugged her knees, buried her head between them, and started to shake. Kate and Mick looked at each other, back at Heidi.

"Heidi?" Kate said softly.

"Just get your coffee please," she managed. "I'll be all right in a minute. Water, please."

Mick nodded to Kate, who turned and went into the kitchen. Mick sat in the chair next to Heidi. She was again wearing shorts and a tank top this time, no shoes. Her hair was drawn back today in a ponytail. Hugging her knees in that deck chair she looked so diminutive. Like a child. Until she looked up at him. There was both anguish and choler in her eyes—eyes that certainly didn't belong to a child. They burrowed into him. He couldn't return the look; it chilled him.

Kate returned with a tray carrying two mugs and a glass of water. She instinctively sensed something amiss with Mick. Almost cautiously she handed Mick his mug and sat on the other side of Heidi, handing her the glass. She took it, uncharacteristically not saying "thank you." After Heidi had taken a sip, Kate asked hesitantly: "Can you tell us what happened with Peewee?"

Heidi stared into her glass, took a couple more sips, wiped her eyes with the back of her hand, and looked at Kate, then Mick. Snot was running onto her upper lip, so Mick reached into his pocket and pulled out a Kleenex. "Here, not sure if it's clean or not, but you're gonna be sippin' snot in a second."

She attempted a smile, said thank you, took the Kleenex, and blew her nose ... more like Peewee might. Both Mick and Kate half laughed. "Sorry, not very ladylike, I guess," she said, eyes red-rimmed. But the anger was gone, replaced by what appeared to be despondency. "Father is fine, but apparently a guard is not. I mourn for the guard, but my apparent affliction is for my father. Something bad, irreparable is going to happen to him. I am sure of it."

"What happened to the guard?" Mick asked, although a breath of relief escaped. "Have the police been around?"

"Father will be there at brunch. Let him explain. I don't want to talk about it, if you don't mind."

"No, no, of course not. Ummm, ok." Mick looked at Kate, who just shrugged. "So, let's take a look at your new poem, another 'plum' poem you said?"

"Yes. I wrote it last night lying in bed, waiting. Waiting to see if my father was going to return. I was sure he would, although I'm not the first person to feel this way. Then we best head over. Mother will have everything ready. She doesn't often get a chance to entertain guests, and, although highly irritated this morning, she's very excited about meeting you. And, in spite of my father's apprehension, mother has extended the invitation to include you, Miss Kate. She's very proud to host what she considers a 'keen' woman. She appreciates what you're doing for the boys. Apparently you made a good impression."

"Oh, oh, good, but that's OK. You needn't invite me, I ..."

"Too late, I'm afraid," Heidi interrupted. "She would be insulted if you didn't accept ... unless ..."

CHAPTER 23

"Unless what?" Kate asked.

"It's an imposition on you for some reason."

"You got something better to do?" Mick posed.

"Oh, shut up! Yes, of course. I'd love to come," Kate said.

"Well then, here." Heidi had been holding the folder the entire time and handed it to Kate. "Why don't you read it? I did the sketch last night, too. I don't think either's very good. I was pretty upset."

Kate took the folder. "Shall I read it aloud?"

"Yes, please."

Kate read:

>Sometimes the
>Darkness
>Filled the room as
>Though
>Confident it were
>Going to
>Stay for more than just
>The night
>
>—H.S.

Of course they could both picture Heidi lying there last night, acutely concerned about what Peewee was up to ... what they were all up to. It registered to Mick why he had gotten the intense, almost accusatory look earlier. She may have been worried about all of them—he, Spense, Kate, and Lottie—but they were all complicit in putting her father not only at risk but in breaking a definitive moral code of hers: in spite of the good they may have been trying to accomplish, someone had gotten hurt—killed, the way it sounded.

"I think it touches on an emotion, a feeling we've all felt at times in our lives. I am very impressed with how simply and exquisitely you paint it with words," Kate said. "And the sketch, also simple, it expresses ... well, with the eyes, that you don't approve, and as a mime, you can't say anything about it. The mouth, the whole sketch, implies helplessness."

"Yes." Heidi smiled sadly. "So, if you two would like to get ready to go, we'd best head out. It's not a long walk. Actually, it's very near the clubhouse, or we could say: 'our new school.'"

Kate managed a smile at that and Mick asked: "Should we take the cart?"

"You'd have to leave it on a very narrow part of the road. Our path is where the scrub gets dense and encroaches on the road. It'd be best if we walked, I think."

"That's fine, Heidi," Kate said. "It's an easy walk, Mick. We'll run up and get ready, hon. Be down in a sec."

They headed out, walking fast and without much conversation. It was difficult for Mick and Kate to make small talk when their minds were congested with concern about what had happened last night.

The day was a little warm, and there was little breeze on this part of the road. Gradually the cottage lawns ended, the

CHAPTER 23

road narrowed, and thick bushes started encroaching from both sides. Suddenly Heidi told them to follow her and she ducked under some branches. Lizards and little critters scurried away in the brittle underbrush.

"Hey, isn't this the same way we took to the clubhouse?" Kate asked.

"Yes. We live near the clubhouse. The path will divide and we head left, around the little coral bluff with the ladder, to the other side of the hill, where the island narrows to a tip, out past the end of the road. Better prepare yourself for a surprise. I wouldn't call our home ... conventional."

"Weird," Mick said. "I've walked down to the end of the road several times. I've never noticed this path."

"No. You don't really see it because there's no break in the bushes. If you were to happen on it, which is unlikely—nobody wanders through this dry, tough scrub—but, if you did, you'd think the path ended at the coral wall. You'll see."

The path climbed gradually and, sure enough, it appeared to end at a rock and coral escarpment about ten to twelve feet high, rough, jagged, and impossible to climb. "This is where they drop the ladder," Kate said. "It was really cool."

"Please follow." HS headed to the left toward the rugged coral. No path was apparent over the coral, so walking it looked to be difficult, but it was easier than it looked. Heidi had stopped and slipped on a pair of flip-flops she had taken out of the little purse, or bag really, that she always carried the folder in. "I don't care how tough your feet are," she said. "They'd be in shreds walking on this coarse coral." They followed her around the promontory.

The brush ended and huge palms appeared, along with sparse, long grasses as the coral dissipated into sand. They

| 345

heard a sound like distant war drums. Suddenly the north tip of the island came into view. It was stunning. Beyond the sand, which sloped down gradually for several hundred feet, was a mix of coral and rocks that stretched off along a rocky shoal that crawled for several hundred yards into the distance until a huge singular rock rose maybe fifty feet. On the left of the rocks were calm pools of water turning turquoise as they blended with the white sand of the Abaco Sea. On the right were the waves of the Atlantic crashing into and up high over the rocks. The sound of drums they had heard as they had neared the wall were waves crashing on the rocks and coral as if they were hollow. It was two different worlds, the peaceful sea on the left, the tumultuous ocean on the right.

As Mick and Kate stood, awestruck by the incongruity of peace and rage, calm and fury, Heidi stepped in front of them and pointed up and behind.

"What the …" Mick cried as he turned.

"It's a … What the hell is it?" Kate hollered.

Built into the side of the hill forming the craggy promontory was what looked like the front end of a large riverboat or cruise ship. Flat stepping-stones led through the sand, twisting through the coconut palms to where, cut into the forehull, were French doors. This was apparently an entrance, which had a canvas awning covering it held up by large bamboo poles. Due to the sand, the entrance was reminiscent of Africa, safari-ish, except for the fact that there was a ship seemingly hovering above.

Several levels of receding balconies wrapped around each side. They had been, apparently, the decks, but because it was only maybe the front quarter of the boat, they appeared more like terraces. Like any boat out of water, the entire apparition

CHAPTER 23

appeared huge and loomed high into the sky. On the first, lower deck, they could see the tops of chairs and a table with an aquamarine and gold-colored umbrella—the colors of the Bahamian flag—one of which also blew in the breeze from the very top of the cabin, which appeared to be a mile in the air.

Kate and Mick were trying to take it all in, mouths wide open in awe, when Heidi let out a loud whistle. Immediately a large head appeared on the second deck, high above. "Welcome!" it bellowed down. "You made it back alive, I see." He lifted one arm in a greeting wave.

"It's you we were worried about, you big oaf," Kate yelled up at him.

"Are you hurt?" Mick hollered.

"Nahh. Heides, show them in. Wanda is making the last preparations." And he disappeared into the … whatever.

As they followed Heidi up the walkway to the entrance, the girth of the hull seemed amazing. They came in through wide French doors into an interior area that had multiple-colored high-gloss cubicles like a large, chic chicken coop, running from the floor to the ceiling on the right, and a row of hooks made out of what looked like some kind of bone or coral on the left. There was a round porthole window on each side. The floor was wood, also high gloss, with a woven mat running the length of the hallway. Just past the hooks was a spiral staircase that twisted up to the deck above. The hallway straight ahead ended at a wide set of stairs heading up on the right side and a narrower passageway on the left that led into dark beyond the stairway.

"Everyone must take off their shoes and place them in the cubicles," Heidi informed them. "Much of the decking upstairs is a polished wood. Only clean, bare feet or slippers allowed. Mother's rules. You can hang anything you want on the hooks."

Kate hung up her purse and hat, and all three put their sandals in a cube. "OK, this is amazing so far," Kate said. "You'd never know you're in a boat, here."

"Except for the portholes, *eh*?"

"Oh, shut up, wiseass," Kate said in typical Kate style.

"We could go up the staircase here," Heidi said, rolling her eyes. "It takes us to the deck off the kitchen. But I'll take you to the main staircase, which gets us up into the main cabin." As they walked down the hallway Heidi explained what was behind each door, mostly the mechanicals of the home and storage. The hallway was dim, lit by electric sconces on the wall between each door. This gave the illusion of a fancy hotel or ocean liner, especially with the wide stairway at the end carpeted with an oriental runner and handrails of brass.

"My god, we're in the Titanic!" Mick exclaimed loudly when they reached the staircase.

A baritone roar rumbled down the stairs: "Come aboard, my old friend and … new friend."

Heidi led them up and into what must have been the original main cabin, but larger than one might expect, and, as warned: high-glossed wooden flooring. There was a ship's wheel along the right side made of a beautiful dark mahogany with brass spokes. A leather, very comfortable-looking captain's chair sat in place by the wheel. The windows, looking forward, also framed in mahogany, must have been that of the original river boat or cruise ship or whatever it had been. The view through the windshield was of the northern tip of the island: slow-rolling sea waves left, crashing ocean waves right, the narrow, tapering peninsula of rocks and coral ending at the

CHAPTER 23

huge rock which was more apparent with this elevated view. There was an island off in the distance.

It was difficult to know where to look around the cabin: a red enamel cone-shaped open fireplace was in the middle of the room, surrounded randomly by floor pillows. Everything seemed random: odd-shaped pieces of driftwood, some serving as tables, were scattered everywhere. Colorful pieces of coral hung from the bead board paneled ceiling. In one corner was an old TV with a couple chairs. All but the back of the room was windows, under which were book shelves filled with books and more books. The back wall had a ship's staircase going up to the next level, probably with the deck that the huge head had appeared from. Next to the stairs was a hallway that also led into darkness.

Suddenly they heard a clank behind them, and they turned to see 'Mother' in the kitchen. She was so small and unsubstantial they hadn't noticed her. She couldn't have been more than four and a half feet tall, but, oddly, looked normal. She had silvery-white hair that hung to her waist. Her skin was island brown and smooth as marble. There was no immediate impression of age. She wore a beautiful, subtly colored gown of a flowing material—maybe silk.

"Sorry," she said in a tiny voice.

Heidi, who had been silent when they entered the cabin, as had Mick and Kate who were speechless in their astonishment, said: "Mother, this is MP ... or Mick—you take your pick—and his *sister*, Kate. This is my mother, Wanda."

Wanda smiled demurely. "Welcome. The food almost ready."

"Is there anything I can do?" Kate asked immediately, and walked toward the kitchen and met Wanda on her way out from behind the counter. "I am so glad to meet you. May I give you a hug?"

"Oh my, yes." And Kate bent, giving her a hug and a kiss on her cheek. "Thank you so much for inviting us. I just love your home."

Mick came over and took both her hands, leaned in, and kissed her on the forehead. "You're simply adorable," he said.

Kate slapped him on the arm. "Don't get so familiar, fool."

"Oh, that awright," Wanda said with a soft, island, sing-songy inflection. "I feel I know both already." She laughed lightly at herself, or something.

"Mama," Heidi said to Mick and Kate, "is a little perturbed this morning." Heidi smiled, Mama looked concerned, more about what Heidi was going to say it seemed. "And, as I said, I am more than a little worried about my father: Mr. T! You've heard him called that? His boys and the island men call him that. Who even remembers Mr. T? Father acts like he thinks he's a super-eagle or something. He doesn't know he can't fly."

"Oh, Heidi. Don't talk. Going to be too much trouble," Wanda warned gently.

"He got shot, you know? Well, sort of," HS said, hands on hips.

"How in the devil can you get 'sort of' shot?" Kate asked.

"Shot where?" Mick asked.

"On the construction site," HS said flatly.

"No, I mean where on his body did he get shot?"

"I knew what you meant. Do you see what I mean?"

"Oh." Mick realized she was being pointedly sarcastic, meaning he was shot in the escapade at the construction site, an escapade she did not approve of. So this was the "tough nut" Peewee had mentioned. "Yes. Yes, I do know what you mean. I assume he's OK?"

CHAPTER 23

She turned, walked over to the bottom of the chrome steps, and yelled up: "Father, what are you doing?"

"Heides, come up here will you, please?"

"No. I go," Wanda said, and like a darling little hen—short steps, chest out, head pointed and meaning business—tapped her tiny feet over to the stairs.

"Wanda," came a voice from above, "you take care of our guests and the food." He cleared his throat loudly. Heidi rolled her eyes and said, "I'll go, Mama."

"C'mon, Wanda, I'll help you in the kitchen." Kate gently took hold of her arm and they walked back into the kitchen. When they got there, Heidi and Mick both broke out laughing. The counters, which looked normal when Wanda was behind them, barely made Kate's thighs. The contrast was marvelous; it made Wanda look normal size and Kate eight feet tall.

Heidi and Mick were both laughing hard, as if the situation needed comic relief. "You should see my father when he's in there. He looks big as a bear." And Heidi burst out laughing again. Mick cracked up at Heidi, Kate and Wanda at both of them.

A remarkably emphatic clearing of the throat echoed around the cabin-room.

"Oh, shoot!" Heidi ducked and ran—for some reason her demeanor had made it seem like she never ran anywhere —over to and up the stairs.

As Mick walked around the counter, heading out toward the deck to check the view, he heard Heidi and Peewee coming down the stairs and turned. Heidi was helping him. His left arm was bandaged, as was the calf on his right leg. "All right. What the hell happened?" Mick demanded. "We were afraid you were dead. HS here wouldn't tell us anything. Said *you* would, so spill the beans."

| 351

He could tell Peewee was in considerable pain, even though he was trying to act as if nothing was the matter. "It's nothing," he came out with when he reached the bottom. "Let's go sit on the terrace and I'll tell the tale."

"No way!" Kate complained. "I need to hear it, too, now. What the devil happened?"

"Let's all go sit down. Woman and daughter, if you don't mind, could you save any more scolding for later?"

Neither Wanda nor Heidi answered, and Heidi held his arm as he limped toward the terrace.

"Here, let me help," Mick offered.

"Nah, I'm fine. Thank you, daughter," and Heidi, without a word, let go and with a disdainful look headed out through another wide French door onto the 'terrace' ahead of them.

Mick held onto the abandoned arm anyway, and they followed Heidi with Wanda and Kate behind. The terrace, or what had been the foredeck of a vessel, was startling. Considering the elevation and a ship's rail encompassing the perimeter of the deck, they felt like they were on an ocean liner, but with sand and palm trees surrounding as if they were sailing the desert. "What a fantastic place, Peewee. What the devil was it?" Mick asked.

They all sat down at a large rectangular, again high-gloss, wooden table. Peewee maneuvered himself into a chair with arms at one end, and Wanda and Heidi into two armless ones side-by-side on the other end. There were long benches on both sides and Mick and Kate sat side-by-side on the one where they faced out at the water. The huge umbrella they had seen from below protected them, and the table, from the sun.

"OK, let's hear about these injuries," Kate insisted.

CHAPTER 23

"You see out the point and past the big rock?" Peewee started, ignoring Kate's demand.

"Yeah," Mick answered.

"That island floating out there in the haze is about a mile away. A reef extends all the way from here to there. At low tide you can see other smaller boulders above the waterline, exposed in the swells. At high tide, you can't see them. Every once in a while, still, boats will try to make the run from the ocean to the sea. Unless they're really small crafts and they know specifically what they're doing, they generally don't make it. Somewhere around the 1940s, one of the original ocean liners around here that made runs from Nassau to some of these outer islands foolishly tried it. It hit, aft, and sunk with its fore above. It was such a beautiful ship, they wanted to save it, so they tried to get it ashore, right here. They cut the destroyed section of the aft off—how I don't know, it wouldn't have been easy—and then, I've been told, they connected cables and lifted what's now our home by two helicopters and dropped it on this sandy spot. Problem was, they also dropped one of the helicopters. Four dead."

"It sat here—in the sun, so it bleached a bit but didn't rot—for years, while they argued about who owned it: Elbow, the Bahamas, the shipping company, or the helicopter company who presented a lawsuit. So first they were fighting over it as an asset, and then as a liability. I got down here thinking I was escaping a fucked bureaucratic system"

"Todd Kjelland!" Wanda warned fiercely, surprising Kate and Mick, but not Heidi and Peewee.

"Uh, my apologies, Mother. But it was a little surprising to find the same bureaucratic failings and foibles down here as well."

"Who got it over here against this bluff?" Mick asked.

"I did ... with a little help from my friends."

"Whaddya do, winch it?"

"Right on, my man."

"Right on?" Kate mocked, laughing.

"Yeah. Far out, too, how it actually worked without destroying the hull or decking. We hooked up some cables they had left and slowly slid it as tight as we could against the cliff. What's really cool ..."

"Uh-oh. I think we're getting a double entendre, unintentionally I do believe, from my father here," Heidi piped in.

"What's that? One of your poetry words?"

"What my father was going to say is that they added on to the back and so the hull here and downstairs runs right into the caves in the cliff, which is not only cool, but 'cool,' he thinks. We store foodstuff in them."

"And could escape through and out if we had to. Is that a triple whatever?" Peewee scoffed. "Anyway, there are cracks and crevices where the rock and coral meet."

"Don't talk no 'escape'!" Wanda again warned, although less fiercely.

"Speaking of escaping," Kate said, "it's time we hear about last night and these bandages."

"How'd you come to own it?" Mick interjected.

"They were glad to get rid of it; got it for a song."

"You better start singing, Buster," Kate insisted, giving Mick a dirty look. "No more beating around the bush. What the heck happened last night?"

"Yes," Mick affirmed, tapping his knuckles on the table. "Tell!"

Wanda and Heidi sat back, folded their arms across their chests, tightened their lips, and hardened their eyes.

CHAPTER 23

"Well, the idgits. I'm escorting the 'hero' down the road, just getting 'im outta harm's way, in case that trailer blew to smithereens, which I assume it just about did. Holy sh—"

Wanda looked at him hard. HS snarled a sarcastic smile.

"Anywho, all of a sudden those other not-so-heroic idgits that had taken off running just jump out of the ditch and start blastin' away, spraying bullets all over the place. I had the other guy kinda in front of me, thinking they weren't gonna shoot him. I suppose it was dark, but they shoot the sh— crap out of him. I guess the bullets went right through him, and then me. One got me in the arm—nothing broken—but I think that bullet got a bit of bone in the leg on the way by. Have to admit, it hurts."

"Whaddya do?" Mick almost yelled. "What happened then?"

"Hell, I dove into the bush. Took off through the mangroves. Then I start worrying my other guys might hear the shots and get into it with them. I couldn't find the blasted walkie-talkie, so I start whistling like a fool bird or sumptin'. It's kind of a signal."

"Grown men whistling signals," Heidi said, shaking her head. "You'd think …"

"ANYWAY!" Peewee cut her off. "I find 'em and we sneak back by the road …"

"You're shot, for crying out loud! What you doing walking around?" Kate spouted.

"They blood all over him when he get home," Wanda said, mouth tight, eyes fierce.

"Ahh, it was mostly from the other guy. I don't know. I guess the adrenaline gets pumping. Anyway, we see 'em drag the dead guy away."

"This trouble!" Wanda, again.

| 355

"Have you heard anything about the police?" Mick asked.

"Nahh," Peewee answered. "They're not going to pay much attention to a dead immigrant Haitian who they probably have no record of even being here. I doubt the Mandelsung's 'll even report it—attract too much attention, red tape. You know they don't give a shit about the guy."

"But what about the site?" Mick insisted. "It looks like a bomb went off! How're they going to explain that?"

"I'll let them worry about that."

"But won't Spense get implicated? It was his boat. They had to know that!"

Pewee smiled. "The harbormaster will attest that Spense's little vessel never left the harbor."

"Why didn't you call us, to tell us what had happened?" Kate interjected. "What happened to the walkie-talkie?"

"I have no idea what happened to it. After I told you to blow the shit up, they fired again and I must have dropped it. I wasn't gonna hang around looking for it with those morons and their machine guns."

"We came back looking for you," Kate said.

"Well, we watched them get to the gate. They threw the guy in a mule ..."

"What?" Kate interrupted, exasperated. "Threw him in a *mule*?"

"A four-wheeler with a little box," Mick explained.

"Oh. OK," Kate said, grimacing, embarrassed.

"When they took off, so did we," Peewee finished. "Let's eat. I'm hungry."

"No matter how much you rationalize, a man is dead," HS said calmly, firmly, like a hammer falling, "or don't we want to mention that?"

CHAPTER 23

Anger flashed in Peewee's eyes. "*I* didn't kill anybody!"

"Yes, you did," she said, and looked at Mick and then Kate, "and so did you two, as well."

Peewee's fist hit the table. "No, they didn't. Now, Heidi Lea, would you and your mother serve the food?"

"I'll help," Kate said, standing up, sensing a stalemate, with the reality of what Heidi was saying sinking in hard.

Both Heidi and Wanda looked nonplussed, sat for a moment staring hard at Peewee, who was looking down at the table. Slowly, they got up and followed Kate into the kitchen.

Mick, feeling like Heidi was right—they were all complicit in a man being killed— looked bleakly at Peewee. He was breathing in short bursts. It was incongruous to see such a giant of a man near to crying. Mick didn't dare say anything ... didn't know what to say ... felt like crying himself.

CHAPTER 24

WHEN THEY got back, neither talking on the way as the realization of what they had caused continued to sink in, Kate went upstairs and Mick checked his messages. There were several from both Lottie and Spense, starting calmly and then crescendo-ing from annoyance to animosity to threats. "Spense and Lottie are pissed," Mick announced to Kate as she walked hesitantly out onto the porch. "What's the matter, hon?"

Kate sat down and looked over at Mick sitting at his computer on the porch table. "I also got an email from Sara."

"Yeah? What's up?"

"Said she heard through the grapevine that Richard now believes, or knows I guess, I'm still here in the Bahamas. Apparently he has visited Canada and South America—somewhere on the coast of Colombia. Imagine that! Spense must have been messing with him. How he expected to locate me, I have no idea, but he apparently is tracking our, my and Sara's, emails now and must have been waiting for us to give away specifically where I might be. He's gotta be really pissed. My God."

"Does he know you're here? I mean on Elbow Cay, or just in Marsh Harbour?"

"No idea. I assume still just Marsh Harbour. But I'd say it's time we figured out how we're going to deal with him before he pops up on our doorstep."

CHAPTER 24

"Well, today's Sunday," Mick said. "I'll email those two and see if they can come over today. I'm surprised they're not here waiting for us. They won't know a guard was killed."

"No, they won't; man, I just can't quite register that, you know?"

"Uh, yeah. What do we do?"

"About what?" Kate asked.

"I don't know. About any of it, I guess. I can't think straight. A man is dead and there was a major, MAJOR explosion, as well as a big frickin' mess. But I guess we'd better focus on this Richard."

"What about Peewee?" Kate asked.

"What *about* Peewee?"

"Well, don't you think we need his involvement? I don't know if he's in shape to deal with this now. Are we sure the police isn't going to be suspecting him?"

"You kiddin'?" Mick spouted. "He'd kill us if we didn't involve him."

"How we gonna get word to him if we meet today? We still don't know his damn number. He probably has email, too. And how's he gonna get here?"

"Don't know how he's gonna get here, but I know he will," Mick answered. "I'll text Spense and Lottie. You can get back to Sara and we'll keep our eyes open for one of your boys."

"Mßy boys?" Kate said, smiling.

"Sure, Teach. I'm not sure how diligent they still are about coming around, but I'd guess we'll see one of 'em. They used to slip by like ghosts; now I've noticed they stop and look or, if there's more than one, they'll talk a little loud. Probably got a crush on that cute little tush of yours."

"Hey! I'm their teacher. There's no tush in teaching. Men!"

"Oh, yeah? Ever had a crush on a cute male teacher?"

"Well, yeah, I suppose, when I was a kid."

"Like about their age?"

"All right, all right. I'll be aware of that. I'll go get my laptop."

They sat side-by-side: Mick texted both Spense and Lottie. Said he'd explain when they got there. Both responded immediately, saying they'd be there within the hour. Then he started on an email to Barney, cc'ing Jim, Jim, Randy, and George. Barney said they'd been pissed they weren't in the loop after Barney had gotten back and told them about all the excitement on Elbow Cay. Barney apparently wasn't in his cubicle, as he didn't answer back. Neither did Jim, Jim, Randy, or George. Kate found Sara at home, so they were having a needed catch-up.

Before they were done, three of the boys wandered by kicking a soccer ball. Kate took a break from her chat with Sara and went to the porch railing to talk to them. Told them she'd see them tomorrow, Monday; she'd meet them at the clubhouse. They said 'no,' that they'd come by to escort her as usual. When she asked if they would check with Peewee if he was up and able to come for a meeting, they laughed. Said if he was in his grave, he'd get up and come to the meeting. But he'd be taking his boat, not walking, and would probably need a ride from Hope Town. Apparently the word about last night was already out, at least to the island folk. Mick said he'd pick him up. They said give him a half an hour.

"What are you frowning about?" Kate asked, looking over at Mick when she was done chatting with Sara.

"Huh? Oh, nothing. Just thinking about my buddies. Wondering where I'm going to go from here, with …" he trailed off.

CHAPTER 24

"What? You mean you're thinking of leaving Elbow?"

"No, no ... not now. Never mind."

"Well ... I might be leaving," Kate said, holding her breath.

"What?" This was the main thing rolling around in the back of Mick's mind, like a pool ball that can't find a pocket. He knew she would be leaving ... but not now, not this soon!

"Well, they're actually making progress. Some sorta big guys have been convicted and gotten time."

"For what?" Mick was actually surprised they were sending some of them away. He thought maybe fines ... which, when you're making $10-$20-$100 million—big deal! But actual prison sentences? Marvelous!

"Right now insider trading, like Sara mentioned," Kate answered. "Interestingly, it's been emails to a great extent that's provided the proof."

"Cool. They deserve it. Some of those assholes have really grown enormous balls."

"Nice analogy, Wordsworth. So, anyway, they're setting some dates. I'm sure it's not imminent—the wheels of the justice department turn slowly—but ... it's rolling ahead. Sara just said to get prepared. They may need me there."

They looked at each other. In the back of Mick's mind a ball found a pocket.

"You could come with me? Give me moral support," Kate almost whispered.

Mick looked away, seeing nothing. Kate, watching him, took a deep breath that caught in her throat. Neither was going to cry; too early for that. No tears, yet.

"What ..." came out a little hoarse and Mick cleared his throat. "... has happened with Barney and Sara. Anything?"

"No. He hasn't contacted her again. She neither."

| 361

"Ah, what a world, huh? The things that keep people apart. I know he's making love to her …"

"Huh?"

He was angry. "You know … in his dreams."

"Gross, Mick."

"Why's it gross? It's all he can do. Wouldn't it be cool if …"

"Don't even go there," Kate cut him off. "I'm not even sure where you were going, but I don't want to hear it anyway."

"Well, if we want this open, unconditional relationship … I imagine you masturbate?" he knew he was being cruel, but he couldn't help himself.

"Mick! For crying out loud."

"What, too personal? I thought nothing was too personal for our close brother-sister relationship? So, do you?"

"All right. If you insist, yes, of course."

"Do you think of a man?"

"Whaddya mean?"

"You know. Imagine a guy … you know … doing it to you?"

"What? No."

"No? What do you do?"

"Mick, this is too personal. It's creepy. What'd your wife say?"

"The subject of masturbation never came up. She probably would've been embarrassed."

"What about me?"

"What? *You* embarrassed?" Again, he knew he was being mean, didn't really know why, but he couldn't help himself. "So, what do you think about?"

"I don't think about anything. I just enjoy … my touch."

"Not somebody else's?"

"Mick! That's not funny. Why don't you ask Lottie?"

CHAPTER 24

"Not trying to be funny. Lottie and I don't have this open, no-holds-barred relationship ... like I thought we did."

"So, what do you guys do? Huh?"

"Some have no imagination, just look at a picture, a naked woman, and pretend, like telepathically, they're screwing her. But, now Barney and I have good imaginations. I bet Barney has made love to Sara in a hotel in Vancouver, on his kitchen table ..."

"Mick!"

"He may have even had a threesome ..."

Kate screamed "Go to hell!" and ran off the porch. He heard her feet pound on the stairs, her door slam.

Now there were tears.

KATE HADN'T come back down. Mick jumped on his cart and headed into Hope Town to pick up Peewee. As he drove up to the pier, two of the boys were helping Peewee get out of his boat—a seventeen-foot center console whaler with a hefty 225 hp Yamaha outboard—and up onto the dock. HS, surprisingly, followed behind. Mick drove partway down their pier, which was against the rules, so Peewee wouldn't have to walk. Just then Lottie's jeep came wheeling in and screeched to a halt in the little parking lot filled mostly by golf carts. She came running onto the pier, right up to Peewee, stopping just shy of smashing into him. In spite of his bandaged arm and leg, she reached up and hit him, hard, with both hands against his shoulders. "Where the hell did you go last night, ya big baboon? We thought you were dead, for Christ's sake!"

Peewee winced through a smile. "It makes my heart leap you were worried about me."

Lottie punched him in the arm, at least his good arm. "What are ya talking about?" she yelled. "We were all worried!" She stepped back and looked him over. "So, what the hell happened? We hear gunfire, you yell 'blow it,' and then you blow us off?"

"Now, settle down, darlin'. It's nothing. I'm fine. Sorry, but I seemed to misplace the walkie-talkie while I was getting shot at. Didn't really have time to look for it."

"So, what's with the bandage if you're so fine? A new fashion for big oafs?"

Peewee was grinning ear to ear. "Yes. To make me look rugged and sexy."

"Like Mr. T?" came the sarcastic interjection from Heidi who had been standing off, arms folded firmly.

Just then Spense pulled up to the pier in his dory, climbed up the ladder almost before the dory stopped, tossed a couple loops around a cleat, and limped over to the group. "You've come back to us, if not all in one piece," Spense said as he, too, looked Peewee over. "Glad to see you're indisposed sufficiently to deter another aerial-lift demonstration." He put out his hand tentatively and Peewee shook it gently. "Am I the only one who knows nothing about these bandages … and what transpired after we lost contact?"

"No," Lottie said, slugging Peewee again.

"C'mon, Mr. T. Let's hear about the bullets that bounced off you." Another shot from Heidi.

All turned toward HS. "So, I assume this is the 'tough nut' we've heard about?" Lottie said and walked over to her and held out her hand. "Nice to meet you … but I'm not sure what to call you?"

"HS will do for now. I can see the reviews I've heard are true. You are very beautiful."

CHAPTER 24

Lottie laughed. "You're not so bad yourself."

"For an immature little girl," Heidi countered.

Lottie laughed louder. "No. It doesn't take a whole lot to see you're no little girl ... and there's nothing immature about your sarcasm."

Spense stepped forward. "May I introduce myself. Spenser Redfern at your disposal."

Heidi put out her hand as if for Spense to kiss it. "I've been dying to meet the owner of that outrageous yacht. You are obviously not our commonplace conventional transient."

"Ah," Spense replied as he kissed her hand. "I believe we speak the same language. Sound mates, so to speak."

"Ah, a good little twist of a cliché," Heidi responded, withdrawing her hand. "Just what is your favorite sound, mate?"

"A clever little wordplay yourself, my dear." Like Mick, Spense found himself smiling at everything she said.

"Well?"

"Ah, my favorite sound? Well ... the answer is of a delicate nature."

"What? Is it the sound of a woman in orgasm? That would be mine, I believe, if I were a man."

Spense sputtered, gasped, choked, and covered his mouth, trying not to laugh.

"My lord!" Lottie expounded. "No, I'd say you're definitely no little girl."

"I coulda told you that!" Mick said, also trying not to laugh, afraid to look at Peewee.

"My God!" boomed Peewee, shaking his head at HS. "Now that the cordials, if you want to call them that, are out of the way, let's get a move on."

"Not until I hear about those bandages ... and bullets?" Lottie demanded, hands on hips.

"I agree," Spense confirmed.

"Later, later," Peewee said.

"Uh-uh. Now," Lottie and Spense said in unison.

"Don't forget to tell them about whom the bullets went through before they bounced off you," HS said in what to Peewee must have been an irritatingly patronizing tone.

Peewee gave HS a stern look, frightening all but HS, who showed no apparent apprehension. He turned to the others, who were holding their breath, and explained flatly what had transpired, ending with: "Sorry to cause the concern."

"Why didn't you call us or something?" Lottie threw in.

"Who? At what number?" Peewee was starting to sound irritated. "Besides, we had to get our asses out of there before …"

"Before anyone else discovered that a guard had been murdered?" HS was relentless.

"Heides! I think that's enough now." There was an authority in his voice that didn't invite any more discussion from anyone, which Heidi also seemed to appreciate.

"I'll ride with Mick," Lottie said quickly, just in case Heidi decided she needed to counter. "Peewee, you and HS will be more comfortable in Spense's 'limo.' By the way, where's Kate?"

"Waiting for us," Mick said. "Peewee, hop in mine and I'll drive you to Spense's cart. It's in his private spot in the lot." He grinned at Lottie. "Lottie can sit on your lap."

"No, that's OK. I can walk," Lottie tried.

Peewee wrapped his good arm around her middle from the back, lifted and set her rear end against his hip, like a mother carrying her child, and limped over to Mick's cart. "Afraid of the beast, my beauty?"

"Put me down, you fool. You'll hurt yourself."

Peewee slid into the cart, slipping Lottie onto his lap. The

CHAPTER 24

cart listed, springs screeching. Everyone but Heidi broke out laughing.

"If it makes it that far," Mick added as he climbed on.

When they all pulled up to the cottage, Kate was on the porch waiting for them. Heidi tried to take Peewee's arm to help him up the steps, but he gently shook her off. Nobody else dared offer. The first thing Peewee did was inform Spense that he and "Mary" would not be implicated in the previous evening's escapade, and that all involved would have sound alibis. After explaining how that was going to work, they had an hour discussion deciding Sara would meet with Richard in New York and discuss with him when he wanted to come down for the meeting. HS asked why they were meeting with him at all here in Hope Town. Why not just meet him in New York or Washington? Mick looked at Kate, who responded that she felt she owed it to him and wanted to know what his angle was before all hell would break loose when she returned to New York.

Mick smiled almost apologetically at Heidi and shrugged: "Good point, but can't argue with Kate when she's made up her mind."

Peewee said he understood and again insisted he provide the escort. When Kate suggested Vernal, Peewee had gone silent for a moment and then informed them that he and his family were still missing. The Haitians were searching for them. Peewee said that when he would meet Richard, there would be islanders at the ferry, on the ferry, and at the dock in Hope Town Harbor … even at the airport in Marsh Harbour to ensure Richard actually landed there. If there was anyone else but Richard, he would know. They were not to worry about him. Mick noticed Heidi visibly biting her tongue when he had said this. They decided the meeting with Kate, in which Mick insisted on being involved, would take place in the little public park adjacent to the public pier—a very visible spot.

Spense and Lottie were not happy to not be involved in the meeting with Richard, but Spense said they would be close by watching. Mick suggested that there be lookouts posted at any potential docking spots on Elbow. Peewee assured him that no associate of Richard could be involved in any way without them knowing.

Kate informed them Sara told her that she would be in New York the next day and would attempt to set a date for the meeting with Richard immediately, but that Richard should only know about Marsh Harbour as his destination. Peewee said that he would meet him there, but his people would be on alert immediately as well … in Marsh Harbour and on Elbow, just in case. Sara was to email Kate when he was coming. They all, with the exception of Heidi, seemed to leave the meeting feeling good about the plan and Kate's security.

Mick had pulled Heidi aside to tell her to bring a new poem any time and would she keep Kate and him informed about Vernal. He gave her his cell number and email and got hers and Peewee's. Heidi told him she didn't like the prospects resulting from the Vernal situation. Said it was trouble, for sure. Asked Mick what was wrong with Kate. Mick had replied "nothing" and had gotten a look that clearly informed him she knew he was lying.

When everyone had left, Mick and Kate sat silently side-by-side on the porch. Finally Mick said: "Suppose we should talk?"

"No," Kate answered. "Let's go up to the perch and just look out at the ocean and the sea."

CHAPTER 24

"Nah," Mick said after a pause.

Kate looked at him. "Really? Why not?"

"I don't know. Maybe."

"I don't think you've ever not wanted to perch up on your perch. What's up?"

Mick, after staring out blankly, finally looked over at Kate. "To be honest, it's gonna make me think of you leaving." Then he slowly stood, said he was sorry for earlier, and walked up the stairs heading to the perch. Kate followed.

They sat quietly for several minutes. A jet, super-sonic type, clamored across the calm sky. "No sonic boom," Mick said.

Several minutes passed. "Nope," said Kate.

Several minutes passed. "I used to love those sonic booms, but hated them."

Kate looked over at Mick. "Don't you have to either love *or* hate?"

"No."

From the perch, they could see palms and flowering bushes down across the road. Over the tops of the low-slung cottages and bungalows, the Abaco Sea stole its blue from the sky, and the candy-cane-striped lighthouse across the harbor stole the scene. Mick spoke, as if to the lighthouse. "The *pop* or *boom* coming out of nowhere excited me. I loved it until I asked my mom what caused it. When she told me that the jet had broken the sound barrier and the result was the *boom*, it scared the shit out of me. How could something come from nothing?"

"From *nothing*! What the hell you talking about?"

Well, you know, usually there's a cause and effect type thing. You love someone, so they love you back. You hit a bell, there's a ring. You know why it rang; you could see the frickin' bell, and you hit it. What exactly did that plane hit?

| 369

The sound barrier? Show me a sound barrier. There ain't no wall, there ain't no ceiling, there ain't no barrier, there ain't nothin'. It was like Frankenstein."

"Frankenstein?"

"Yeah … a Frankenstein of love … sound, I mean."

Kate hit him on his arm with the back of her hand. "Where do you come up with this shit? A boom's a boom. You either love it or you hate it, Einstein."

Mick looked at Kate. "Nope. You're my Frankenstein. You're my sonic boom."

She hit him again. "Not!"

"Yup. You showed up out of nowhere and I loved it … you … and now I hate you're leaving."

"Mick, I have to go back."

"I know, one big boom out of nowhere and then you're gone. Not coming back. Like you're not real."

Several minutes passed, Mick finally, almost whispering: "How long you going to stay in New York?"

"Only as long as I have to."

Several more minutes passed painfully by. "What about Rashi and your boys?"

Kate didn't respond. Both stared blankly out past the lighthouse.

After several poignant moments, Mick finally breached the smothering silence. It was hard to breathe. He had to say something. "Where will you go?"

"Go? When?"

"When you leave New York."

Several more minutes. "Home."

Mick spun in his chair and looked the other way, out over the Atlantic, the waves breaking hard over the reefs.

CHAPTER 24

Kate continued to stare out past the lighthouse. "I have to admit," Mick said. "Often when I'm up here on my perch and I squint my eyes, there are times I can almost feel a crisp, late-summer breeze; see a lake, waves brushing the shore; a pine-studded island disappearing into the twilight-turned-to-dusk; a streak of moonlight shimmering across the water, pointing at me, pleading with me to stay; and I can hear loons trilling despondently in the distance out past a rocky point, in a distant bay as if mourning my leaving."

"Home," Kate said sadly after a few moments, and slipped downstairs to her room.

CHAPTER 25

DATE: Tuesday, March 13, 2012, 10:00 a.m.

Sara: Kate, you there? Time to chat?

Kate: Good timing, sis. I've been sitting on my bed staring at the computer screen, thinking about what to say, or trying not to. What's the news?

Sara: You OK? I can almost feel something amiss. I can hear it in your tone.

Kate: Everything's fine. Did you talk to Richard?

Sara: Don't tell me everything's fine. I can tell it's not. Anything new with Peewee?

Kate: He's OK.

Sara: Gee, don't overload me with information. What about Vernal?

Kate: Heidi will tell us if they hear anything.

Sara: What do they think happened?

Kate: They don't know, but I'd bet it's got something to do with Ajax and Arthur. Tell me about Richard.

Sara: Yes, we talked. He said he wants to meet with you—only you, nobody else. He'll land in Marsh Harbour day after tomorrow at 5:30 p.m. Said he'll be by himself.

CHAPTER 25

Kate: Only me, eh? Tough shit. How'd he seem?

Sara: Controlled anger, I'd say. He's been all over the place. He's got to be pretty frustrated.

Kate: Yah? Well, tough-titties. No chance I'm meeting him alone. But he doesn't need to know that.

Sara: Right. I assumed that. Who'll meet him?

Kate: Peewee will escort him to Hope Town. Mick and I will meet with him. I'll be well protected.

Sara: Good. I really can't imagine him trying to harm you. He may try to charm you, though. That's the impression I got. He told me how much he misses you, that he still loves you. He thinks he's God's gift to women, I can tell.

Kate: You believe him?

Sara: About what? That he still loves you? Heck no. He's phony as a $22 bill.

Kate: I believe that's a $2 bill, sis.

Sara: No, he's phonier than that. You still got any feelings for him?

Kate: Hell, no. I don't know if I ever did. He was just rich, tall, dark, and handsome, with a nice, safe apartment in the big city. I never really even got to know him.

Sara: Like you know Mick?

Sara: OK, what's up now? I've sat here for over a minute waiting ...

Kate: We just discussed my leaving for NY.

Sara: I've been worried about that. What happened?

Kate: Nothing. I just said that I had to go back to NY to testify pretty soon. He asked if I was coming back down here. I said he could come with me.

Sara: And?

Kate: He said no. I said I would like to come back, to visit, but that I wanted to go home.

Sara: And?

Kate: And, nothing.

Sara: Kate, hon, you've got to talk to him. You do love him, right?

Kate: As a brother.

Sara: Bullshit! Sorry. You can't fool me.

Kate: What if he loves Lottie? Hell, I love Lottie. She's great—and he's having sex with *her*!

Sara: Please talk to him. It's not fair to him. You know that. It's not fair to you, either.

Kate: We'll see. Thanks for setting it up with Richard. I'd better get going.

Sara: Oh, Lord, Kate. I want to be there. I'm worried.

Kate: Don't be. With Mick, Spense, Lottie, Peewee, and his islanders, I'll be safe. Bye, hon. Did you talk to Barney?

Sara: No. Bye, sis. Take care, please.

Kate had stayed in her room last night until she fell asleep. She had wanted to avoid any further conversations with Mick. Whatever they would talk about was bound to be painful. But now, this morning, she had to tell Mick about the meeting.

CHAPTER 25

She was to have her first session with Rashi, surreptitiously, at eleven o'clock at the cottage; and then the boys would be coming by around one p.m. to get her for their session. She welcomed the diversion and was excited about both classes, but the excitement was tainted by a bittersweet anticipation: of her mission here with the boys and her desire to get NY over with and go home. Yet, she felt she would be abandoning her boys ... and Mick, of course.

Mick wasn't downstairs or on the porch, so she ventured up onto the perch and found him slouched at the drafting table that he used as his desk, paper in front of him, but blank.

"Good mornin'," Kate said, sitting in the rickety wicker from Jack's.

"You eat?" Mick asked.

"Ah, no."

"Me either."

"I didn't see any coffee?" Kate asked, both talking quietly, cautiously.

"Hungry?"

"Not really. I talked to Sara, though."

"And ... ?" He perked up.

"He'll arrive at the airport in Marsh Harbour tomorrow at five thirty p.m., alone."

"That's what *he* says," Mick said, turning and sitting up straight. "We better get word to Peewee. I've got Peewee's number, finally, from Heidi. Someone should probably be at the airport, even now. I'll call him. This Richard may not fly in on an airline. He might be flying privately. We'd better watch Elbow Cay, too, just in case."

"No, Mick. Remember, all he knows about where I am is Marsh Harbour. He said he wants to meet just with me."

"Tough shit."

Kate smiled. "Same thing I said, pretty much. You know what I just thought of we haven't talked about?"

"Huh?" He looked at her for the first time.

She pulled off a sweatshirt she had been wearing. The day had started off on the cool side with a dawn breeze from the east, oceanside, today. But the sun was warming the perch now at midmorning. He watched her remove her sweatshirt guilelessly, feeling no need to avert his eyes. She had a T-shirt under the sweatshirt and, naturally, he could tell, nothing under it. She had apparently slept in an old pair of his boxer briefs ... a vision that not long ago would have gotten his heart racing. It felt good to look at her fondly, a free spirit with no promiscuous intentions. He still thought the freewheeling relationship was a bit awkward, but he felt himself easily moving toward wanting her as a sister, not a lover. The thought of sex now gave him the shivers.

"Remember that day I went into the Sotheby's real estate office to make copies?" Kate asked.

"Yeah?"

"Well, Gretchen, one of the agents, and I have kind of become friends. She told me some stuff about Peewee and Heidi."

"Yeah?"

Everyone knows Peewee lives somewhere around the North End, but nobody dares walk up that path, and his place is not accessible by the east ocean side because the beach ends at the cliffs and, even though he keeps his boat on the west, sea side, it's all rocks and reefs, generally considered inaccessible by land or sea. He gets out, somehow, in his whaler, though. The clubhouse, or whatever, is on his property, and he uses it as a courthouse as well as a sort of boys club."

CHAPTER 25

"A courthouse?"

"Yeah. I guess if any of the island boys do anything wrong, they have a trial, Peewee as the 'judge,' and the other boys are the 'jury.' It sounds like this was part of the agreement with the business owners. She told me it was amazing. With nothing to do, out of boredom, many of the boys are tempted to drink, use drugs—crack and marijuana mostly—and get into trouble. Now—nothing. I guess that one kid that won't come to the classes, not Rashi, but the big, fat one, Harvey, used to be really bad news: a bully and always in trouble. I guess he's still a bad egg, but he's afraid of or respects Peewee, so he stays on the straight and narrow. The story is that the last straw was he tried to force himself on one of the young island girls. Now, if he does anything again, island justice is his due."

"Which is Peewee?"

"I suppose. Peewee and his 'kangaroo court.'"

"Gretchen said Heidi and her friend, probably the one in the story, wouldn't go to school and were real hell-raisers."

"Like what?"

"It didn't sound like anything too severe ... mostly pranks. Like, if one of the store owners didn't allow any of her friends in the store, she and her friend would use the Internet to dig up dirt on the owners and post their findings around Hope Town. Apparently not helping business."

Mick was laughing. "Where's the friend now?"

"I don't know; she didn't say. But Heidi was ill, I suppose her heart, for quite a while. Everybody thought she was supposed to die. I guess she was in some kind of an asylum for a while. Why in the hell an asylum, do you suppose? Gretchen talked about her like ... I don't know ... like she was sort of a mystery. I guess she never went to school, but must have been educated because, the way it sounded, the flyers or whatever were really clever and well-written."

"Maybe the friend wrote them."

"No. It sounded like they knew Heidi wrote them. It sounded like the friend had the devious mind and came up with the pranks, but Heidi did the writing. Why? You're *not* surprised?"

Mick chuckled. "No, I'm not surprised. Why would I be? She could probably be good at writing obituaries." This thought stifled the chuckles.

"What time is it? Oh shit, I'd better sit down and figure out what to do with Rashi," Kate spouted. "Any suggestions, Teach?"

"What? You're the teacher."

"But I've never had any formal training."

"A wise man once told me: 'Teachers are born, not made.'"

Kate thought for a moment. "Cool. I guess I believe that. But, c'mon, you've at least got experience, right?"

"Actually, when I think about it, I do have something. In a class of problem kids I had was this kid that couldn't read, Nick Von Hortan. He was overweight and looked like shit. Didn't even try to take care of himself. But, I could tell in about ten seconds he was smarter than shit. When I gave them all a writing assignment to see how their writing skills were, he didn't do it and refused to write—anything. Said he had never written anything and that's why he was in this problem-kid class. They didn't know what else to do with him. He would have nothing to do with special ed, just like Rashi."

"Whaddya do?" Kate asked. "Why wouldn't he write anything?"

CHAPTER 25

"It turned out he had a severe case of dyslexia, and ..."

"Explain dyslexia," Kate interrupted.

"Well, I'm no specialist. I know it's a kind of cognitive impairment that, with Nick, although he was super intelligent so could, through context clues or whatever, comprehend what he read, but when he wrote, the letters were jumbled or backward. Like he wrote 'the' as 't-e-h.' He thought it made him look stupid, so he chose not to write."

"And ... ?"

"I hooked him up with my senior editor of the literary magazine: Lana Holmstrom. She was a year older and really cute, a stunner—a beautiful, remarkable, nice young lady. Although not a stunner himself, he knew a good thing when he saw it. He wrote: no attention to spelling. She interpreted or just transcribed, really, when he read to her what he was trying to write. He started to write a lot, if you get my drift?"

"It worked?"

"Well, yeah! His senior year he won a big English award and got a college scholarship. There's no greater motivator to a guy than the attention of a beautiful woman."

"Like Lottie?" Kate stuck in, like a shiv.

"Like a beautiful woman you *can't* have," Mick stabbed back, pointedly, eyebrows raised. "As it turned out with Nick, as well. Nick ended up taking his own life, though. He ended up wanting Lana, but there was no way." Nick had his Lana; Rashi had his Heidi; Mick had his Kate. He wasn't sure if she followed this drift. Anyway, he was growing weary of this apparent jealous bullshit with Lottie. He was screwed up enough as it was without trying to figure where that was coming from.

Kate stood, turned her back to Mick, and didn't move.

"Heidi then?" she asked. "To motivate Rashi?"

Mick felt his throat involuntarily tighten. "Yes, I suppose," he squeezed out. "Then when you leave, you may have started something Heidi can carry on, depending on their history, but I don't know how she'd do with the rest of the boys."

Kate stood still for a while, then nodded her head, said almost under her breath: "Maybe ... you?" and headed down, off the perch.

THE DAWN arrived, dark and ominous. Mick woke shivering, sheet and blanket clutched tightly, pulled up under his chin. He scrambled out of bed and grabbed his now infamous, at least in his mind, sweater and walked to the window. A spring storm was brewing. The Abaco was steel gray, the lighthouse dull and dismal, the bushes colorless, cheerless, all seemingly unsympathetic to the dawning day. When he looked down he didn't see Heidi on the step. He shivered, sneezed, pulled on a pair of flannel loungers, and wrapped his sweater tight around him. On his way out he listened in at Kate's door and her breathing was rattling in her throat more than usual. He opened the door as silently as he could, walked to the bed, and pulled a blanket up from the foot of the bed, covering her. She stirred, groaned, coughed, but didn't wake.

He shuffled quietly out of the room, closed her door gently, and headed downstairs. He put on a pot of coffee and stepped out on the porch while it was brewing.

He walked to the railing and did his ritual breathe in, breathe out and shook his body vigorously to get his blood flowing.

"Quite the morning routine," floated out from behind him.

In spite of a voice as smooth and soft as his flannel pants, he grunted, flinched, and turned abruptly. "My God, Heidi! You about gave me a heart attack ... again!"

CHAPTER 25

She was seated on the settee, her ruana as well as another blanket wrapped around her, leaning back against a pillow.

"Sorry, sir. Didn't know what to do when you didn't see me. I apologize for coming up on the porch without an invitation, but it's a rather blustery morning."

"Look, you can come up on the porch anytime. You don't need an invitation. You could come in and make yourself tea if you liked. You're welcome here … you know that."

"I'm glad to hear you say that, sir," and she pulled a steaming cup out from under the blankets. Smiled feebly.

"Good. Glad to see you helped yourself. I'm going to get myself a steaming cup of java and I'll join you on the settee."

"Better grab a blanket. It's a bit wintry this morning—not your Minnesota-type winter morning, I'd guess, but still bitter and unwelcoming."

As usual, he couldn't help but smile at her choice of words. He got himself his coffee, grabbed a blanket, and joined her on the settee.

"Well, do you have something for me today?" he asked as he settled back, the blanket wrapped around him. The wind was swirling, and an occasional biting gust swirled into the porch. "We could go inside today. Get out of this wind."

"I'm fine if you are. We wouldn't want to wake up your sister." She always said "sister" with an odd little emphasis that perplexed him.

"Why do you always refer to her as 'my sister'?"

"Because you say she's your sister."

"What do you mean *I* say she's my sister? She is my sister."

"If you say so, sir."

"What do you mean, 'If *I* say so'?"

"She's never told me she's your sister."

[381

"Well, why should she have to? She *is* my sister."

"I believe you think so, sir."

"What? Are you implying ... I don't know ... what are you implying?"

"My father wants to see you this morning. Can you pick him up at the dock in the harbor?"

"What? Of course. Answer me, will you?"

"They discovered that Vernal and his family, when they were accosted, were escorted back to Haiti," she said calmly, matter of fact. "Where, by the way, they're in danger. Vernal's political activism has made him some enemies there. Apparently that's why he and his family were here in the Bahamas."

"Huh? What? Wait ... what? How do you know this?"

"My father talked to the Haitians in Marsh Harbour. A gang of Haitians—not so friendly ones I'm afraid—were hired to abduct them. They were aware, of course, of the danger he'd be in Haiti."

"Really? My gosh. Are they OK?"

"We think so. Physically, anyway, so far, according to Vernal's friends in Marsh Harbour. The gang's also been hired to assassinate my father, we've been told."

"What? Assassinate! This gang? Hired by whom?" Mick was off the settee, blood now flowing hot as his coffee.

"They said by the Mandelsung brothers. They weren't too happy about the other night. They were apparently behind the kidnapping of Vernal and his family, too."

"Jesus! Uh ... how'd they find out about Vernal's involvement here?"

"We have a mole in their gang, I guess, and apparently they have a mole in ours. That's why they knew ahead of time about the other night. And Vernal had to spill all the beans to

CHAPTER 25

prevent them from harming his family. He came into work, they grabbed him, took him to the big Mandelsung boat, and they already had his family there."

"No shit! Kill your father? Is he safe?"

"As long as he's on Elbow. Nobody can get to him as long as he's here, especially with his devoted islanders watching out for him. That's what I want to talk to you about."

"We have to contact the police," Mick blurted out, pacing the porch.

"Uh, ri—i—ght," Heidi said, bitingly sarcastic. She hadn't moved from the spot on the settee and had remained confoundingly calm. "The last people we would want involved are the authorities. Try explaining the other night: expensive machines ruined, a burnt crater ... not to mention a dead guard. Let me repeat: my father is safe as long as he remains on Elbow."

"What do you mean?" Mick asked, knowing a second after he asked what she meant.

"He was talking to our islanders, and I heard him say he was going to meet your sister's ex-fiancé in Marsh Harbour and escort him here. Correct?"

Mick stopped pacing, faced HS searching for a response, but couldn't think of a thing to say.

"You don't have to say anything, sir. There'll be no talking him out of it anyway. He thinks it's humorous that they want to kill him and that he'll be in Marsh Harbour ... right out in the open ... in their neighborhood. This is just another dam his river will, hopefully, flow around."

"No. I could talk him out of it. Just not allow him to participate. This is Kate's and my problem—this guy from New York—not your father's."

Again HS laughed a scornful, sour laugh, far too acerbic and caustic for a young woman her age. "I thought you knew my father better than that? No. There'll be no dissuading him. He could not live, anyway, feeling he was a prisoner on his island. Believe me, I understand that. No, what I would like you to do is devise some scheme, some design to put an end to all this. If you don't, I know in my heart it will be the end of him."

Mick could only stand there, helplessly, looking pleadingly at HS.

"Maybe talk to that Spense fellow. I'm guessing he could devise a plan. Between your odd foursome, I believe you could come up with something. Talk to Kate's sister, Sara. I got the sense she's no dummy. Please?" she begged, showing a first sign of distress.

"All right. Yes! I'll get ahold of Spense and Lottie ... the reach-out to Sara surprised him ... get them over here, before we meet with your father. Tell him I'll pick him up at the harbor at noon. We'll see what we can come up with."

Heidi unraveled herself from the blanket, walked up to Mick, leaned up, gave him a kiss on the cheek, and hugged him ... hugged him hard and held on. He wrapped his arms completely around her. God, he thought, I love this young girl, or, rather—wizened woman. I can't let her down.

She gave him one last squeeze and, as usual, slipped furtively away.

Rather than text Spense and Lottie, Mick decided to call them. Spense answered immediately and after hearing about Vernal, Peewee, and the arrival of Richard, said he would be there in less than a half hour. He said he'd call Lottie and have her drive the jeep into town and ride with him on his cart,

CHAPTER 25

since no cars were allowed on the north end.

Kate hadn't come down yet. Mick realized he hadn't shut the porch doors and it was freezing in the cottage. He closed the doors, turned on the unsubstantial space heater in the living room, and, as he headed up to check on Kate, heard rain start to splatter against the windows, realizing Heidi was going to get wet. By the time he got upstairs he was shivering again. He opened Kate's door and was hit by a cold blast of air. Kate's window was still open, and the wind, now swirling, the storm coming in from the Atlantic, was whistling in through Kate's open window. He shut the window and knelt on her bed. She was on her side, breathing hoarsely, and her nose, which was about the only thing exposed, was running with shiny snot covering her upper lip and drool soaking her pillow. He laid down next to her on top of the blankets and put his arm around her. She inadvertently snuggled against him, but her breathing calmed and he could tell she was waking.

"Uh non't fee gud," she said, her nose completely stuffed.

He kissed her on the cheek, barely exposed, and asked, "What can I get you? Besides a Kleenex and towel?"

"Heat," she rasped. "I'm freezing."

He rubbed her back and arm vigorously, through the sheet and blanket. "Gotta get your blood flowing," he said. "I have the heater on downstairs. Why don't you take a hot shower, bundle up, and come on down. I'll make some breakfast."

"I non't wandah ged up," she said, and sniffled.

"We'll have company here in less than thirty minutes," he told her. He explained why they were coming.

"Nesus Cwrist! Why nidn't you dell me?" and she threw her blankets off. "Do make someding t'eat. I be wight down."

He wasn't sure when he was supposed to have informed her of the pending events, but he headed downstairs and scrambled some eggs and figured orange juice would help, so poured her a glass as well as a cup of coffee. She was down in no time, bundled up in sweats and a robe. She obviously hadn't taken time to shower or brush her hair … and it was wild. He thought of telling her that she might want to take a look in the mirror, but one of the things he was learning to love about her was her carelessness about how she looked. Much like she might with a brother. Of course, it didn't matter: wild hair, no makeup, any old clothes—she still looked good. Wild hair actually suited her.

Mick explained more over breakfast, and just as they were finishing, they heard Spense's cart rumble up … less than twenty minutes from the call.

They all settled on chairs around the heater, Kate all bundled up. Lottie had given Mick a kiss and hug and whispered in his ear that she could have used a warm body last night. "Me, too," he had whispered back. Although there were two women he would have loved to keep warm last night, Lottie was the only one he planned on consenting to.

After Mick told them what he knew, filling them in on everything HS had told him, Spense stood and in his usual pose, hand to chin, started pacing. "I've been thinking about this," he said. "The only way to put a permanent end to this dismal affair is to somehow discredit the Ajax brothers. I believe Peewee will find a way to keep himself safe and out of harm's way, for now at least, in this current intrigue regarding Richard. We can't be sure what connivances our villain might bring to the table, though, so let's deal with that as it unfolds. But, we must devise a way to remove this Ajax and his family from the equation. Agreed?"

CHAPTER 25

They all looked at each other, shrugged, and nodded.

"Dow we gonna do dat?" Kate said, and blew her nose.

"Kate's got a cold," Mick informed them.

"No shit, Sherlock," Lottie said, and in another typical 'Kate fashion' slugged him on the arm. What was with these two?

"Sorry, my dear," Spense said. "Although most happy you're a tough broad and can carry on in spite of the sniffles. So, let's discuss dow we gonna do dat?"

Kate's turn: she backhanded Spense on his hip and snuffed: "Chut op!"

"OK," Spense started, "we've got to figure out a way to get the A-hole brothers, as our Mick has astutely dubbed them, to do something that either gets them eliminated from the situation violently if we have to or, hopefully, by some nonviolent, clever means."

"Eliminated violently?" Lottie questioned. "You mean like ... killed?"

"Or at least incapacitated," Spense suggested, shrugging.

"Dow bout dwe durn the Datian gang gainst dem? Dat ud be gud dymitree."

"You mean feed, like, false information for their mole to bring back to them?" Mick said.

"I like it," Spense said, "except we'd be betting a lot on this mole. Does Peewee know who the mole is in the gang?"

"Don't know, but we could ask Peewee when he gets here," Mick said.

"When's he coming, again?" Lottie asked.

"Noon," Mick said, just as they heard a cart, an hour early if it was Peewee, pull up in the back. He went into the backroom and opened the door.

Peewee and Rashi followed Mick back into the living room. Rashi sat behind the others on the floor. Peewee grabbed a chair, testing it before he put his full weight on it. Everyone was silent. There was suddenly tension in the room but nobody really knew why. Finally, Peewee decided the chair would support his bulk. He had to sit with his bandaged leg sticking straight out, taking space, increasing his dominance in the room. Everyone felt small, and, oddly, guilty and just waited for Peewee to speak.

"I don't understand why you're meeting without me, but, regardless, I'm here now."

Everyone swallowed, and waited.

"This is Rashi. He's my chauffeur today, and he's not as dumb as he looks."

Rashi smiled too broadly, crossed his eyes, and shook his head, flinging his braided dreads from side to side.

"So, what's up?" Peewee asked, crossing massive arms over a massive chest.

"We heard about that threat to your life," Mick answered. "We've decided that the way to end all of this is to, somehow, expunge, uninvolve the Mandelsungs ... and their money. The sooner the better. We've been discussing how to do this."

"I agree. What have you come up with, if I might ask?"

"Blease non't bangry," Kate said. "I non't want dyou ..."

"Don't go there," Peewee said, frowning at Kate and with a conviction nobody was going to argue with. "I'm in. Everything's set. Eyes are everywhere, and I'll be meeting this guy, today, one way or another—if he shows up. Now, what have you come up with to get rid of these assholes? Permanently, I might add."

Mick explained their thought concerning the mole.

Peewee said it was an interesting idea, but: "There no longer is a mole ... not theirs, anyway."

CHAPTER 25

The rest all looked at each other. Mick asked where he was. "Where a mole belongs," was Peewee's answer. Nobody said anything. Peewee slowly grinned. "No, not in a hole, but back with us. Poor Harvey is easily tempted to stray by the allure of money. He has been offered one more reprieve. We'll see." Without looking at Rashi, Peewee said: "Rashi, what you think we should do about this family?" Everyone but Peewee looked at Rashi.

Rashi looked down at his hands in his lap. "Just so you know," he started, "Peewee does not want anybody else getting killed or even injured. That includes your guy, Miss Kate," and he looked up at her, smiled, and then back to his lap.

"To permanently get rid of this big money family responsible for the offenses against the island, I would figure, would take the intervention of the government … if we don't want violence. But, we can't connect what happened the other night to whatever we do now in ridding ourselves of these people."

He looked up again at everyone. "And I want you to know, Mr. T had no intention of anyone getting hurt that night either, much less killed. I know a friend of mine feels you're all responsible for that guard's death. It is not your blame. They killed their own man. But, since the government may be persuaded to think otherwise, we must divert any attention away from us and those fireworks. No matter what we do." He looked up and smiled again. "Great job, by the way. You have the gratitude of all the islanders."

"So, I've talked this here over with Peewee and my friends: there is a protected island, a wildlife sanctuary, where it's forbidden to trespass. The government, although they feel they need development to help bring in money to pay the bills, is very protective of a place like this. Anyone sets foot on this island without direct permission from the government is in bad trouble. Native Bahamians all know this. Every once in a while a tourist or part-timer pulls a boat up on shore to explore or whatever, but since there are signs well-posted, the government gives them no slack. They're actually prosecuted and even, possibly, imprisoned if caught. If we draw them—it would have to be these two or other members of the family—if we draw them to this island and make it appear as if they were not only trespassing but planning to or doing harm to the sanctuary, it's likely the government would not let them continue here on Elbow ... or maybe anywhere else in the islands. The family, not just Ajax and Arthur, would be considered contemptible. They would be discredited. Their money should not get them out of this trouble."

They all looked at each other. Peewee smiled broadly; the rest raised their eyebrows and shrugged to the affirmative. "How would you suggest setting something like this up?" Mick, impressed, addressed to Rashi.

"Well," Peewee took over, "the Mandelsungs won't know I know they plan on killing me ... those miserable little shitheads. Anyway, Harvey, who they presently believe is their mole in our midst, sets up a meeting between myself and them, calling for a truce, pretending it's an attempt by me to negotiate."

"Won't they be suspicious?" Lottie asked.

"The Haitian gang, although not on our side, really, are pretty pissed at the Mandelsungs. Our mole in the gang told us the Mandelsungs ..."

"Mick calls them the A-hole brothers," Spense interjected.

Peewee's laugh boomed, and at the same time a loud burst of thunder reverberated around the room. It was hard to tell one from the other.

CHAPTER 25

"It sounds like a doozy of a storm," Spense said. "Glad to be hunkered down in here. Mary does not relish this weather." No one ever knew if he meant his wife or the boat.

"A-hole Brothers! Ajax and Arthur, right? I like it!" Peewee said. "Anyway, the A-holes wouldn't pay the gang, who had been hired to protect their shit at the site, because of what happened. So the gang's pissed: they lost a man *and* the A-holes stiffed 'em. We figure we'll have Harvey go to the A-holes, all contrite, and tell them the gang wants revenge like they're blaming it on me. Tell the dumb shits, who probably aren't bright enough to figure something out themselves, that if a meeting is set up on this island, they could kill me and leave me there, that nobody'd find me for a long time, if ever, because nobody's gonna be going to this forbidden island."

"Won't Ajax and Arthur know it's forbidden to go there?" Lottie asked.

"You think those shit-holes give a damn?" Peewee answered. "They think they're above the law anyway. But in this case, they're wrong. This island has been protected as a sanctuary, from way back. There's even sort of religious, sacred connections, all the way back to the original native Bahamians. The government might be short-sighted when revenues, jobs—what they see as progress—is involved. But they believe in the integrity of their ancestors. There's like twenty or so national parks in the Bahamas and like almost 700,000 acres safeguarded. The Bahamas National Trust that manages these areas is very powerful. We have the third largest living coral reef—the Andros Barrier Reef—in the world. This island contains several endangered species. No, this sanctuary is, indeed, sacred. If they catch anyone on this island, their asses are in deep doodoo. As a matter of fact, we'll have to be very careful, ourselves, to do no damage, not disrupt anything."

"How do you plan to do that?" Lottie, again.

"We figure us boys," Rashi took over, "will go to the island first, plant some of the explosives we confiscated from them on the shore of a little harbor that's the only landing spot. Make it look like they were going to do something destructive. There are always various wildlife dying of natural causes and whatever around the various islands. I don't know if you realize, but there's like seven hundred or something islands and thousands of little cays that make up the Bahamas? So, anyway, we'll get the word out around the islands, besides the Abacos—Eleuthera, the Exumas, any of the Family Islands as they're called—and collect dead turtles, conch, lobsters, birds. We'll find a dead flamingo or two—they're especially treasured, our West Indian flamingos—and plant them on and around the beach. Make it at least look suspicious how they might have died. The Mandelsungs will, of course, deny it, but how could they explain what they were doing there? Along with the explosives and some other shit … guns, whatever … it should get their asses thrown in jail for a long time. At least put any of their developments on hold."

"And implicate the entire family," Peewee interjected. "If all goes as planned, that family should, hopefully, be put out of business—at least here in the Bahamas. Then, of course, we may have to deal with the Chinese, but this will for sure set things back."

"How you going to get them out there?" Lottie asked. "Again, won't they be suspicious?"

"We'll figure that out," Peewee said. "From what I hear, those two aren't the brightest stars in the universe."

CHAPTER 25

"We'll have to convince them that this is the best way to get at Peewee and best place to leave him dead," Rashi added.

A flood of lightning lit up the room and six faces. A second later a ball of thunder rolled over them.

"That was close," Mick said. Suddenly rain pelted the windows and palm leaves started slapping the cedar shakes. It grew almost as dark as night in the cottage. Spense, however, had stood and started pacing the room, chin in hand, seemingly oblivious to the storm raging outside. "Uh-oh," Mick said. "Spense is going to enlighten the room, I believe."

"'Bout time," Peewee rumbled. "You've been pretty quiet, you and cute Kate."

"Oohm nettin an old," Kate groaned out.

"I've got something to take care of that, later," Peewee promised. "Wanda is great with all kinds of remedies. What's up, my twisted little wizard?" he directed at Spense.

Spense paced over to the heater, stopped, and faced them. "How pissed are the Haitian gang?" he asked Peewee.

"Pissed!" both Peewee and Rashi answered vigorously.

"Before you arrived," Spense began, "we were discussing symmetry. Perhaps there's a way to put harmony back into our little world here."

"Let's hear it. I'm all for balance in the universe," Peewee said.

"OK. The Haitian gang, or at least Harvey, gets rehired to set up Peewee and to guide Ajax and Arthur to this precious island to assassinate Peewee. Harvey demands his money up front this time. I assume the A-holes want to rid themselves of Peewee bad enough, they'll agree. So, Harvey and the Haitian hoodlums escort these bums in the Mandelsung cruiser. Will it be able to navigate into this little harbor on this island?"

Peewee and Rashi looked at each other, both shaking their heads. "That's a pretty good size boat they've got. Probably too deep a draft to get in," Peewee said. "They'd have to moor a ways out."

"That's good: a good reason to justify the use of a smaller boat," Spense said. "So, the faux assassins deposit the A-holes ashore and then head out, leaving them there. There'll already be a smaller boat there, the assumption being it's Peewee's, appropriately disabled. The Mandelsungs will be stranded on the shore staring at a cache of dead, exotic animals, explosives, guns, whatever. So Harvey and cohorts, long gone in the other smaller boat, receives his restitution; the Mandelsungs are left trying to explain to the authorities, who have been alerted, what they are doing there and what they were up to—why their yacht is floatin' off this island. We will, hopefully, have achieved balance and harmony in the universe. Although the Mandelsung family has gotten away with previous atrocities they have committed, they will be 'done in,' poetically, by the atrocities they *haven't*!"

"I'll drink to that!" Peewee, yes, bellowed, and once again the room and smiling faces were illuminated by a blast of lightning. Everyone held their breath, and as the thunder punctuated the moment with what almost seemed a sonic boom, everyone cheered, stood, and high-fived, low-fived, hugged ... except Rashi, who looked on, grinning and shaking his head.

"Genius. Absolute genius," Peewee, yes, roared. "Whatcha got to drink, mon?"

"I've been harboring a little bottle of Red Breast, no cheap joke by the way, for a special occasion. I'd say this qualifies," Mick shouted.

CHAPTER 25

"I have no idea what 'red breast' is, or whose," Peewee yelled, "but I like the sound of it."

"It's Irish whiskey, fool," Lottie said and, naturally, slugged him on the arm.

"Red Breast for Redfern! Red Breast for Redfern!" Spense chanted and everyone joined in, replacing their name for Redfern, including a 'Web Bwest fo MaGindy.'

Mick retrieved the bottle and they all camped around the heater, wind rattling the windows, each making a toast, one more inane than the next, as they passed the bottle around … until it came to Kate.

She grabbed it to her breast. Mick started chanting: "Red Breast! Red Breast!" and they all picked up on it.

When the chanting stopped, Kate, shaking her head, announced, "I non't wont to sober yup, but doo dings: won—Wichard; and doo—I hup disall goes noun as smoothie as dis Wed Bwest."

They all roared this time and cheered again.

"OK, everybody. Hang onto that Red Breast for a moment, my dear. I'll get you a glass—with that cold—if you don't mind. Let's all focus on this Richard, now. Everyone, sit down, put your head back together," Spense ordered.

They all sat but Peewee. "What to discuss? I'll meet him at the Marsh Harbour harbor. I'll know whether he landed at five thirty or not. One of my guys will have located him and will drive him in his taxi to me. I'll take him, well-protected, naturally—almost everyone on the ferry will be our people—to the village park here in Hope Town; Kate and Mick will meet with him there. They'll have their little discussion, never at any risk because a lot of friends will be in the proximity and watching. Nuttin' to wurry 'bout."

"What if ..." Mick started.

"Not to worry!" Peewee cut him off. "No one will get on this island without our knowing it. Understand? Neither myself nor our little Kate will ever be in any danger. We decided we had to draw him here. If he comes and no games, no problem. We'll know if anyone else is involved in any way, shape, or form."

"We're afraid there might be, Peewee. You know that. A bigger asshole than Richard could be involved," Mick said.

"Unless he or his cohorts are invisible, we will know. I repeat: we will know if they try to get on the island."

"What if they have weapons?" Mick cautioned. "These guys, if there are any, could be tough."

"They better hope they don't try to play tough," Peewee said, implying to Mick and the rest there could be more fireworks. "You wanna do this or not?"

"Yef, abfolutely," Kate sniffed out, and they worked out some of the particulars, all leaving feeling confident. The wind, thunder, and lightning had abated. Frequently small squalls blew through the islands, but Spense, Lottie, Peewee, and Rashi headed out into a still serious rain, some serious thoughts starting to sink into the less-frequented spaces in their minds. Some serious shit was, again, going to start happening.

CHAPTER 26

MICK AND KATE got the call from Peewee at 6:05 p.m. Richard had landed on the five thirty flight, alone. They were now on the six o'clock ferry to Hope Town. Mick called Spense to let him know. He and Lottie had retreated to the Mary to wait—Spense had been spent after the meeting. Mick felt a little pang of jealousy, realizing Spense was probably getting some TLC from Lottie, thinking he wouldn't mind a little TLC himself —"C" meaning more than "care." Not wanting to miss out on any of the excitement, they would head back into Hope Town in the dory and pick a spot up the hill between a couple of town cottages and watch through Spense's high-powered binoc's. He said he would even have a pair of infrared along in case the meeting lasted longer than the sunlight. Spense and Lottie were not going to miss out on the meeting with Richard just because they weren't participating.

Mick and Kate hopped on the electric cart and hummed into Hope Town. Peewee had sent Heidi to Mick's cottage after the meeting with an island concoction that had pretty much cleared up Kate's congestion and, along with the adrenaline, had her feeling much better. Heidi, on the other hand, was not in good spirits and barely spoke to Mick or Kate, except to wish Kate good luck, and had left right after dropping off the island remedy.

BACK TO THE ISLAND

Mick pulled the cart into the parking lot that was between the pier and the little park. Fortunately the storm had passed and the rain had stopped completely, but it had remained humid and cloudy. Rashi and a couple of the boys met them and directed them to a picnic table in the center of the park, explaining they would be surrounded by island folk, all inconspicuously milling around, looking as if they were enjoying an outing after the storm.

Spense and Lottie had pulled Spense's dory up to the pier, waved, and pointed up the hill to where they would be watching. Mick felt comfortable that nothing bad could happen. Kate seemed calm, but as they sat and waited, her left leg never stopped moving up and down in a rapid staccato beat.

"Nervous?" Mick asked. He had thought of asking Kate that a hundred times, but it seemed an inane, rhetorical question.

They sat side-by-side at the picnic table, facing the harbor, figuring Spense would probably want a good view of Richard, who would be facing the cottages on the hill. Kate, who, in spite of her drumming leg, had been slouching, sat up straight, grabbed Mick's hand, and, with a penetrating gaze, smiled and almost whispered, "No, not really. Especially with you here. Thank you." And she gave him a warm, friendly kiss on the lips. "I think I'm more ... excited, maybe. It's weird, isn't it? I've been afraid of what he or they might do if they found me, yet here we are inviting him to us. I find that comforting." Mick noticed her leg had stopped drumming. "I feel like we're in control. I almost feel sorry for Richard."

"Sorry?" Mick was taken back. "The guy's a bastard, a crook. Why in the devil's name would you feel sorry for him?"

CHAPTER 26

"Because now he's trapped. And don't get me wrong, I no longer have any feelings for him, but he isn't a bad guy, and he's totally screwed. He's really just a pawn."

"Bullshit! If he's a compliance officer, he had to know about all the shit they were pulling. It's the universal soldier conundrum. He *can* think for himself. He doesn't have to do what he's told if he knows it's wrong. He frickin' has free will. I'm guessing he got paid well for his *lack* of compliance."

"It's not that simple ... or that black and white," Kate answered.

"It is to me. Did you love this guy?" They really hadn't talked much about their relationship. It had seemed a taboo subject.

"Let's not go there. Not now."

"When, then?" Mick knew this was a really inappropriate time to even think about this, much less discuss it, but he couldn't help himself.

"Why do you even care?" Kate asked, sounding glad he did.

Mick couldn't answer. Why did he care? He was jealous, he knew. Stupid. He knew he had to get over it.

"Here comes the ferry," Kate said as it rounded the point and entered the harbor. Both Kate and Mick scanned the waterfront and turned to look up the hill at the cottages terraced along the cart and walking lanes, the top ones silhouetted against the gray sky over the Atlantic. Neither could locate Spense or Lottie, but many people were strolling and lingering on corners. Lights were starting to come on in some of the cottages as the sun dropped behind the lighthouse on the other side of the harbor.

"I don't see anything or anybody suspicious," Mick said.

"No, me neither." She recognized a couple of her boys sitting on the steps between two of the walkways. She waved by simply wriggling her fingers; they just held a hand up for a second, obviously watching them closely.

The ferry had rounded the boats moored in the harbor and was making its way toward the pier. For a moment it disappeared behind Cap'n Jack's, their dock and pier empty today. "God!" Kate exhaled. "Am I glad it's Sunday. What if you guys all had to go to work?"

"What? There's no way I'd leave you alone to do this. Nobody would have gone into work, fool."

Kate leaned into Mick and gave him a hug. "Thanks, bro."

Mick gave her a quick squeeze back. "Ready? They're pulling up to the pier."

Peewee came up the ladder onto the pier first. The ferry and pier were in full view across the little parking lot from the park. He took his time and looked around, then motioned for someone to come up. The man who had appeared had slicked-back blond hair, was dressed in typical tourist-wear: Hawaiian shirt, Bermuda shorts, Tommy Bahama loafers—sans socks—and a Panama hat. Mick disliked him even before he was sure it was Richard, although this guy looked like the photo. It was hard for him to tell his height as Peewee dwarfed him, but the others climbing up onto the pier behind them were all shorter than what must be Richard.

Peewee wrapped his fingers around the guy's biceps and led him down the pier, perusing the area the entire time, head swiveling like the lighthouse lantern. The guy's steps were shorter than Peewee's, so his arm led him out front and he semi-trotted to keep up. Mick smiled to himself: no question who the alpha was.

CHAPTER 26

When they got to the end of the pier, Peewee stopped and looked both ways up and down the road. When he looked up, he nodded, more than likely to one or more of his fellow islanders, informing them all was right. When Peewee turned and headed toward the park, the guy sort of stumbled as his arm left with Peewee before his feet did. As they got closer, Richard noticed Kate and started a wave, an obviously forced smile on his face, but the smile vanished as he noticed Mick. Peewee must have increased his grip as he grabbed at Peewee's hand and winced. Peewee looked down at him and must have given him his flesh-ball look as his glance up at Peewee caused him to noticeably cringe.

They walked up to the table, the guy no longer attempting to smile. "This the fella?" Peewee's voice gruff and threatening.

"Hello, Richard," Kate said, blankly yet clearly, her nose no longer stuffed due to Wanda's island remedy.

"I thought we were supposed to meet alone," Richard said, attempting but not succeeding to not sound petulant.

"Listen, asshole," Peewee said, pulling Richard to his toes by lifting the arm he still had in his grip, "this ain't going your way. And if *you* aren't alone, you'll regret coming down here, hear?"

"As I've told you, I'm alone," he whined, his voice rising an octave. "I've come in good faith. Now if you would let go of my arm, I could say hello to my girlfriend."

Peewee lifted him higher and looked at Kate. "You his girlfriend?"

"Ah, no," Kate said, starting to worry about Richard's health.

"Then apologize, asshole!" Peewee growled in his Mr. T mode.

"Sorry, sorry, for Christ's sake. You're hurting my arm."

| 401

"Any more lame-assed remarks like that and it won't be just your arm that's hurting. No fuckin' bullshit going on here. Understood?"

"Yeah, yeah!" Richard answered, wise-cracky, trying to regain a little dignity.

Peewee lifted him right off the ground by his arm. Richard whimpered and stretched his toes to reach the ground.

"Wanna play wiseass with me?" Peewee asked, eyebrows raised.

"OK, OK. No. Ahh, shit, my arm, man. I'm sorry. Please put me down."

Peewee smiled down at him, set him on his feet, and let go of his arm. Richard rubbed it tentatively, as if checking for broken bones.

"I'll be over there, watching," Peewee told him, gave him one last glare, and walked to the far side of the park.

"Sit down, Richard," Kate said as he turned to face her.

"Kate, I've really missed you, hon," he said as he sat.

"Fuck you, Richard. If you're going to start playing your Wall Street charm game, I'll get that little fellow—we call him Peewee—over here again. I am fully aware you have not been chasing me around the planet to reconcile our romance. Did you enjoy Prince Edward …"

"Who's this guy?" he interrupted, looking coldly at Mick.

"He's my fiancé," Kate answered, and hooked Mick's arm.

It took Mick a second to register what Kate had said, expecting her, naturally, to say "brother."

"So, where's the ring? I see you're not wearing mine? Been fiancé-hopping while I've been island hopping?"

Hmmm, Mick thought. A vain attempt at a sense of humor—mean-spirited.

CHAPTER 26

"Look, Kate, I'm sorry," Richard said, backtracking. "That's just jealousy speaking. We had a good thing going, didn't we?"

"Apparently you had a good thing going," Mick said. "Too good?"

Richard's look at Mick altered from cold and expressionless to disdainful and arrogant. He looked back at Kate and tried a smile. "Didn't we?"

Mick shook his head, leaned into Kate. "Suppose all these Wall Street guys are sociopaths? They must be to be able to sleep nights." He straightened and bent forward across the table. "Do you really think you can charm Kate into acquiescence? Do you spend so much time high up in your office that you're that out of touch with reality, you pompous prick?"

Richard lifted a bit off the picnic table bench, as if he might want to hit Mick, then looked over at Peewee, who smiled and waved to him, then back to Kate. "So, you brought this guy and that goon along for protection?" He looked at Mick. "Good thing you got that goon along."

Mick laughed. "So, we're done with the charm? Good. I believe you've figured out the romance angle ain't going to work, you egotistical moron. Too bad."

He started to say "fuck off" to Mick, hesitated, looked back to Kate. "Hon, I've been chasing you all over the globe. I was not going to give up until I found you. I was hurtin', babe. I really miss you."

Kate's turn to laugh. "My God. How stupid do you think I am? For love or money, huh? Well, let me guess: it's money?"

"No, screw the money. I just want you back, I …"

Suddenly Peewee was behind Richard, pushed his head into the table, and handcuffed him behind his back. Immediately there were several islanders surrounding them.

Peewee grabbed him by the hair, pulled his head up, and gritting his teeth, growled: "Came alone, huh?"

"What? What?" Richard whined. "What you talking about?"

"What happened, Peewee?" Mick asked, standing up.

"Some of this asshole's friends landed a helicopter in my own frickin' yard. Broke into *my* house!"

"I know nothing about that, honest," Richard pleaded.

Peewee slammed his face back into the table. "Shut up!"

"Where are Wanda and Heidi?" Kate asked, panicked. "Are they all right? What happened?"

"Honest," came Richard's muffled cry. "I know nothing about that."

Peewee ground his head into the table. "Wanda and Heidi got out the back, through the caves. They just called me. I've got a bunch of my guys headed there, already. I've got to go." To his men who had materialized around them: "Lock this guy in the cell in the old police station, arm yourselves, and stand guard."

"You've got to believe me!" Richard wailed.

Peewee took his hand off his head, scowled at it, and wiped the grease from Richard's hair on Richard's Hawaiian shirt. "You'd better fucking be right, asshole, or you'll regret being born."

"Really ..." Richard started.

"Shut the fuck up!" Peewee yelled and slapped the back of Richard's head hard enough his head bounced off the table, plopped back down, and didn't move.

"Be right back," Peewee said, looking apprehensively at the motionless head. Spense and Lottie came running up, asking frantically what was going on. "Why don't you guys go back to Mick and Kate's? Wait there. Spense, mind if I borrow your cart?"

CHAPTER 26

"Sure, why? What's going on? What happened to Richard?" Spense sputtered and handed the keys to Peewee, who took off without answering. The island men started dragging an unconscious Richard away.

"We'd best head back to my place," Mick said. "We'll clue you in. Shit. I can't believe it. This ain't good."

When the four of them got back to the cottage, the sun had slid down and dusk came early due to the low hanging clouds. The cottage was in shadows. The wind hadn't picked up, but with low temperatures and high humidity, it was chilly out and clammy when they got inside. Mick and Kate filled them in on what had transpired as they all huddled, once again, around the heater in the living room.

"Oh, I forgot to tell you, Kate and I are engaged," Mick pronounced.

Spense raised his eyes, Lottie scrunched hers, and Kate rolled hers. "It just came out," Kate explained. "It seemed like a good idea at the time ... you know, after all Richard's devout declarations of love. You know, if I'm engaged ..."

"Didn't work," Mick said. "You shoulda heard the guy: 'Oh, I'm hurting, babe.'"

"Apparently he didn't think you looked like much competition," Kate said and glared at Mick.

"'We had such a good thing going ...'" Mick didn't get the hint.

"Quick thinking," Lottie directed at Kate.

"But as I said, it didn't work." Mick's little controlling organ, the good old amygdala, was twittering at full speed.

Kate didn't say anything, eyes riveted on Mick's, boring into them.

"'Oh, I've really missed you, hon'," Mick mocked, overdramatically.

"The guy sounds like a real asshole," Lottie said. "You're doing a pretty good imitation of one yourself, Mick. Why don't you let up a bit?"

They heard Spense's cart rumble up, heading south toward town, and all ran for the porch. The cart looked like a third-world bus with men piled on and hanging off the sides. Peewee was driving and on the back seat, surrounded by burly looking island men, were three guys in dark suits.

Peewee stopped in front of the cottage and waved up at them. "Meet us at the police station. I know it's Sunday, Lottie, but could you round up some food? Maybe just throw some pizzas in the oven at Jack's?"

"Sure, um, yeah. I can do that. Some beer too?"

"Nah. How about some good old-fashioned Coca-colas?"

"For how many?"

"Three or four pizzas, a dozen Cokes."

"OK, no problem."

"See ya'll there." And he was off in a cloud of heavy dust, Spense looking skeptically at his overburdened cart.

No one had dared approach the issue of the break-in at Peewee's. They all were afraid of what horrors might accompany such a breach. Now they breathed a little easy, assuming these must be the men, and they were not only alive, but all in one piece.

On the way into the old police station, Mick and Kate dropped off Lottie and Spense at Cap'n Jacks. The police station was up the hill from the pier.

Mick and Kate pulled up in front of the abandoned-looking building with the Police sign above the door so faded that

CHAPTER 26

if you didn't know what it said, you wouldn't know what it said. They were told to go in by the group milling about. Rashi said he'd take the cart and go get Lottie and Spense and the food. When Mick and Kate walked inside, it looked like any old-fashioned sheriff's office. There was a desk, a table with the standard bare light bulb above, with the three guys on one side and Peewee seated on the opposite side facing them, and a door to the right which probably led to the cell Richard was in, hopefully conscious. Only the six of them were in the room.

"Pull up a couple of chairs. We were just about to start our conversation." Peewee faced the three men who sat calmly and silently, almost at attention. They were like triplets: short hair, no sideburns, white shirts, dark suits, dark ties—definitely looked government, a stereotype of every movie or newspaper clip of something like Secret Service. All were about thirty, six-two, lean, and athletic-looking. A hint of worry and anxiety—a nervous odor —permeated the little room, but the three appeared calm and looked straight ahead, unblinking.

"Well, guys," Peewee started. "Do you realize that was my home you broke into?"

"No, sir," the one in the middle answered. "We didn't break in. The door was unlocked."

"Were you invited in?"

"No, sir."

"Did you know my wife and daughter were in the house?"

The other two, one who had been looking down at the table, glanced at Peewee, and the one talking raised his eyebrows: "There was no one there when we entered, sir."

"Wrong. There was when you entered, but they didn't really like the looks of you goons and since they hadn't invited you in, they decided to leave."

The three remained stone-faced.

"How did you come to land your copter on my property, and why did you enter my home?"

The guy in the middle shifted uncomfortably in his chair.

"You're going to have to answer some of my questions. Please believe me. You will eventually answer. And, they get harder."

Mick was surprised Peewee was so temperate, but he could tell the three guys were unsettled by it. They didn't look like the type to be easily intimidated, but having to gaze upward into that broad, oddly smiling face, pretty much set the pecking order. Mick looked at Kate and she crossed her eyes.

"Well?" Peewee encouraged, still smiling. Mick thought if he were one of these guys, he'd be shitting in his pants.

"We were just following orders," the guy on the right said.

The guy in the middle gave him a stern look.

"MP, you believe in free will?" Peewee asked pleasantly.

"Uh ... yeah, as a matter of fact, I do."

"If I told you to shoot this guy ... what's your name?" he directed to the guy in the middle.

He didn't answer.

Peewee's smiled faded and that little flesh ball look came into his eyes. "I'm not going to ask you again ... because you won't be able to answer if you don't TELL ME YOUR FUCKIN' NAME!"

"Gerald, sir," Gerald answered immediately.

"OK. Mick, if I tell you to shoot Jerry here, would you?"

Mick looked at Kate, then up at Peewee. "No, I couldn't."

"Why not?"

"Because it wouldn't be right."

Peewee leaned toward Gerald. "What would your mother say if she knew you walked uninvited into my home and

CHAPTER 26

frightened my wife and daughter? Would she be proud that you were doing something 'right'?"

"We didn't know …"

"Who sent you down here?" Peewee interrupted.

Gerald immediately answered, "We can't tell you that, sir."

Peewee looked back and forth between the other two and suddenly stabbed a finger at the guy on his left, who jumped back. "Whaddya wanta bet, if I break this guy's left … you right handed?" The guy nodded slowly to the affirmative, unable to hide the fear in his eyes. "So, after I break his left arm in six-seven places, when I start on his right, he'll tell me everything I want to know? Whaddya wanta bet?"

All three swallowed hard, looked down, and remained silent.

"But I'm not going to do that. You know why? Because it ain't right. I don't know about your mother," looking at the guy in the middle who was now meeting Peewee's eyes, "but my mother would not be proud of her son if he did that."

Peewee leaned back; Mick and Kate were rigid on the edge of their chairs. "Look. It's obvious you're government goons, with your helicopter, suits, and 'sirs.' So I know there's some things, well maybe only one thing, I know you can't disclose. That's who sent you here."

"Ask him if it's a senator, Peewee," MP suggested.

Gerald looked at Mick, then back at Peewee.

"We'll find that out, anyway," Kate said.

All three looked over at Kate for the first time. They had been avoiding looking at her.

"I'm going to start asking simple questions. Ones I believe you feel you can answer; please do. I don't want my dear mother rolling over in her grave. Why my place?"

| 409

"We were told that was the most strategic place to land."

"And … ?"

"And we were told we'd have to neutralize you, if …"

"Skip the government bullshit. What does 'neutralize' mean? Kill?"

"No, sir. We were told you would be the biggest … hurdle … to our mission."

Peewee leaned forward and down, his face inches from the guy's face. "There you go again: 'mission!' OK, what was your mission?"

"He can't …" the guy on his left started, but Peewee, without looking, backhanded him across the face. The guy, along with his chair, flew into the wall several feet away. He didn't get up.

"Sorry, I wasn't talking to him. You got something to say?" Peewee directed to the guy on his right.

He shook his head, quickly and vigorously.

Peewee looked back at Gerald. "The mission, Jerry?"

Gerald shifted in his chair. "We were supposed to escort the lady," and he looked at Kate.

"Kate. My name is Kate."

"She's my sister," Mick said.

"And she's my friend," Peewee said, leaning toward and looking down at Gerald inches from Gerald's nose. "'Escort? There you go again, Jerry. OK, escort her where?"

Leaning back, looking up at Peewee, Gerald answered, "Back, that is if she didn't come voluntarily with the Wall Street dude."

"Back where?" Peewee eased back into his chair, smiling sardonically.

"Ah, well, back to Washington."

CHAPTER 26

"Why?"

"No idea, sir."

"Wouldn't that be a little like kidnapping, Jerry? If she didn't want to come?"

Gerald didn't answer.

"You married, Jerry?"

"Yes."

"Kids?"

He didn't answer.

"KIDS?" Peewee demanded in a voice that would strike fear in King Kong.

"Yes."

"A sister?" Peewee asked, more calmly.

"Uh, yes."

"What if we flew your copter back, landed in your front yard, entered your home uninvited, scared the shit out of your family, drove to your sister's home, and 'escorted' her down here to Hope Town? How would you feel about that, Jerry?"

He looked down and didn't answer.

"Piss you off, Jerry? You see my dilemma?"

"We were just following orders," the guy on the right, sitting right across from Mick said.

Mick leaned across the table and swung a fist at the guy, but he saw it coming, ducked, and Mick's fist bounced off the top of his head.

He lunged across the table at Mick and what he didn't see coming was the fist of Peewee's right hand. The jab sent both the chair and him flying into and bouncing off the opposite wall from his comrade. He didn't move either.

MP was hunched over, holding his hand, when Peewee spoke. "Once again, little guy, I have to come to your rescue."

"Yeah, thanks. Shit, that hurt."

"You think that hurt? What about poor Allen down there," Gerald said, trying to stare angrily at Peewee but unable to suppress a little grin.

"Let me look at it," Kate said and put her arm around Mick's shoulder. "My hero," she cooed sarcastically in his ear and reached for his hand.

"I'm fine. It'll be OK," and he pulled his hand away.

"So, you do see my dilemma, Jerry?" Peewee continued. "If I called in here a couple of my machete-carrying soldiers and ordered them to cut these guys' heads off. Should they do it? They'd be following orders."

Gerald looked steadily at Peewee. "We work for the government of the United States of America. Apparently you didn't like … his answer," and he looked at the last guy to bounce off the wall, "but it's the truth."

"My soldiers work for the United Islands of the Bahamas, which is where you have, of your own accord, come to do illegal things. MP, go get a couple of the guys and have them bring in a machete."

"Wait," Gerald said. "We weren't supposed to hurt the lady …"

"Kate," Kate said.

"Kate. We were just supposed to bring her back. The orders were to not harm her … or you."

"Oh? What about the people you turn her over to? They gonna take her out to dinner? Buy her a cocktail?"

Gerald just looked at Peewee.

"So, rather than bring my men in here, I'll just turn you over to them? See what happens? I'm free of guilt, I have no idea what might happen. It's not my fault."

CHAPTER 26

"This is the government of the United States I'm talking about, not a bunch of ... savages."

"Hah!" Peewee burst out with. "You know the truth? If I turned you over to those 'savages' out there, you know what they'd do? They'd take you all home and care for your guys' wounds. I think the savages are the ones you'd be handing Kate here over to."

"You know why they want her kidnapped?" MP interrupted, ineffectively trying to sound tough. "Huh?"

Gerald looked tentatively at Mick and then Kate. "Sort of."

"She's going to put away some Wall Street savages who screwed the American people out of billions of dollars. What do you think the people or person that sent you down here might do to protect themselves from prison and losing all the money they've accumulated fucking over you, me, all Americans?"

Gerald didn't answer.

"Are you proud of yourself?" Kate asked. "Now that you've seen me, are you proud that you were going to kidnap me and turn me over to ... whomever? Who might do ... whatever?"

"To save their fat, cheating asses!" Mick finished.

Gerald didn't say anything. The first guy Peewee had back-handed started to groan.

"And me?" asked Peewee. "As you can see, I'm not that easy to neutralize. How did you land there? How did you know about my place and me?"

Gerald remained silent.

"Sorry," Peewee said. "You're going to have to answer that one."

Gerald looked Peewee steadily in the eye.

"Now!" said with as much definitiveness as Mick had ever heard from Peewee, or anyone for that matter.

"Don't be an idiot," Mick said flatly. "You have to realize you're on the wrong side here. Not worth getting mutilated, man."

Gerald looked at Mick, at Kate, back to Peewee. "Apparently this Wall Street asshole—yeah, I think they're assholes, too—I was told found out that Kate had worked at Sears or whatever. Two brothers, from some wealthy family that owns Sears, told him Kate was staying with her brother on this island. These two guys also told him about you, said you'd be the biggest problem."

"How'd these two find out where I lived?"

Gerald's gaze at Peewee remained steady. "I'm afraid you've got someone in your ranks who's not as loyal as you think."

Peewee sat up and leaned forward, once again inches from Gerald's face. "You better be damn sure you're telling me the truth."

Gerald didn't waver. "That's quite a remote spot you've got there. How else would we or anybody have known if it wasn't somebody in your confidence? It doesn't even look like a house." Gerald smiled. "I apologize, seriously. I understand your animosity. I'd be pissed, too, if I was you. That's one of the coolest places I've ever seen. Believe me, we were careful … there's no damage done. We had no orders to and no intention of hurting you, weren't told of any family. But our tactical plan necessitated dealing with you in order to … make contact with Kate. Again, we were hoping she would be convinced to return with this Wall Street guy we were informed of. We underestimated you, obviously, and," he looked at Kate, "I can tell just by looking at Kate here, there's no way she'd go back with some Wall Street asshole."

Mick glanced sideways at Kate and raised his eyebrows.

CHAPTER 26

"So, you've talked to and know Richard?" Kate asked, ignoring Mick.

"Who's Richard?" Gerald asked, still looking at Kate.

"Don't fuck with me," Peewee warned.

"If Richard is this Wall Street prick, no, I never met him."

"How'd you get the information then?"

Gerald looked back at Peewee. "You know I can't give you that."

"Even if your life's at stake?"

"I'm a dead man anyway, I give you that information."

"Whose side you on: right or wrong?" Mick asked.

Gerald managed another smile. "That's not my decision to make. I do …"

"We know," Peewee finished, "'what you're told.' One last question: did this Richard know you were showing up here as well, Jerry?"

"I don't know. I really don't."

There was a knock on the door. Peewee yelled "come" and Rashi stuck his head in. "Food's here, T. And we got the Cokes."

"Bring it all in," Peewee said. "Maybe a couple jugs of water, too."

"OK," Rashi said, and held the door open as a couple guys brought in the pizzas. A third followed with a twelve-pack of Coke and several jugs of water. "Figured you'd be needing some water," he said and smiled.

"Good man," Peewee said. "I'm gonna have you and someone else, you pick who, stay in here with these guys. I'm putting them in the cell with the other guy. Set up a schedule; have replacements trade every four hours. Got it? Leave us for a minute. I'll come out and get you when we're ready."

"Sure. No problem," Rashi said. And the three of them left.

"Any way you could let the three of us go?" Gerald asked. "We're done here. We'd head out and you'd never hear from us again."

Peewee leaned back, putting his hands behind his head. The chair creaked; everyone held their breath expecting it to break. "You know, I almost trust you. You seem like a man of your word. Can't say that about these two here, though." Both guys had come around but had stayed on the floor, not daring to move.

"They do what I say," Gerald said.

"Follow orders, huh?" Mick said. "Have *your* orders changed? Still supposed to capture Kate here, aren't you? Isn't that your duty?"

"You have my word," Gerald answered. "We're out of there; you let us go."

Peewee rocked in his chair, the joints screaming. "Good question, MP? Duty or honor? Right, Jerry? Quite the dilemma."

Gerald didn't answer. The guy on the left, the first one Peewee had smacked, started to argue. Gerald told him to shut up before he got anything decipherable out.

"You're catching on, Jerry. Excuse me while I go get Richard. You know Richard, the Wall Street asshole?"

Gerald just frowned and nodded his head.

"MP, Kate, watch Richard's face closely when I bring him out. See if you see any signs of recognition in his face when he sees these guys." Peewee looked at Gerald. "I hope to hell you're telling the truth, Jerry. I do hope you all eventually walk out of here ... well, walk to your copter and fly out, I should say."

Gerald held Peewee's glower. He was either honest and straightforward or so ingrained in his 'duty' that he'd lie,

CHAPTER 26

do anything he could to fulfill his mission. Mick decided he wouldn't trust their word. They had orders. They were government and loyal, he guessed, to their careers—right or wrong, ethical or not. He hoped Peewee felt the same.

Peewee disappeared into the room behind the only door. Mick whispered to Kate that he'd watch Richard and she should watch Gerald, see if there was anything in his expression when he saw Richard. When Richard walked through the doorway, hands still cuffed behind his back, Mick watched his eyes closely. There was fear and something like bewilderment, almost embarrassment. Richard's eye went first to Kate, who wasn't looking at him, then Mick, then they settled on Gerald for a second, maybe a second too long, then scanned between the two guys on the floor, flicking back for a second to the guy on the floor on their right, and then back to Kate, who finally turned and looked at him. It was then Mick noticed the stain on his Bermudas, probably the source of the embarrassed look.

Peewee followed Richard through the doorway, put his arm patronizingly around Richard's shoulder, and looked at Mick. Mick grimaced and shrugged his shoulders. Had he looked at Gerald out of recognition or puzzlement? Why did he glance back at the other guy? He couldn't be sure. Mick nudged Kate, who looked at him and shrugged as well.

"Ricky, here, is a little embarrassed," Peewee said, managing to sound both mocking and compassionate. "As you can see, he has peed his shorts. Ricky, have you met Gerald before?"

"Uh, no. I haven't," he answered, a little too quickly Mick thought. And how did he know which guy Peewee was talking about? Shouldn't he have asked which was Gerald? Or have said something like: "I don't know any of these guys?" Or could it be he was just scared shitless or that Gerald was the only one seated at the table?

"Jerry, you don't recognize Ricky here?"

"No. I have never seen him before." It came out formal, almost like a response scripted by career training.

"And Ricky, you going to stick to your story about knowing nothing about these guys?" Peewee asked and pulled him hard against himself, intending it to be an intimidating "hug."

"Who are these guys? I have never seen them before," his voice slightly trembling.

"How about that guy?" and Mick pointed to the guy on the floor to the right. The guy on the floor didn't look up at Richard.

"No. Who is he?" his voice still quivering.

"You know," Peewee said, "we were planning on just letting you have your little powwow with Kate, see what you had to say, and send you on your way. If I discovered you knew these guys were along for the ride, I'd be darned pissed, you know? I never know, myself, what I might do when I get pissed. You know? And now, if I find out you're lying, I hope you got some of that fancy disability insurance. You know: if you physically can't work anymore? Know what I mean?"

Richard looked at Kate, pleading in voice, but a different, hard look in his eyes: "Sweetie … ," he started, but Peewee, his hand encompassing Richard's far shoulder, squeezed him in a sideways bear hug so hard Richard yelped and cried out.

"You his sweetie, Kate darlin'?"

"Ah, not even close. But I think you're hurting him," Kate said.

Peewee eased his squeeze and Richard's legs almost buckled. "Nuff with the sweet talk, asshole. All right? She don't like you

CHAPTER 26

no more. Got it? MP, why don't you take one of these pizzas and a couple of Cokes out to Rashi? And I assume Spense and Lottie are hanging around? Bring 'em in."

Peewee let go of Richard and told him to sit in the empty chair on Gerald's left vacated by the guy on the floor. Mick brought Spense and Lottie in, told Lottie to take his chair next to Kate, and pulled over two more for Spense and himself. Peewee opened the boxes of pizza; handed Cokes to Mick, Kate, Lottie, and Spense; and slid a jug of water in front of Gerald.

"Eat up, everyone," Peewee announced. Richard immediately reached for a piece. "Kate, your ex here isn't much of a gentleman. Apparently he's never heard of 'ladies first.'"

Richard's hand stopped just as he started to pick up a piece. He withdrew his hand quickly and put both his hands in his lap like a contrite child.

"We're fine," Gerald stated.

"I insist you and your buddies eat. If you haven't figured it out, you're not getting out of here for a while. We'll be talking to Richard alone. I have a feeling we may be able to encourage him to tell us the whole and nothin' but the truth. What do you think, Jerry? Think Ricky looks like an honest guy? I think he'll want to come clean, with a little persuasion maybe, but I'm sure he won't lie to his old sweetie. Whatcha think?"

Gerald stared steadily at Peewee, as if studying him. Richard's eyes flitted around. His body quivered like he had Mexican jumping beans stuck up his ass.

"Ladies, please take a piece of pizza so Ricky can eat," Peewee said, giving Richard his flesh-ball stare. "Spense, you seem to be a man of unusually keen instincts. You get a feeling Ricky knows these other gentlemen? They maintain they

[419

don't know him. If I find out they do, we get to see how long a helicopter floats."

"The US Government knows we're here, you know," burst out the guy on the floor on their left.

Peewee laughed. "I understand a certain senator," he looked directly at Gerald, "whose identity I'm confident we'll discover with or without your help … a big-assed senator maybe knows you're here. You really think he's going to risk his fat ass for your expendable one? You think the US Government wants an international episode exposing all these noble deeds you're up to down here in paradise? What do you suppose Interpol might think?"

"There's a shitload of money at stake," the guy on the left started.

"Shut the fuck up!" Gerald snapped at the guy.

"Spense, whaddya think?" Peewee asked casually, as if he was enjoying himself.

"Well, and this is out of nowhere, but our Richard keeps wanting to take a sideways glance toward the awkwardly inclined fellow down there on the right. I definitely get the feeling they know each other. No real idea why. But I definitely get those vibes."

"You know," Mick cut in, "when Richard walked into the room, he did sort of a double-take at him. I also feel he recognized Gerald. And the way he asked 'Who are these guys?' doesn't seem copasetic. Really, he knows who they are, because of what happened in the park. It just doesn't seem like what you'd say, you know?"

Peewee looked at Gerald, eyebrows raised, but didn't say anything for a while. Finally: "You know, you seem like a smart guy. I'm sorry to say I wouldn't trust you, because you

CHAPTER 26

think you're a soldier, but you'll all be a lot less screwed if you come clean. And I really, really don't want to hurt Ricky here. Next he'll shit his pants. But in my search for truth in the universe, I've just gotta know if Ricky knew you guys were coming along."

"What are you going to do to him if he knew?" Gerald asked.

"What, you have a conscience? What do you care what we do to a Wall Street prick who's been screwing you and your family? And your pension?"

Gerald managed a little smile. "I don't know him, but my understanding is he's just a pawn."

"Like you?" Mick stuck in.

Gerald kept the smirk and looked at Mick, back to Peewee: "A compliance guy, not one of the big assholes who call the shots."

"But he knew what was going on!" Mick retorted. "And he did nothing."

Still with a lingering smirk, Gerald said: "Hell, Washington knows what's going on. The former chairman of the Securities and Exchange Commission went to work for Goldman Sachs. So did the adviser to the Treasury Secretary. The big banks —Sachs, JPMorgan, and the like —fund the campaigns of the people who are supposed to be making the laws regulating them."

"So you know what's going on? And you've done nothing! You do know why they want Kate back?" Mick was getting worked up.

"What can I do?" Gerald said and smiled at Kate. "But, yeah, I hear she's giving them some really good shit, actual proof; maybe we can get one of the really big assholes for fraud. He snickered: "Blew their cover. Way to go, ma'am."

"Then why in the hell are you down here kidnapping her —excuse me, escorting her —I assume back to a senator who would be maybe the biggest asshole of all? Huh? Why?" Mick was close to fuming.

Gerald shook his head. "That's not the way the world works. Personally, I hope you fry all of the big cock suckers. But, in the real world, I *am* just doing my job."

"Ever think that's why we're down here? Escaping the *real* world? " Peewee asked calmly.

Gerald held Peewee's gaze once again. "What do you plan to do with Ricky?"

Peewee glanced at Richard, who now looked like he was about to cry *and* shit in his pants, and then back to Gerald: "Something a hell of a lot less gruesome than if I have to find out the hard way."

"Look, I'm guessing you wouldn't really damage the little prick, but you sure as hell could scare it out of him. Yes, he knows Allen over there. You were right. He may know who I am, but I really don't know him. Never seen him, honestly."

"I believe you," Peewee said. The women were still holding their pieces of pizza. No one had dared even move, much less eat. "You and your guys will be our guests tonight in the other room. Sorry you won't be able to go out to dinner, but it's Sunday and nothing's open anyway. We'll be taking Ricky with us."

"What? Where?" he wailed. "I wanna stay here."

Lottie leaned into Kate and whispered, yet in the small room everyone could hear: "My lord. What a fucking wimp. Sorry, but I can't imagine what you saw in this guy. You know, in spite of him sitting there whimpering, he's still been staring at my tits."

CHAPTER 26

"No shit?" Peewee said, sincerely annoyed. "MP, you must defend your girlfriend's honor. Smack him, only *not* with your fist; use the base of your palm." Instantaneously, MP, who had pulled his chair up at the end of the table next to Richard jabbed out with the palm of his right hand and caught Richard on the side of his mouth. Blood and a couple teeth, surprisingly, flew and splattered on Gerald. If there was any harm done to his hand, Mick had no idea; it felt so good to nail him.

"Mick!" Kate yelled, surprised. Lottie pumped her fist.

They put Gerald and the other two guys in the cell. Rashi gave them three Cokes, the water, and pizzas. Peewee, along with the others, walked Richard down to the pier after letting Kate clean him up a bit. Mick had caught him with the base of his palm on the left side of his face, splitting both his upper and lower lip, loosening several teeth and knocking out two. Mick apologized to him, saying he wasn't aware that his palm would do that much damage, even if he did deserve it. He wondered if it had been a setup by Lottie, but he figured Richard deserved it anyway.

The pier was across the street and down a ways from the police station. They walked Richard out the pier. Peewee and one of the larger islanders held Richard by the feet, hands re-cuffed behind his back, and dangled him upside-down over the water, Richard shrieking unintelligibly. After dipping him a few times, Richard, coming up sputtering and coughing water each time, gave up the name of the senator. Kate, who kept complaining that they were torturing Richard, pleaded that Sara probably knew his name anyway. Peewee said Ricky owed this information to them for lying.

BACK TO THE ISLAND

It turned out the senator was a wealthy 'good ole boy' from a southern state. Richard, nearly hysterical, would probably have given up his mother by this time. He informed them between dunks that this senator was involved because he was a 'silent' and secret board member of Richard's firm. If the CEO of the firm went down, so could this senator. Mick pointed out that, maybe, wasn't it time someone realized that this was a slight conflict of interest. Richard squealed that even if the senator was able to insulate himself from legal problems, his stock options in the company would take a huge beating. He said the senator's assets would be pretty much wiped out, as would his own, by Kate's testimony and the evidence, supported pretty conclusively by the emails Kate had 'stolen' off his computer, at which point they dunked him another time for good measure.

When they pulled him out and stood him up on the pier, Kate, to Mick's horror, wrapped a beach towel around him that had been lying on the pier. When she asked him what he had planned on accomplishing by coming down here, he said he had the authority to make her an offer that was pretty hard to refuse—an offer that would make her a wealthy woman. At which point, to everyone's delight, she shoved him off the pier back into the water and stomped away.

Mick said a quick goodbye to Peewee and Spense, gave Lottie a quick kiss, said he'd call her tomorrow, and caught up to Kate. They climbed on the golf cart and drove back to the cottage, Kate crying, Mick not knowing what exactly for and afraid to ask.

The rest stood, no one feeling guilty in the least, watching Richard, hands still cuffed behind his back, trying to keep his head above water by desperately kicking his feet. Peewee

CHAPTER 26

finally yelled at him to stand the fuck up, he was only in five feet of water. He then hauled the screaming, hyperventilating Richard out of the bay, back up to jail, and threw him in the cell with Gerald and his cohorts, telling them he had given up the senator's name, and asked, to Richard's horror, what they would do about it.

CHAPTER 27

WHEN MICK opened his eyes, he rolled over onto his back and just laid there. He didn't want to think. The sun must have been up because the room was bright. It must have been warm, as his window was wide open and he wasn't cold. The most prominent sounds were the whistle and chirps of the birds in the bushes outside his window. He listened farther out and could vaguely hear waves washing—must be from the ocean side. Then the distant growl of an outboard motor—must be from the harbor. The brittle leaves of the palms rattled lightly. A horn in the distance—must be from Hope Town. He looked at his door; it was open. He listened for Kate's sleeping rattle. Nothing. She must be up already. Then a nauseous dread contracted his groin. He better get used to there being no rattle, no breathing, no sister. He closed his eyes. Buried himself in his pillow. He listened in. His heart pushing blood past his inner ear blended with the waves, pulsing in, pulsing out. He heard a noise downstairs, probably in the kitchen.

He took a deep breath, swung his legs over the side of the bed, and sat up. Just sat there. Like an uneasy rain, the events of the last few days slowly dripped on him. My God, he thought, the last few days hardly felt real. He heard two women's distant voices: Kate and Heidi.

He stood, pulled on his loungers over his boxer briefs, slipped on a T-shirt, and headed for the bathroom. A pee

CHAPTER 27

and some cold water splashed on his face made him believe he was ready to head downstairs and face half of what were now, the four most important women in his life. One was gone; he knew one was leaving. But there was Heidi. Was there Heidi? He had the feeling she may need to fly her nest, but then there was Lottie. Lottie?

He could smell bread being toasted as he made his way cumbersomely, slowly, down the stairs, as if his mind was still deep in his pillow. As he shuffled into the kitchen, he could see Kate and Heidi out on the porch, each with a cup: Kate with her coffee and, of course, Heidi with her tea. The toast popped up as he walked through the kitchen. He detoured over, took the two pieces of toast out, planted them on a plate lying on the counter, plopped two more slices in the toaster, and poured himself a cup of coffee—a cup that was conveniently by the coffeemaker. He was going to have to learn to discard memories like this. He almost smiled as he remembered her chastising him that first morning: "Mind if I keep a couple cups BY THE COFFEE POT?"

"What ya want on the toast?" he yelled out to the women.

"Oh, he's up," he heard Kate say.

He heard her bare feet scratch on the porch floorboards as she stood and padded through the French doors into the kitchen. "Morning, bro. How about some good old peanut butter and jelly toast? Whatcha say?" and she gave him a gentle peck on the cheek and nudged him out of the way. "Heidi," she called, "want peanut butter and jelly on your toast?"

"Got any of those blueberry muffins?" she called back, jokingly. "Peanut butter and jelly would be great. Thanks, Kate."

"Oh, did you hear that?" Kate squealed. "She called me Kate!"

Mick walked out onto the porch with his mug. "Still no muffins at your place, *eh*?"

Kate yelled out to "shut your trap."

"It's a good morning, sir, eh?"

"Oh, great, there's two of you now. So Kate's Kate and I'm still 'sir'?"

"Yes, sir." And she smiled her impish grin at him.

Mick pulled over a chair and sat. "With sir, Mikael, M, MP, and Mick, I think it was Dylan who said: 'I'm not who I am most of the time.' So, what have you and *Kate* been talking about here?"

"Aren't you going to do your morning routine, Mr. MP?"

Mick chuckled. "I usually do that in private, unless there's a little urchin hiding in the shadows spying on me."

"Urchin, I am?"

"Oh, yeah! You know what it means?"

"Not entirely. I know there are sea urchins. Spiny little creatures. I doubt you are considering me spiny, although I've read of street urchins, somewhere."

"Right. The 'street' kind, mischievous little things. One meaning is 'juvenile delinquent,' if you were to look it up."

"You mean 'Google it,' sir?"

"Oh, yes. I hear you and your friend were quite adept at 'googling.' Googling while you should have been in school?"

She studied him for a while. "Who have you been talking to, might I ask?"

"Oh, I have my sources, and here comes one right now."

Kate came out of the kitchen and handed them each a plate with their peanut and jelly toasts. "You two look like you've been up to something."

"Your *brother* just called me a juvenile delinquent."

CHAPTER 27

"What? Why would anybody call such a sweet thing like you a juvenile?"

"Very funny," Heidi said, feigning insult. "So, Miss Kate, you've been listening to rumors and slanders about me?"

Kate laughed gleefully. "You've quite the rep."

"Well, I don't really have much competition on a little island like Elbow, do I? And somebody's got to keep these backward island people on their toes."

"Like your mom and dad?" Mick snuck in.

"My father would be disappointed if I didn't have some fun, raise a little hell."

"Your mother?" Mick asked.

"My mother is a sparrow that left the nest and did experience a bit of the wild world, so, since she *did* return to the nest, her island, she's a little more skeptical of what kind of fun or hell I might find out there in the big, bad world."

"Why'd she come back?" Kate asked.

"It was home. She came for what she thought was a visit and stayed when she found Father, who had made this his home. Speaking of Peewee, I'm surprised we aren't discussing the events of yesterday. Denial?"

Both Kate and Mick hiccupped a little laugh. "At least nobody got hurt, or worse," Mick said.

"That's not what I heard. Rashi told me you popped that Richard fellow pretty good, and then Peewee almost drowned him."

"No, that was Kate who almost drowned him. She shoved him right into the harbor with his hands cuffed behind his back."

Heidi grinned. "I know. I heard from Rashi."

"Just what is your relationship with Rashi?" Mick asked.

| 429

Heidi looked thoughtful for a moment. "You've read a little about our relationship."

"You mean he's the one …"

"We were in love. He still thinks he is."

"With you?"

She gave him an incredulous look for an answer.

"Well, so … what's up now?" Mick was unsure if his questions were over the line, but he felt toward Heidi as if she were a daughter, he imagined, since he had never had one.

She held his gaze for a while then looked down at her hands playing with the hem of her shorts. "He can't really be in love with me, can he?"

"Why?" Mick asked.

"Because," she continued to play with her hem, "because I will be leaving Elbow, and … he won't be. And … I … can't love him."

Both Mick and Kate sat silently, afraid to look at each other, not knowing why she felt that, not knowing how to respond.

Heidi looked up at Kate. "It's what I was trying to get up the courage to ask you this morning. But I hate to talk about it in front of MP here."

"What do you mean?" he asked.

"Well, and I am sorry to bring this up. I'm guessing it's why we aren't talking about yesterday. But …" She started playing with her hem again. Then, like she had summoned up the courage from a deep breath: "When you go back to New York, Kate, could I go with you?"

Kate skipped a breath. "Uh, jeez, Heidi. You really popped that one on me. Holy cats! Why? What would you want to go to New York for? What would you do there?"

CHAPTER 27

"I wouldn't expect you to take care of me. Just maybe help me get set up in an apartment or whatever. I'll get a job."

"Doing what?" Mick asked, immediately realizing he was sounding pessimistic.

"Who knows?" she said. "Isn't that the fun of it?"

Nobody said anything for a while.

"What would you do for money?" Kate asked, cautiously.

"Father will set me up for a while."

"You've talked to your parents about this?" Mick asked, wondering where in the hell Peewee got his money.

"Oh, yes. Of course. He expects me to … explore my destiny, I guess."

"And, again, your mother?" Mick said.

"She doesn't say much, really. But what can she say? She flew the nest. They'd both feel much better if I was accompanied by someone they trust, of course. Especially if you both were going, but I can tell you don't plan on leaving, at least not now, sir?"

Kate looked at Mick and grimaced. "But I could be leaving pretty soon, hon."

"If you're not comfortable with me accompanying you, I understand."

"No, no, that's not it. I'd love to chaperone you. Seriously. But," another grimace, "it could be any day. When would you be ready?"

"I've been ready since before I met you. I think I knew I'd have to leave that day my friend and I watched that ship sail away. And then she left."

Mick, remorsefully resigned to what he was hearing Heidi say, but knowing he was being selfish, felt a brooding need to change the subject. "So, what do we know about what Peewee's plans with those guys he's got locked up?"

"You'll have to ask him. He's not too pleased about that metal albatross, as he calls it, parked in our yard. He stomps out onto the deck, stares at it, and stomps back in, over and over again. He's 'fit to be tied.' Is that the cliché? The blades made quite a mess, there's sand blown everywhere and a crater where it landed. He says he won't let them go until they clean it up. Mother pointed out that they also had to leave the same way they came, so what good would that do? Then he stomps around again. I assume everything went OK in your meeting with this guy, Kate?"

"First he played the romance card, then offered me a jackpot if I refused to testify."

"That's when he ended up in the drink, I imagine?" Heidi asked, grinning from ear to ear.

"Yeah, you got it. I was really pissed off first—that he thought he could court me back, second—that he could buy me. What a dick. Excuse the French, Heidi."

"Hey, we going to be travelling buddies, no reason to apologize. He probably couldn't understand you not being interested in the money."

"Yes. To him it is all about the money, obviously. I suppose that's what infuriated me the most, really. I guess I was hoping for a sign of something like repentance. It's at least what I wanted. Stupid. I should have known better."

Listening to this didn't help Mick's mood at all. It just firmed up his dejection. He loved her ... Marilyn or Kate? He wasn't sure which, but he had done his best to convince himself it should be Kate. She had wanted to meet Richard down here so he could make it right. He saw that. And loved that. She had to have been at least somewhat close to him. They were engaged, for Christ's sake. She wanted to give him the benefit of the doubt, hoping he had realized he had just been a pawn, knowing he should have done something and would repent, seeing the error of his ways. Instead, he thought machismo and money would win her over? Were men, and even women, in positions of self-perceived power, really like that? Obviously some, hopefully not most. Or was it the inevitable curse of the 'capital' aspect of capitalism? At least of capitalism gone awry?

As if by reading his mind, Heidi asked: "So, what's the problem? What is it about the system this guy's a part of that you and Father hate so much?"

"Can't speak for your father," Mick started, realizing no one had ever really outright asked him this question. "I guess … I do believe capitalism, with a little socialism mixed in, is potentially the world's best system for both an economy and community, if the freedom it encompasses is not used, I guess I'd say, unfairly, to take advantage of people. People and businesses have to make money—even as much as they can—and there's nothing wrong with growing and prospering, if done ethically. Mick crossed his arms and looked down at her. "You know who the Dalai Lama is?"

"Yes, sir. Isn't he like the CEO of the world's philosophy?"

Mick had to laugh. "So, it doesn't surprise me that you've heard of the Dalai Lama, but how do you know what a CEO is?"

"You forget I've been home schooled by my father. He loves the Dalai Lama but says most CEOs are short-sighted narcissists."

This cracked Mick up, coming from what appeared to be an innocent young island lady. "Well, your father and I have a lot in common. First, you're right, it's almost like the Dalai Lama should be the CEO of the United Nations. He seems to have a perspective that transcends governments and politics. He once said that freedom, democracy, and justice were American principles but that for some people economics are more important, but that that was a mistake. That in many countries, like Syria right now, without these principles human life becomes worthless. He felt that without moral principle, truthfulness, there is no future."

"Your United States are that bad?"

He was still smiling, couldn't help himself. "Not on the same scale as Syria, no. But the decisions made with only profit—not fairness, justice—as a guideline, like what's happened on Wall Street in New York, doesn't take human life into account. They don't kill people, just their dreams. Because of the system that allowed individuals to do what they did with people's savings, innocent people lost jobs, homes, lives, dreams, all because of the greed that drove these individuals—people without moral principle—that Kate is hopefully putting behind bars. So I, and apparently your father, have chosen to escape that system down here.

"You so sure you're escaping it down here?" HS said. "And, if you believe the system is good but has gone awry, why run from it? That surprises me, sir."

Mick lost the smile.

"If Kate is going back to battle the system, why don't you go along? Make more of a difference there than hiding out down here?" Heidi smiled sadly. "Well, I can certainly understand why you and my father are friends and, I guess, have both tried to escape to our little island, but … ? Anyway, I wish you both luck." Then she stood and grabbed each of their hands, pulling them up. She wrapped her arms around them, pulling them toward her. "I love you both," she said, voice breaking. "The folder is on the table." And, as usual, she glided away.

CHAPTER 27

As they stood watching Heidi head up the lane, Kate grabbed Mick's hand back. "I've got something I need to talk to you about. Look at me."

Mick relaxed his grip. "I'd really rather not talk about it. Not now, maybe later."

"No, what I have to talk to you about is, well, it's not what you think. Please …"

They heard the rumble of several carts coming toward them from the direction of Hope Town. "Mick …" Kate started.

"Look!" Mick shouted, leaning out over the railing, craning his neck to look south down the road toward town. "There are several carts coming and I see Peewee's head already, sticking up above one of the windshields. Guess we're gonna find out about last night."

"Mick …"

"They've got Richard and the other three guys with them it looks like. Let's go down and meet them."

Mick headed off the porch and down the steps. Kate followed reluctantly. Peewee pulled up with Gerald next to him and Richard sandwiched between the other two 'chaperons' in the back. A parade of about ten other carts were following full of islanders: men, women, and children all, it seemed, providing a lively escort. Peewee pulled up to Mick as Kate settled at his side.

"We're off," Peewee announced. "Nobody, but maybe Ricky a bit, thanks to you, tough guy, worse for wear."

Gerald actually smiled and nodded to both Mick and Kate. "Good luck, ma'am."

Kate stepped up next to the back seat, the three of them squished together. Nobody was tied or handcuffed. "Richard, I am sorry for what will probably happen to you."

BACK TO THE ISLAND

Richard, looking petulant, whined: "You've totally ruined my life. I'll lose my job, my investments, I'll be blackballed—unemployable. They'll probably sue me. I'll be the one behind bars, and I didn't do a fucking thing."

"Exactly!" Mick exclaimed.

Richard ignored Mick and remarkably whined one last feeble entreat at Kate: "Don't you have anything to say, babe?"

"Yes. Yes, I do. Don't ever call me 'babe' again!"

Richard raised up and threateningly pointed at Kate: "Listen, bitch! You fucking cunt!"

Gerald swiveled and nailed him with his elbow smack dab in the middle of the forehead. Richard slumped backward, out cold, and once again the other two squeezed him between them holding him upright.

"Sorry, ma'am," Gerald said to Kate. "He really embarrasses me."

"Hey, Gerald. You're all right. Think about that universal soldier idea, will ya?" Mick said.

Gerald saluted with a finger, his middle finger Mick noticed, and laughed.

"Enough of this!" Peewee growled. "As I said, we're off."

"How do you know they're actually going to leave?" Kate directed at Peewee.

Peewee looked at Gerald. "I'd like to believe him. But, just in case …"

"Ma'am," Gerald said, "we won't be back. Again, fry their asses for me, will you?"

The cart jerked ahead as Peewee took off, the line of carts following, all smiling and waving at Mick and Kate, the kids screaming as if it were a parade.

CHAPTER 27

Mick and Kate retreated back to the porch, heated their coffees, and sat side-by-side at the table, Mick checking his computer, Kate nervously watching him. He found multiple emails from Spense and Lottie: Spense wanting to know 'what the bullocks was going on,' Lottie telling him she wanted to see him, wondering when they could trade backrubs, Mick thinking he'd love to get and give a rub he didn't have to feel guilty and tense about.

Kate had earlier found an email from Sara—one she'd been dreading. "Mick," she said, trying not to sound ruffled, "we need to talk. How 'bout a walk on the beach?"

"Oh, man! That sounds great. Get our minds off everything. I mean, holy shit! I came here because it was supposed to be a quiet, lazy, peaceful village. Of course, then I met you. Peaceful met stormy."

"Well, so—o—ry," and as she gave him a hug whispered, "a nice, peaceful walk then."

"Oh?" he said, turned, and ran yelling, "Last one to get their suit on gets thrown in." Mick ran off the porch, and as he started up the steps, Kate leaped and knocked his foot, tripping him. He fell, smashing his shin onto a step-edge and sliding down to the bottom, screaming like he'd been murdered and grabbing his leg. Kate tried to jump over him, but he grabbed her leg and pulled her back. She slipped back and landed, knee-first, solidly in his groin. With Mick now curled at the bottom of the stairs, groaning and screaming, Kate spun off and took a step up, but Mick leapt and wrapped his arms around her left leg and yanked. Kate fell, this time nicking her tailbone on the edge of the bottom step, and now both were screaming. Mick threw his arm around her and pulled her to the floor, rolled on top of her, and pinned her arms to the ground. Kate started thrashing and tried to knee him in the already tender groin. So he sat on her stomach, pinning her arms under his knees. She started pummeling his back with her knees, so he leaned back, holding her legs with his hands, rendering most of her helpless, except ... her head.

She snapped her head up and chomped at the target only inches from her face, latching onto the crotch of his loungers between her teeth and whipped her head back and forth, snarling, like a terrier with a bone. Mick, startled and rather concerned for his own bone, tried to stand up. But Kate, clamped onto his loungers, didn't let go ... and down came the loungers. Fortunately Mick had on his boxer briefs and felt fortunate all Kate had chomped onto was the loungers, which were now around his knees. He fell over backward on the steps, now his tailbone cracking the same step edge as Kate, which had him "ahhh ... shitting" in pain. She let loose her grip and, once again, tried to leap over him up the stairs. Mick blindly reached up and found the waistband, unfortunately, of both her pajama bottoms and her underpants. Kate pulled clear of both, kicking them off, leaving Mick with a handful of bottoms and a view of his sister's bouncing up the steps.

Not to be deterred, he kicked off his loungers and, albeit painfully, scrambled up the steps after her. She had thrown her T-shirt off and was trying frantically to step into her bikini bottoms when he grabbed her around her waist from behind and started dragging her toward his room ... and *his* suit. When they reached the doorway, Kate grabbed the frame and Mick found himself, with only his T-shirt on, bare-assed, arms around his now entirely naked sister, one leg under each of his armpits, Kate stretched horizontally, hands firmly holding onto the doorjamb ... when both heard a rather startled:

CHAPTER 27

"WHAT THE … ?"

Both froze, turned their heads, and there was Lottie, standing at the top of the stairs, more than a little surprised by the scene unfolding in front of her.

Lottie turned and ran back down the stairs, yelling "Oh … my … God!"

Mick assessed the scene, looking down at Kate's naked body stretched out before him, released her, dropping her feet and, consequently, her to the floor, and took off after Lottie. He stopped at the bottom of the stairs to pull on his loungers and, by the time he hit the porch, she was on a cart, barreling through the dust back toward Hope Town. He yelled "Lottie" as loud as he could, but she wasn't going to hear him over the roar of the cart speeding away. He debated chasing after her in his cart, but even if he did catch up with her, he couldn't quite picture the explanation happening in public in Hope Town village. As a matter of fact, he couldn't imagine what any explanation might look like anywhere.

He slowly clomped, heavy-footed, back up the stairs, wondering how they hadn't heard the cart, trying not to imagine what Lottie might have thought she had seen. Well, anyway, he thought to himself, Kate *was* his sister, so unless Lottie thought him a total incestuous pervert, which was probably what she was thinking—why not?—he would simply have to tell her the truth, whatever that was, and hope for the best.

He found Kate, now in her bikini, both top and bottom, sitting on her bed cross-legged, hand over her mouth, staring at him wide-eyed as he looked in.

He leaned on the doorjamb, shaking his head. When he realized her mouth was muffling a grin, he broke out laughing, and Kate followed.

"Ah, shit. Well, I don't think she'll really suspect me of trying to have my way with my sister. I hope! I'll somehow try to explain. She's pretty reasonable and, hopefully, really open-minded. Thank God you're my sister, though. I doubt I could explain this away if you weren't."

Kate quit smiling. "Mick, we gotta talk. Let's go for that walk."

They mixed themselves a gin and tonic in thermos mugs and headed over the dune for the beach. "I beat you; I get to throw you in," Kate claimed, climbing down to the beach.

"Uh-uh! No fair," Mick retorted. "I would have won if we hadn't been interrupted."

"Oh, how you figure that?"

"I'm bigger and stronger than you are. I had you wrapped up. I could have dragged you into my room to get my suit."

"Right! And how were you going to continue to restrain me *and* put your suit on?"

"I wouldn't have to; by the time you ran back to your room, I'd have my suit on."

"What if I grabbed your suit?"

"I'd still overpower you."

"Like you did downstairs?"

"No fair. You cheated."

"How?" And she dropped her thermos glass and took off running toward the waves, yelling, "Last one in is the cheater."

"No fair!" he yelled, tossed his glass, and took off after her. Before she reached the water he faked stepping on a piece of coral, hollered, falling in the sand and rolling around holding his foot as if in dire pain.

Kate stopped, came back to check on him as he continued to roll in the sand, yelling about his foot. As she bent over

CHAPTER 27

him, he leaped up, knocking her over, and took off running toward the waves. As he reached them, he slowed, turned, and let her catch up to him. She grabbed his hand as she raced by, dragging them both into the water.

After they both dove into a breaker, Kate laid on her back, arms and legs spread, floating up and down with the waves. Mick, bobbing upright, contemplated her. Thank God she had her suit on. He realized how unbounded she was, and a wave of melancholia washed over him as he was pretty sure he knew what Sara's email had said. He was expecting it but didn't want to face the fact that his sister, with whom he felt at that moment an intense closeness, was really leaving. He looked at her as she slowly was carried into shore. He tried not to think about how much he was going to miss her.

He let himself drift in as well and they both washed up on shore. The waves were moderate and they both laid in the sand, letting the waves wash over them.

Finally Kate got up and sat just out of reach of the wave's wash, and Mick crawled up to her. "So, when do you have to go?" he asked.

She paused, first looking down for several minutes, and then at him. "Tomorrow. They're sending a plane to Marsh Harbour. They want to get my deposition. They're thinking they might get a pound of flesh from a couple of the big bulls."

"Jesus! Tomorrow?"

She shrugged. "Day after tomorrow I'm scheduled with the attorneys in New York."

"How can you leave that fast? How can you even get ready?"

Kate hesitated, still looking at Mick. "I don't think I'll ever be ready to leave. I don't want to leave; you understand that?" She started to cry. "I *have* to," and she put her head between her knees.

Mick crawled up next to her and hugged her. "I know, hon. I know. It just ain't easy. I love you, goddammit."

Kate looked up at him, eyes red and pleading. "Promise me, if I tell you something, you won't hate me?"

Mick leaned away, gently pushing her chin up so he could look right at her. "How could I hate you? You're my sister. I love you."

"Promise," she said.

"What? Of course I promise. We're family. I'll always love you. I promise."

Kate looked up at him, eyes streaming and face twisted.

"Look, I promise. What the devil is it?"

She looked back down again. "You know that father of yours—Mac McGennity?"

"You mean that father of ours?" Mick said.

"Mick ... he ... adopted Sara and me," she said into the sand, looking as if she wished the waves would wash the words away.

Mick froze. His mind flipped around, at first not able to settle it on what she might mean. "What? You mean? WHAT?"

Kate tried to grab onto him, but he abruptly stood and looked down on her. "Mick ..." she entreated.

"You're serious? You're not joking?"

"Mick, I wouldn't ..."

And he took off running down the beach.

"Mick, you promised ... !" Kate screamed after him, crawling to her knees.

Mick ran wildly, like he was trying to outdistance the meaning of what he had just heard, splashing in and out of

CHAPTER 27

the waves as they washed up onto the shore. He ran fast, faster than his body would allow him, afraid to slow, that if he did Kate's words would catch up with him. Finally, he tripped and fell, exhausted. He laid there, panting, shaking his head from side to side, trying to escape the thoughts that were banging against his skull.

He got up again and ran, stumbling as the sand got deeper until he was against the cliff on the north end. He stood, panting, looking at the wall as if it might disappear. He looked up, the top at least thirty feet up, and it extended out into the Atlantic tapering to a reef. No way around it. Dead end.

Suddenly a loud irregular whirring sound came from over the hill. At first he didn't know what it was until it slowly gained force and merged into a deafening roar. The helicopter! He never saw it but he imagined it lifting as the decibel level increased into a loud whine and quickly dissipated as it flew away.

He couldn't focus. He stood there a long while looking up at the cliff. Finally he decided he should go talk to Peewee, see if the three, or four, of those guys got off without further incident. It had been … how long … since they had left the cottage? An hour? Two hours? Four hours? His mind wouldn't track time. He felt a sense of relief that he could focus on this, a new need. Out of sight, out of mind; out of … what? He transferred his sentience to the need of checking on Peewee and Wanda and Heidi, that's all.

He started running back, thinking only of Peewee, Wanda, and Heidi. He knew there was a path through the brush that led to the road. He had taken this path from the road to the beach, but not from the beach to the road. He figured he'd run along the sand edging the high hill until it leveled and look for the break into the brush. Several times he stopped and backtracked, almost in a panic. Where was the break? He was sure it was there. Where was the path? He knew it was there, but he couldn't find it! His running slowed as his breathing got more and more labored. Finally he saw it. He had to run. He had to go see how Peewee was. He dodged and ducked under the brittle bushes, scratching himself. He was barefoot and all he had on was his swimming suit. He saw blood on his arms, but there was no pain.

When he got to the road, he turned left and ran toward the cottage and Hope Town. Suddenly it struck him that he was running the wrong way. He stopped, stumbling, out of breath, and turned and ran the other way. How far was the path to Peewee's? He'd only been there once and he had followed Heidi's lead. Would he recognize it? He remembered it was hard to find. How would he find it? When he took a look straight ahead, down the road, he saw someone coming. Who would be walking on the road?

As he got closer, he realized it was Heidi. He slowed, tried to compose himself, but he was out of breath and heaving to catch air. He stopped and waited for Heidi to reach him.

She stopped a little short of him and waited, silently, for him to calm down. When he started breathing normally, she stepped up to him and held his hand. "You could come with us, you know? Even if for a while. They're picking us up in Marsh Harbour in a plane. I'm sure there'd be an extra seat."

"So you know you're leaving tomorrow?" Mick asked, breathing slowly, feeling a sudden odd calm coming on. Everything slowed down. He looked down at his hand in Heidi's.

CHAPTER 27

"Yes. I got an email about an hour ago from Kate." Mick realized that Kate must have emailed her before they had left for their walk. "I'm going there now. I assume she's there? You know, to make a list of what I need to bring." They looked at each other for a while without talking. "Where are you headed, sir?"

"Uh ... to your place. I heard the helicopter take off and I thought I'd check with you guys."

"You heard the helicopter from your cottage?"

"No, no. I was on the beach."

"You must have taken the path through the brush then? Although it looks like you made your own path. How'd you get so scratched up? You're bleeding in several places."

"Can you show me the path to your place? I'm not sure I can remember where it is." His breathing was almost normal now, but his mind was still spinning, just slower.

"Sure." She started to lead him by the hand like he was her child and looked up at him, seeping sympathy. "You look like you're taking Kate's leaving pretty hard, sir. Why don't you come along? Cap'n Jack's will survive."

He looked down at her face and worked up a smile. "There's Lottie. I can't just walk out on Lottie, can I? And there's Spense, your dad?"

They walked a ways. "Excuse me, sir. Maybe this is out of line, but my father will be fine, Spense comes and goes, the way I understand it. And, well, I like Lottie too, but ... well, who you going to miss more: Kate, Sara, or Lottie?"

He stopped abruptly. "You know about Kate and ... er ... me?"

"Know what, sir?"

Her perused her face, probed her eyes. Apparently Kate had not told her, could not have told her, of course. But a

 445

remembrance hit him like a flash. "You know Kate's my sister, right?"

She looked quizzically up at him. "That's what you've always said, sir." They started walking again as she led him by the hand.

"Why do you say it like that?" he asked.

"Here we are, sir. The path entrance is almost impossible to detect, as you can see. The landmark is here, on the other side of the road. See how those two large bamboo trees cross each other. X marks the spot. Oh, and since you're barefoot—they look a bit beat up, too—I've left my flip-flops where the path trails off over the coral. They'll be a little small, but you'll need them to get over the coral to our place. If you're not back by the time I leave, I'll bring a pair of yours and trade with you. OK, sir?"

He leaned down to her and kissed her on the forehead. "Thanks, hon."

"Kate is at the cottage, right, sir?"

"If not, she should be on the beach just over the dune."

"OK, sir. Bye, now. Please consider coming along. My father and mother would like it, too."

"Bye, hon. See you for sure before you go."

She tightened her lips in an "OK, be-that-way" look, turned, and sauntered away.

Mick followed the path and as he came around the edge of the promontory, he expected to see a real mess. There was a wide but shallow crater, but not sand everywhere like he expected. Everything else looked about the same as he remembered it. He walked up near the front entrance where the stepping-stones led him and yelled up. Two heads showed, one peeked over the railing, the other towering over it. "MP!

CHAPTER 27

Hello! Come on up," Peewee yelled down. Wanda made a quick little wave and turned away.

MP walked up the spiral staircase and found Peewee on a lounge, book on a table by his side. "Come on, have a seat. Need anything to drink? Some bandages, perhaps?"

Mick was parched, he realized. "Water, please."

He got up to go get it, but Wanda was already carrying out a pitcher of iced tea, a little smile on a little face.

"Ice tea OK?" she asked as she set the tray on the big table.

"He looks a little dry," Peewee said. "I'll get him a glass of ice water, too." And he limped in through the French doors. Wanda walked over, gave Mick a weak smile, and set an insulated glass with the lighthouse emblazoned on it on the side table next to him.

"Thanks, Wanda. Looks like your *company* has departed?"

She sat on the chair next to him without responding.

"You OK with Heidi leaving?" Mick asked, trying another topic.

Peewee returned with the ice water and handed it to MP, sat on the lounge, and let Wanda answer. "I worry. But glad she go with Miss Kate," and she gave him the same weak smile.

"She needs to go," Peewee said. "She seemed to think she'd be going with both of you?"

"No. No. She did try to convince me to go with her and Kate, but …"

"She tried to convince you? When?"

"Just now. I ran into her on the road."

"Looks like you ran into some bushes too, there, little guy. You'd think someone with even half a brain would walk the path, preferring not to scratch the shit out of himself. But no, you mustn't have even a half up there. Kinda *empy* is it?"

"Real funny, big guy. Hey, you know it looks pretty good

around here. I thought I'd find a mess. How'd it go with those guys? I heard the helicopter. That's why I came."

Wanda nodded to Mick, gave him the same almost sad smile, and went into the main cabin.

"You heard the helicopter? Where the hell were ya?"

"On the beach."

"What were you doing there?"

"Umm, we went for a swim, Kate told me about leaving tomorrow, and she went to pack. I took a stroll this way."

"A stroll? You look like you've run a marathon. You having trouble with Kate leaving?"

"Tell me about what happened with the guys!" Mick wasn't too interested in talking about how he felt about Kate at the moment; he didn't know how he felt about Kate at the moment.

"Yeah, we came back here. I gave 'em rakes, a broom, rags, and a vacuum cleaner. When they had come, the windows were wide open and sand was fuckin' everywhere, and a good size crater, bigger than that one they left by far."

MP took a sip of his water, stood, and walked to the railing, attempted a chuckle. "You made 'em clean up?"

"Hell yes. They made the mess. Gave Ricky the vacuum. Told him if I found a grain of sand, I'd throw him off the deck up here. He did a damn good job."

"How's the crater smaller now?"

"Gerald …"

"It's 'Gerald' now?"

"Yeah, he's an all right guy. Said when they landed, they had to hover for a while and the downdraft caused quite a cavity. He made the other guys work their asses off to fill it in. Apologized like hell. Said, taking off, they'd cut slide sideways before laying the foot to the metal, so to speak."

CHAPTER 27

Peewee walked up next to Mick, stood on one side of him, putting his hand on MP's shoulder. They stood silently for a while gazing out over the wonderful north point of the island: ocean still pounding the rocks on the right, waves massaging them on the sea side. "You doing OK, MP?"

"Yeah, yeah. It just came up so fast—her, they, both leaving."

"Better that way, don't you say? Less time to fret over it."

"Maybe. Yeah, you're probably right." It seemed right for them concerning Heidi. They seemed ready and resigned to let her go. She might come back. Kate wouldn't. He wasn't ready for Kate to be out of his life; not Heidi either. It was like life was just rolling … well, not actually rolling but bouncing along and, all of a sudden: wham! A lot of unfinished business hanging in the air, especially after what he'd just found out. What exactly did he find out today? His mind still wouldn't quite wrap itself around it. It felt like the realization was poking at his skull, but it couldn't quite get through. Maybe Peewee was right: probably good she was leaving, soon.

"Wanda's packing for Heidi. I probably should go check on her. Maybe you should go help Katie."

Katie? He never thought of her as Katie. Funny. No, he didn't want to go help Katie, Kate, Marilyn, whoever she was.

"Who was the mole?" he suddenly asked Peewee out of nowhere.

"Didn't I say? You know, Harvey. The big dummy," Peewee scowled.

"Harvey? The big fella that's been some trouble?"

"That's the fella. Got offered some money for information and couldn't resist it."

"Oh, yeah, that's right." Mick couldn't think straight. It was like his brains had been scrambled. "So, what's going to happen to him?"

"Oh, we'll have the hearing tomorrow."

"Hearing?"

"A trial, so to speak."

"Oh, yeah. I remember Heidi telling me: a jury of his peers."

"Yup. He's already been given too many chances. This is liken to treason. He'll most likely be banished."

"Banished? To where?" Mick asked.

"That's his choice: where. Just not here on Elbow. He can take his payoff as far as it'll take him."

"Then you'll have an enemy out there."

"Better out there than in here," Peewee said and turned. "You get home and help Kate. You hear? Get out of here."

Mick was in no hurry to get back. He pretty much sauntered, stopping to look at insignificant things. The road, actually just a lane here, was quite pretty he noticed. A hedge of flowering bushes ran along one side. Toward the very north end, before it dead-ended, the lane was all soft sand, bushes encroaching on the road. Two carts could not pass. There were no cottages. In one place a little back, closer to his cottage, was the little backwater seaside harbor they had seen kayaking. Here it neighbored the road. There were several small boats moored at slouching, crooked docks—fishing boats mostly. As the road got nearer his place, there were lawns and cottages on the right as the road neared the sea, and still a rise on the left. More pretty, flowering bushes in the sand in places, but no homes on the east side, the ocean side, until his. The road was full of little ups and downs and rather rutted. It smoothed out at Mick's and widened, fortunately, for Spense never pulled around back, and there was space by the porch in front to park.

It was empty now. Mick trudged up onto the porch. No Heidi. No Kate. She, or they, were probably up in her room ... packing! Fuck.

CHAPTER 27

He sat down with his computer and tried to make contact with his old confidant.

DATE: Friday, Mar. 16, 2012, 2:12 p.m.

M: You there wackin off in your cubical, big boy? Looks like yur online?

Barn: Yeah, yeah. Funny man, M, MP, Mick, or whoever you are. How is everything? I've left you several emails. No reply. What's up?

M: Got something I need to talk about. Bad.

Barn: Bad? What do you mean? Why? What?

M: Kate. She's not my sister.

Barn: What! What the hell you talking about?

M: I don't know what to think, so I don't know what to say, but Kate just told me she and Sara were adopted by my biological dad, McGennity.

Barn: Whoa, baby. No shit! Jesus, Mary, and Joseph. Really? When did you find this out?

M: About an hour ago, maybe two. It's got my mind fucked up. I can't even keep track of time.

Barn: You never could. But, holy shit. She told you? What did you do? You didn't do something stupid, like resurrect your temper?

M: Well, before I did something stupid, I just took off running. We were on the beach, and I just took off.

Barn: Man, M! So, you haven't talked this over or even talked to her since she told you?

M: No, I'm on the porch. I just got back. She's upstairs packing, I think. She's flying back to New York tomorrow.

To get deposed. I guess it looks like some of the big honchos might have their tits in a wringer.

Barn: Tits? What, are some of the big guys women?

M: What? You don't have to be a woman to have tits.

Barn: Yes, you do. Men only have nipples.

M: OK, OK. I'll think of another idiom.

Barn: Idiom?

M: Idiom, you idiot. A little saying that isn't literal. Never mind. I need help!

Barn: OK. I know you never do what you're told. So, questions. That's the right way to do it, right?

M: YES!!

Barn: OK, OK. Calm down. So, how do you feel about this?

M: What! How do I feel about it? That's like a psychiatrist asking his patient what his problem is. If he fricking knew what his problem was, he wouldn't be talking to the fricking psychiatrist! Would he?

Barn: OK, Jesus. Settle down. OK, so, what do you think you might want to say to Kate when you next see her?

M: Very good. Nicely and safely put. I suppose I will gather my wits, calmly sit down with her, and then I'm gonna frickin kill her! OK, I just had to say that. OK, really: I don't think I want to talk to her now. I have no handle on how I feel. Shit, man. Not really my sister! This is all way too weird. I'm sure Martha's up there, if there is an up there, getting a real kick outa this. You know, I actually think I do love her. All right. I'm afraid I do. But, how? I've done

CHAPTER 27

my darndest to think "Oh, whoopee I've got a couple new sisters," and although they're very different, they're both really something, and it's not fair now that they're NOT MY SISTERS. You know how difficult it's been with her traipsing around? It's probably good that she's leaving tomorrow. When I think about it, of course, it's why she just told me about it. She told me about it now because she's leaving. Ahhh ... she can't do this to me.

Barn: Are you angry? Why?

M: Why? She's lied to me, a big fat lie, and I'm the fool.

Barn: Why are you the fool? Think about it. If you knew she wasn't really your sister, you would have been trying to get into her pants continuously. She couldn't tell you.

M: Yeah, yeah! What am I supposed to do about Lottie then? Huh? Like I want to hurt her?

Barn: I have no idea. Wait a minute. It's supposed to be me asking you: What are you going to about Lottie? Do you love her?

M: I was beginning to think so. I was certainly getting there. I mean, she's great. Man, is this screwed up! I can't win.

Barn: Well, it isn't really a game, is it? There's nothing to win. You could look at it positively. You have two women you love. I, for example, don't have one.

M: Three women, you mean—four actually. Nice try, tho. You're happy slapping the lizard there in your cubicle, anyway.

Barn: Slapping the lizard? Where in the hell did you get that one? Four? Who else you talking about? Anyway, I guess the most important thing right now is what you're going to say before Kate leaves. Can you make it a positive parting? Do you think she loves you as a brother, or otherwise?

M: Positive parting! Aren't we the poet? Do you even know what alliteration is?

Barn: Not a clue. I know, the illiterate tax professor. So, can you? Does she—which?

M: How can I make it positive? I'll try. How does she love me? Let me count the ways! I have no idea and I'd gander that she might not, either. I better go. Thanks, Barn.

Barn: Wait. What does Sara say about this? I'm assuming she was aware of the situation?

[MP thought about this and decided he didn't really want to think about Sara.]

Barn: Why aren't you answering? Are you angry with Sara? Well, keep me informed! That's an exclamation, not a question.

He couldn't work up any anger toward Sara. She must have been really uncomfortable being caught in the middle. He now realized what was behind some of the little skirmishes she and Kate had had. Why was he so dammed oblivious all the time! Sara?

When he shut his computer, he noticed the folder on the table next to it. When did she drop this off? He opened it. Goddammit! This was coming to an end, too. He really looked

CHAPTER 27

forward to that little urchin every morning. He had grown accustomed to it. Mornings were going to seem empty. Life was going to seem empty. He read:

> I wanted,
> And I received.
> Not always what I wanted
> But after, it was always what I seemed to need.
> Therefore I was lonely from time to time,
> and from time to time my loneliness was caused
> by my own yearning for the soft and subtle
> ministries of silence.
> Or perhaps it was vanity that caused me to cast
> my thoughts upon the nothingness of sea or sky
> to have them come back to me as a sunset, or starlight.
> Or to test the validity of my convictions, when carried
> on the different voice of a calming sea or raging ocean.
>
> —H.S.

Mick reread. Then reread again. Was she talking about herself, or Kate and him? "Not what I wanted, but what I seemed to need?" He didn't want Kate to go away. But, as Barney got him to admit, it was probably better now that she did. Would he be lonely? Shit, yes. Despair—"nothingness of sea or sky" but coming back as "sunset or starlight"—hope?

Wait a minute. Interpreting Heidi's poem this way would mean she would have had to know he and Kate weren't really brother/sister. Right? Or maybe he was reading too much into it. She did know Kate was going to have to leave, go back to New York to testify. But she didn't know about that until this morning. Huh. Maybe he was so into sudden self-pity that he'd start interpreting everything in light of his new confounded dilemma; and a bastard of a dilemma it was.

He heard footsteps on the stairs, something he wouldn't likely be hearing again. Well, there was Lottie. Could he find solace in Lottie? Should he even look for solace in Lottie? She could spend the night now. He certainly wouldn't mind the sound of her bare feet padding down the stairs. Lottie. He heard Kate and Heidi come into the kitchen. Heidi put her hand on M's shoulder as she passed but didn't say anything. Mick was afraid to look at her as she left.

Kate came out and sat next to him at the table. Neither looked at each other nor spoke. Kate picked up the folder and read the poem. She seemed to study it for a while. "You know," she smashed the silence as if it were crystal, "I always felt like Heidi knew."

Mick blanched but didn't answer.

"Knew that our relationship was more than brother/sister. You know?"

He still didn't answer, thinking: Why in the hell didn't *I* know then?

"Oh, Mick ..."

"MP," he interrupted.

She looked at him. He stared straight ahead. He wasn't going to look at her.

"You going to drive us in to the ferry tomorrow, or should I have Spense?"

"I will. You at least. I imagine Peewee and Wanda will bring Heidi in."

"Are we going to talk before I go?" she asked.

"I don't want to talk. I don't know if I'd be talking to Kate or Marilyn. I've got to figure that out."

CHAPTER 27

"How we going to do that if we don't talk?"

"Don't know."

"So, you're angry?"

He finally looked at her, expressionless, but close to erupting. He'd always heard there was a fine line between love and hate, although he had never before experienced this dangerous dichotomy himself—and had doubted he ever would—until now. He looked away without answering.

Quietly Kate got up and went into the kitchen. He smelled bread toasting. Another thing: no getting up and smelling coffee brewing, Kate waiting to hand him his cup. No muffins baking, bacon frying. All of his old friends, including maybe now his favorite—Sara—thousands of miles away. The two women ... two people ... who were two of the three most important in his life were leaving his life here in the Bahamas, and he couldn't shake the feeling that he'd never see either of them again. There was Peewee ... and Lottie.

Kate came back out and sat at the table with a glass of milk and two pieces of toast—one with peanut butter, one with jelly. Something he had done all his life. The realization just that they had that in common overwhelmed him. He got up, gently touched her shoulder as he passed, and went up to his bedroom. He lay down on the bed and, although it was only the afternoon, immediately dropped into a dark, dreamless sleep.

PART IV

Well, What Do You Know ...

CHAPTER 28

Date: March 17, 2012
To: Lottie
From: M
Subject: Not what you think

Today is the first day of the rest of my life

Lottie: Hi, babe. I hate clichés and platitudes, but this one fits me today. I took Kate and Heidi to the airport in Marsh Harbour this morning. Kate is going back to New York for depositions tomorrow. Heidi is accompanying her ... flying the nest, testing the waters, and all *those* clichés. Kate said to say goodbye to you and Spense. She didn't want to do it in person because, she pleaded, she'd never be able to say goodbye and leave. Said she'll be back. We'll see.

When we get into work tonight, I'll explain the scene you happened upon. I can't even imagine what it looked like, but I hope you trust that it wasn't what it looked like. It was a bet—I'll explain at work—just a stupid brother-sister thing. Well, what I thought was a brother-sister thing. The timing on this is significant. We were heading out for a walk on the beach together that ended up a solo RUN on the beach for me. I considered putting off telling you this, and I don't know if it will or if it even should affect our relationship, but I just feel that I should tell you this right away. I don't know why, but I do. So, here goes: Kate told me on the walk that my birth father *adopted* her and Sara.

CHAPTER 28

I remind you, I found this out after the debacle you came upon. At that time, what was happening might have been stupid, but it was honestly a wrestling match with whom I thought was my sister. I know, I know ... why were we wrestling naked? You'll have to wait for that explanation.

I know we were going to head over to your place tonight after work. I'm still up for it if you are. I think I might need somebody tonight. You? I can't think of anybody I'd rather be with right now.

Love, MP

Date: March 18, 2012
To: M
From: Lottie
Subject: Sorry

I am sorry I avoided talking to you last night, at work or after. Something I couldn't get out of my mind—you signed MP? I thought Mick was Kate's brother? If I recall correctly, MP was attracted to Marilyn? Just who, exactly, are you? You signed off "love?" You mean it?

Although I ran at the vision I came upon (what would YOU have done?), I trust it was not what it looked like. Let me rephrase that, I HOPE it was not what it looked like. I can get over that (I think—it was still, even for me, pretty fuckin weird!). I have no idea what it would be, but I'm sure you've got an explanation. I think I know you well enough to believe you weren't trying to have your way with your sister. Of course, SHE'S NOT YOUR SISTER! OK, I believe you, that you didn't know at the time. But I think I need a little time to think this over. I mean, I was falling for you, you asshole.

BACK TO THE ISLAND

Date: April 1, 2012
To: Sara
From: M
Subject: April Fool

Hi Sara. How are you? I miss you. I'm sure Barney misses you, too, but I miss you more, even if you aren't my sister. *April Fool!* I'm sure you now know I know?

Anyway, how did the deposition go? Is Kate in any danger in NY? I don't trust that senator, especially. Power and money with lack of ethics and principles is not a healthy combo. Richard turned out to be a wimp. I doubt we have anything to worry about from him. But what about his bosses? Is there a risk of a 'gun for hire?'

Your sorta-brother, MP.

Date: April 2, 2012
To: M
From: Sara
Subject: Deposition

Mick, oh Mick. What to say? Even though I knew, of course, when I met you, that you weren't really my brother, I might be stuck always thinking of you as Mick and as my brother. I'm not sure what I think of that.

Since you emailed me, rather than Kate, asking about the depositions, I assume you're not on emailing or speaking terms with her? Please contact her. She's totally lost. She went through the depositions, I guess I'd say, resolutely. She's articulate and composed on the exterior, but a shamble of nerves and contradictions and pandemonium inside. She needs you to talk to her, or email her or something. We discussed telling you the truth, you know—no,

CHAPTER 28

I shouldn't say the "truth," the truth is hard to define and not always prudent, I'm discovering. From a distance, I encouraged her to come clean. When I was down there, I understood what she meant. Could you two have lived together, platonically? One too many drinks one time, too much marijuana, you two would have been in the sack. Look at what almost happened between Barney and me, and we're the righteous, conservative ones! Who knows how things would have turned out "if?" I totally understand Lottie confuses things. But, you know Kate—once her mind is made up, there's no changing it. She felt she needed to do what she did and that was that. Sound a little like your pal, Barney (which is interesting)? Do see the big picture: the good she is hopefully doing now?

I do believe she's safe. She has around-the-clock protection, which she abhors, but, once the depositions are done, the proof is then a matter of record. I know she's dying to get back to Spokane and put everything behind her. Everything but you.

Please contact her.
Love, Sara.

Date: April 3, 2012
To: Kate
From: Sara
Subject: Your brother

Katie, I get the feeling he's not ready to talk to you. You can't blame him. He's bound to be a tiny bit confused. Let's try to find some time tomorrow to discuss this. He's worried about you and emailed me today asking how things are. Why don't you at least email him?

Love, Sara

BACK TO THE ISLAND

Date: April 3, 2012
To: Sara
From: M
Subject: R & R

Hey, it just hit me: Since we aren't brother-sister, want a little reckless rendezvous? If you're not going to make it with Barney, a dedicated, Bible-totin' Christian, how 'bouts me, a dedicated fun-lovin heathen? Perfect weather down here this time of year.

Love 'n' fun, MP

Date: April 4, 2012
To: M
From: Sara
Subject: Sister/Brother

Oh, so sorry, bro. I've got a couple other affairs going currently, so tied up (not that way, fool; get your mind out of the gutter) and I'm really fond of the incessant rain here this time of year. Sun and fun sounds terrible.

Very funny, MICK! Believe me, you saw MORE of me than you most probably ever will again! I don't know what got into me down there. Thank God it wasn't Barney. Ha! That just wasn't me. Blame it on Kate. You want a rendezvous, give the hot one a call.

Your SISTER, Sara.

Date: April 5, 2012
To: Sara
From: M
Subject: Hot one?

Give the hot one a call? What's yur #? Or you mean Lottie? Just kiddin'. Don't get yur knickers in a bunch. But you're the hot one.

CHAPTER 28

Your butt, not your sister's skinny little ass, was the cutest bouncing into the ocean in the moonlight that night. You do know I know that Barney didn't 'get into' you down here. Who you saving yurself for anywho? And, I said 'love' and 'fun!'

Date:	April 6, 2012
To:	M
From:	Sara
Subject:	a 'line'

More than one step over the line, way more, you heathen! Kate, contact KATE, skinny ass and all!

Date:	April 7, 2012
To:	Lottie
From:	M
Subject:	Talk

Hey, babe: When we gonna talk?

Date:	April 7, 2012
To:	M
From:	Lottie
Subject:	RE: Talk

What do you mean, Mick? We talk every night at work.

Date:	April 8, 2012
To:	Lottie
From:	M
Subject:	Dinner

Right. Very comical. We have the same night off tomorrow. Want to come over for dinner? I don't know if this matters, but I haven't talked to or emailed Kate. I miss 'us.' By the way ... why are you stressing 'Mick?' There's no Mick. I'm MP.

Date: April 8, 2012
To: M
From: Lottie
Subject: RE: Dinner

That's what I'm afraid of: MP and Marilyn! Talk to Kate. Then maybe we can talk, and have dinner and? I miss 'us,' too. I mean it wasn't that I was thinking of making babies or anything yet. Making love was good enough for me ... but? Talk to her, Mick. You need to figure things out before we move on.

Date: April 9, 2012
To: M
From: Barney
Subject: update

OK, I've waited long enough. I want a daily update. You hear? DAILY! So, what's going on?

Date: April 9, 2012
To: Barney
From: M
Subject: Relax

You there? Doing whatever you do in that cubicle? No? What's the proprietor of your humble abode look like? Are there any cute librarians in your part of the world? That's what you might as well find, seriously, since you spend so much time in that library writin those infamous lessons of yours: a cute, big-boobed bibliotechian.

Hey, I almost need to talk, I mean really 'talk' to you like we used to. Not there? OK, here goes: Lottie is freaked out. Won't talk

CHAPTER 28

about *us* until I talk to Kate, anyway. Which I understand. And that's cool. I mean, I guess it answers the question about how 'casual' she thought our relationship was. Right? Can you discover if you love someone by making love to them? I know you think you should love someone before making love. See where that one's got ya? You know, it's almost like that thing: you want what you can't have? You've mastered that one. Anyway, all right, I have to confess: I cry. Yeah, I've been fucking crying! I haven't cried since Martha died, and the time before that was when I shit my diapers. I don't cry! You hear? And I'm crying now.

OK, I'm over it. That's gud. A lot's been going on. I really need to talk to you so I'll call and clue you in. Yes, I'm getting int'l calling. Next on the agenda: Spense, Peewee, and Rashi—this weird, smart island kid—have devised a plan to rid the Bahamas of Ajax, Arthur, and the Mandelsung family. Cool. Action galore!

Tell me what to do, Barn! HELP!
Please—M.

Date:	April 10, 2012
To:	M
From:	Barney
Subject:	Relax

Call Kate. At least email her if you still can't make calls. Do change that, dude? Get overseas calling or whatever. Again, CALL KATE! That's all I got to say.

Date:	April 10, 2012
To:	Barney
From:	M
Subject:	Why?

BACK TO THE ISLAND

Why shouldn't she call me? She's the one who lied. Why don't you call Sara?

Date: April 11, 2012
To: M
From: Barney
Subject: It's not the same

That's why she can't call you. You know she feels terrible. Be a gentleman, asshole. Call her!
—Barn

Date: April 12, 2012
To: M
From: Kate
Subject: Us

Hello, Mick. I'm making a guess, it's just a hunch, that you're mad at me? Can't imagine why. I also can't imagine talking this through via emails. What do you think? Can we talk?

Heidi is so dear. That old student of yours whom you had come on to while trying to teach her grammar (just kidding—notice my proper use of whom? Proud of me, eh?) has taken Heidi under her wing. She really is quite pretty and seems like a great person. For some reason I can't understand why she still holds you in high regard! She has two sons but no daughter and has hired Heidi in her publishing business! She was totally taken with her as well. Says "sky's the limit" for her, and Heidi is so excited. She has wanted to email you some new stuff, but says she won't until you contact me. Ha! I don't think this counts, since I'm the one contacting you. No pressure—but? I helped her get set up in an apartment near Spanish Harlem. It's like a dormitory just for women, mostly young.

CHAPTER 28

She has an efficiency unit, really small, but that's how things are in Manhattan. It's a safe place and I trust your old student to take good care of her, so I'm heading back to Spokane.

Mick, I can't say what I did was the right thing to do, but it was what I thought I needed to do. Sound familiar? You know—Heidi's poem. I have no idea now what is the right thing to do or what I need to do, except go home. I'm really worn out. This has been stressful and draining. I just sure shit hope it does some good. They tell me it will. Things HAVE to change on Wall Street.

I just can't go down there, now. What I'd like is for you to come visit me in Spokane. I think we need to be face to face for a good tete-a-tete. Any possibility of that?

Love, Kate

Date: April 13, 2012
To: Barney, Sara, Kate
From: M
Subject: News!

Great news! The plot to discredit, disenfranchise, disgrace, dishonor, disparage, degrade, demean ... add any others you can think of ... Ajax, Arthur and the whole damn family has worked. Peewee and the boys had their little tribunal at the clubhouse and Harvey either had to accept banishment as his retribution or make amends. It was Rashi's idea. That kid is a smart little pecker. He and Peewee decided either it was time for Harvey, the island kid that had ratted out Peewee and that Vernal guy, to move on and that with the 'fees' he got, he would have enough funds to get far enough away. Or, Harvey had to go to Ajax and Arthur and convince them, that for another 'fee,' he could set up Peewee for the Mandelsungs; that they would think Peewee

| 469

would be on this off-limits island, this certain night, where Harvey told them he was storing the explosives he stole from them. That they could ambush him, kill him, and no one would find him on this 'forbidden' island. That Peewee's disappearance would really make an example to defer any of the others from any more ideas of ecoterrorism.

They believed Harvey, probably because they're dumb shits and, of course, Harvey had proven himself twice already to be a traitor. So there they were, on this island with the explosives and some already dead exotic, some endangered, birds and animals that had been planted there. So the Bahamian police, who had had an 'anonymous' tip, showed up. Ajax and Arthur left stranded, with a disabled boat so they couldn't escape, just as planned. And what were they going to say: we were here to kill Peewee Springer but he fooled us? Anyway, it sounds like they threw the book at the A-hole brothers, affecting the entire family. Their days of development and habitat destruction are over. At least for now. Hooray!

Another thing that's really cool is that Harvey agreed to use his two 'fees' to defray the costs of bringing Vernal and his family back from Haiti. Talk about symmetry and balance in the universe: Ajax and Arthur, who sent him and his family away, paid to get them back. What we need now is a little more symmetry in Washington and Wall Street. Cheers to Kate for attempting and hopefully succeeding in helping to attain a fair balance in what's now an unfair, unbalanced system.

Raise your glasses to Kate. Lottie, Peewee, Spense, and I already have. And to Sara, the 'good' sister who was there all along supporting Kate.

P.S. I've attached an article I wrote about it that appeared in the *Bahama Journal*, the *Bahama Post*, *The Freeport News*, and *Nassau Guardian*.

CHAPTER 28

Wealthy Tory Family Implicated in Scandal

Two members of the well-known Mandelsung family were found by authorities on Albury Cay, a protected wild life sanctuary. Non-authorized individuals are forbidden access to the island and surrounding waters. Ajax and Arthur Mandelsung were arrested on the cay. Apparently a dory that carried them ashore from their yacht had become disabled, stranding them. The Freeport police had received an anonymous tip informing them of the serious trespassing transgression.

The family is known as a significant developer, along with the Chinese, of resorts and casinos, dating back to the time of the early development of Nassau and Paradise Island. They have numerous projects currently in process. The Bahamas National Trust, which is responsible for the management of all the national parks and protected areas, has filed suit against the family, as explosives and several dead, protected animals and birds were found at the scene. The Mandelsung brothers were unable to explain why they were there and what they were up to. The Trust has put a halt to any further development by the family until the investigation is complete.

Date: April 13, 2012
To: M
From: Kate
Subject: RE: News!

Hey, what's that supposed to mean: the "good" sister? Eh? Give Lottie a hug and kiss for me (I assume you'll have no trouble fulfilling that request), include Wanda in that as well (only on the forehead, fool. I don't suppose it'd do any good to instigate a "forehead rule'" for Lottie?). High-five Spense (even if he's hanging upside down) and Peewee for me. Tell Peewee even at concern for life and limb, I'd let him give me a hug for his major coup. Tell Rashi

BACK TO THE ISLAND

I'm proud of him. Really—success! All those shenanigans weren't for naught! So cool!

I'm back in Spokane already. The renters (of my place) had agreed to move out before I returned. Although most of the world will not know what I've gone through, I am a hero in my hometown. I can thank my meddling sister for that! I had a difficult time leaving Heidi—she goes by HS even in NY by the way—but she seems happy and, as I said, I feel I left her in good hands. It must be gratifying to have students out there from your past that feel grateful to you. I think that had something to do with her decision to hire HS, but I know she'll be happy she did.

Speaking of students, is anything going on with the island boys? It was really touching that they showed up at the pier to say goodbye to Heidi and me. We both cried in the plane on the way to NY. But it wasn't for leaving the boys that I couldn't stop crying.

That was a great story about Rashi and Harvey. I feel the worst about Rashi. HS is writing to him and encouraging him to just write to her about what he feels, regardless of spelling, grammar, and the like. I worry about him, too, as does Heidi. She says he feels he loves her, and with her gone, he'll languish in that small corner of the world—beautiful as it is. Can you help with that?

That's all for now. Call or e-me if you like. I've got a new cell: 509-983-6425. Check your phone to see what 6425 spells.

Love, Kate

Date: April 13, 2012
To: M
From: Sara
Subject: RE: News!

CHAPTER 28

Mick: That's great news! Sometimes the stars are just simply aligned. I miss you and all the excitement down there. It makes my life up here seem so mundane.

CALL KATE! Yours to the three of us DOES NOT COUNT!

Love (so far), Sara

Date: April 13, 2012
To: M
From: Barney
Subject: RE: News!

Good Lord: There's enough going on down there to write a novel about. Holy shit! Sounds like the right thing happened, on several levels. And nobody was killed. Imagine that!

How are things with Lottie? Did you call Kate? You have to, you know? You know that, right? I've got a lot of shit on you. I'll blackmail you into it if I have to.

CALL HER!

—Barn

Date: April 14, 2012
To: Barney
From: M
Subject: Dear Abby: HELP!

#Hey Barn? You there in your 'pent-acle?' Your bachelor 'pad-icle?' No? OK, well, yes I'm going to call … email, whatever … Kate. I know I have to. I just, really, have no idea what to say, how to say it, when to say it … whatever 'it' is. No need to blackmail me. I'm already being blackmailed into it. I'm really missing my poetry sessions with Heidi. Did I tell you she went to NY with Kate and

BACK TO THE ISLAND

Kate got her a job and found her a place to live? Anyway—she won't write to me or send me anything until I talk to Kate. So, nice friend you are, you won't have to do the blackmailing.

Of course things with Lottie are not good. I HAVEN'T TALKED TO KATE, yet. C'mon, Barn. What do I do? I had just come to grips with loving Kate, and, I mean really loving her, as a sister and seeing where it was going with Lottie as a mate.

HELP! I need advice, Abby. Advice much clearer than those tax laws yur so fond of.

Date: April 15, 2012
To: M
From: Barney
Subject: NUTS

You are nuts, always have been. (I'm in my sex cubicle now. You there?)

No? E me later, asshole.

Date: April 16, 2012
To: Kate
From: M
Subject: MP and Marilyn? Mick and Kate?

Sorry. I know I should have written sooner. What do you mean what do I mean Sara's the 'good' sister? You tortured me daily. Does that sound like a good sister? And, no, no 'forehead rule' for Lottie. How can I come to Spokane? What would I say to Lottie? I told her, you know, **SIS**! She now knows! Made my explanation of our little naked grapple a little more difficult. She was mentioning babies the other day, so can I just run off to Spokane?

CHAPTER 28

I'm glad you're home safe and sound. I'm proud of you. Whether it does any good or not, I'm proud of you for trying, being conscientious, being strong, morally and physically.

I'm carrying on the lessons with the boys. Went up to the clubhouse today. Yes, cool. Really cool. I am going to help translate what Rashi writes and send it to Heidi ... *if* she sends me her stuff. An eye for an eye; a blackmail for a blackmail.

Best, MP (I think it was Virginia Woolf who wrote: 'Trapped by destiny.' *Trapped*! Know what I mean?)

Date: **April 17, 2012**
To: **M**
From: **Kate**
Subject: **Trapped!?**

About time! Why "trapped?"

Date: **April 17, 2012**
To: **M**
From: **Heidi**
Subject: **a verb and an adverb**

Sir: It is very interesting here. I really like your old student and she says I am doing very well. I can't say I like New York. There are so many people. When I wrote of "not always getting what I wanted but always what I seem to *need*," I do think of you. "Therefore I am *lonely* from time to time." You, too, I suspect? It was "ironically" funny to me that you actually thought she was your sister. I'm dying of curiosity to see how you reconcile that—is "conundrum" the right word? I imagine you *miss* Kate (sorry, almost as bad as your attempts at humor). Me too, now. But I have my mother and my father. Rashi. You. You have me (lucky dog) and Spense and Lottie, Sara and "Miss" Kate. At least it is a double entendre? You do know, I hope you have or will have Kate somehow in your life? Please straighten things out with her. I don't enjoy seeing people I love suffer.

I feel almost guilty for feeling lonely. This morning while waiting for a taxi an old man walked by. Inspired me to write this poem. I'm afraid I've been so wrapped up in my new job, new life, new everything, I haven't had time to be inspired. I need you to inspire me, sir. Could you do that?

Thanks for carrying on with the boys. I'm very curious to hear what Rashi might have to say. You always told me I was special. So, I am. So is Rashi, especially with you to teach him:

> the man and his pocketed world
> poured out onto the avenue
> and the rusty cans and newspapers
> and stray dogs, like him,
> rolled along, or were kicked along,
> or blown along, or whatever.
> and the street crowd moved about him
> like some strange and crawling gray space—
> denying any resemblance,
> offering no home.
> he lighted up a cigarette,
> and stared off into some memory,
> "i am the only lonely man," he mumbled,
> "mine is the only soul that aches."
> —H.S.

It is odd to be lonely when surrounded by so many people. Thank you, sir.

CHAPTER 28

Date: April 18, 2012
To: Heidi
From: M
Subject: 'Verbs'

HS: It's hard for me, you know, to call you HS. Heidi seems so much more, I don't know, endearing, I guess, even if you are a spiny little thing. But, at your request, HS it is and I'll just have to get used to it. Yes, I do *miss* the 'Miss' (as well as you)—clever double-e. I'm sure you must be missing your island, especially since it's city lights replacing your starlight and skyscrapers blocking your sunsets. But then again, when you have a sunset almost every day, you may start to take them for granted?

Next email I'll include something from Rashi! I still have to convince him that I don't think he's dumb because he can't spell or whatever. I don't really know how to deal with dyslexia except to not let it deter him from writing. So, we'll see. Could you, maybe, write the next poem to him, about him and for him? May provide incentive?

I'll be holding my breath until I see it.
'Love' (can I say that?) MP.

Date: April 21, 2012
To: M
From: Heidi
Subject: New Poem

Sir: Sorry it's been so long. I have been working on a project. She has given me quite a lapful of responsibility on this one. It is remarkable how the need to fulfill a responsibility can consume you. It's all I've been able to think about, night and day. Talking about consuming: here is one for you—(a little risky?):

[477

BACK TO THE ISLAND

> I called out your name
> last night while standing
> on the edge of a tear ...
> "but don't you cry,
> don't let him know,
> you mustn't let down now!"
> And I closed my eyes, held
> My pillow tightly and painfully
> waited for the night to
> sleep the day away
> —H.S.

Thank you, sir.
Love (can I say that? What is love, exactly?), HS

Date: April 27, 2012
To: Heidi
From: M
Subject: Rashi

Hello, there, hon:

How's the project going? Making any friends? Liking NY any better? Spring's coming; maybe, from what I understand, the best season in the city. The seasons are much less subtle in the northern hemisphere. I imagine you got a good taste of late (real) winter when you first got there?

Everything's gud here. Have a lot of time to write now that I'm not living with a lunatic and having visitors and blowing up things. Close to finishing *If I had a Million Dollars*. Working on my fiction piece, too. Not sure what I'll title it. For now, it's *Serious at Sears*, but I think a better title will come to me.

Here's Rashi's first "Plum Poem":

When you wish upon a falling star
Wish that it doesn't strike you.

CHAPTER 28

I think it's great; he's clever, but I'm not sure I like the tenor of it. What do you think? I'm not sure if it's a result of your poem? When I read yours to him, he took it and read along as I read it to him again. I think that's good for him to 'need' to read, as you and what you say are important to him. He didn't respond or say anything, tho. He's an intense young man. Smart, too. Hard to read, no pun intended.

Love, M

Date: May 1, 2012
To: Sara
From: Kate
Subject: Mick

Hey sis: it's been nice having you home for a while and having someone to talk to. Now that you're back in Washington for a while and I can't talk to you, I thought I'd email you. You there?

No? Well, OK. We've avoided talking much about Mick, or, at least, *I* have. I know you'd like to hit me over the head, but get tired of telling me what I don't do. You've never had much luck with that. Sorry I am so stubborn. Then, of course, I always turn the tables and talk about you and Barney. Why do we do this to each other? Why do we do this to ourselves?

Sally and I are going down to Coeur d'Alene and staying at our place for a long weekend. It'll be nice to get a break. I think I overdid it picking up two PR gigs at the same time, especially when I can't get that fool Mick out of my mind. After he finally emailed me, he didn't respond to my response! Dick!

I've had a couple of dates, well not really dates. I've gone out for drinks with some of the guys we used to hang around with. Remember "Bode the Bod?" You were just as hot for him as I was. We had a few too many the other night and when he walked me out to the car, he kissed me. Just as I decided "what the hell, I'll kiss him back," his tongue went down my throat and his hand tried to find my little booby. I actually gagged and pushed him and ran away bawling my eyes out. I pushed away Bode the Bod! Who we used to lie in bed and drool over! What's that about? OK, I know what that's about.

I don't think Mick is going to initiate calls or emails, as won't Barney, either, it looks like. So, I'll make you a deal. I'll email Mick, even if he didn't respond, if you e Barney. I've hesitated pursuing him because I really do feel bad about Lottie. They must be getting serious. Mick said she brought up babies! I suppose I should suggest that we reestablish our brother-sister relationship. Think that'll work?

Love you.

Date: May 3, 2012
To: Kate
From: Sara
Subject: NO, Don't know

No: I don't have quite the same intense history with Barney as you do with Mick. I can't see working on a long-term relationship with him hunkered down in that library stall in Mpls. So, no, I won't be contacting him. I suppose if he contacted me, which I doubt he will, I'd respond. But, then what? I just can't see it working.

Now, don't get angry, but I understand MP's point of view. I don't know if he's "in sex" with Lottie or "in love." I do believe he may love you, but that did happen when he believed you were his

CHAPTER 28

sister. The question is I doubt if you can accept that? If not, what are you willing to do to change it? I doubt you can do it in emails from Spokane.

Love you, too.

Date: May 5, 2012
To: Heidi
From: M
Subject: Rashi

Hey hon. Thought I'd send you this one from Rashi. It's pretty funny considering …

wsh tht thr wr n vwls n th lphbt.

Haven't seen anything from you for a while? Everything all right? Love, MP

Date: May 10, 2012
To: M
From: Kate
Subject: Sara and Barney

Hi Mick, how are you? It's getting nice up here. Last weekend a friend and I drove down to Coeur d'Alene where we have a cabin—remember? It's on Rose Lake in Idaho, but not far from Spokane. Mountains and lakes—what's better, huh? Especially lakes? And—no mosquitoes!

Anyway, Sara won't contact Barney in any form or fashion. I believe she would like him to. I think she's just old-fashioned. No, I *know* she's old-fashioned and expects him to get in contact with her. Didn't you think they were a good match? She's got nobody she's interested in right now. Says she doesn't have time for a

| 481

relationship, which isn't true. She's way up there with the SEC and can pretty much work when she wants to and where she wants to. She pretty much just delegates shit to her subordinates, especially now that the Richard ordeal is over with. If Barney was interested, she could work it out. Has he got anybody serious now? If not, why don't you encourage him to at least email her? See what happens. You know, it would be copasetic, as you used to say.

How are Spense and Peewee and Wanda? Please say "hi" to them for me. You and Lottie made any babies yet? How is the writing coming? Should have more time since I'm not around tormenting you? How are the boys? Rashi?

I know you've been corresponding with Heidi. (I just can't refer to her as HS. Maybe when she's famous.) Apparently she's done some good things at work, but I worry about her. I don't think she really likes the bustle of the Big Apple. Do you?

Anything else exciting going on down there? Peewee must be bored? At least he's alive, and, I hope, healed by now?

Love, Kate.

Date: May 12, 2012
To: M
From: Heidi
Subject: Busy. Maybe too busy.

Hello, sir: Wow, I heard the other day that this town "never sleeps." It might be hyperbole and a trope, but true. How about that: "hyperbole & trope"? Picking up some new words in this profession. But it is very ironic: I'm so busy working on publishing, I don't have time to write. What good are new words if I can't use them? The only nature I see is pigeons, and they are as restless as the

CHAPTER 28

people. People don't seem to be able to relax here. Everything's so hectic. I hear sirens all the time and think to myself that I'm lucky, somebody's worse off than I am. But then I dream the sirens are coming for our Peewee. What I should be worried about is them coming for me, I suppose.

Rashi's little plum poem is really quite clever, but not much meat to it. You know, I don't sound like myself. I don't even realize it until I write to you, sir. I hope I've prepared you for the piece I'm sending you.

> Retractions
> Hands pull away from me.
> Hands break away,
> tearing flesh.
> I know.
> Time to heal,
> Time to rest.
> I know.
> Space to breathe,
> To know yourself.
> I know.
> All drained out;
> Save yourself.
> I know.
> I know the sound of falling leaves.
> —H.S.

Who are you falling for lately: Kate, Lottie, Sara? You must be quite the perplexed paramour. There's always me to be there for you. That's a sketch of what I've become and look like now. Look interesting, sir? Your style?

Good luck with that. Love. Bye. Thank you, sir.

483

BACK TO THE ISLAND

Date: May 13, 2012
To: Heidi
From: M
Subject: Sara?

Heides: 'Perplexed paramour?' Very nice alliterative accusation (ha, ha). I can see you throwing Kate and Lottie into that mix, and you're correct there. But where did Sara come from? You know something I don't? And I'll always be there for you, too, no matter what you become, although I'm sorry to say: No, you do not, now, look like my type. Too skinny!

Date: May 13, 2012
To: M
From: Heidi
Subject: RE: Sara?

A lot of time to speculate when one is lonely, sir.

Date: May 14, 2012
To: Barney
From: M
Subject: Summer visit

Hey, Barn. I know you're not in your cubicle because it's three a.m. Haven't been sleeping very well, so I write into the night. Actually it's a productive time: fewer distractions and I love to see the lights on the masts in the harbor swaying back and forth and the light in the lighthouse swiveling around and around. It's mesmerizing, helps me think … almost like meditation.

I need to respond to Kate's last email. She's adamant you at least email Sara. She's got no love interests and, I assume, there's no sexy librarian spending time in your sex-icle with

CHAPTER 28

you? Anyway, Kate says Sara's old-fashioned, as we know, so she won't contact you; expects you to contact her. Why don't you? Maybe this summer I'll come visit Mn and we can arrange something with Sara and Kate? I have to admit I can't get either out of my mind. It's pretty stupid not seeing them. In Kate's last email she was heading down to her old stomping grounds in Idaho with a boyfriend or something. Shit, Barn. I still really don't know what to do. Lottie and I have been getting along great—at work. The other night we stayed late and had a few nightcaps with Spense. When I walked her to her car, we, like, attacked each other. Hot and heavy for like ten seconds, and then she pushes me away and starts to fricking cry. It was not the right time for makeup sex, that's for sure. Then she just jumped in her jeep and took off. Crap! I have three women in my life I love (Heidi, too) and I can't 'make' love to any of them. There's always Ma—you know, Jack's mother. Never mind, bad, sad joke.

Anyway, if you guys are coming down here during your summer break, best to do in June before the horrid heat and hurricane season sets in. Talk to the guys and see what's a good time for me to come up. I'll check with Kate, you can check with Sara. Maybe they can come to see us together? Sound good?

See ya soon.

Date: May 15, 2012
To: Kate
From: M
Subject: More trouble

Kate: what's going on up there? May already, so spring has sprung I assume?

BACK TO THE ISLAND

The government can't decide what to do with the mess on the west side of Elbow. We may have stopped or maybe it's just slowed what they were trying to do there, but we did add to the onshore mess. It looks a little like a bomb went off, which is pretty much what happened. I wrote some articles in various periodicals about how fortunate we were to prevent the destruction of the coral and preserving the environment and habitats and natural shoreline, etc. But the government seems to have whet its appetite for revenue and what it sees as progress.

Peewee is working with the National Trust or whatever it is to try to get it declared, something, to render it undevelopable. You know him, he's not going to give up. And Vernal, now back, has been trying to unite the Haitians and prevent the violence between the various sects and gangs. Man the world is tribal, and it's mostly stupid religious dissention it seems, even with the Haitians, I guess. There's been some clashes and, of course, Peewee is there to back his friends: Haitian, Bahamian, or otherwise. I'm finding out the island is cliquey. People start petty little rumors. It's kinda like a small town, maybe worse. I'm tired of it. It doesn't seem you can get away from shit: it's one form of scat or another, even here in paradise.

No, no babies with Lottie yet. Can you get down here for a visit? Spense is leaving pretty soon. He escapes the hurricane season. Says Mary gets nervous. Heads north ... mentioned Boston. Says he'd like to see you before he goes. This summer I plan on visiting Barney and the guys in Minnesota. Barney said if I invited you, he'd invite Sara. One place or another we can have our face-to-face tete-a-tete. Better leave your boyfriend at home, though, or come on down here and we can double-date.

Best, MP.

CHAPTER 28

Date: May 16, 2012
To: Sara
From: Kate
Subject: Boyfriend?

Sara, did you tell Mick (he signs off as MP—suppose we should start calling him that? I don't know if I can). Anyway, did you tell him I have a boyfriend? Why would you do that? I mean, I've decided I'm not going to really date. I mean, why? I do love the asshole, so I don't want him to think I'm dating or have anybody else! Shit momma. But what do I do? Pray for Lottie to fall in love with Spense, who I assume can no longer make babies? Nice, huh? Babies? Shit, fuck, fart. Lottie must be pretty damn serious. Even if we're willing to try and work things out, our long-distance relationship would be more difficult than yours and Barney's. At least you've got the time and the dough. Think Mick'd ever live here? We have lakes, too, for crying in the fish! And without all those damn mosquitoes.

Did Barney get in contact with you? MP—ahhh!! I'll have to come up with another new one, maybe I'll try just "M"—said he was going to and he wants us to meet the two of them in Minnesota this summer. Maybe we could get the two of them out here—if you're ever out here? Mick wants me to visit down there, but I'm not going to.

He doesn't sound like he's in a very good state of mind. He says there's more trouble in paradise, and he's also worried about HS (don't like that moniker, either—but of course, her choice I guess).

Love, Kate

Date: May 16, 2012
To: Kate

BACK TO THE ISLAND

From: Sara
Subject: Wow!

Kate: first—No! Why would I say you have a boyfriend? I didn't say anything about even a date or whatever. But straighten that out!

Second: Yes, try to get him and Barney out here. I'm willing to take a break in Minnesota, though. Heck, I fly right over it and, I have to admit, think of MP and Barney every time. We'll see if he contacts me. He obviously hasn't yet. Maybe *you* and Barney should make a go of it? Never mind, bad idea. Don't know where that one came from. Are you sure you can't go down there for a visit? I would make time, if you do. BUT, I know, how would you deal with Lottie? Could picture a big battle, knowing you two? Maybe I could be the conciliator, the arbitrator?

Love, Sara

Date: May 20, 2012
To: M
From: Richard
Subject: Asshole

Congratulations, asshole. Surprised to hear from me? Don't remember that I can read all your emails to Kate and vice versa? Well, you two totally fucked up my life. I got fired, blackballed, and lost all my investments. Hope I can pay you back someday. I wouldn't rest too easy, either. The Mandelsung family, who naturally has some of their family money on Wall Street, ain't too happy about what you did to them, here or there, and it's not only those stumble-bum brothers either—Ajax and Arthur. They're not going to just forget about you, you know? You and that big fucker better watch your backs.

CHAPTER 28

What really pisses me off is I didn't do a goddamned thing wrong and I'm suffering, and the kingpins will probably get off. I've got lawsuits against me and possible litigation. Those big guys can afford big-time lawyers, so, just to let you know, they're going to get off and I'll end up the scapegoat and I didn't do a fucking thing.

Just so you know, your "fiancé" was quite the whore in NY. I know she's actually your sister, but you probably know how good she is at blow jobs. She was great with me. Must be fun to have a sister like that? Just so you know, the guy she's shacking up with now is a broker in Spokane and I know him. He's a big fucker. Went with her down to Curdalane. Must have been a fun weekend for her. She always liked them big, so you're probably just a sympathy suck, you little prick.

Fuck off.
Richard.
P.S. Who's this HS you two are worried about? I'm going to have plenty of time now, maybe I'll look her up.

Date:	May 20, 2012
To:	Kate
From:	Richard
Subject:	Thanks

Hey, even though I never actually fucked you, you really fucked me big time. That blow job trick works pretty good, bitch. Where'd you learn that, from your fat ass sister? The word is she's more of a tease than you are. You know what you did to me? I've lost everything because of you. The big guys will get off anyway and I'll probably end up in prison. Thanks, cunt.

Speaking of cunts, they say that girlfriend of your fiancé, ha, nice try—brother—is quite the whore. Better watch out for AIDS next time you screw your brother.

BACK TO THE ISLAND

Thanks for chasing me around the globe with your stupid emails. That was on my buck, you know. And I've heard the Mandelsung family has sent some guys, and I mean bad-asses, down there to deal with your brother and that big asshole. I hope they die a slow painful death. I heard they saw your brother and his whore screwing right outside that dive they work at. Real classy.

Have a nice fucking life, bitch. And watch your back. You've made big time enemies.

P.S. Think I'll look up this HS you're so worried about. Maybe we can shack up. See if she's as good at blow jobs as you. You show her how? Since that's all I ever got from you, maybe I'll screw her.

Date: May 20, 2012
To: Kate
From: M
Subject: Richard!

Kate: I just got an email from that asshole, Ricky. Why didn't we think to change our emails? Shit! A new address, password, whatever? He's been following our emails! Damn! I've already talked to Spense (he's still here for a while), and he's fixed mine somehow. My password or whatever is now encrypted, so he, or anybody, can't hack in. Check with somebody up there and change yours, too. Spense talked to Heidi, too, just in case. God, are we dumb!

He threatened he might try to reach Heidi: Christ! What can we do about that? Do you think he's blowing smoke? Should have drowned the asshole when we had the chance.

Date: May 20, 2012
To: M
From: Kate
Subject: RE: Richard!

CHAPTER 28

Yikes! I got one, too. A really gross one. Yes, I'll change whatever I need to. There's a guy I know here that's really good with technology. He'll do what I need to and I'll let you know.

Man, I don't know what to do about Heidi. I suppose we should at least warn her to keep an eye out. Mick, I don't really think he's a dangerous guy. He's obviously being an asshole, but he really wasn't a badass. I honestly don't think Heidi would be in any danger from him, but I suppose we should warn her, even though that's not good either. Believe me, I know what it's like to be looking over your shoulder. Just what she needs being new in New York. FOR SURE don't tell Peewee. He'll end up in New York going after him, probably kill him or close to it.

Love, Kate

Date: May 20, 2012
To: Kate
From: M
Subject: ?

What if something were to happen to Heidi, and Peewee finds out we knew about the threat?

Date: May 20, 2012
To: M
From: Kate
Subject: RE: ?

I don't know! I'm taking some pills and heading to bed.

Date: May 20, 2012
To: Kate
From: M
Subject: RE: ?

BACK TO THE ISLAND

Alone?

Date:	May 20, 2012
To:	M
From:	Kate
Subject:	RE: ?

What the hell is that supposed to mean? And look who's talking!

Date:	May 21, 2012
To:	Sara
From:	Kate
Subject:	What the hell?

Right after we talked the other night and I told you about Richard, I had told MP (it should be MF, if you know what I mean) I told him I was going to bed and he comes back with "alone?" What the hell? When are you coming home? I'm sick of my pillow—I need a shoulder to cry on.

Date:	May 21, 2012
To:	Kate
From:	Sara
Subject:	RE: What the hell?

I'll be finishing up this week. Coming home this weekend. I'm the one usually needing your shoulder. Glad to offer you mine. Hold on.

Date:	May 22, 2012
To:	Richard
From:	M
Subject:	Assfart

Hey asshole, now I have your email address, not too smart yourself, not that you'll ever hear from me again. I'll be changing my

CHAPTER 28

password as soon as I send this. You won't be able to contact Kate, again, either. But, two things before I say sayonara: first, as I already told you, when anybody, but especially you Wall Street jerks and, I suspect most politicians, see something WRONG and do nothing about the shit that was going on, that's just as bad as doing it. So forget trying to convince yourself you're innocent. You're guilty *because* you did nothing.

Second: if Heidi even sees you, you're a dead man. Capeesh? You met Peewee—he'll hunt you down and 'neutralize' you, and I believe you know that. That's even if she sees your face in a crowd.

Fuck yourself if you want, assfart!

Date: May 26, 2012
To: Heidi
From: M
Subject: Rashi

Hi, hon. It's a Saturday, I thought I might catch you at home. You there? Haven't seen anything from you? Busy at work? Everything all right?

I hesitate to tell you this, but I fear I have to. You know that Richard guy, Kate's ex-boyfriend? Well, he emailed me and threatened to stalk you. He intercepted some of Kate's and my emails and so knows you're in Manhattan. I hate to encourage you to tell your father, but if something did happen, he'd never forgive me and I'd never forgive myself. For now keep an eye out, and please be careful. He's probably just blowing smoke. Spense said he'd scan that picture we have and send it to you. Maybe be on the lookout, just in case.

Love, M

BACK TO THE ISLAND

Date: May 26, 2012
To: M
From: Heidi
Subject: work, work, work

Hello, Sir. How are you? Is it always this rainy and cloudy? Where's the sun? What does everybody need to become happy? A mother, a father, a sister, a friend, a lover? Here's what I look like now, sir. Do I look inviting?

Why don't you go visit Kate? She's not going to come down there. You should know that. Who do you love, sir? Who's your sister? Who's your friend? Who do you want for a lover? Probably not me, the damaged back-island girl.

Bye, darling (can I say that?)

Date: May 30, 2012
To: Kate
From: M
Subject: Heidi

I'm worried about Heidi. I don't think she likes what she's becoming living in a big city. Is she worried about her heart? She referred to herself as damaged! Do you know anything more about that?

God, I wish we could adopt her.
MP

Date: May 30, 2012
To: M
From: Kate
Subject: Funereal

CHAPTER 28

I had to look it up funereal. I don't like that word. She sounds happier when she writes me.

Adopt? Who—you and Lottie? Not making any babies of your own?

Kate

Date: June 4, 2012
To: M
From: Barney
Subject: visit

M—we're having trouble finding a time to come down there. Me, Jim, Jim, Randy, and George all want to come, but every time we try to decide on a date, somebody can't do it. I've got a suggestion—why don't you come up here for a visit first? Jim Rank's dad's best friend is selling his place on Lake Vermilion up by Ely. I don't know the lake, do you? I guess it's really beautiful, they tell me. It's by the Boundary Waters Canoe Area. It's pretty big—lots of islands, big pines, etc. Anyway, he wants to sell it. I guess the place is amazing. It's like an East Coast type place—cedar shakes, dormers, porches—and has a boat house and a couple guest cabins. The guy, I guess he's loaded, wants to sell it to someone he knows will take care of it. He had it built in the 1980s, although I guess it looks like 1800's. He told Jim's dad that if Jim was interested, he'd sell it pretty cheap, you know, without a realtor and all. Maybe we could all go in on it? He said we could come up for a week over the 4th of July and stay in it for free to see what Jim (we) think. The guy'll be out of town. I guess he's getting old. It's a lot to take care of, and it's pretty remote, I guess. Can you make it?

I emailed Sara and asked if she could get to Minnesota around that time, while you were here. And to get Kate to come as well. I

| 495

haven't heard back yet. How are things with Lottie? Have you been talking to Kate? How's she? What are you thinking? Are you thinking?

Barn

DATE: Thursday, June 5, 2012, 11:46 a.m.

M: Barn: Help! You online? I messed up. I believe you asked two questions yesterday. Answers are: 'yes', and 'I don't want to.'

Barn: Yah, I'm here in my cubicle. I might have a little trouble typing, though, I've got a librarian in my lap.

M: In your dreams.

Barn: You were going to leave me hanging with "yes" and "I don't want to" weren't you?

M: Maybe. But ... would you like to finish up with the librarian and get back to me?

Barn: Nah. I can get it anytime I want. So, "yes"? That mean you can come up here over the 4th?

M: Yes.

Barn: And the "I don't want to" ... what? (you got me using these damn dots ...). Since I asked you "what are you thinking?" you're saying you don't want to think? I assume you've done something stupid?

M: Yup.

Barn: Don't make me drag it out of you. How did you mess up?

M: They're ellipses.

Barn: What? You drunk?

M: Those dots ... are called ellipses.

Barn: I don't give a damn about what they're called. I'll never use another one. *What did you do?*

CHAPTER 28

M: OK, OK, relax. Jeez. Lottie and I had a screw-it-all screw the other night. I think Kate's got a guy—going on weekend trips—so I'd guess sleeping together. So I said 'screw it' and told Lottie I didn't love Kate—that way, anyway—and the rest will go down as spectacular carnal splendor. Not a lot of love, but the passion had obviously been saved up and was spent in splendid fashion.

Barn: OK, so is there something wrong with that?

M: Yes.

Barn: C'mon asshole. What? You don't want to talk about it?

M: No.

Barn: You do too. Tell me, prick.

M: When I think back on it, I'm pretty sure I could have loved Marilyn. So, I didn't lie: I don't love Kate—that way, anyway, I think. Is that bullshit? I know we've gone over this a million times … but—I'm SCREWED UP! Now what do I do? I don't want to hurt Lottie. I don't want to hurt Kate. I don't really want to hurt myself. I could end up with neither Kate nor Lottie. Wouldn't that be the bee's knees?

Barn: Screw the bees! Look—I already said this. Excuse me if I'm not overflowing with sympathy. I'm here in my cube contemplating a nonexistent librarian and you're all sad because you don't know which beautiful, gorgeous woman you love the most. Forgive my lack of empathy.

M: OK, OK, relax! Anything up with Sara?

Barn: No. Enough of this shit. When you going to come up? The 4th is a Wednesday. So, all the guys are trying to get the week off from the 4th to the 11th. It looks like it'll be only the guys, no wives. So, when should I tell Sara?

BACK TO THE ISLAND

M: I don't know: before or after. It doesn't matter. Just let me know. Actually, after is better: I'll come up for the week and then stay as long as I want to.

Barn: Are you going to talk to Kate? What does Sara think of your dilemma?

M: God, don't bring Sara into the mix. Why don't you have her work it out with Kate, and let me know if they can come after the 11th. OK? See ya, big guy! Can't wait. I'm excited!

DATE: Sunday, June 10, 2012, 11:25 a.m.

M: I just realized something … I miss you, you know? You there? Wanna chat? I need a hug.

Sara: Don't get fresh. Yeah, I'm here but I feel like I shouldn't be. Ya want a hug, talk to Kate.

M: Can ya hug in a chat ? . . that would be cool. Anyway, you're more fun to hug.

Sara: Knock it off.

M: Looks like I'll be seeing you. Excited?

Sara: Yes, I have to admit I am excited to see you. So is Kate. Who you going to hug first, eh?

M: You?

Sara: Wrong.

M: Who you gonna hug first, me or Barney?

Sara: Neither.

M: What? That'd be downright "un-family-ish."

Sara: We're not family, if you might recall.

M: So, then, it could be a really good hug.

CHAPTER 28

Sara: I do believe you're about to step over that line. I am excited to *see* you—don't get any ideas. I can just hear those greasy, lecherous wheels turning. Goodbye.

M: Goodbye? This was just getting fun.

Sara: Well, that's all the fun you're getting. Again, bye.

M: Did you really leave?

M: I hate computers.

Date: June 11, 2012
To: Kate
From: Sara
Subject: Minnesota?

Hi, hon. How you doing? Barney emailed me FINALLY. MP is going up there (Minn.) for a week over the 4th. Asked if we wanted to fly into Mpls for a few days. What you think? Like around the 11th of July? Can you make it? Or, really, do you WANT to make it? I think you should. You two are really dumb playing all these stupid games. Barney said M (that's what he calls him most of the time—can you live with M? And I mean it both ways—one of M's double entendre jobbies) said he and Lottie weren't sleeping together. I know you won't go down there. I understand, but you two should figure out something quick before one of you screws something up. By the way, Barney also said he thought you have a boyfriend? Is there something you haven't told me? I'll be coming home again this weekend. I plan on staying for a while this time. I'm excited, actually, to see those two again. I guess I miss Barney, just as a friend by the way, but I REALLY miss M.
Love, Sara

BACK TO THE ISLAND

Date: June 14, 2012
To: Sara
From: Kate
Subject: RE: Minnesota?

Sara: (Miss M!—as a friend, right? Watch it!) Really? He's not sleeping with Lottie? He talks about Lottie wanting to "make babies." How can they do that if they're not sleeping together, eh? Maybe they're together but not sleeping! I think Barney'd cover for him. I don't know where he gets the idea I've got a boyfriend. I feel like I'm walking around wearing a damn chastity belt and he thinks I've got a boyfriend? You know, one of the reasons I thought he and Lottie were still hot and heavy is because of what that asshole Richard wrote. I guess that's pretty dumb. He'd obviously lie like a rug to get back at me. You don't suppose Mick ... M ... got that idea about me from Richard? He emailed M, too, you know? But he'd be smarter than to believe that prick, wouldn't he? Of course I almost did. I always sign off "Love, Kate" He signs off "Regards" or some shit like that! I'm going nuts, Sara. I'll talk to you about the land of 10,000 mosquitoes when you get home.

Love, Kate

Date: June 15, 2012
To: M
From: Kate
Subject: M

Hey, dude. How the hell are ya? I checked, I haven't heard from you since May 30th! I suppose you know Barney finally contacted Sara. She just told me you're going to be in Minnesota over the 4th of July and we're supposed to meet you two on the 11th in Mpls? Sound right? And what's this shit about me having a boyfriend?

CHAPTER 28

I haven't even been on a date! One night I had a few too many and I let an old friend try to kiss me. When he stuck his tongue in my mouth I almost barfed. I don't know how else to say this, but to just say it:

I am sorry our relationship developed the way it did. You just have to believe that I thought it was the right thing to do. I just couldn't have lived with you otherwise. I also apologize for what you call "tormenting you." I couldn't help myself. YES! I admit I was attracted to you right away. And I loved you NOT as a brother. But, see, nothing happened. Now we could start fresh, from the beginning, like we should. And like when Lottie saw us wrestling naked—think what an unconditional, unrestrictive, cool relationship we had. I love you, goddamnit! You hear that? And I know you love me. I just know you do. I wish you'd jump on a plane and fly up here tonight. God, I get the shakes just thinking about holding you. Kissing you again—for real—I promise I won't barf. And, making love. God, think of it!

All right, sorry, I had to take a little break there. If I have to wait until July 11th to see you, fine. But if you don't love me, please tell me now—and I don't mean "love" as a sister. If I have to love you as a brother, I don't know if I want to love you at all.

LOVE ME, PLEASE. Kate

Date: June 15, 2012
To: Barney
From: M
Subject: Love?

I just got a love letter from Kate! It really didn't sound like her. I figured she'd be way too proud to 'declare' her love for me. I really, really don't know what to do about that. Kate says she

BACK TO THE ISLAND

doesn't have a boyfriend, not even dating—so what did she call that weekend in Coeur d'Alene? Oh, what the shit!

Oh, I've got the plane tickets. I'll be coming in on the 3rd. I'll get you the particulars later.

Thanks for listening. MP

Date: June 16, 2012
To: M
From: Barney
Subject: Love?

Right! I'm the lucky one! See you on the 3rd, asshole.

Date: June 17, 2012
To: Heidi
From: M
Subject: Where are you?

Hi, hon! Haven't heard from you a while. You OK? I worry, you know, when I don't hear from you. Here's Rashi's latest. I can't believe how quickly he picks stuff up. He's now pushing me to meet every day. He also sits in when I meet with all the guys, which I only do a couple times a week. I've been going like bonkers on both *A Million$* and *Back to the Island*—my new title for the novel. My typist can't keep up with me!

Is Rashi in love with you? Do you love him? I really don't like the tenor of this one! E me will you, please.

—MP- a worried man (who can't sing) singing a worried song.

> When I had looked in your eyes
> I got nothing
> All I wondered
> Vaguely

CHAPTER 28

> If I could find something better
> Than your mouth
> To put my fire out

Date: June 17, 2012
To: Sara
From: Kate
Subject: Worry

I know you just got home and I could just call, but if I did I'm afraid I would just blubber. He hasn't gotten back to me, and I laid it on the line. I mean I, and you know me, told him I REALLY loved him, and—nothing. Fucking NOTHING!!

Date: June 17, 2012
To: Kate
From: Sara
Subject: RE: Worry

Give him time, hon. I know, you know, Barney believes he loves you. I'll come over and let's go for dinner and a movie.

Date: June 17, 2017
To: Sara
From: Kate
Subject: But ...

But does HE know? If he doesn't respond TODAY—to hell with him. See you later. Thanks, sis.

Date: June 18, 2012
To: Kate
From: M
Subject: Sorry

BACK TO THE ISLAND

And sorry, sorry, sorry. I sat down immediately on seeing your e and stared at the keys. My fingers wouldn't work. Well, I guess it was probably my mind that wouldn't work, but it seems the heart does. Yes, I think I love you. All right, I know I love you. So, yes, I love you.

Now what?
LOVE, M … P … or ick, I suppose.
P.S.—I'm worried about Heidi.

DATE: Monday, June 18, 2012, 7:00 p.m.

Kate: Where the heck are you? You're online it looks like. I called but I didn't leave a message. NOW the SOB emails me! A week after I profess my unbridled love for him, he finally writes back. The son-of-a-bitch.

Sara: I'm here. I was just checking my emails when you popped up. I didn't have my phone with me. Sometimes I just have to get away from that thing. It wasn't a week, it was two days. Two days! So what did he say?

Kate: No, it wasn't! It was three. It seemed like a week! He says OK, all right, yes, "I *think* I love you." What a dipshit!

Sara: What do you mean? What'd you want him to say?

Kate: I don't know. I wanted him to email me back two days ago. I don't want him to "think" anything. Why'd it take him so long?

Sara: Are you sure you're not looking for trouble where there isn't any. What did he say about Lottie?

Sara: Where are you? Answer me: What about Lottie?
Kate: I know he's sleeping with her. I can tell.
Sara: How!
Kate: The way he said he loves me.

CHAPTER 28

Sara: Sis, you're nuts. I guess you always have been, but now you're driving me nuts. I'm going to bed. Nite.

Date: June 19, 2012
To: M
From: Heidi
Subject: love

Hello, sir! There's nothing new here. Work is good. I have nothing new to send you. Too busy.

I used to read to Rashi, like he was my child. I told you he thinks he loves me. Whom do you love? Doesn't seem love is so simple, like it should be, right, sir?

Bye. Don't worry (very funny about not being able to sing. And, please, don't be worried long—I love that song, too.)

Date: June 20, 2012
To: M
From: Kate
Subject: What now?

"M?" You told me you didn't like that. Reminded you of a girl's name. So if we love each other, which now, can I assume(?) we both realize, or at least acknowledge, what do I call you? Barney calls you M. I like it a lot better than that damn MP. I can call you that when I'm mad at you, which I assume will be a lot since you're such a dumb shit—self-proclaimed, remember.

What now, eh? I don't really know. I can't come down there, you realize that? Right? I couldn't face Lottie. I'd love to see Spense and Peewee and Wanda, but—I really couldn't face Lottie. I think Lottie is great and I'm guessing she loves you ... not as much as I do, though! Don't ever forget that, jerk. You hear?

BACK TO THE ISLAND

Why can't you come here? Sara's dying to see you, too, and I certainly don't want to wait until July 11th to see you. That's ages away. I need a backrub NOW! It will be so weird to ... I don't know ... make love to you, I guess. You see, I've wanted to since before I moved in. You actually got me that first day. I think the "tipping" thing was symbolic—you know? I want you to be my anchor, my stability. And I can smack you around when you get out of line. Sara says you don't have a filter. You don't know where the line is. She told me you wanted to fool around with her since she wasn't really your sister! The first thing I'm going to do when I see you is smack you for that one. You just leave my little sister alone, you hear. And remember, I'm not your sister, but she is, ya hear?

Oh, Mick, I'm so excited. Fly up tomorrow, will you? Please? Maybe we can get Heidi a job here in Spokane. Get her out of that big city. She doesn't belong there. Tell me about your book, or books, I guess. Just tell me anything. Mostly, when we're going to see each other—please before July11!

Say hi to Spense, Peewee, and Wanda. Tell Lottie I'm sorry. I'd like to be friends, but I won't hold my breath on that one. I really am sorry for idly sitting by and watching and letting that develop—that's why I tormented you, you know. I was just trying to keep you interested. I understand that. Do you? Can't we actually talk? I'm scared.

Bye. Love you. See you soon? Kate.

Date:	June 23, 2012
To:	Lottie
From:	M
Subject:	trip

I've wanted to talk to you about this at work, but it never seemed

CHAPTER 28

the right time. This being a Sunday and all, I'm being a chicken and e'ing you instead: I told Jack last night after close that I would be taking a little leave for a while. I'm taking the week off, getting *A Million Dollars* ready for the publisher I've got in Mpls, and then visiting Barney and my friends for a couple of weeks in Minnesota. Things are really slowing down on the island, anyway. I think Jack was relieved he didn't have to lay me off. I've got my place rented for the first three weeks of July so expect to be back soon after that.

Should we take a break until then and assess just how serious we are? It's likely I will be seeing Kate, as Barney is arranging a visit for her and Sara while we're in Minnesota. I'm going to try to reestablish what I thought our relationship was—brother/sister. Once I have that relationship orchestrated in my mind, we can move ahead in our relationship without any reservations. Does this sound copasetic to you?

I miss us. The comfort I felt connecting again was remarkable and reassuring.—MP

Date: June 24, 2012
To: M
From: Lottie
Subject: Bullshit

Yes: bullshit! That wasn't you writing that email. That was a poor excuse for a dildo. So take those cautious, carefully versed words and stick them up your ass. You were so "comfortable connecting" i.e. fucking, the other night that we're going to take a break for a week when we aren't going to see each other for almost a month? I believed you when you said you didn't "love" Kate, fully intending to mean "sexually." That makes me no more than a whore. God, I am so gullible. Why don't you just stay in Minnesota? You think I'm dumb?

Date: June, 25 2012
To: M
From: Lottie
Subject: Bye

What? No retraction? No, "Oh, you're taking this all wrong. I love you and let's make babies?" Look, I more hate myself than you for going to bed with you the other night. I guess I should have said: "I *wanted* to believe you when you said you didn't love Kate. I needed some arms around me. So, I'll take the blame for being stupid. I am afraid it's past the point of "let's just be friends." I have to admit, I'm hurt and pissed. I am trying to just look at you as a stupid warm dildo that gave me what I needed the other night, and the other times. But, unfortunately, you're more than that. Too much more.

Bye, Mick or MP or whatever. Nice knowing you. Lottie the Hottie.

Date: June 25, 2012
To: Lottie
From: M
Subject: More than sorry

Lottie: I am. I am sorrowful, distressed, disconsolate, contrite, repentant ... I could keep going. I honestly think I do love you. I don't know how you thought about me, but you're the coolest woman I've ever met. I mean it. And, yes, 'Lottie the Hottie'—one of the most beautiful, inside and out. You deserve absolutely the best. If I can't give it to you, I hope with all my heart you find the person who can.—MP

CHAPTER 28

Date: June 25, 2012
To: M
From: Lottie
Subject: RE: More than sorry

Take that thesaurus and stick it up your ass, too.

Date: June 26, 2012
To: Barney
From: M
Subject: I told you

Hey Barn, you there? No? Well, I told you I screwed up. When I told Lottie about coming up there and I suggested we take a break now until I get back, she got REALLY pissed. I am such a dumbshit and an insensitive asshole. She called me a dildo, which is pretty demeaning ... and clever, actually, and pretty darn accurate. She told me to just stay in Minnesota and she doesn't want to be friends.

Yelp! I don't want to let either of them go and I'm afeared I'm going to lose both of them!
—M

Date: June 29, 2012
To: Kate
From: M
Subject: July 9th!

Hi there. Won't be long now! Can't wait. Everything gud with you? Are you two renting a car or are we picking you up? I spose Barney and Sara have that one worked out?

See you soon. Love, M.

Date: June 29, 2012
To: M

BACK TO THE ISLAND

From: Kate
Subject: RE: July 9th!

Hello, yurself. Forget how to spell, did ya? I'm sooo excited! Really, I have to pee constantly. How did Lottie take this? I feel really sorry for her. I liked her.

Soon, love me.

DATE: Friday, June 29, 2012, 4:11 p.m.

M: Just sat down and saw your email. You there?

Kate: Hey, I am at my computer, too. Working on a PR contract I'm trying to finish up so I can come see ya. So, Lottie?

M: She's pissed.

Kate: Why? I can see hurt, but why pissed?

M: I don't know. I can't imagine, but I guess she thought she loved me. I sorta, you know, love her, too. You know, she's great.

Kate: You didn't sleep with her again, did you?

M: What do you mean? When?

Kate: Mick! You did! Tell me exactly what day.

M: I don't know exactly what day. What's the problem?

Kate: What do you mean—"what's the problem?" You finally admit you love me, and then you sleep with Lottie?

M: No, no. It was a while ago. You know, like back when you were, or I thought you were, sleeping with a guy.

Kate: What in the hell ever gave you that idea? I told you I wasn't even dating.

M: Well, you told me, you know, you kissed that guy, and then you went on a weekend trip.

CHAPTER 28

Kate: I went on the weekend trip with Sally, my and Sara's friend, and we didn't have sex! And that guy tried to kiss me, I didn't kiss him back. You said you weren't seeing Lottie.

M: Well, what do you mean? We work together.

Kate: You are really pissing me off. Don't act stupid, even though I'm beginning to think you are. When did you last sleep with Lottie? E me back and give me the date. And if you lie, I'm never talking to you again.

Date: June 29, 2012
To: Kate
From: M
Subject: RE: YOU

Kate. Hon. I don't know. It was back in April, maybe early May. It was before I knew you weren't dating, and it just happened. I thought at that time you and I weren't going to happen. It was before we decided to meet up in Minn., and, and, you know, before when we, you and I sorta just admitted we loved each other. And it was only once. We weren't seeing each other outside of work because of you. And I've avoided her ever since.

I love YOU!—M

Date: June 30, 2012
To: M
From: Barney
Subject: ?

What the hell happened? I'm almost afraid to ask. Sara just emailed me and said they're not coming! What did you do?

BACK TO THE ISLAND

Date: June 30, 2012
To: Heidi
From: M
Subject: Everything ok?

Hello, hon. How are you? Is everything OK? I'm traveling to Minnesota & will be gone for a few weeks, so I won't be checking my emails regularly. Why don't you shoot me one right away, if you can, to let me know not to worry. It's been awhile since I heard from you. You haven't seen that Richard fellow, have you?

Date: June 30, 2012
To: M
From: Heidi
Subject: I'm ok

Hello, sir. I'm OK. Don't worry about me. I don't think I've seen him. There's a lot of guys in Manhattan that look just like him, dress just like him, and probably act just like him. Vacation times have arrived and so I'm filling in for people, doing double-duty. So, very busy. No time to write anything worth sending.

You appear to be doing a great job with Rashi. I'm really impressed with his writing. But, as I warned you, if you discovered his soul, you'd uncover his demons. He's too big, I believe, for that little island, yet he'll never leave. A fatal flaw, I'd venture. He always wants, as I've said, what he can't have. I hesitate writing to him. I fear fueling his despondency. It is a burden to have a person love you, right, sir? Especially if you love somebody else? I will, though, write to him in your absence, both to encourage him to continue writing and to attempt to give him hope. What is more destructive than despair? How painful when we see it in people we care for and, more poignant and painful, when we find it in ourselves? Right, sir?

CHAPTER 28

Have fun with your friends in Minnesota. Are you going to see Kate, Sara, or both?

Love, HS.

Date:	**June 30, 2012**
To:	**Kate**
From:	**M**
Subject:	**face to face**

Kate: Barney said you and Sara have cancelled. Do you really want to do that? What you're doing is unfair ... to me, to Barney, and to Sara. Your anger, or whatever it is, is unwarranted. Honest. We definitely need a face to face. Don't you agree? Really? I'll call you when I get to the States.

Love, M.

Date:	**June 31, 2012**
To:	**Sara**
From:	**M**
Subject:	**Please come to Minn**

Sara: Is there no persuading 'pig'headed, 'Kat'tankerous Kate into reconsidering your visit to, as she says: the land of 10,000 mosquitoes? Don't you think she is being unreasonable? Are you mad at me? You know, Sara, I really do think I love her, but ... but, I'm afraid it is as a sister. I'm afraid I can't help it. I really don't even know if I can explain it. This may sound gross to you, so sorry, but I just can't think of her sexually now. I don't even understand it myself. There is no way I can consider, in my mind, having sex with her. It gives me the chills—seriously. Please don't tell her this. You know, it's almost weird how much I trust you. I know if I ask you not to say something I know you'll honor that request, even when it involves your sister. What does that mean? I know I shouldn't have had sex with Lottie when I did, but the regret is because of Lottie, not Kate. Do you know what I mean? I don't think I betrayed Kate. I just don't. I really thought we were done, you know, in that way. So, what does that mean? I do think I betrayed Lottie, not because we made love ... well, I'm not sure I'd call it 'making love,' but 'having sex.' I don't know if she felt we were making love. She was ... sorry, I don't want to talk about it with you ... but it seemed more like she wanted sex than she wanted me. Does that make sense? Or am I just rationalizing? You know she wouldn't have anything to do with me when I told her that Kate and you actually weren't my sisters. That's why I think I feel guilt or remorse or whatever. It's driving me bozo. I think I actually do love Lottie, too. I mean she's great, you know? But even if I convince her that my feelings toward Kate are only 'brotherly,' which IS how I felt the last time Lottie and I had sex. You know, maybe I wanted to believe Kate was dating and sleeping with a guy. It was like I was almost relieved. I believe her that she wasn't, but is it weird that I felt I was off the hook? Is that ... I don't know ... does it make any sense? You know, these are usually things I talk over with Barney. Why I'm unloading on you, I don't know.

So, sorry, I do feel awkward telling you this kind of stuff about Lottie. I hope you don't hate me for it? But, since it's really all about Kate and how she feels about me and me not being able to reciprocate, I feel I have to involve you. When I think about it, you are the last person I want feeling I'm not a good person or whatever. Lottie has made it clear she's pissed. I'd love to have her as a friend, but I believe I could live without her, so I'm

CHAPTER 28

guessing that means I don't LOVE her, right? I'm afraid what Kate might feel, but if I think of her as a sister, she can be angry, but has to forgive her brother, right? I don't think I can live without Kate ... and you. When I think about it, you're the one I'm almost most worried about. What the devil does that mean, do you suppose? So, are you angry with me? Don't you feel Kate's being unreasonable? Can't you talk her into coming?

Love, M.

Date: June 31, 2012
To: M
From: Sara
Subject: Sorry

Dear M: No, I don't want to talk her into going to Minn. It breaks my heart. She knows, I think.
Miss you. Love, Sara.

Date: June 31, 2012
To: Sara
From: M
Subject: ?

Knows what?

CHAPTER 29

(One month later)

Date: September 27, 2012
To: Barney
From: M
Subject: The lake

Hey, Barn: I'll be flying in tomorrow. Then Mon we close, right? Are you all right with the way we divvied it up? I plan on normally being at the cabin May through Sept. God, the minute I heard the loons I knew I had to be up there. It's weird. Are the sounds you heard in the womb always there to seduce you? And the property! My Lord: the ledge rock is really cool, don't you think? You may not realize it yet, but a sand beach like we've also got is rare on Vermilion and other Boundary Waters-type lakes. And there must be a hundred towering red and white pines that seem to dwarf the lodge and cabins. Those lakes and woods are just in my blood. Lake Vermilion is gorgeous, don't you think? Aren't you glad we found this place? It almost found us. You remember Lake V is where I vacationed with my parents when I was really little? Even in the womb, do you think we contract a sense of where we belong as we become?

So you are fine with me buying the lodge and little cabin, you taking the other bigger one? If Jim or any of the other guys want to buy in later, those two storage buildings can be remodeled

BACK TO THE ISLAND

into cabins, I think. Just add on a screen porch and decks. So, my three-fourths and your one-fourth is OK, right?

I plan on staying up there now until sometime in Oct. Fall's beautiful. It will depend a little on when the Bahamas cottage is rented. Summer into fall is hurricane season down here. But that's something I've never experienced, so I might run down there and check it out. It is protected from the ocean side anyway. Guess I'd want to be there to see how sturdy my little place is and how resilient to the more robust elements. No renting in hurricane season anyway. That'll give you some time alone at the lake with all your sexy librarians. But I'll want to get back up some in Jan and Feb, catch a little bite from old man winter, and then probably back down in Mar and April—no good up there at that time anyway, snow's bad and the lake doesn't open up until mid to late April. But with all those spruce and pines, it's totally beautiful in the winter, I remember. And I miss cross-country skiing. You'll have to try it. Great exercise. What are you planning?

I'll be getting in late, so I'll take a taxi. Thanks for keeping my car at your place.

See you tomorrow, M

Date: September 27, 2012
To: M
From: Barney
Subject: The lake

I'll pick you up. I've already got your flight information. Meet me outside baggage claim.

Yes, I'm fine with the deal. You know me, hard to leave the comfort of my cubicle, so I won't be up there a lot, anyway. I'll see what I can do about sexy librarians, though—you might be surprised!

CHAPTER 29

Yes, I could see it in your eyes when we got to the property. I knew you wanted it. But, you know me—I don't know a red pine from a beaver.

See you at the airport. Barn.

Date:	October 10, 2012
To:	Heidi
From:	M
Subject:	visit

Hi, hon. How are things? I talk to your folks pretty often, I'm sure you know? I realize you're busy, but your mother really worries about you; so does your father even tho he tries not to act like it. Try to keep them informed more frequently, if you can. OK?

Can you get away before the snow flies and come visit me up here in Minnesota? There's still some good color left. The birch and aspen are yellow and gold. The maples are a bright burnt red, some already turning a more subtle russet. We have a deciduous pine—tamarack—that turns almost fluorescent yellow before it drops its needles. The loons are still around. You haven't lived until you've heard the cry, which is a poor word to describe the sound—there actually is no word in the English language to describe it adequately—of the loon. "Trill" is probably the closest. There are eagles, osprey, wolf, moose, fox, and deer galore … an occasional bear. What do you think? You can fly directly into Mpls/St. Paul airport and either Barney, Jim, or Jim can drive you up, or Mike, a friend of mine, can fly you up in his hybrid sea plane. Think: taking off on land and landing on water … sky blue water. Can you make it?

BACK TO THE ISLAND

Date: October 2, 2012
To: M
From: Heidi
Subject: RE: visit

Hello, sir. Thanks for the invitation. Where you live sounds like where you belong. I'm sorry, but I just can't come. What if I wanted to stay? Anyway, father is flying in tomorrow. That Richard fellow—I never saw him in person when he was down in the Bahamas, but I recognized him from that photo—I saw him a few times here and I thought it an odd coincidence or that maybe it was someone that looked like him. But I kept seeing him and then I was especially vigilant one evening and observed him following me back to my apartment. Unfortunately, I mentioned it to my mother who, in turn, mentioned it to my father and ... well, he's flying in tomorrow. Can you just see him in New York City? I have to admit, I'm concerned. There was no talking him out of it. Once again I am torn: I realize he wants to protect me, and, maybe, I need it. I certainly don't feel this guy has good intentions. But in his anger, Father may turn to violence. I'd like to say I can take care of myself, but my strength is not in the form of muscles, and I am spooked. If you have any ideas, please let me know.

Oh, another thing that's a bit distressing: Father wants Vernal's Haitians to move back to the site and clean it up. Re-squat, so to speak. I expect more fireworks. Poor Mama.

I fear for this Richard. Mr. T's anger is a concern ... and I am the reason why. You've got me using ellipses, sir. Are they a crutch or a useful transition? (That's me, the publicist, speaking.)

If you have any insights, I would appreciate it.

Thank you, sir. Love, HS.

CHAPTER 29

Date:	October 2, 2012
To:	Sara
From:	M
Subject:	Gosh!

Sara, hi: It seems like forever that we've talked. Where are you? You're not there at your computer, phone, pad, whatever, are you? No? Shoot!

Will you be in New York tomorrow or the next few days? When Richard threatened to 'check out' Heidi, I told him if he did, Peewee would certainly come track him down. Well, Richard's been following her around. Peewee's flying in tomorrow. I was hoping there might be a cool head around, in New York? You know Peewee. I wouldn't be surprised if he exterminates the rat. You know he'll find him. He's too big to be angry. It's definitely dangerous. This is his daughter. I think I'd consider killing someone threatening my daughter; hell, I'd kill somebody threatening Heidi. T-r-o-u-b-l-e with a capital T.

Well, get back to me when you can. I mean, I don't really know what you could do anyway, but you are a cool head. (Cool rest of you, too, just in case I haven't told you.) Again, I trust you implicitly.

Shit (sorry), to involve you. I don't know what else to do. It smells dangerous.

Call me or e me. Thanks, hon.

Miss you, dear. Love, M

Date:	October 2, 2012
To:	M
From:	Sara
Subject:	RE: Gosh!

Hey there M. *Dear!* What's that about? Where are you? In Minn. or Hope Town? How are you? Yes, it does seem like a long time not seeing or talking to you. Funny: I feel you're close by, and yet I don't even know where you are and either place you might be is not so near. Yet, I just flew over Minnesota on my way home. I could feel you. Is that where you are?

I'll be visiting you in the heavens, again, on my way to NY on Mon. the 8th. Hope I can talk to Peewee. Yes, I agree, Peewee on the loose on a rampage in Manhattan sounds like trouble. That dumb shit (excuse, please) Richard! Maybe it's his way to commit suicide. Sounds like he has no future. Too bad he got it so bad. He's going to be behind bars soon. The sooner the better for his sake. I know he was complicit in allowing or standing by and watching some real ugly stuff going on in an awfully important realm of our country. Greed will not regulate itself. The guys that are able to create nothing out of nothing, worth nothing, and profit from it are a frightening piston in the machine. If we can just get one or two of the biggies, maybe we can stop the momentum of this runaway train. Sorry, Kate is always yelling at me for mixing my metaphors. Sorry, also, for rambling on about Wall Street, but in my job with the SEC, it's a focus in my life. (Sometimes we don't do so well ourselves at the SEC: think Madoff.) I am really proud of my sis, although you should be too.

I never got your side of this current fracas, but I understand what you told me. I had told Kate that when she was down there she had made her own bed and it was her fault you were not in it. I would love to see you, I sincerely miss you, but until you and Kate clear up this misreckoning, I'm going to keep my distance. Being caught in the middle of such an impervious state of affairs with two people I love dearly is not my idea of bliss. Why not try an email, at least, or call Kate, if you can. I have no idea how to suggest a means to repair this relationship without leaving a scar, much less an open wound. I am so sorry. You have no idea.

Love, Sara.

CHAPTER 29

Date: October 5, 2012
To: Heidi
From: M
Subject: Peewee

Hi, hon. Anything new? Would you please keep me informed? Now I'm not only worried about you, but your father.

Love, M

Date: October 5, 2012
To: M
From: Heidi
Subject: Why Worry Now?

HS: My father is here safe and sound. He even looks bigger here because all the Irish, Italians, and just about all the Europeans, I guess, are a little short ... like us, sir. He also doesn't have any warm clothes and it's getting pretty chilly here in this concrete city. It's weird: this summer the sidewalks were steaming, the concrete radiating heat. But now the sidewalks are like whisky stones (see, I am becoming so cosmopolitan), cooling the already frigid temperatures.

Other than my concern for what my father might do, everything is fine, sir. There probably is reason for worry, but why bother? I gave up a long time ago.

Love, HS

Date: October 6, 2012
To: Sara
From: M
Subject: I'm so lonesome I could cry

Hi, *sis*: "It's Saturday night and I ain't got nobody." I am, actually, at my cabin here in the woods all by my lonesome. Blow me a kiss as you fly over. Lottie has been gone from Elbow for quite a while. She's rented out her place ... long-term rental I'm told, by the same rental agency that I use. Don't tell Kate, OK? Don't know why, really, but let me when I'm ready to go there ... you know, without Lottie in the picture. Lottie had told Jack she was flying to Boston to see her sister. Her parents are both dead, I guess. Must be where her $ came from. Then, apparently, Spense, who left back in May, is going to meet up with her in Boston before he heads south for the winter. She was considering joining him on the Mary. I plan on staying up here at the lake until sometime later this month until my cottage is no longer rented on Elbow. But with Spense and Lottie gone, not even mentioning Kate ... and you, it's gonna be lonely down there, too. It's weird, I escaped to that little island to get away from it all. When I look back, I guess I was probably really looking for a new life—one distant and disassociated with the one I had with my wife. You don't really think you're starting over, but, really, what choice do you have? I thought I was also escaping a system I was so—I don't know—fed up with, I guess.

But there's a saying: 'No matter where you go, there you are.' So, where am I? Alone! And I found the system I thought I was escaping from has permeated even the white sands of paradise. So I am up here now in God's country, but when I'm given audience to one of nature's splendors—like the other night there was a fantastic colorful northern lights display—it's almost existential: If I'm the only one to see it, did it really happen? I say to myself what the hell difference does it make? I still witnessed it for crying out loud. But, sometimes that's what I feel like doing. It's actually what I do do at times, and I don't even know what or who I am longing for. Martha, still, maybe? Or do I start all over again, again? I want to share this up here with somebody.

CHAPTER 29

Help me, hon. What should I do? God, sorry for sounding like a simpering wimp.

Anyway, I plan on spending Christmas in Hope Town with Wanda and Peewee, if he's not in jail. I've invited Heidi up here, but she says she can't come. Why don't you (and Kate?) head on down for a warm-up sometime in Nov or Dec? Even Christmas would be great? Having been an only child, I spent all my Christmas mornings also alone, sniff, sniff ... without two sisters I never knew I had. Can I guilt you two into coming down? I know it'd probably be as hard for you as me to miss a white Christmas. At least the sands are white.

I know you're going to NY on Mon. I really am worried about what Peewee will do to Richard if he finds him stalking Heidi. I'm also concerned about that little urchin. God, I sound like a drag. Sorry. Don't mean to be a downer. I'm actually pretty content most of the time. But I do miss you and Kate. Thanks for helping out.

Love 'n' luck—M

CHAPTER 30

Sunday, October 7

THE PHONE rang. She almost didn't answer it. She was tired. Could just fall asleep and fade into the couch. Her mind had been straying quite a lot lately and quite a distance. But she suddenly jerked out of it and scampered for the phone. It could be Sara; it could be Heidi.

"Hello?" Kate answered flatly. It could be Mick.

"Hello there, yourself."

"What? Mick?"

"MP. M if you prefer, please."

"Yeah, yeah. OK. M, I'll try."

"Just how are you doing? Good fall color over there?"

"My summer tan is fading …" she started. A smile apparent in her voice now, replacing the funk.

"Yeah, yeah, very funny. How'd you get a tan anyway? Heard you were working your little tail off."

"Keep my tail out of it, will ya? We hardly know each other anymore."

"No problem," a skipped heartbeat but trying to maintain a half-hearted happy-voice as well. "So, how are things?"

"Mostly good," Kate answered.

"What? Mostly? What's not good? Everything's all right with Sara, right?"

"Yup."

CHAPTER 30

"Your work?"

"Yup. I'm busy, anyway."

"So, with what or whom are things not good? Eh?"

"Ha, ha, eh? Gee, I don't know. How's Lottie?"

An awkward silence crept in. He knew what she was after with the Lottie question and it made him happy somehow that she didn't know about Lottie's absence. "What about Heidi?" he asked. "That's why I called. You been talking to her?"

"Speaking of talking, how *am* I talking to you?"

"Got a new phone … a sorta smart one."

"Lotta good that'll do ya."

"Look who's talking! Anyway, I'm in Minnesota at the lake now, anyway, but I did get overseas calling or whatever." He wasn't sure how friendly he was comfortable being or that she was comfortable with.

"Gee, welcome to the twenty-first century, fool. How can you afford it? Spending a lot of money lately, aren't you?"

He assumed she was referring to purchasing the lake place. "Heidi?" he asked, changing back the subject.

"HS, you mean?" she was trying to toy, he figured; keep it fun but not personal. There was pain in the personal.

"God, I just can't call her that."

"Me either," Kate sighed. "I don't know what to think. As always she's in her conundrum: need for her father but fear for his methods."

"Nothing's happened yet, then?"

"No. She said he checked in with her, approved of her apartment, and she hasn't seen him since. He told her not to worry … nothing would happen to harm her. She was just to carry on as if he wasn't there. She hadn't seen Richard since he followed her home two days ago."

"I fear there's to be an ambush," M said.

"That's what I'd guess too," Kate agreed. "Hopefully Richard gets a glimpse of Peewee first and gets scared off."

"If that cocksucker gets near enough to see Peewee, Peewee will have already seen him."

"You're probably right. So, either Richard gets smart or … shit! What'll you suppose he'll do?"

"There's no way of knowing, except I'd bet a lot of money that Heidi never sees Richard again. Well, anyway, let's keep in touch … about Heidi, I mean."

"Yeah, sure. If I hear anything, I'll let you know. Vice-versa."

"Sure. Think Sara could moderate Peewee's … methods?" Mick really didn't want to end the conversation. It felt good to hear her voice.

"No, well, maybe. Sara's as rational as they come, and I would think Peewee would respect Sara enough, even if it was just to listen to her."

"Listen, yes. But to be honest, if the goal is to get Richard out of Heidi's life, I'd trust Peewee's methods more than Sara's."

"Yeah. I agree, I guess. How are things at your new place? You said you're there now, right?"

"Lonely," Mick answered, and regretted saying it immediately.

"Why don't you have Lottie with you … making babies?"

"For all I know, Lottie and Spense are making babies," Mick said, figuring he might as well tell her.

There was a long pause. "What … what do you mean?"

Mick considered what to tell her. Prominent in his memory was that the truth was not always the best policy. Should she know Lottie was apparently out of the picture? That would mean he was free and clear … but for what? No reason then to not go out there. But he didn't want to, and he assumed

CHAPTER 30

she didn't want to come to the land of 10,000 mosquitoes. But, anyway: "Lottie went home to Boston for a visit and is maybe meeting up with Spense and cruising down to South America or wherever with him."

Another long pause. "Really?"

"Really," Mick answered, and felt this was a good spot for an exit. "Let's talk tomorrow and see what the other knows."

"OK," Kate answered. "If anything happens we call each other. If there's nothing to report, I'll call you tomorrow night anyway. That OK? You be around?"

"I'll be around my cell. Tomorrow night then?"

"Yeah, OK. Night."

"Night." Mick looked at his phone for a while, as if her image would appear in the window, and finally hit 'end.' He didn't feel like he was going to cry. He was getting past that.

Kate did the same. She sat and stared at the phone, not wanting to hit 'end' either, not wanting the conversation to end, not wanting … to be angry.

She immediately called Sara on her cell. She never knew if Sara was tied up or could answer her phone—no matter what time of the day. She was frequently on conference calls day or night when she was in Spokane. But today was Sunday.

Sara answered immediately. "Hi, sis. What's up?"

"I just talked to Mick."

"M, you mean?"

"Did you know that Lottie wasn't down there anymore? That she's in Boston or sailing with Spense?"

"How'd you find out?"

"Mick—M—just told me."

"Told you? He emailed you?"

"No. He told me. He called."

"Uh, well, good. That's great, right?"

"Did you know Lottie was gone?"

"Found out yesterday. M emailed me."

"When were you going to tell me?"

"I wasn't." Sara was holding her breath but also her ground.

"Why the hell not?"

"He asked me not to tell you."

"You're my sister, for crying out loud."

"And he's my ... friend. He told me something in confidence and asked me not to tell you. So, I wasn't going to tell you."

Sara heard a deep sigh on the other end of the line. "You mad at me?" she asked Kate, and cringed waiting for the reply.

"I don't know. Yes! God, I don't know."

"Look, sis, if M asks me not to say anything, I will respect that. I hate to say this, and don't fly off the hook, but it's yourself you should be mad at."

"I know he slept with her!"

"So what? She probably loved him. I don't think he ever really loved her, but that's most likely because of you. Put yourself in his shoes. You're down there like an inadvertent energy boost to his testosterone, but he believes he can't use it to any end with you, yet one of the sexiest women I've ever seen is willing to offer him some TLC."

"TLC?" Kate almost screamed.

"Yes. Care, comfort, companionship ..."

"Coitus, you mean."

Sara laughed. "Sorry, sorry, but that was quick. Funny."

"It's not funny!"

"Look. You've got to see both sides. If you had told him you really weren't his sister, Lottie would have been no more

CHAPTER 30

than a great person to work with. You know that. He would more than likely have loved you like you think you want to love him."

"He slept with her AFTER I told him!" she almost screamed.

"No, I believe you have the timing wrong. Kate, dear. Look at it with perspective, would you? Both he and Lottie—give Lottie credit—they agreed not to pursue their relationship until he figured out how he felt about you."

"Yeah? Well, what'd he figure out by sleeping with her? That she was a great fuck but that he loves me? I don't know if I could ever trust him again."

"You know, I know you pretty damn well. Probably better than you know yourself." Sara's dander was aroused. "I think that issue is a disguise."

"A disguise? A disguise for what?" Kate was backing off a bit. She could tell Sara was getting upset, which didn't happen very often.

"A disguise for the fact—maybe I should say you're using it as an excuse—an excuse for not facing reality."

"What are you getting at, Sara? What reality am I not facing?"

"The reality that you're afraid. I don't even know what of: that by putting Minnesota in the picture that you're 'giving in?' That you so love Spokane and Rose Lake that you can't leave it all even for love? That he'd have to move out here to prove his love? One might pick up and start new roots to live with the love of their life. But for a brother? Or to not leave because of a sister? No. I think the real reason you're not going to live in the Bahamas or Minnesota is because if you go there and proclaim your undying love and want to live with him as husband and wife, that he can't ... because you're, by your own doing, in his mind his sister. And I really think you're afraid of him moving out here and you love him … as a brother. So the reality is you're avoiding facing the real issue. That he and Lottie had a last fling … I mean, don't get me wrong, I don't condone what he did … but that's understandable, considering their past relationship and completely forgivable considering …"

"Considering what?"

"Considering … for Christ's sake, Kate, how could he not be confused, discombobulated."

"Discombobulated?" Kate broke out laughing. "That is not a word you use, sis. Where did that come from?"

"Oh, shut up," Sara said jokingly. "Don't get off on a tangent. You know you drove him nuts. I know he loved … loves … you and was attracted to you, but you made him believe you were his sister. Come on!"

"How do you know so much about how he felt … how he feels?"

"What? You don't think we've talked, sent emails? Really, I love him … of course I love him … as a brother, and he loves me, too, I'm sure … as a sister."

"You sure?" Kate asked.

"What's that supposed to mean?"

"Just what I said."

Sara steered away from that topic. "When you wouldn't go to Minnesota for the visit this summer … sorry, I've been leery of breaching this subject: I felt then like you were looking for an excuse not to go."

"Why the hell would I be looking for an *excuse*? I had a good fucking *reason*," Kate howled.

"Oh, really? OK, let me ask you: would you move to Minnesota to live, with me staying here? And don't bring up

CHAPTER 30

Barney. He's a great guy, but that's as far as it's going to go. Barney and I are not going to happen. So, would you move, leaving me here?"

"No, I can't see myself abandoning you here?"

"So, you're saying you won't leave Spokane or Coeur d'Alene, not because you're so attached to your roots, but because you are attached to me?"

"Both, I suppose. But, maybe, if I felt I could trust him …"

"Would you please quit bullshitting me." Sara exhaled a large sigh. "What if I were to get hitched to a guy in Washington, DC? What if I moved there?"

"Yeah. What if?"

"Would you feel like I was abandoning you?"

"What are you getting at, Sara?"

"Do you feel like you'd be abandoning me if you moved to Minnesota?"

"Well, yah, I suppose. You'd be all alone here."

"Am I supposed to feel the same, Kate? How would you feel if I moved away?"

"Do you want to move to DC?"

"That's not the point."

"What is the point, Sara?"

"Grr … you know what I'm getting at and you're still trying to avoid the issue."

"Guess I'm not as smart as you are, dear. You're going to have to condescend to explain just what the issue is."

"Don't get petulant with me. Maybe you are unaware of what you are doing, I don't know, but if you had gone to Minnesota, made love to M, which I'm guessing may have happened, incestually or not, you would have had at least to consider moving to Minnesota, to be with him."

| 533

"What about Elbow Cay? I couldn't live there."

"M, either. It's obvious he sees that lake up there as where he wants to be. If he keeps the cottage on Elbow, it'll only be for getaways."

"Why can't he move here, live with us? I'd be willing to chance that there's nothing *incestuous* involved!"

"*Us?*" Sara shot back immediately. "See, you think of Spokane as *our* home."

"Well, I've got you here. What does he have in Minnesota?"

"Well, his roots, for one thing."

"Well, our roots are here, damnit!" Kate almost shouted. "Why would we have to pull up ours?"

"We? You can't lay that on me. That you won't leave *me*."

"Well," Kate took a deep breath to calm down. "Why don't you marry Barney, I'll marry Mick, and then both of us can move to Minnesota?"

"You know, I thought of that when we were supposed to visit. I mean Pat, Barney, is the first person with whom I've even considered a … well, a long-term relationship. So, the thought entered my mind, but you squelched that possibility."

"First person? Is there a second? You didn't put up much of a fight about cancelling. Why's that? You want to move to Minnesota?"

"Maybe if I loved somebody that lived there!" Sara sighed. Kate could feel her shaking her head. "But that's not the issue here."

"Oh, what is? You would move to Minnesota?"

There was a long pause. "No … maybe."

CHAPTER 31

October 8, 2012

MICK WAS sitting on the dock bench holding photos of Hope Town and other places on Elbow but looking out across the large bay he lived on. Lake Vermilion was known for sunsets, lending the water a rosy 'vermilion' tinge. The wind had died and the water was a mirror, unusual for Big Bay. The sun was reflecting purple off a dark cloud. The point to his left was honeyed, the late autumn sun illuminating it. Some of the islands in the distance were lit bright, others in dark shadows. The varying dimensions were amazing: the tip of a near point in light; a little farther, darkened Jackrabbit Island; a little farther the gap between Cherry and Ely Island not usually distinguishable in the distance, but apparent now in the lower light. Farther in the distance, maybe ten miles away, a lower ridge glowed with a higher dark one rolling down on top of it.

He was hoping to find a picture of Elbow worthy enough to use for the cover on his novel. He had named the novel *Back to the Island*. It was pretty easy to set the story in Hope Town. It was a remarkable place. He knew Heidi would have to go back to her island. He, himself, had some pangs of regret buying Vermilion. He knew he would love it and want to live here among the rivers, lakes, and forest, *and*, surprising him, there were almost no mosquitoes! There was almost always a breeze coming off the bay and no stagnant, standing water to breed the bastards. But, that would mean Elbow would be relegated to only cold weather visits. He'd see little of Wanda, Peewee, and Heidi, whether she returned to her island or not. Of course, winter was lovely up in the Arrowhead, the name given to the northeast corner of Minnesota. There was nothing like a good blizzard blowing off the lake, and facing it straight on in the sanctuary of a hot tub. But, unless something changed, he'd be in the tub alone. Nobody to share the scene with, like now. You couldn't explain a scene like this to somebody; she had to be there to experience it with you.

He felt his cell vibrate in his pocket. He saw it was Kate. "Hello, you. Having a good day, are ya?"

"Good as can be expected," she responded.

"Meaning what? Are your expectations high or low? Heard anything from Heidi, by the way?"

"No. Nothing has happened yet. My expectations, actually, are not being met."

"Nothing? How long has Peewee been there? Almost a week? What expectations?"

"He's only been there six days."

"Give me a break, six days is pretty damn close to a week!"

"No it's not. It's a whole extra day. Peewee could annihilate Manhattan in a day. A day's a long time in his life. My expectations of happiness."

"Annnnywayyy … ," drawn out in a parody of exasperation, "what is he going to do, you suppose? What are your expectations for happiness?"

"I imagine he's lying in wait, for the ambush, you know. I expect I may need to be with you."

CHAPTER 31

His heart literally leapt in his chest. "You're probably right," he came out with.

"Right? Right about what? That he's lying in wait, or I am?" she asked, tentatively.

He had trouble suppressing an involuntary grin, and it took him a second to respond. "Both, I hope."

"But I don't wanna live there," she said.

"I don't wanna live there," he said.

So, what we goin' to do? they both thought.

"Wait!" M said. "I got a call coming in. It's Heidi. I'll call you back."

"HEY! HOW are you, hon?"

"Hello, sir. It's nice to hear your voice."

"Likewise! I was just talking to Kate."

"Oh, good, sir. I'm really glad. You like me to call you back?"

"No, no, that's fine. I said I'd call her back, which I'll be doing after I talk to you. It's great to hear your voice." He realized he hadn't actually spoken to her—only emails. She didn't sound the same. "You sound older."

"I am, sir."

"Ha, ha. OK, more—more worldly, then."

"Is that good or bad, sir?"

For some reason it wasn't bothering him that she kept calling him "sir." Guess you can get used to anything if you accept how it is, he realized.

"Good. Good ... or is it? What's up with your father?"

"He just left. He took me out for a drink. That was a first, and then left to catch an evening flight."

"Really? What happened with Richard?"

"I have no idea, sir. Really."

"You didn't ask him?"

"No. If he had wanted to tell me, he would have. I probably don't want to know. All he said was I wouldn't be seeing that guy anymore."

"Holy shit. I wonder?"

"I've chosen not to, sir. I am relieved, though. Tell me what you're up to. How are sales with *A Million Dollars*? I really enjoyed it. Everything makes sense. I like that you equate 'rich' with being 'independent,' doing what you want with your life. Gives a little different feel for the meaning of money. How is it selling?"

"I've been so busy with *Back to the Island*, I haven't done any marketing myself. Right now I'm on my dock, the sunset behind me illuminating the islands and far shore, and just figured out what picture of Elbow I want to use for the cover on the novel."

"Color cover, sir?"

"I'd like it to be. I'd also like some cool color pictures, if not at the beginning of each chapter, at least each part."

"How many chapters? How many parts?"

"Thirty-five chapters; four parts."

"Pretty expensive to do color on that many chapters, sir."

MP laughed. "Our roles are reversed. I need you now to help me."

"Oh, I already have, sir. Your old student, my boss, Desiree, knows people in publishing. She says she can get appointments with some agents and publishing houses regarding the novel."

"No shit! Thank you very much, Heides."

Her turn to laugh. You're the only other person than Father to call me that. It's your friend that you'll be owing the thanks to, though. You might even consider self-publishing, sir. I

CHAPTER 31

can't see you getting on with most editors, I must say. You can be your own boss, do what you want with the book, and you make a lot more if it sells."

"Hey, what do you think of this marketing idea: the song 'Back to the Island' is the same allegory as the book. So, I wrote to Leon Russell ... you know him?"

"Yes, sir. Remember our conversation? I told you I also loved that song, and you were so surprised a back-island urchin, one of those delinquent, spiny things, like me had ever heard of 'Back to the Island.'"

"Back-island urchin, huh? I don't know about spiny or back-island, but, I have to admit, I did think of you a little urchin-ish."

Heidi giggled. It was good to hear the young-Heidi laugh. "I do like the metaphor, sir. I believe I understand it well."

"I was afraid of that. Anyway, wouldn't it be cool if an audio copy of the song could accompany the book somehow? In *A Little Short*, something I had started before *Back to the Island*, I have some lyrics from a song, with the same metaphor as the chapter, preceding each chapter. Seems like a cool idea ... almost a new genre: a disk could accompany the book. I also wrote a letter to Emmylou Harris and Mark Knopfler."

"Wow. You are optimistic, sir. What did you want of them?"

"What do you think of taking a number of great ballads and giving each to a good writer and having them create a short story of the song? You would buy the book with a CD that comes with it? That'd be like a new genre, no?"

"Very clever, sir. You're a lot smarter than you look."

"Hey, that's my line. Watch it!"

"Good luck with Leon. I've heard he's pretty private and not that accessible," she told him. "Don't know much about

BACK TO THE ISLAND

Emmylou and Mark, but I like them, and they write some great songs."

"Can't hurt to try."

"Even if you fall?" she snuck in, referring to her old plum poem.

"Would you laugh?" he came back with.

"Would you cry?" she countered.

"Oh, I really miss our sessions, and you. Got anything to send me?"

"They're coming out rather dreary these days. Almost as disheartening as Rashi's. He occasionally sends me something. You'd be really concerned by some. This one, for instance, I'll send it you; no, I'll read it. Listen," she read:

> **Fresh**
>
> Life is like a fresh oyster
> Swallow it whole, alive
> Or it's unbearable
>
> Everyone's trying to chew life up
> Why am I trying to swallow it whole
> It might be too big for my throat
> And burst my larynx
> Pop out and roll down my chest
>
> Don't even try to swallow
> Fresh oysters live
> Just loll them in your mouth
> Till one of you
> Starves to death.

"Holy shit," M said.

CHAPTER 31

"Yeah. No kidding. I am so worried about him. I don't dare send him one of my poems; they may just depress him more. I just write things—I don't know—I just try to talk to him like a friend. But I don't want you to think I'm depressed. I'm really not. Lonesome, I guess, for you and Mother, especially after seeing my father … and then not that much of him. He's a strange fellow."

"He's a great father and great friend," M said. "I think I'd trust him as much as anybody in the world. He sounds like he accomplished what he went to New York to do. I can't imagine him wanting to be there for very long."

"No. I think he was in a hurry to get back. You know those Haitians that were displaced because of the planned development site?"

"Yah."

"Well, they had moved back in and were cleaning up the mess. My father's guys, including Rashi, were helping Vernal and his Haitians. But the government asked them to clear out and when they didn't immediately, they threatened to arrest them. Peewee had arranged, before he came up here, for some islanders to temporarily take in all the young ones. I can't help but assume he anticipated more trouble. There are currently four young urchins Wanda is caring for. I know he was dying to get back to try to 'fix' things. He had been talking to the land trust people to annex the site to protect it. It sounds like the government is addicted to the idea of the spot creating money for whatever they have in mind."

"Did the articles we wrote have any impact?"

"Oh, yes. There are a lot of islanders all over the islands that would like any undeveloped land protected. But money talks. I hear that obnoxious cliché almost every day here."

"Crap. None of that sounds good."

"No, sir. Sara is coming over in a few minutes. She'll miss my father, of course, but I'll enjoy seeing her. She seemed like the sanest one of you all. Pretty, smart, and nice, too. I assume you agree?"

"What are you two going to do?" M asked, avoiding her question, almost afraid of what the little urchin might be implying.

"I'm making dinner and she's bringing a movie. Yes, I broke down and bought a little television, and a DVD player. I guess they're almost obsolete. Hard to keep up with the future in your United States of America."

M realized he had had a shit-eating grin on his face almost the entire time he was talking to her. Nothing new there. "Then I'll let you go. Let's talk often, OK?"

"Call me anytime, sir. I'll try to find an acceptable poem to send to you."

"You have my address up here in case you want to send me something?"

"Yes. I got it from Kate. But why not just email it?"

"Uh, yeah right, I suppose. Do you two communicate often?"

"Pretty regularly, especially lately of course, with both Kate and Sara," she answered. "I'm waiting with bated breath to see what, which, or who has the stronger pull, attraction—which you yield to."

"Huh? The strongest pull? What d'you mean?"

"Later. Let's see what happens. Bye now, sir. I better get back to my cooking. Don't want to burn anything."

"OK. Bye, hon. Have Sara call me, will you please? It sounds like you'll be safe now."

CHAPTER 31

"Don't worry about me, sir. Take care of yourself. Bye."

And she was gone. What did the little shit mean? He was learning her instincts; her perceptions and intuitions were unerring, almost unnerving. Which has the stronger pull? Hmmm.

He punched up Kate. After several rings he hung up before it went to voicemail. He couldn't shake the feeling that she was in a relationship. Sara had said she wasn't dating, but he found that hard to believe. He, when he thought about it, almost hoped she was. In spite of her professing her love, she just didn't seem like the type to sit at home pining away. A shiver seized him. It had been a clear, warm-for-October day, Indian summer they called it in this neck of the woods. But as soon as the sun sunk behind the trees this time of year, in the shadows a chill set in, the wind hinting of the winter, whispering through the pines: "I'm on my way."

PART V

"Well what do you know the comedy's a tragedy."

.
.
.

CHAPTER 32

M ENJOYED winter kayaking and paddled until the lake froze over. It had been an unusually warm and late fall so the ice came late, but even before the lake froze hard, an early blizzard blew in, dropping several feet of snow, allowing for both great kayaking, and cross-country skiing earlier than usual. He loved the look of water bordered with snow. The white looked whiter and the blue a remarkable shade—bluer than blue.

Because of all this he had put off going back down to Elbow, and now it was late November, almost Thanksgiving. He often talked to Heidi. He wondered how long she would last in New York City. She said the job was good; she had made some friends. She had had some dates, and although there was nobody special, several of the guys had become friends. She said the creep that had ogled her before was benign, that she had scared him off. M, surprised, couldn't convince her to make a visit to Vermilion. He had had a nice talk with her boss, Desiree, his old student, and apparently HS was upbeat at work, was an excellent employee, and had been given a hefty raise. But, he could more *sense* something and hear it in her voice. She was always happy to talk to him, he could tell, and so appeared upbeat. But, there was something; she just wasn't the Heidi he used to know. Of course, she was getting older, growing up, living in the big city. But something was

CHAPTER 32

... what? Definitely different but more like something was ... he couldn't put his finger on it.

He had emailed both Sara and Kate about meeting him and Heidi on neutral ground in New York and then possibly accompanying them down to Elbow for a respite from the cold. He hadn't heard back from either.

An email popped up on his computer on Sat., Dec. 15, a few days before the trip. There was no message, only:

Date:	December 15, 2012
To:	M
From:	Heidi
Subject:	Cold

The singing summer sidewalks
turn to cold December death walks.
Must we always see the green to have
faith enough to sing?

He immediately tried to call Heidi but had to leave a message, so emailed her as well. He was alarmed, although not really surprised. It was getting near Christmas, so

| 547

she was bound to be lonely and homesick. Except this didn't really sound like lonely; more like despair. All he had emailed was: "Call me!"

He emailed her again later when she hadn't returned his call. He called her. Had to leave a message.

After several hours of fitfully roiling around in his bed, he got up and checked his emails. It was three a.m. and there was one from Heidi:

Date: December 16, 2012
To: M
From: Heidi
Subject: What do you know

Sir: Rashi's dead. They, the authorities, say it was suicide, which shouldn't surprise me, considering what he writes, but it does. Here is his last email:

Dancer

I am dancing
A slow, complicated dance
Alone, I fear
In a hall
Of glittering gems, dazzling lights
And a bitter chill

I can see nothing
Save the shadows and blurs,
I may be alone
Or
We may keep dancing together
Kept apart by shadows and blurs

CHAPTER 32

I should call her
But I can't
If I find out I am alone
The cold will kill me

Perhaps we are dancing together
She seeking me
I seeking her
The shadows and blurs hindering us

But most likely
I am a fool
Dancing alone
With blurs to protect me
Shadows to hide me
And the cold to keep me company

He knew I was coming home. He knew I was considering staying home. Why would he kill himself?

Peewee, Vernal, and the other people squatting at the settlement site have been arrested. The police say it wasn't them that did the arresting. We don't know where they are, except for Rashi, of course, whose body shows up inexplicably. Suicide, my foot!

I must go back to the island. My mother needs me. My father needs me. I'm afraid Rashi needed me. I might need you. I'm going to try to get a morning flight.

Love, HS

CHAPTER 33

M TRIED calling Heidi again. Why wasn't she answering? He left a message saying he was heading down to Elbow. He'd have to drive down to Minneapolis and try to get a flight out to somewhere that had flights to Marsh Harbour. He threw some warm weather clothes in a suitcase, packed a sandwich, and filled a thermos with coffee. It was still dark as he got under way at about 4:15 a.m.

He called Sara and Kate on the way to tell them what had occurred. He had to leave messages for both, of course, it being the middle of the night. Sara had called back right away. Anxious to get home early for the Christmas season, she was already in flight from DC to Spokane on an SEC private jet. When M told her what was going on, she said she'd talk to the pilot and call him right back. Within minutes, she called back. She told him the pilot said "no problem" landing at the Minneapolis/St. Paul airport, especially since they were flying right over it, assuming he could get clearance, and would pick up M and would fly them to where they needed to catch a flight to Marsh Harbour.

M at first refused. This was way too much to expect. He asked if she wouldn't get in any trouble using an SEC jet for personal reasons. Sara responded that she might feel a little guilty for the extra fuel to get them to, probably, Fort Lauderdale, since it was the least busy airport that had flights

CHAPTER 33

to Marsh Harbour, but that this was pretty much her personal pilot that flew her all over the US. He was fine with it as long as it was a domestic destination. She said she had no superiors who would question her. She pointed out that it was one of the busiest travel times of the year over Christmas, so it would be unlikely M would find a last-minute seat on a commercial flight out, and so not to worry or argue; this was the only solution to getting them there. They would check, in flight, to see if, indeed, Fort Lauderdale was the best choice or if either Miami or Orlando might be better.

M had noticed Sara kept saying "them." When he asked her why, she said she would be going with him. He was so shocked he didn't argue on the phone, assuming he would talk her out of it later. It was a three-and-a-half- to four-hour drive from Vermilion to the airport, but by the time they got permission to land, taxi in, and arrange to pick up M, the timing would be pretty good, especially since M would get there in less than three hours. When they rendezvoused in Minneapolis, M would argue then that this was too close to Christmas and Sara should be in Spokane, with her sister.

When they connected at the airport, Sara simply responded to his objections with: "Priorities," and uncharacteristically: "Shut up! I think we're going to need some of my contacts to get to the bottom of this. So drop the argument and the apologies."

It turned out to be best to fly from Minneapolis into Fort Lauderdale, the only airport to have a flight they could make—at twelve thirty p.m.—on Bahama Air direct to Marsh Harbour. All the later flights went to Nassau and were full. If they missed the one in Fort Lauderdale, they'd just spend the night in Fort Lauderdale and catch an even earlier flight the next morning. Fortunately the outer islands in the Bahamas, like Elbow, were not hot tourist spots for Christmas, like Nassau and Providence Island. More people were flying *out* of Marsh Harbour than *in*. The pilot said that getting there in time would be close, that it would depend on when they got clearance to land. Fort Lauderdale, although not as busy, was not as big an airport and so they might not be as lucky getting clearance right away.

Everything had gone smoothly in Minneapolis as, being a large international airport, they didn't have to use the main terminal. There was plenty of room in an adjacent area used primarily for the government, where M could leave his truck. They were not so lucky with Fort Lauderdale, though. It turned out they had to circle for several hours before they got clearance and missed the flight to Marsh Harbour.

They found an available room at the Airport H & L (hotel and lounge). The hotel had a shuttle from the airport. By the time they got to the hotel, they were starved. When they checked in they found out that the reason this room was available was because it was one usually reserved for airline personnel and was small and utilitarian: no sofa, and only a double bed. M had winked at Sara and bumped his hip against hers. She had responded by telling him: "Relax, buddy. You get the carpet."

They brought their stuff up to the room and headed right back down to the restaurant. They slid into an overused and cracked-vinyl booth, each taking a deep breath, leaning their elbows on the table, and for the first time relaxed enough to really look at each other. At first neither knew what to say, do, or think about this new adventure they were embarking on. So, for several seconds they just gazed, both feeling a little

CHAPTER 33

foolish, at each other. Slowly a smile snuck onto both their faces, and they broke out laughing.

"Well, isn't this interesting?" M finally said.

"Oh, and just what do you find so interesting? The double bed?"

"We—e—ll, no," he lied. "But you, for starters," he answered, not lying, ignoring the allusion to the bed, knowing it was an illusion but definitely finding the predicament interesting. "You know what you've done here for me is something you'd only do for … family, I'd say. You know? And I can't thank you enough."

Her smile dwindled as she sprawled back in the booth, uncharacteristically casual, not removing her eyes from his. "Listen, you've thanked me enough, OK? No more thanks. You'd a done it for me."

"Sure, if I had a private plane at my disposal. OK, but one last time: Thank you!" He felt like he was on a first date. It was weird. He wanted to be gracious, for sure, but also clever, witty, interesting. Why he was feeling like this, he didn't know. Wasn't this just Sara?

"Oh, by the way," she said, "I really don't want to talk about this now, but besides Kate's testimony nabbing Richard, they're appealing, but the CEO has been found culpable as well. So it'll be very interesting to see the ripple effects."

"God, wouldn't it be cool if Kate's testimony sets a precedent and they start to clean up the investment banking business?"

"We hope so," Sara sighed and slouched even lower in the booth.

A bored waitress appeared and plopped a couple menus down on the Formica, asked if they wanted anything to drink, and looked at M first for some reason.

"You want to go first?" M asked, nodding to Sara.

The waitress shifted her weight from one hip to the other, rolled her eyes, and looked at Sara, who laughed. "I'll have a glass of water and a glass of white wine, please—just your house white."

M noticed that, although Sara seemed soft-spoken and unassuming, there was a precision to her tone and choice of words that lent them a finality, a completion there was no arguing with. It was the first time he had been with her in *her* element, separate and divorced from the influence of her overbearing 'older' sister. Sara *was* the majorly successful one, after all. "Sara got the brains," as Kate had told him. She had also said Sara had gotten the looks. This new vision of Sara in this new context, not just-the-other-sister, surprised and even stunned him a bit.

The waitress shifted to her other hip and looked down at him with half-open eyes. He must be slap-happy, he thought as he found this hysterical. Laughing, probably inappropriately he felt, he told her: "I'll have a glass of water as well, please, and a martini. Do you have Boodles gin?"

"What?" was all the enthusiastic waitress could muster.

"What what?" M asked, trying not to laugh.

"Uh, what's Buddles?"

M looked sideways at Sara, who still had a little smile on her face but was shaking her head, telling him to cool it, he supposed. "Might be a type of gin?" he answered, unable to tone down the sarcasm, starting to feel a little bad that he was making fun of her, even though she deserved it. "Tell you what: ask the bartender if he has Boo-dles gin. If he does, throw a splash of vermouth in with it, on the rocks. If no Boodles, try Bombay Sapphire instead. Thank you."

CHAPTER 33

Miss Charm, who had been holding her pad, ready to write in apathetic anticipation, dropped it, along with the hand, and said in a pathetic attempt at attitude: "Bombay *what?*"

Sara, stifling a laugh and fearing M, being tired and hungry, might display his Irish temper—much like his father might have—said: "Just bring us both a Tanqueray martini on the rocks with a splash of vermouth and a couple onions—cocktail onions—on a skewer."

"Toothpick?" M stuck in. The way she was looking at Sara pissed him off, but he knew he was showing off, trying to appear clever and 'the man' for Sara. He knew immediately this wouldn't work with her.

"Please," Sara said. "Thank you."

Miss Charm turned without writing it down and slugged off, shaking her head.

"Temper, temper, my dear Irishman," Sara said, still shaking her head. "Being a cheap little bar and restaurant in a cheap airport hotel, I'm sure she's been hardened by weary, ugly travelers." She certainly wasn't one of the 'ugly' travelers. It was weird. Had she been this remarkable-looking in Hope Town?

"When we get our martinis, I'm switching—she's gonna spit in mine," M kidded.

"Uh-uh! No way. You deserve it. You asked for more than spit."

"Heck, *she* was the one with the attitude."

"Heck, eh? Thanks, I guess, for trying to be polite to me, I suppose. Why let poor unhappy people affect you?"

"There's that 'eh!' Is that Spokan-ese?"

Sara laughed. M wasn't too sure how entertaining he was being, but she seemed to be enjoying herself, maybe in spite of himself. It worried him that he might be acting a

| 555

little over the top because it was so important to him that she like him.

"Kate uses 'eh' more than I do. She spends, except the last year or so, more time in that neck of the woods than I do. Spokane's not too distant from Canada, you know?"

"Cana— what?"

"Oh, shut up, fool."

The second time she'd told him to "shut up." Was that good or bad? M leaned back in his booth as well, and they both sat there, sprawled, appraising each other, both with just a suggestion of a shit-eating grin. Neither said anything for several minutes, M not feeling uncomfortable in the silence. Sara maintained the slight smile. Her eyes crinkled when she smiled, M realized; Kate's did not. Both continued to calmly, silently gaze at each other. He got the feeling that Sara maybe felt like Kate should be here, too. Sara had not really said anything that actually implied that, but it was a feeling he was getting.

Suddenly M, feeling he needed to do or say something, popped up like he had been probed. "Should we discuss anything more about Kate, Peewee, or why we're down here?"

Sara slowly shook her head. "Nah. I'm rather burned out. Another topic, please."

"Well, I'm feeling pretty guilty you being here on my account this close to Christmas."

The slow shake continued. "I seem to remember me telling you to 'shut up' about that. You hear me complaining?"

Hmm, another "shut up," sort of. "Then tell me something about my, our, father—other than he skied through the window of the bar he had gotten wasted in. Kate wouldn't talk about him."

CHAPTER 33

Sara now leaned up to the table as well. Her face nearing his disconcerted him, sending a little electric jolt to his senses. "Hmm, let's see. He was a good father. He was important in our lives. He was a lot like you ... and Kate, even though he wasn't her biological father. I took after our mom."

"How like me? And what about the part of him that's like me did Kate not like?"

"That's a pretty combobulated sentence you've put together there."

"'Combobulated?' Now that does not sound like you. Is it even a word? Isn't it 'discombobulated?'"

"Discombobulated sounds like you're not combobulated, which to me sounds like 'confused.' See, you and Kate are just alike."

"How's that?"

"I had told her that you had had to have been discombobulated down there in Hope Town. She said the same thing you just said—that it didn't sound like me."

"But we're both right. It doesn't."

"That's one way you're like your father ... and Kate: competitive, combative, important that you're right."

"Hmm, interesting. What was Kate's problem with him if he was a good father?"

"He may have been a better father than husband. Kate felt that way, anyway. She thought he was unfaithful to our mother. He never got caught or anything," she added quickly.

"Then why did she think he was unfaithful?"

"He sort of implied it. It was like he held it over Mother's head ... maybe in an attempt to try to control her, by making her think he could have another woman, anytime."

"Doesn't sound cool," M said, thinking back, wondering about himself. Is this why he was so friendly to all his woman friends? He hoped not.

"It wasn't cool; it was a weakness. Personally, I don't think he had other women … that way. He was charismatic, an engaging guy. But insecure. He could be charming and used compliments very effectively. Women were drawn to him and liked that in him."

"Wouldn't anybody?"

"Of course, but he was exceptional at it. It infuriated Kate. You realize, you sleeping with Lottie is like proof of her suspicions about your father. Plus, because she suspected him, she felt protective of our mother, which just exacerbated the situation. His self-aggrandizement, his self-promotion irritated her to no end. Of course, as you know, she is much like that, herself."

"You?"

"Me? As I said, I am more like my mother. She wasn't as concerned as Kate about his little flirtations. I understood my father. Kate didn't. He kind of had a 'little man' complex, even if he wasn't so little. Just a little short, like you. He had to show he was good at something, that he could do anything better than anybody. Of course he couldn't. So, rather than get infuriated with him, my mother and I realized this was a shortcoming."

"I don't follow; maybe I'm too short?" Maybe he didn't want to follow.

"Ri—ight. Simply: he was always trying to prove himself. *And*, he was a very successful businessman. We were well off, and Mom was well taken care of. But he was never satisfied. It's what killed him: he couldn't go fast enough. His tragic flaw, literally, as it turns out."

CHAPTER 33

It was rather frightening for M to hear about deficiencies in his natural-born father, whom he never knew, that may have been passed on to him genetically. He knew he was too aggrandizing at times, too competitive. "So," he asked Sara, "how would you abridge a comparison of Kate and me?"

"I don't think I want to do this. You and Kate need to work out your differences ... similarities, actually."

"So, we *are* a lot alike?"

Sara sighed. "Yes, of course. You know that."

"Very difficult to analyze ourselves. People like us don't have very good self-perception. We're too busy promoting what we're not, which is quite the irony."

Sara laughed. "But I would want to point out that that statement was actually pretty darn self-aware. I'm impressed. Maybe there's hope for you after all."

"Thank you. Oops, I'm not supposed to say that."

Sara rolled her eyes. "If you want the abridged version: the word I would use for you both is 'pugnacious.'"

"Pugnacious? You mean argumentative?"

"No. That's why I didn't want to do this. Argumentative has negative connotations, and so is a judgment. I am not judging!"

"So, you mean that I'm ... we're ... tenacious?"

"No, no. That has connotations, too ... usually positive, at least. But that would still qualify as a judgment as well."

"Doesn't every word carry a connotation?"

Sara leaned into him across the table. "Let's just leave it at this: you asked, I answered. Pugnacious. That's it. You take it the way you like."

Just then, as it was time to change the subject, they both realized they hadn't seen a glass of water, a martini, or a

| 559

waitress for quite a while. Both could use a drink and were hungry.

M raised his arm to get her attention, first sticking up one finger, then two, then his whole hand, then waving it calmly, then waving it maniacally, then …

"Waitress!" Sara snapped, not angry, but resolute, impossible to ignore. M, impressed, smiled, thinking of the movie *The Graduate*.

Miss Charm turned abruptly, moped over to the table, but looked concerned.

Sara addressed her calmly: "Throw those two watered-down martinis away that have been sitting on the bar, and have the bartender make two new ones; go get us two waters, now please; then get and bring us the martinis; by then we will be ready to order. If we aren't served in fifteen minutes, we will not be paying for our meals or our drinks. Thank you. Shall we call over the manager to ensure he approves?" Somehow, she did this inoffensively. Mick knew, of course, he or Kate would have been angry and probably obnoxious and gotten nowhere.

The change in Miss Charm was remarkable. She straightened, looked over her shoulder, like she thought the manager was right there, replied: "Yes, ma'am; I mean, no, ma'am. I'll take care of it right away. Excuse me." The waters arrived in twenty seconds, the fresh martinis in two minutes, and the burgers which they ordered, although not M's choice companion with martinis but probably the safest bet in this joint, in fifteen on the nose, as it turned out.

M had watched in fascination. So this was how she managed all those number crunchers and whomever else she was in charge of. He smiled to himself: of course, how else could

CHAPTER 33

she have risen to the top of a large organization like the SEC without chutzpa?

While drinking their martinis and waiting for what turned out to be mediocre burgers and under-fried fries, Sara did bring up Kate: "One reason why Kate is so angry with you for your latest liaison with Lottie, I believe, is as it relates to her feelings about not trusting your father. This is obviously deep-seated. For her to cancel that summer visit, affecting her, you, me, and Barney couldn't have been easy for her."

M got the feeling there was more to it and that Sara was covering for her sister, creating excuses, even for why she wasn't here, now. "You realize that …"

"Please don't go into it," Sara cut him off before he could start rationalizing. "I am not holding anything against you or judging either of you … in this combobulation you two have created."

M broke out laughing just as Miss Urgency humbly hurried over with the burgers, causing her to freeze, platter in hand. "No, sorry," he explained, "not laughing at you. Let's see those burgers. We're famished."

When she had left, between bites, M asked: "So, that's it, you think? Kate and I are done? No brother-sister, no … you know?"

Sara looked over her burger at him while taking a bite. When she was done chewing: "You mean no nookie-nookie? No husband and wife?"

"Yeah."

"Could you be satisfied and content with a brother-sister relationship?"

"Don't know."

"When will you know? How will you know?"

| 561

"Don't know. Sorry, but I thought we'd figure everything out on that summer visit. It seemed intriguing, too ... you know Kate and me, you and Barney."

"Why? To make it easier for Kate to move to Minnesota because I'd be there, too?"

"Sorry, that was mean. Look, let me make this perfectly clear. Forget about Barney and me, OK? I like Barney. He's a great guy. That was four days under very unusual circumstances down there in Hope Town. Not gonna happen, OK?"

"OK," M answered, and he felt relieved ... about what, exactly, he wasn't sure. "So, Kate and I?"

She diddled with a fry, flapping it around, trying to get it to point at him. "Damn thing's flaccid," she finally said.

He realized that downing the martini fast on an empty stomach must be affecting her. Her speech had lost that precision, as had her way with the fry. "Flaccid?" he repeated, and laughed.

"Oh, shut up!" she told him, again, for the fourth time. Then, out of nowhere she threw the fry at him and said, not angrily but slurring a tad: "Ya think I enjoy being caught in the middle of your combobulation? Huh? I'm done talkin' 'bout it, hear! Now finish your shitty burger and let's go to bed."

"Now that sounds like a good ..."

"Shut up, you! I already told ya," she interrupted, "You know what I mean. Prepare to grab some carpet."

Fifth time.

He muffled his laugh by sticking the bun and dry meat in his mouth, taking his final bite. Sara plopped hers, half-eaten, down on the plate, pushed it away, and drained her water.

On the way up to the room, she insisted that a break from work was no problem, that she could, pretty much, work when

CHAPTER 33

she wanted to, that over Christmas and even with New Year's the SEC pretty much shut down anyway. She said that typically Washington, DC did too, but that they were paying the price for their stubborn partisanship pandering this year, and the politicians had to hang around to the last minute to fix the fiscal cliff impasse. The entire economy was on the edge of a precipice, causing the country to suffer from acrophobia. Served the damn politicians right, she said. They should have and could have come to a compromise a long time ago. They could work on Christmas day if they didn't pull their heads out of their asses.

When they got to the room, M, still smiling at this 'new' side of Sara, wondered how the martinis might affect the sleeping arrangements. They both stood staring at the bed. "OK, listen," Sara proposed, "we stay fully clothed—no nighty, got it? You face one way; I, the other. No spooning and no inadvertent rolling over and trying to remove anything or you're on the floor. Got it?"

"Deal," he said, and stuck out his hand to shake on it. She looked at the hand and slapped it away. Maybe she was more like Kate than she wanted to admit ... with one exception: she wasn't trying to hurt him.

They took turns in the bathroom and cautiously climbed into bed, back to back. Although exhausted, both had trouble going immediately to sleep, gripping their own precipice: their side of the narrow bed. Eventually they both fell into a light slumber, jolting each time they felt their butts bump. But the bed sagged toward the middle, drawing them together. Eventually they just gave in and went to sleep, both inadvertently sporting a little grin, butt firmly to butt.

They awoke early, at the same time, neither feeling very well rested. They both showered quickly, taking turns in the bathroom, went down for the complimentary breakfast, and caught the shuttle for the airport and first flight of the day at nine a.m. for Marsh Harbour. There were several open seats on the early flight.

They got off fine, but it was going to be a windy landing, and the twin prop puddle jumper pitched up and down and swayed back and forth as it neared the runway. Sara held on tight to M's thigh as if he might land safely even if the little plane didn't. M, of course, didn't mind.

They caught a taxi to the ferry, and after a choppy crossing, jumped on M's cart, dropped their stuff off at the cottage, finding it sandy but not damaged, and continued down the lane to the path to Peewee and Wanda's, pulling into the bushes as much as possible to park. Mick led Sara up the path and when they rounded the corner of the coral crop, Sara's interest was piqued as she thought she heard drums, letting out a surprised whoop when she saw the ship protruding from the coral wall behind it.

"Oh my God," she uncharacteristically shrieked as she circled around, looking up at it. "You both described this to me, but … my God! It's so wonderful. What a place to live. And the view!" she exploded. They had talked little, M serious in contemplation as they got closer to facing Wanda, and Sara respecting that. So this release of pent-up emotion surprised M. Sara, even drunk playing on the beach, had always been much more reserved than her sister. M was pleasantly surprised at her spontaneous, if for her a little inappropriate, outburst. Everything about her now seemed a new adventure to him. Kate wore all her emotions on her

CHAPTER 33

sleeve. What you saw was what you got. Sara was more of an enigma, a curiosity, a curveball, a mystery ... much like a little urchin he knew.

They both stopped and looked up at the decks looming above them. Suddenly they noticed Wanda's head peeking over the railing on the first deck, almost as if she had just materialized there.

M and Sara waved. Wanda did not wave back. "Oh, Mick ... I mean M," Sara whispered, "do you think I offended her by wailing away the way I did? I'm sorry."

"Nah. She's probably just worried. Let's go talk to her and Heidi."

M walked Sara in and down the hall to the main stairway, skipping the spiral staircase that led up to the deck they had seen Wanda on. Sara vociferated the entire time but more subdued, yet hardly able to contain herself as they reached the top of the stairs and came onto the main cabin. They found Wanda behind the kitchen counter scrambling to find food and drink for her unexpected guests.

They took cheese, crackers, and fruit juices out onto the deck to get the lowdown from Wanda on the recent events. They noticed several children playing on the rocks down below by the calmer seaside. Several of the island boys—really, young men—were down there with them.

"Wanda," M said, as they sat at the table, "this is Sara, Kate's sister. She has a very important job with the government of the United States. She's here to help."

Wanda nodded to Sara and attempted a smile.

"Wanda, I'm so very glad to meet you. I'm sorry I was so loud when I saw your place. It is so wonderful," Sara said, apologizing.

Wanda garnished another little smile and pushed the plate with crackers toward M.

"Where is Heidi, Wanda?" M asked cautiously, concerned that she hadn't been there to greet them.

Wanda looked at her hands folded on the table. They were trembling, M and Sara noticed. Sara laid her hands over Wanda's and gently squeezed them. "Heidi says she can't come home for Christmas. Say she must finish up her work so she can stay home when she get here."

M could tell there was more. "When's the last time you heard from her?"

"I called and email her yesterday and today, but she not answer yet. Her boss, she email me back. Say Heidi in hospital."

"What?" M said, shifting to the edge of his chair. "What's wrong with her? Did something happen?"

Wanda shrugged. Although she was trying very hard to keep her composure, they could tell she was close to the edge. Her entire little body was starting to shake. "Sometimes she have problems," she managed to get out, her voice trembling. "Don't want to talk about it, please."

M looked over at Sara, who grimaced. "Can you tell us the latest on Peewee, I mean Todd?" M asked, wondering if he should even bring this up, now.

She continued to look at her hands, but Sara's holding and caressing them was seeming to calm her. "We don't know where they are. Police say they don't have them."

"What about Vernal?" M asked.

"No one knows what to do. Todd always the one to take care of everything. We're just waiting. Police not giving us any answers."

"*All* the people from the site are gone? They, whoever, have taken them *all* somewhere?"

CHAPTER 33

Wanda nodded. "All but the children that Todd made leave. There are some here, now."

"I know. I noticed them down by the water." Peewee must have been expecting trouble, M figured. "What about Rashi? Heidi said he was staying here to protect you? Do you know what happened to him?"

Wanda again shrugged. "He took the boat into Marsh Harbour to get food ... and never came back. The police say he committed suicide." She started to cry, pulling her hands from under Sara's, and covered her face.

M and Sara gave each other a worried look. "Dear," Sara started in a remarkably calm and reassuring voice, gently hugging Wanda's shoulders, "we will find out what happened and where Todd is, I assure you. I will also have the authorities in New York City check on Heidi. I'm sure she's fine, but we will check."

Sara looked over at M. "I think we should go so I can contact whom I need to." She leaned in close to Wanda, almost whispering in her ear. "I have many contacts in our government who will check with the authorities here in the Bahamas. We will get to the bottom of this, I promise you. We'll make sure Heidi is OK and safe, too. OK?"

Wanda turned, wiped her eyes, and grabbed Sara's hands. "Thank you, Sara." Then at Mick: "You are very good friends. Bless you."

"Will you be all right if we go? Do you feel safe with the boys here?" M asked.

Wanda nodded.

On the way out, M walked down to the water to talk to the guys. They said they had been told Heidi felt guilty leaving her boss and company in the lurch during the busiest season of the year and so had decided to stay until just after Christmas, tie up all loose ends with her apartment and job, and come back to the island for good. When M asked about the hospital, they looked at each other, finally saying that wasn't anything really new. Once, she had been gone for a long time.

They hadn't heard anything from Peewee or Vernal. Before Peewee had left for New York, he had gotten permission from the government to let the squatters move back if they agreed to clean up the site. But they needed to be prepared to leave at any time. Peewee had told them he had made headway with the land trust, especially since the squatters were cleaning up the site. But, as with all bureaucracies, it was going to be slow going.

Apparently the government still had an interest in developing the site. They didn't say with whom, but it had been suggested that it was the Chinese, but that was maybe just a rumor because it had been the Chinese that had developed Providence Island where the casinos and nightlife already were. When Peewee had returned from New York, he made sure all the children had been removed from the site. He had left Rashi back with Wanda to watch over his place, and had camped out with some of his islanders at the site because much larger, foreign-type boats had been moored out off the reef for several days. Then, one day, with both Peewee and Vernal there, all the squatters had disappeared. The paper reported that they had been arrested, but the Bahamian government denied any involvement.

M asked what they knew about Rashi's death. They looked at each other and explained that they didn't know much. The story was that he had cut his own throat, killing himself. Rashi had been sad and maybe depressed they said, but why go to

CHAPTER 33

Marsh Harbour for groceries and then take your own life … especially by cutting your own throat?

M asked where Harvey was. They had looked at each other, shrugged, and said they didn't know.

M and Sara left, stopping to check one more time on Wanda, telling her they would return the next day. Wanda insisted planning on them for Christmas. Sara insisted she would come to help. Wanda didn't put up much resistance.

MP felt bad leaving her, but at this time of the year it wasn't going to be easy for Sara to get ahold of the people she needed to. She said she'd be calling in some 'markers.' Wanda was used to Peewee getting in scrapes and disappearing for a while, but he had always returned. MP had a queasy feeling in his gut about this one, though. Sara had given Wanda a hug and told her to try not to worry. M had reminded her that, after all, this was Mr. T., which he had immediately regretted when he got one of Wanda's hard looks in return.

On the way back to the cottage, Sara told Mick that she would make some calls right away before it got to be too late in the day to catch anybody. It was less than a week away from Christmas but, ironically, due to all the politicians still in Washington for the fiscal cliff fiasco, there would be a lot of security people still around as well. With the first call to her office in Washington she was able to get a subordinate to agree to get an SEC 'protective detail' officer in Manhattan to run over, first to the hospital, then to Heidi's apartment if she wasn't there, then to her boss's place if she wasn't there, finally to where she worked. They'd find her and ensure she was OK.

Rather than have M hover, Sara told him to go get them something to eat in Hope Town. She said she'd have to make several phone calls and probably several emails to get to the right people that would have access to and clout with the Bahamian and possibly Great Britain's government.

He asked how in the world she would be able to get government officials, who took years to get anything done, if ever, to move this quickly ... especially something of seemingly little importance to anyone but Sara and M.

Her answer was pretty cynical: anyone in a position of power and authority had something to hide, financially. They all knew it would behoove them to do what they could to be on the good side of the Securities and Exchange Commission. M asked if that didn't hint of blackmail. Sara shrugged and said it was reality and that they didn't know favors would pull no weight with her anyway. You can't con an honest man, she said, but you can certainly con a con. And, today in politics, that would be a con 'person.'

Mick took off in his cart to pick up a couple chicken dinners from Munchie's, a Bahamian-owned little carry-out shack reputed to have the best chicken in the Abacos. All the way into Hope Town he was grinning ear to ear and shaking his head. Who woulda thunk it, that a cute, plumpish, mild-mannered, soft-spoken, pleasant, loveable, squeezable, nice, understanding, nonjudgmental, sincere, compassionate, loveable—had he already said that—sweet lady could control government officials? Obviously he should add 'intelligent' and 'powerful' to the list.

Could she actually cause that which made the system so corrupt—greed—to backfire on the transgressors? Use it against the abusers? There were groups camping out, protesting, running airplanes into buildings, writing diatribes pages and pages long, bitching (including himself) in any ear available, trying to get back at a system that they felt was unfair and

CHAPTER 33

corrupt … when all you really had to do was to understand what caused the corruption—greed—and be in a position to say: hey, asshole, do what I want or I'll not only look and find what you've done, tell everyone what you've done, but put you behind bars just for the fun of it if I want to.

When M got back, Sara was upstairs showering and establishing herself in Kate's old room. M threw on a fresh pair of pants and a sweatshirt and waited for Sara on the porch. When she came down, she had on her familiar fuchsia terry cloth running suit. They warmed up the chicken dinner in the mike and sat at the table on the porch to eat. Sara said they would hear back anytime about Heidi, but that it would be tomorrow before they would possibly know anything about Peewee.

After eating, they both grabbed a windbreaker and took off for a walk on the beach. December weather was cooler, cloudier, and more variable. Storms were always a threat. Hurricane Sandy had blown through in October with strong winds but no rain. The result was less damage to buildings, but many plants, bushes, and trees had been left dry and ravaged. M had been glad he wasn't here for it but had been anxious to get back to check on the cottage. On the beach they saw much of the sand had been blown off and washed up against the dune, altering the shore significantly. It didn't look like the same place.

While they were walking, Sara got a call from her office. To get out of the wind they had huddled behind a large tree that had been washed up. She was told by the security officer that located Heidi in the hospital that she had been walking home from work early on Tuesday the 20th because she was going to be going back into work later that night. She had turned the corner in the hallway of her apartment building, a supposedly well-secured building, and had been surprised to see someone at her door messing with the doorknob. Scared, she had hustled back to her workplace, and Desiree, her boss, had taken her to her own apartment, but when they had arrived an ambulance had been summoned. The security guy couldn't discover what the medical problem was.

The police had already been informed about the break-in and were going to investigate, which might take a while since there was a lot more serious shit going down in the naked city. Apparently Heidi had just wanted to try to get home to Elbow, but it had been decided she should stay put in the hospital for now.

M and Sara speculated on their way back what would precipitate first, the need for hospitalization and, second, the guy at the door. It was probably not related *directly* to Richard, since they assumed Peewee had taken care of that ... but *indirectly*? The timing of both Peewee *and* this seemed pretty coincidental—*and* Rashi on top of it! Sara decided she would get ahold of her office and request that, if a couple security people were available, to keep their eyes on Heidi's apartment and guard her hospital room. M guessed someone would be available.

When they got back to the cottage, M found an email from Heidi, and Sara had one from Kate. Heidi's basically retold what they already knew, apologizing for causing any concern, that she was fine, not elaborating. M called Wanda while Sara went up to her room to call Kate in private. Wanda had finally gotten an email from Heidi as well, and M felt he eased her apprehension when he told her somebody official would be keeping an eye on Heidi, that maybe they could get her home

CHAPTER 33

for Christmas yet. Wanda didn't want to talk about Heidi's ailment or whatever it was, either. M didn't really know what to think of this, but he felt until they figured something out about Peewee, she might be safest under guard. This was really beginning to piss him off. What was wrong with her and who or what the hell was behind this?

When Sara came down, she handed the phone to M, telling him it was Kate.

"Hello?" he ventured, having no conception if he was excited to be talking to her, irritated, lonely for her, or ... what?

"Mick! It's me, Kate."

He figured he must be irritated because he wanted to yell: "MP dammit!" and "Don't ya suppose I know who it is?"

"Sorry to hear about Heidi, Peewee ... and Rashi! He was a really cool kid. I really feel bad about that. He was destined to be someone—a leader. But it sounds like Heidi's OK, right?"

"Did you get an email from her?"

"No, but I'm going to email her when we're off. It looks like she can get emails in her room, right? How are *you* doing?"

"I'm pissed!"

"Oh, I'm really sorry I can't be down there. I just can't. I'm right in the middle of two Christmas PR campaigns. Can you maybe fly back with Sara, even by Christmas? Wouldn't it be fun for the three of us to spend Christmas together?"

OK, this irritated him, too. It seemed self-centered of her to think it was her, not the situation with Heidi and Peewee, that pissed him off; and she was obviously more concerned about *her* not spending Christmas with him and Sara, Sara being the one she was probably most concerned about, than maybe a life and death situation with her old friends. Was he like that? Was it even egocentric for him to believe that his concern for Peewee and Heidi was more important than Kate being with her sister? Why should he visit her in Spokane when she wouldn't come to Minnesota? Being around Sara was making him more cognizant of his own behavior, he realized. What was that about? And what would Sara do now—stay with him until they knew what was going on, or head home? She had told Wanda that she would help her on Christmas. But from what Kate had said, Sara must not have told Kate that.

"Don't know," he answered. "I mean, yes, it would be fun to be together on Christmas, but I don't think I could enjoy myself until whatever is happening here and with Heidi is cleared up."

"Won't the authorities handle it?"

"Maybe." He didn't want to talk to her anymore. "Kate, I have to get going. If you find out anything new with Heidi, let us know … and vice versa, of course."

"OK, sure. Deal. Bye, love you," she answered as he hung up. He hadn't had time to respond back with a "love you," or had he?

M and Sara started to clean up the cottage. There was no structural damage, but sand was everywhere. After a couple minutes of cleaning they both realized they were both beat and needed to head to bed. M complained that he was scared and needed someone to sleep with him. His back was all tense and he needed a backrub. Sara told him to shut up, for what—the sixth time that day? That she had seen a stray cat in the bushes if he needed something to scratch his back and butt up against.

The next day they spent the entire morning sweeping and vacuuming sand out of every crack and crevice. There had been a little coffee left by the last renters and this got them

CHAPTER 33

to late morning when they decided to run into Hope Town for some groceries and to grab an early lunch at Cap'n Jacks. It was really an odd, empty feeling not having Lottie there.

Not minutes after they got back, Sara got a call from Washington, DC. M watched Sara mostly responding, "Um hum, um hum" for almost an hour." When she hung up, she stretched, sighed, and said, "Mostly good news, I'd say. It isn't the Bahamian authorities or the Chinese or the Mandelsungs that have Peewee and Vernal. It's the British government, rather, as I thought. The Mandelsung family has money and connections. They went to whomever their connections are in England and told their version of your and Peewee's great adventure." With this she looked a little askance at M, eyebrows raised.

M laughed. "Nice try, but its *Pee-wee's* Big *Adventure*, fool."

"Well, at least you got it."

"Like there's that much to get?"

"Hey, shut up!" (Seven!) "I'm trying to lighten the mood here."

All right, what did this "shut up" shit mean? "Hey, you're supposed to be the 'nice' sister. Kate was always yelling at me to shut up. You used to be so sweet."

"Well, maybe Kate's the nice *sister*. Ever think of that?"

"No!" He also, being uncommonly sensitive to inflections, noticed that she had emphasized "sister." Now what did *that* mean?

"Oh? Well you never know. Now shut up (Eight!) so I can finish telling you what's up. So … the Mandelsungs gave their side of the story to whomever over in England and, of course, Peewee and his crew are depicted as murderers, rapists, and terrorists. So, the Crown sends over some official posse and

| 575

rounds them all up and hauls them into Nassau, which has a strong British influence and contingency, and locks them up. So, at least they're safe and not in the hands of blackguards."

M was amazed by and proud of his nonsister. "Who in the devil did you contact?"

"Ever heard of Interpol?" she asked him.

"Yeah, in James Bond movies. Is it for real?"

"Of course. It stands for 'international police.' Its headquarters are in Lyon, France. It promotes international cooperation between policing units around the world. If the U.S. has a citizen incarcerated in another country, generally the FBI, which has a broad presence around the world—fortunately in Nassau for our purposes—gets involved. Interpol, the FBI, and even the SEC, when necessary, work hand in hand: we uncover the crooks, the FBI arrests them, and Interpol arbitrates. So, we'll be meeting our FBI agent in Nassau—arranged by Interpol."

"Well, what now then?"

"Is Peewee still a U.S. citizen?"

"I don't know," M answered. "I can call Wanda. She should know."

"Let's let it be for now. If you heard me, I told them he was."

"Yeah, I assumed. What if he isn't?"

"If we want to accomplish anything, we need to have the U.S. involved, so they'll have to believe he is. Without a U.S. citizen in custody, they're not going to get involved and then I don't know what might happen. I'm guessing the Bahamian government might be just as happy to have this out of their hands, especially since some of Peewee's people are probably illegal Haitians. Getting Interpol involved guarantees cooperation."

"So, what do we do?"

CHAPTER 33

"My contact said Peewee had thrown around a couple names. One: yours—obviously didn't mean shit to them."

"Gee, thanks."

"But Spenser Redfern did. Any idea where he is?"

"We've been in contact. He and Lottie met up in Boston and sailed south to where he winters near Santa Marta, Colombia. They should be there now."

"Think he'd, I'm guessing he would … he'd have to fly, I'd imagine, to Nassau? I will need to go as our contact, you, Spense, and Lottie, if she's with him, will be like witnesses on Peewee and the others' behalf. The British authorities have got to hear the other side of the story."

"The A-hole brothers got arrested for trespassing on and destroying protected land, you know? I thought they would be behind bars."

"Well, maybe, but their family apparently has a shitload of money. But my contact is working on getting the Bahamian authorities to hand over whatever evidence and files they have regarding that 'incident.' They will have to cooperate with Interpol. It holds higher authority in the pecking order. Maybe their influence won't get them out of this if Interpol's involved."

"You know who would be totally anti-Mandelsung?" M realized. "The National Trust that polices protected land."

"OK, we'll work on that. You get ahold of Spense and find out when he can get to Nassau, if he's willing or able. The sooner the better now, before Christmas, or we'll be waiting a while before people get back to work after the holidays. We'll have to try to find a flight as well. It worries me, though, that the whole protected island thing with the Mandelsungs was actually a setup. But we need to go and get Peewee and the rest of them out of there, and the sooner the better. Email Spense now."

M emailed Spense, telling him the situation. Spense emailed back an hour later. Said he and Lottie were "in" but would have to get to Barranquilla, which had an international airport. They wouldn't be able to get a flight until the next day. They would stay at the Graycliff, a hotel in Nassau. He knew the proprietor and she would hold rooms. He wanted to know if he and Sara needed one or two rooms. M wondered what was going on in that twisted mind of his. M emailed back, telling him that all the flights into Nassau had been full over the holidays. Spense got back saying he would charter a plane and pick them up in Marsh Harbour the next day at two p.m., on their way to Nassau, and asked again: one or two rooms? M decided to leave him guessing, since he had no idea why he was asking that or what he might be insinuating. He supposed that probably rooms were at a premium near Christmas. Yet, another butt to butt with Sara might not be the worst thing in the world, anyway, he thought. Everything seemed to be working out today, at least so far so good. But the Heidi thing had him spooked.

They had a quiet, contemplative meal, sat on the porch with a glass of wine, and hardly noticed the sun innocently and slyly slink down behind the lighthouse, the swivel of the light a reminder that when the sun came around again it wouldn't be so innocent: shit was going to be happening … again.

PART VI

Maybe ...

CHAPTER 34

M WAS the first one up, and he put on some coffee and went out onto the porch to perform his morning ritual. He got his cup of java and settled into one of the Adirondacks. For a second he almost wondered where Heidi was. The sun was up behind the cottage, but the porch was still in shadows. There was a mild breeze but it was pleasant in just his flannels. There was no rush this morning as they would be catching the noon ferry. He started to slip into an uneasy contemplation of how the day's events might unfold, changed his mind, and eased into an easy contemplation of Sara.

She was really very little like Kate. Rather than Kate's hard edges, hers were mellifluous and mild. Rather than a thorny temper—Kate could get pissed at a bowl of cherries—she was even-tempered with a gentleness that soothed. Kate had so driven him crazy and to distraction that when Barney was there he hadn't really ever thought of Sara other than as Kate's sister and a match for Barn. Now that that wasn't going to happen, it appeared, he thought of the naked wrestling match with Kate. Could that have happened with Sara? Number one, she wouldn't have been tackling him, fighting over who could race up the stairs and get swimming suits on first. That was something you'd do with a sibling—a combative, spontaneous, free-wheeling sibling. He had loved Kate for it: for her abandon, her spirit. But, oddly, when

CHAPTER 34

he was grappling with her, naked, it wasn't sexual, which startled him now when he thought about it because he had been, basically, between her thighs. No, it was competitive. Like with a brother or sister ... well, an open-minded, no-holds-barred sister. If that had been Sara ... well, again, number one: he couldn't imagine Sara wrestling with him naked or not. Number two: it didn't strain his imagination to see himself cuddling with her, though. And the thought, he realized, didn't leave him nursing any guilt. She was much more nuzzle-able than grapple-able... like Kate.

Sara arrived, cup in hand, and settled solemnly next to him in the splendor of her fuchsia terry cloth running suit. He realized she didn't have much of a change of clothing along. He offered her some fresh clothes of his. (Hey, why not?) She had attempted a smile at the suggestion but retorted she was fine for now, but looked a bit weary, not giving him any shit back. He could feel something was not right.

Sara's limp smile easily soured to a scowl. She told M she had just gotten an email from her contact in Nassau. The Mandelsung family was there, in force, and apparently the reason Interpol had known Spense's name was that there were international warrants out for his arrest. "You know what that means, right? If we go to Nassau, Spense, and possibly you and Lottie, all will be arrested. We've got to get ahold of them."

"So, you think this is all related to one of our little escapades? Not just the 'squatting' issue with Peewee and the Haitians?"

"I don't think the Mandelsungs think of either your bombing mission or the restricted island chicanery as a 'little escapades.'"

M immediately emailed Spense to warn him. But he didn't respond.

"Of course, you realize without Spense and Lottie you will have no one present to corroborate your story, whatever that might be. If we don't get word to them, the upside is we have that. Of course, if we're all in jail will they even listen to us?"

"You know with you, Spense, and, Lord—Peewee—on our side, I'm just not worried. My God, the three people in the world I'd most want on my side in a fight. Lottie's no slouch, herself. I ain't gonna worry. What about Kate? Could Interpol go after her? And I don't even want to think about Heidi."

"We've done all we can with Heidi. No sense in worrying. And, I'm not going to tell you how, but I should be able to get Interpol's cooperation. I should be able to keep or get you all out of the hoosegow, and protect Kate. But we should still try to warn Spense. Why don't you try a call?"

M smiled at her. "What, are you the most powerful person in the world? I assume there must be some greed rollicking around Interpol?"

"Let's just say there's politics in any aspect of government, and I am in what you might call an influential position, if I need to be."

M tried to call Spense, to no avail, then emailed him, again to no avail. They both resigned themselves that they weren't going to be able to warn him off, but that if they knew Spense, the warning wouldn't stop him from helping his friends anyway. They both had laughed at this and Sara nodded her head, remarking that she believed he'd probably have an exit strategy anyway. Peewee probably as well. M agreed, and they decided it made no sense to worry about it: it would be whatever it would be, regardless. Although the fate of Peewee, Vernal, and the rest of the Haitians and islanders

CHAPTER 34

had been bothering the devil out of him, he put it out of his mind. Sara was what was on his mind.

While they waited, hoping Spense would at least acknowledge the message, they decided that rather than speculate and stress out over what could go wrong today, they'd get down and personal and discuss some of the personal issues they'd been avoiding. When, after a very entertaining and enlightening conversation about light issues like tragic flaws, platonic sex, and dollops, they now found themselves standing on the porch in a comfortable hug, neither feeling terribly brotherly or sisterly.

Sara had told him, almost a whispered sigh in his ear, that she or Kate's living in Minnesota was: "Not gonna happen … maybe."

The "maybe" had seemed to echo, a breezy puff that entered M's ear but wouldn't escape his head. "Not gonna happen … maybe? Hmm," M had whispered back, fingers interlaced on Sara's lower back. "What's the "maybe" mean?"

"Let's start with Kate," Sara suggested, softly, and pulled her head back, pushing forward a part of Sara M was starting to regard with affection, but not alarming him yet, and, so, still holding on.

"So, what?" he breathed. "Kate's made it pretty clear she isn't moving to the land of 10,000 mosquitoes. So, what? She and I are star-crossed lovers?"

"Do you love her?" Sara asked, flatly, pressing for a definitive answer.

They were standing at the railing nose to nose, both holding on. M had been realizing and now acknowledging to himself, guilt-free, that he had been finding Sara more and more captivating and, although he had really enjoyed going

| 583

butt to butt with her, was finding the flip side currently more intriguing. He had been resisting thinking of Sara as a sexual accomplice, a sexual partner, a lover, but: that 'maybe?' seemed to be the somewhat sudden, most invigorating question in his mind. He decided they better break the encouraging embrace before he got embarrassed, which was imminent he realized. He reluctantly let loose and headed back to his Adirondack. Sara followed suit, the uncharacteristic scowl having returned.

"Yes, for sure, but, I think, it is as a sister," he said as he sat.

"Not as a lover … or a spouse?" Sara asked and now sat sideways in her chair, facing M, her legs hung over the arms of the Adirondack, bare feet dangling between them.

Mick scrutinized her feet. Kate's were skinny, bony, and veined. How they had turned him on, M couldn't imagine. Sara's were like a Sara Lee roll: full, roundly shaped. Not fat or puffy, but like every other part of her: soft, and almost begged to be squeezed. "No. I couldn't make love to her. It wouldn't seem … right. Her feet are way too skinny and bony. Fine feet for a sister, though."

He took one of Sara's feet gently in his hand and perused it. "Now this foot is just right."

Sara, now smiling, waited for him to continue.

"If Kate, someone, was to be my spouse, I'd definitely visit her 'island' if she wanted me to, but she'd have to be willing and able to," squeezing her big toe, "fly into Minnesota, settle in with me at the cabin, see how she felt about living in the north woods of Minnesota—and …" holding the next toe: "be willing to slap a few mosquitoes. She or whoever …" moving to the next toe: "would have to be willing to sit in the front of a tandem kayak without complaining, and …" onto the next toe: "roll over once in a while rather than sleep butt to

CHAPTER 34

butt, without making me feel like a pervert, and ..." onto the fuchsia-painted pinkie: "be able to head all the way to our home whenever I needed her to." He squeezed the entire naked foot: "This person would have to be willing to do the same when I'm down here. Consider 'home' wherever I am. Maybe make several visits each winter. Maybe even check out a hurricane. What you think about that?"

Sara wriggled all her fuchsia-painted toes. "They could do that."

Sara's and M's phones rang at exactly the same time.

Her foot stilled. She looked at the phone for a second, then looked at M, who still held her foot. "It's Kate," she said, losing the smile and starting to stand.

"Lord, it's Wanda," M said, squeezing Sara's foot, not letting her go. "Why would she be calling?"